Acknowledgements

To Romelle Henry, my 10th grade English Teacher,

You were the first to challenge me with writing for an audience.

It's only fitting that you be part of that audience now.

Thank you for inspiring me to give back to the world with my writing and with becoming an English teacher, which I am today.

Thank you to my family, who kept me on my toes even when I felt I was limping towards the finish line of achievements in my life.

Special Thanks to:

Mom, Dad, Bobby Pentecost, David Roland Rhea, Spencer Lesley, Joe Norton, Nate and Shelley Taylor, Katherine McBurnett, Carrie Varble and Chip Hullet.

To Stacey Singleton, who was there when this story first started but never knew more would be made.

And to Richard Hodgkinson:

whose own writing inspired me to finish mine.

Thank you, Richard!

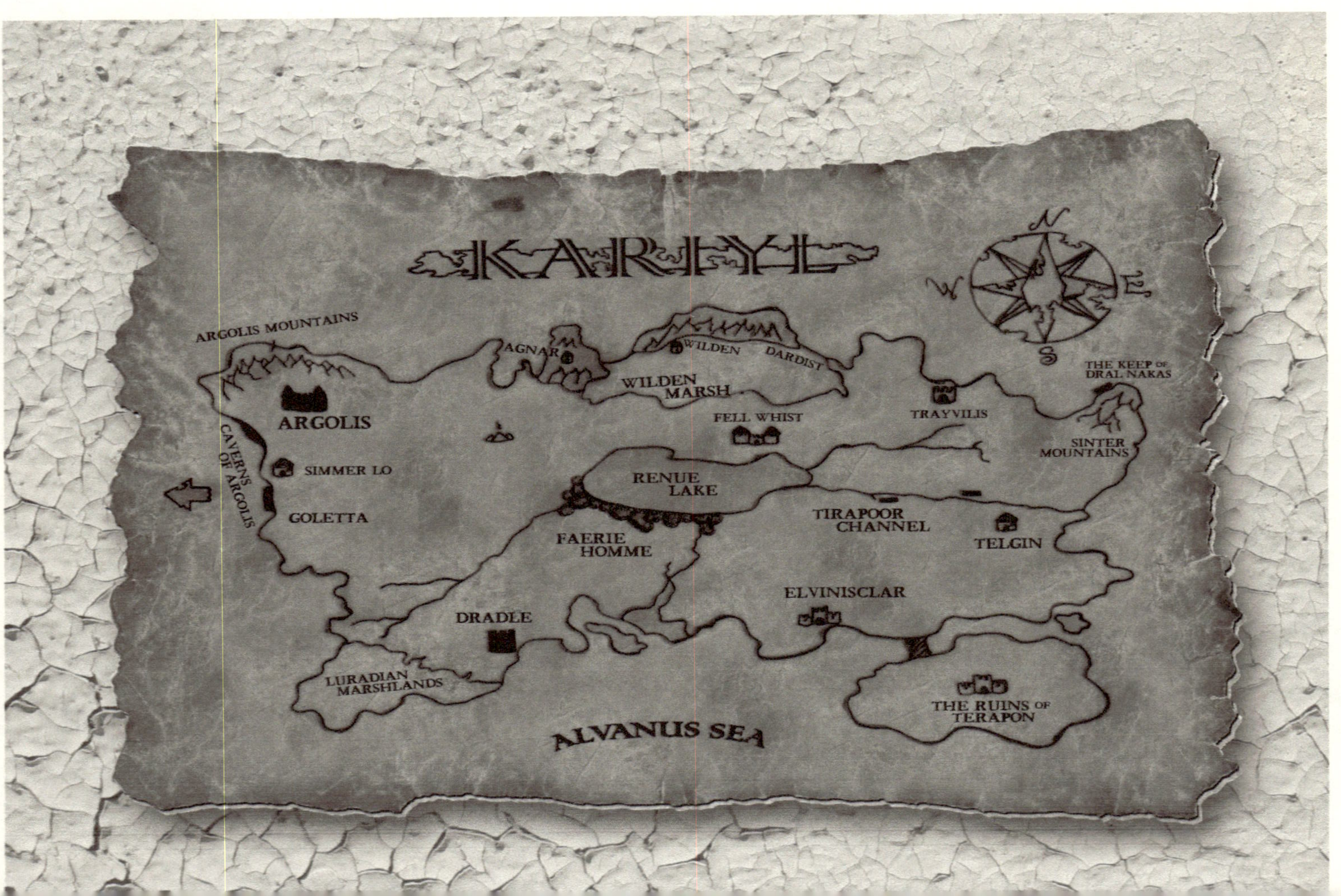

KARHYL
N
S
E
W
ARGOLIS MOUNTAINS
AGNAR
WILDEN
DARDIST
WILDEN MARSH
THE KEEP OF DRAL NAKAS
ARGOLIS
FELL WHIST
TRAYVILIS
SINTER MOUNTAINS
CAVERNS OF ARGOLIS
SIMMER LO
RENUE LAKE
GOLETTA
TIRAPOOR CHANNEL
FAERIE HOMME
TELGIN
ELVINISCLAR
DRADLE
LURADIAN MARSHLANDS
THE RUINS OF TERAPON
ALVANUS SEA

THE CHRONICLES OF AR SOLON

Book XIX:

FORGOTTEN ANGEL

BY

RILEY S. BROWN

Baltimore, MD

The Chronicles of Ar Solon

Forgotten Angel

Book XIX

"If you lost your mind, then you are going down in history as a famous artist!"

Laura C. Kirchner, High School Art Teacher and colleague

Foreword

By Riley S. Brown

For many of you, simply reading a book is enough. But, for some, like me, it's more or less how the book came to be that is the more interesting part. That is why I write this foreword. I grow tired of hearing statistics and publishing hoopla that takes a dozen or so pages to write. And, since this is my first book, I feel that it is fitting to let you know the purpose of the book as well as the purpose of me writing. I could say that the world has been kind or harsh to me and let that be it; but there is much more. For everyone that has ever wanted to write but never had the chance to, I give you this advice: DO NOT STOP. So, with that said, let us start this journey into my past.

It all begins here. It was sophomore year at Hunters Lane High School in Nashville, Tennessee. I was taking an English II class with a teacher by the name of Romelle Henry. She saw my interest in reading and writing and took it upon herself to ask me to write her something. It wasn't until I had written her something that I realized that she wanted me to try and publish it. I was all of 14 or 15 at the time and knew nothing about publishing or how to go about doing it. I didn't even know how to write a professional letter requesting publication. So, there begins the….well, beginning of what I would call my writing career. It was nothing of a career, really, but more of a hobby. I would spend countless hours reading Margaret Weis and Tracy Hickman or Terry Brooks novels at school and at home, during the summer, or even during breaks at work while I would cram fast food in my mouth.

I would also like you to know something about the crowd I hung out with and how they influenced me to become an avid reader. It has to start with

Spencer and Joe. I knew that I was a reader before I met them but it wasn't until after my eighth grade year during that summer that I knew that I loved reading. I was 12 going on 13 and my mom, my brother and I moved into an apartment complex called Archwood Apartments. It just so happened that I had a friend named Spencer that lived there and he introduced me to Joe.

Amid the carefree days of swimming at the pool and running through the woods nearby, we would spend nights playing Dungeons and Dragons and eating junk food to keep us awake. This is the place where my imagination began to go wild. Playing a role-playing game with my friends late into the early morning hours forced me to come up with ideas, with scenarios about make-believe characters that I controlled. There was something about this; this dream-type environment of creating things up from scratch that made me begin to understand that I loved to create stories.

We soon met some neighbors (*Nate and Shelley*) and they introduced us to the Evil Dead films, Franken hooker, and a myriad of novels that sat on their bookshelf that they had read. They let us select anything from it to read. It was like choosing the Holy Grail in Indiana Jones and the Last Crusade; we were allowed to choose a book and each of us chose a different book. My first book that I chose from their library, I will never forget, was *The Sword of Shannara*, by Terry Brooks. That book and the sequel to the story, *The Elfstones of Shannara*, began to change how I saw books. In my eyes, *The Elfstones of Shannara* had changed the way that I saw characters in a book. I didn't know it at the time, but that one book would change my life forever. It was a gateway drug to all the other books in the world. I soon knew what my one addiction was; reading fantasy novels. I would, from then on, spend much of my time doing just that.

I would also really like to tell you the origins of how this novel, Forgotten Angel, came about. First of all, this book has been long in its transformation as a book. I started it late 1999 as a short story and Christmas gift for a girlfriend. Of course, I never thought an entire novel would come of just that single chapter. Originally, it had been a preview chapter, a standalone story that would soon get placed in as Chapter One. The Prologue of the book wasn't written until after I had written up to Chapter 16 or so. The prologue, for me, was one of the hardest things in the book to write.

I began writing the book throughout my second through fourth years in college. I worked, went to college, and wrote on my novel in the spare time that I had in between those two things and having a life. The bulk of the novel was written during 2001-2004. I do not recommend doing this at all. I took a brief hiatus from writing the book to write on some film scripts, finish my minor in college, complete a master's degree, move to another state, get married, have my second child, buy my first home, and take on a teaching career. All the while, Forgotten Angel lay dormant in my mind. It was always in my mind, but it never materialized into a final novel until the summer of 2009.

Small snippets of ideas had begun materializing from the abyss of my mind, the story of the Forgotten Angel finally coming together as a whole. I had always known how the story was going to end; that was the easy part. However, getting there was what filled me with dread. You see, I was always scared to end a story because that seemed to be the end for the characters and their adventures.

Many people have seen my working novel and read various chapters of it, but none have seen it come as far as it is now. And to those people, the patient ones who have waited, this book is for you, too. It is not simply something of my imagination, but also a creation of those who have waited for such a long time for me to finish it. This novel had always been something on my list of things to do that just never got done. Now, as you see it before you, it is done. Enjoy the fruits of my labor and I hope you take as much from it as I have put into it.

-Riley S. Brown

Baltimore, MD

April 2010

Prologue

The quill pen scratched softly on the newly-made parchment, the aged, old fingers moving across the page slightly and then into a gradual turn, adding small details to each letter and word to the otherwise plain writing style of the scribes. He had just finished one tome of history only to reach for a second leather bound volume, its pages still having stories to tell.

And tell it will, thought the old scribe, mumbling to himself, his beard dragging across the page in time with the quill, almost as if they were twins; just alike, yet altogether different. He had dreamt of this history several nights before yet continued on with his duties as a reproduction scribe during the day, engaging in this particular one during the night only while all other scribes slept. The other story he was copying had ended none too well and he hoped that this one would be different.

He began on the first sentence. If anyone were staring, they could make out a smile from beneath the white beard, his lips stretching slightly apart as the story began in front of him.

'It is far in the eastern part of Kariyl that this story takes place; past the elves in Trayvillis and Elvinisclar, far to the south of the Sinter Mountains. The town, which is small in comparison with many of the others that dotted the eastern side of the Tirapoor Channel at one time, was named Telgin. It was named after Melcho Telgin; a human.

He was a businessman, one of the first, in fact, and was responsible for flourishing the industry of trade throughout the eastern half of Kariyl. Once well known, he claimed a piece of land and built a thriving trade center that is still well known today.

Years after Melcho's death, one of his many grandsons took over as town magistrate and built onto the city a trading port that used the waterways of the Tirapoor Channel, located just on the outskirts of the town, to increase business. Being that the Channel flowed to the south, the grandson built a small receiving port near the end of the channel so that merchants and vendors could convert from boat to wagon and forge on to the other populated towns across Kariyl. This saved on food, meal for the animals that pulled the wagons, and utilized a natural resource for trading purposes.

But as time went by and the town grew, the glimmer in the eyes of the townspeople grew faint when the Telgin family gradually relinquished their hold to another magistrate not of Telgin blood. And soon the story of Melcho became just another of the many stories that was forgotten.

Moreover, time began to wash away the freshness of the world, as it had with Melcho and his dream, just as it did with the other cities and towns on Kariyl. There were so many Melchos in the world, all from different times, all from different races.

The cobblestone walkways everyone had come to see in Goletta were now cracked and crumbling to pieces as the days passed by; the halls in the Agnar Courts that housed the carvings of the great dwarven kings were now faded and hid away from the other races. The great books in the libraries of Argolis were shelved and unknown to the new generations that came and went, never knowing the truths that were shadowed to them, never taught that what once was a mistake could be mended and made whole again.

No; they made the same mistakes as their previous generations had made, their mistakes scarring the world. The island town of Terapon that had been built with such hope to mend the parted races was beginning to fade in the eyes of the inhabitants, slowly becoming nothing more than a dream in the lives of those who strove to make Kariyl a better place.

It had been over two centuries since the War of the Races. The humans, elves and dwarves that comprised the races on Kariyl still saw the land as delicate from the battle that they had waged upon it, nearly tearing it apart in their blinding rage. The War of the Races could be compared to a natural disaster in worldly terms, what the inhabitants liked to call a useless tragedy, for it served no purpose in bettering their lives, only burdening their future generations.

'But tragedies happen one step at a time, as does this one I am about to tell. I've found it calming to write as if I'm speaking to one that lives on this land, as I do now. For, you see, I am alone in this world, have been chosen to be, really; writing day after day, yet my inkwell never runs dry.

My name is Gilden Felves, but all who know me call me the Chronicler, which has a meaning all its own. I am the writer of histories, the chronicler of the races of Ar Solon, in hopes that others will read these great tomes so they do not have to share the same fate. I have been chosen to do this for over a hundred years here on Kariyl. Soon though, I will be passing the quill to another to write the past for the future.

Argolis, Trayvillis, Agnar, Elvinisclar and all of the other cities that populate this soil are in these pages I scribe: looking, seizing, loving, and laughing; all in these pages that I write. But, of course, let me not waver from the path I write. I seem to do that a lot as my time draws near.

Once upon a time, in the far reaches of the clouds, angels lived, taking delight in their heavenly ways and perfect world that spread out before them. The clouds were glistening with a magical presence and, if you looked hard enough from the earthen realm, you could almost see shapes forming in the sky. Mythical creatures, fairy tale heroes slaying evil dragons, even the castles that lay far in the southern wilderness where the elves resided could be found in the clouds. It was here, in the clouds, where the angels congregated, meeting since the beginning of creation, discussing the habits and nature of the beings that existed below; those that they called the inhabitants.

Each angel had their own responsibilities that had been bestowed upon them since time began by the Creator, ruler of the clouded world, and many were to oversee their tasks by making trips down to the world and watch in silence, observe the inhabitants and bring inspiration to the populace. Once this was done, they were to return with reports of their progress to the Creator and he would decide if they needed to continue on the path they had taken or if they needed to change it to better the inhabitant's world below. But most of the time the Creator chose for them to stay in the clouds, to remain above and watch what they had done from afar. Many inhabitants were inspired while others were not; the ones inspired using their abilities given to better their lives, to make a barbaric world civil.

It is two-hundred and fifteen years after the War of the Races, the Creator watching his inhabitants as they come together at last, how he had always planned it and begin again, to rebuild what they themselves had torn asunder. But that was the way of the inhabitants. Sometime during creation, the land had darkened and darkness populated their minds, making their ways warped, violent, and without purpose in the grand scheme of things.

In the beginning, the Creator had instilled the grand scheme inside all of his inhabitants, with hopes that all would find it inside of them when the time came. But, as the world began to flourish, the Creator took notice that the grand scheme was nowhere to be found in their lives and, in seeing this, sent his angels to help guide them back in the right direction. So, though he disapproved, the Creator dispatched angels to the world and let them live amongst the inhabitants; one third of his angels that he had created were now on Ar Solon while the other two thirds remained in the clouds with him.

However nice this may have seemed, the responsibilities of the angels were not without rules. One rule that the Creator had sent them out with was not to physically interfere in the inhabitant's lives, for it would send things spiraling out of control and an outbreak of chaos would begin. The Creator had seen this chaos occur several times and it had been foreseen that it would happen again in the near future, so he sent only his most trusted angels to make sure that this would not occur.

The Creator noticed also that, as he sent his angels down to the world he created, when they returned to the clouds from time to time, they had begun to change; they began to take on some of the traits the inhabitants had become accustomed to using, almost as if his angels were becoming inhabitants themselves. This perplexed the Creator greatly.

Yet, he too, had sworn not to interfere, and so he stayed above in the clouds, watching, the angels putting their skills to use, trying to better the inhabitants' lives in any way possible, trying to find hope in each, something special in each, helping to reveal the grand scheme to the inhabitants so they could find purpose, so they could find a place in the world.

The Creator knew that it would be centuries before the inhabitants would develop to the point where he could actually return to them, as he had before in the beginning, even before he had created the angels.

He looked down at his creations and watched as they grew, generation after generation, understanding the world, harnessing it's energies that were stored in their minds, their souls, some even harnessing energy from the environment around them, what the learned inhabitants had come to call *magik*. The more the inhabitants used magik, the more they understood why the Creator was there and why he had created the world the way he did. Many even discovered the truth of the grand scheme but passed away before they had a chance to reveal the truth to their kindred. Nevertheless, some knew the secrets yet kept them hidden to themselves, many times watching as their kin suffered, died, even slipped into madness for the secret that they themselves had known all along.

Yet, there were others; others that began to spread the truth. Scribes, priests, and wizard guilds sprouted within the flourishing towns, giving truth to those that were ready to hear it. But, as the years passed, the darkness everyone had inside of them began to increase, sometimes blinding them from any truth they could ever see.

The Creator knew this would happen also. He remembered when the darkness had started, had lifted itself, rearing back, as if triumphant, and then disappeared into his inhabitants. He had blamed himself for the mistakes they made but knew that he could not take the full blame. *The One* had been the real culprit. That's why **he** was down there, with all the other outcasts he had created, trapped beneath Ar Solon's surface with his daemons, fighting, maddened that he had ensnared himself in a trap of his own design.

Many times, the Creator had heard that the One had escaped from his holdings deep in the mountain cliffs; then several other reports would deny the escape completely, stating only that his efforts had failed. The Creator had no emotions towards this except for a fatherly kindness and could not display regret at his inhabitants that fought, in a constant state of turmoil, or even to his first creation that trapped itself within the world that they had worked together to create, the One watching as the inhabitants thrived and became kings, bishops, high-ranking officials, governed by rules they had created as they learned how to speak and reason amongst themselves.

But, as the world played out, the One **did** seem to have a semblance of control over the darkness that he had instilled inside the inhabitants. In fact, in some instances, the reports the angels brought back to the Creator, the One had taken over lands, towns, sending several inhabitants raving mad into the sea with but a thought. The Creator needed to dispose of the One yet knew no way to without harming the inhabitants themselves.

The Creator knew that the One would do his best to destroy Ar Solon from the inside out if he could but he, too, would die himself. All of the One's powers were stripped when he was cast down into the world. He would have to overthrow all of Ar Solon one continent at a time before he would be able to harness enough power to return to the clouds.

And here is where the story stands, on the precipice of all of Ar Solon, on a continent that has been split from the others and named Kariyl by an outcast elven race from Parthenia. But to call them outcasts would be wrong. They began to make the barbarous world of Kariyl civilized, bringing an amount of life all of their own to the trees, to the mountain chains bordering the northern tips of the land, and to the pieces of the Alvanus Sea that broke into the land, forming rivers, lakes, channels that crossed almost the entire continent before ending in its winding path to the Reune Lake. To the east, in the city of Telgin, this tale of sorrow begins.

One

"Look, that's where the angels fly, right there!" Timothy pointed, falling back onto the ground behind him, hands out in front of him as if he could catch the clouds and hide them in his pockets. His older brother Ranyll laughed, smacking his brothers' hands out of the air.

"You're crazy Timothy. Only the gods live up there. There are no angels. Those are just stories, sort of like myth; just a legend like unicorns and all the other faerie creatures in the storybooks." Nevertheless, he knew Timothy would just shrug him off, just as Ranyll was doing with his younger brother's ideas.

People believe what they want to believe. No one can change that. Ranyll looked up at the clouds now.

"They are beautiful though, Tim. It's hard to believe that we only get to see the belly of paradise. I wonder what life is like up above the clouds. Is it like down here, you think?" Ranyll paused then looked over at his little brother when he didn't answer. "Tim?"

But Timothy was up, back on his feet, pointing to a new set of clouds that approached them from the west, just now beginning to pass over them. The white, fluffy clouds that they had seen only moments before seemed to veer away from the darker clouds coming nearer and nearer, as if they were afraid of them. Timothy jumped up and down in excitement at seeing this.

"What are those clouds, Ranyll?" Timothy's curious blue eyes brightened, waiting for his older brother to respond. Ranyll slipped his boots on and gathered his sword and other things that lie beside him on the ground, poking at his brother with the tip of his scabbard.

"Those are storm clouds. It looks like it's going to rain, Tim. I think we better get back to Telgin where it's safe, before it decides to pour on us."

Timothy stood there and watched as the first flashes of lightning broke through the gray forms, then gathered his things also, watching as the white and gray clouds collided above them. A slight drizzle began around them and they ran for the cover of their beloved city of Telgin.

*   *   *

High in the clouds, above Kariyl and all the cities that were nestled upon it, the angels whispered. The words they spoke were a chant, a solemn oath and prayer that could touch any humans' heart. There was controversy in the clouded world above and, today, a trial was at hand. An angel accused was being shown the intolerable injustices that their actions could cause. The Creator was the first to arrive in the courtroom. A puff of smoke began to fill the space in the Creator's chair and he appeared.

All the others were soon there, too.

Shilinda, angel of the faeries, her elegance radiating as she stood out in the crowd of angels, looked out at the other angels, watching the other overseers of the world below as they congregated together. Divlo, the angel of honor and justice, his eyebrows furrowing, stood out also, his flaming red beard hanging over his brown robes. His huge arms were crossed as he stared out into the crowd, watching as the rest of the angels made their way into the columned courtroom. He had not been in the clouds for some time, but he only came for attendance of this trial.

The courtroom was made of solidified cumulus clouds, some white, some gray. There were long rows of pews that filled the center of the room, almost completely filled now with angels who had gathered in no time at all.

It was very rare for angels to have a trial for the sheer fact that they did not spend enough time in the clouds to concern themselves with such matters.

However, today was different.

Drudas entered, angel of forest and trees, along with Gweeden, angel of art and writing, trailing behind, fingers interlocked in front of him, twiddling his thumbs as he walked. The two angels at the entrance of the courtroom waited for the last of the angels to enter and, when they did, pushed the huge double doors shut.

Silence filled the courtroom. All of the angels were dressed in their ceremonial garbed robes, the hems of the robes hanging down on the clouded marble floors, covering their angelic feet. With a nod of his head, the Creator began the bells.

The bells were hung high above the angels, deep in a layer of clouds within the courtroom. The bells were a sweet tone, made of happiness and beginnings, as were the bowed heads that listened attentively as the last rings of the bells faded into the clouds. The Creator began. He motioned to the double doors that had just closed and for all to take notice.

A roll of thunder broke through the council hall chambers and the accuser walked in. It was Greditto, angel of song and music, his face flustered and a furrow on his brow, wings batting behind him furiously. The crowd of angels parted quickly and let him through, his massive body towering over the other angels. He stepped up to the Creator.

"This is intolerable! I will not stand for this any longer! You have to do something. I have warned her, I really have. But she's gone too far this time!"

The Creator did not speak, just watched Greditto and leaned to the side to watch as the crowd parted again, making way for the accused.

The most beautiful of the angels, Gabriella, floated past the others. She was softer, quieter than that of the boisterous Greditto, stopping to bow to the Creator respectfully before speaking. The Creator acknowledged the courtesy and nodded for her to begin. Her voice was gentle, seductive sometimes, even to the angels that lived around her when she spoke the right words. She stepped forward, her soft, lithe figure covered in white silk.

"I come today before you, mighty Creator, to tell of my journeys. I have been down on Ar Solon for the last several seasons studying . . ."

Greditto interrupted. "She's been fraternizing with them, Creator." The angels in the pews gasped. Associating with the inhabitants was forbidden among the angels.

The angel of song and music continued. "I've seen this with my own vision. It is prohibited that we influence the inhabitants, especially the humans, in everyday activity. The nymphs and sirens are enough on the humans." Greditto stopped and looked over at Shilinda, a deep scowl on his face. Shilinda looked somewhat insulted. She began to rise from her place, her wings tensing on her back, when Greditto started again.

"We don't need another influence in their lives, taking them over and distracting them. They must . . ." Gabriella pushed past his insulting tone with her own, her voice suddenly hard and solid. She had meaning in the words she spoke now and her features showed that of surprise at what Greditto had accused her of.

"Yes, I associate with the inhabitants. I know of their wants, their needs. I even feel their passion towards wanting another." Gabriella looked around the room, waiting for more oohs and ahhs, but there were none, so she continued.

"But I also learn from them more up close more than I ever could by watching from a distance. *Feeling* is not within me. I see their joy and can feel nothing. I haven't the ability to feel what they feel and are but a dream in their short lives, a wish that is always on their tongue. I do not disturb them from their lives, but study them and care for them as anyone else would. So, if I am to be judged, mighty Creator, judge me by what I do by trying to help. My intent is not to harm or injure these beings. No angel here can say that they are not interested in the goings on down on the fractured continents of Ar Solon. There is much to learn from these races."

She had said her peace. She bowed again, stepping away from the Creator. One set of spoken words was all that was allowed from the accused and accuser. It had become customary since ancient times. The angels agreed long ago that a heated debate would get them nowhere and this had become the best course of action. Greditto stepped away also, bowing quickly, impatience pushing him away, following easily the path that his anger made as he left the courtroom completely. He pushed past the other angels and made his way back to his chambers. Gabriella looked at the Creator for guidance.

The Creator waved his hand and a rush of light penetrated Gabriella's silky white gowns, pushing into her being, filling her with visions of obsession, lust, passion for the unknown, and, finally, murder from jealousy and rage. It was only a glimmer of moments, but the truth of the world that she frequented every day seemed foreign to her now. She had not seen such deceit, such betrayal ever in her servitude as an angel. Her wings fluttered and she focused to keep her balance.

The Creator then released her, Gabriella backing away, tears streaking her soft, white skin. She looked to the Creator for answers but found only the puffs of smoke in his seat at the stand, disappearing slowly from sight, his visions the only thing she could cling to.

*   *   *

There was a fierce storm in Telgin that night. The wind shook the shutters off the windows of cottages and the horses whinnied most of the night while the wind pelted the otherwise quiet river town with sheets of rain. Telgin, before the War of the Races, had been located between the trading towns of Maleg and Draycrest. Shortly after the razing of both Maleg and Draycrest, Telgin had become greater a town that it had been before, letting in the remnants of the townspeople from both other towns, its population doubling almost overnight. It had become well known for its fishing trade and water purification methods all over Kariyl.

Gabriella made her way there quietly, the rain passing through her lithe form as she floated above the town, watching as the local lamplighter's extinguished the town lanterns for the night. The angel pushed past the big cottages and inns and made her way through to the small homes situated in the rear part of the town, across the Tirapoor Channel, a river that flowed through the middle of the town. She searched for the cottage and found it within moments, looking at the etching on the front door: *Tolver.*

She had heard this name many times and had seen the young man pass by her, seemingly unawares of the passion that he held, of the grand scheme that was strong within his bloodline. It was the young man's family name that was scribed on the door, what the races used to distinguish themselves from others within the town and to continue a legacy for the next generation of Tolvers.

Humans have such weird tendencies, Gabriella thought, moving through the door with ease, her transparent form drifting to his room, through his door also, and to the sleeping form of Ranyll Tolver.

*   *   *

That night, Ranyll dreamed. He remembered the storm earlier that night, remembered his brother's interest in the clouds above. But something in his dreams made him remember even more. A woman was there now, floating in from the clouds, her face a vision of loveliness, her hair blond streaks of sunlight. Her fingers found his chin and lifted it, keeping his eyes even with hers. Her eyes flashed before him and he could feel them stare right through him; it saw the good in him, saw how hard he worked for his family. She saw how much desire he held within, how much he wanted to be needed by someone. She tapped into that and looked into his eyes and, this time, he was watching her more intently than before.

"I am here for you, Ranyll. I have come for you." He fell into her embrace. *So warm, so much feeling at once.* His heart beat fast, his mind raced as she moved over him. She was in his dreams, yet he could touch her, feel her form between his fingers. Her flesh was transparent but could be felt as an immense heat. Her smile was the sunrise and her eyes the stars in the sky. She had to be a fantasy, a rich dream from which he hoped never to wake.

Ranyll lifted himself quietly from his place in bed and gathered his belongings together; a tunic, a pair of breeches and a belt along with his sheathed sword and his pair of boots. He followed the form out of his room as he dressed and through the main hallway of the house and to the front door. Ranyll opened it just as he slipped on his belt and continued to follow the floating form that stood for a moment, unmoving, staring deeply at him. The young man could not blink.

In fact, he did not want to blink. To him, this is where his happiness could lie forever and he would never want to leave. He was scared also that, if he blinked, the form might disappear and he would wake, lying in his bed, and never know her name or touch her delicate face again. The form blinked and then Ranyll did as well, watching as she moved again, this time making her way to the woods just outside the city's borders.

Ranyll lay in the woods, deep in the woods, not far from his home in Telgin, yet far enough away from where his family dwelled. It seemed like days had gone by while this angel loved him. He could see the daylight pass them by, the sun setting over the trees in the west. It was all dream-like, surreal to the young man that had, until now, lived a quiet, somber life after his father had passed away. He knew that this was a dream of sorts because the beauty did not speak. She just looked at him, almost staring through to his soul; her eyes windowless, almost without a purpose but to be next to him. Her touch was gentle and fair, yet it emanated a power behind it that he could not ignore. She had him in a trance. He knew that was why all he could feel is what she let him feel. No cold, no pain, hurt, or death could touch Ranyll. He felt completely safe at her side.

The moon was high in the sky, over their heads, and the young man looked up at it. The beauty looked up as well. The world seemed to stop for that one moment. Ranyll looked over at her shining form and could almost see a smile there, something he had not seen earlier. He had not spoken in the time they had together either, frightened that his own voice might break the serenity of the night. Ranyll looked up again.

There was a cloud moving over the moon, blotting out the light, slowly shadowing them in darkness. It was the same kinds of clouds that Ranyll had seen earlier that day. The angel suddenly stood up. She looked to him for a moment then looked back up into the sky, at the clouds, and began to move away from him. Ranyll stood also, his body bare even in the darkness. He couldn't let her leave without knowing her name. He held out his free hand as he grabbed at his belt and sword with the other.

"What's wrong? Wait! Don't go! At least tell me your name." The creature looked at him, her soft eyes and even softer face holding him in place. Her hand reached out into his.

"My name is Gabriella, Ranyll. I am the angel of . . ." Suddenly, a bolt of lightning struck and scorched the ground between them. There was a rumble in the clouds and another one struck out, almost hitting Gabriella this time. The form of Gabriella moved further away from Ranyll and deeper into the forest. Ranyll tied his belt onto his waist quickly and began after her, trying to keep up with her the best that he could in the darkness. She floated through the trees, past the huge elms, pushing towards a place far from Ranyll for his protection.

Ranyll, please do not follow. She could see the poor boy follow her, far behind, and pushed herself faster through the brush. The cloud was following above her as well, lightning striking again against a nearby tree, bursting it into cinders.

Her powers could not hold out much longer in the realm of the inhabitants. She'd have to make it back to the heavens and gain strength before returning again to Ar Solon. This had been the way of things since angels had come to Ar Solon to help the inhabitants and Gabriella never had to worry about the state of her powers before, for she had always been in control of her visits to the surface. But the cloud was in pursuit of her even faster now, gaining in speed, the lightning crashing closer and closer with every strike. She could feel what power she had ebb away even more as she darted through the woods. Ahead of her, the woods started to clear and she could make out something ahead.

It was Telgin! I can't go there. The lightning would kill the humans for sure.

She stopped in her place. The cloud slowed and came to a stop above her. She cupped her hands around her mouth and yelled up into the sky.

"Greditto, come out and talk to me. Do not hide in the clouds. You can't stop me from doing what I believe in. The Creator has granted me passage here. The Creator showed me the consequences. I believe that my will is strong enough to discourage them from the wrongs they do. Stop your foolishness and I'll explain it to you." Another bolt of lightning struck this time, and Greditto appeared then, a firm stance between the town and her, the ground below his feet still smoking from his arrival.

Greditto was covered within the shadows of the forest, his eyes dark and solid. He peered down at her and watched as the human boy came into view not far from the two angels. He turned his gaze back to Gabriella.

"So, you will still not listen? Believe that what you stand for is right? Is that it, Gabriella? You hear my warning but do not take heed? You even hide the truth from your inhabitants in the form of a dream. Do they even know that you are not a dream?"

Greditto motioned to the wings that Gabriella held hid behind her silky robes, almost indecipherable from the robes themselves unless you looked hard at them. Gabriella drew forth her wings and stretched them out behind her.

"I hide myself from them because of the past with the inhabitants. I do not want the inhabitants thinking that I am an idol or deity of sorts to worship, but their own abilities stored within."

Greditto just shook his head. "You will never learn that is your absence of thinking that made me do this."

Lightning erupted from Greditto's hands, cascading out onto Gabriella's small form. She dropped to one knee, watching as the ground scorched under her, screaming in pain at the power of the angel's wrath. The lightning scorched the air between them as well, Gabriella feeling the bolts tear into her form.

*   *   *

Ranyll was at a loss for words. His body had gone numb yet his eyes refused to close. He was seeing all of this unfold before him. What he thought to be was his dream suddenly turned into a nightmare right before his very eyes. The other angel struck again, this time more fierce.

*   *   *

Gabriella hit the ground and felt the earth for the first time, felt it shudder under her. It was like a child in her arms, feeling the cold wind of winter on its face for the first time. And she could actually see the trees move away from her, the limbs stretching forth to the Creator, looking for some kind of justice for the wrong that was befalling them. But the clouds were silent; calm, white and fluffy, like all dreams are at first, then comes the waking from them.

The grass under Gabriella was burnt and black now, like her silky gown that fell about her shoulders, threads only of a former version of itself. Greditto let the bolts fly again from his hands, scorching her skin, her hair now a charcoal black. Instead of the beautiful streams of sunlight that had shown their selves so proudly, shadows trailed over her face, down her back, in a mane of black hair that lay tattered and still.

The lightning was still inside of her, burning her angelic soul, tearing down her strength. Her powers were gone, her skin as real as Ranyll's and the other townsfolk in Telgin. She was slowly turning human. And she couldn't stop it. Her wings were scorched black from the lightning and her skin was a grey, pasty shade. She looked up at Greditto and reached out to him, only to feel the scorch of lightning piece her right hand in response. Bolt after bolt dropped her to the ground, face buried in the dirt, hands grabbing for any means to stop this vicious angel that tore at her being.

Ranyll approached then, face a pale white, watching as this . . . angel tore at another of its kind with ferocity. The young man stopped for a moment behind a nearby tree and gathered his thoughts.

What can I do against him? He is nearly invincible. Nearly. He looked over to the broken form of Gabriella on the ground and looked then over to the larger angel bearing down on her, growing closer by the second.

I wonder if it works both ways.

Suddenly, Ranyll pulled off his belt and wrapped it around the handle of his sword, covering the metal from view. He gripped it with both hands and, looking at the trail of lightning that came from the angel's hands, made a dash for it, striking as hard as he could between the two angels, hoping to severe the pain that was being inflicted upon Gabriella.

The lightning blazed to life and sparks littered the ground as it came in contact with Ranyll's sword, running through the length of the blade as though it were stroking the simple weapon. With the lightning channeled through the blade, Ranyll struck it back at the standing angel, a wild charge of lightning reflecting back from the blade. It struck Greditto and he flew backwards into the trees, his thick body smashing into the forest, splintering several trees in his fall. The remaining trees pulled their branches closer to their trunks and watched as the angel stood up from his own blast, wings flapping furiously.

"You've made a terrible mistake, boy!" The voice echoed through the forest and it seemed to multiply the angel several times over, but Ranyll knew from whence it came. The youth raised his sword with both hands and stood, somewhat shaken, but at the ready. The larger angel stood up from the shadows and moved the trees that he had torn down with his fall from his path back to Gabriella.

Ranyll continued. "You will not hurt her anymore. Not as long as I'm standing here."

Greditto was furious. "Do you not understand, boy? She has got you under a spell! You are just a pawn in her game. You have no meaning; now get out of the way! Let me deal with her!"

Ranyll took a step forward. The boy was scared, shaken now by Greditto's commanding presence, but not willing to let this angel get to Gabriella.

"I don't know what kind of angel you are, but I can't watch you do this to her. Now leave her be!"

The fury had suddenly settled in Greditto's eyes. He looked onto this human boy.

I've already been seen too long. Interference was not in Greditto's plan. He had set out with a plan yet this boy stood in his way. He looked at the boy then over at Gabriella. "So be it. Goodbye, Gabriella."

She looked up with her pale blue eyes and watched as Greditto floated into the air. He spoke one final time before leaving her on the face of Ar Solon.

"'And the forgotten one watched as the last vision of the clouded world disappeared from sight, looking now through a set of mortal eyes so it could see the very pain it had induced upon the poor races.' Goodbye, my forgotten angel."

She had heard the solemn verse many times in the Great Halls in the clouds. However, she never thought it would apply to her. Her hands fell limp in front of her and her head dropped to the ground, eyes flittering shut, trying to hide from the pain that she felt throughout her body. All soon became a barren wasteland of darkness within her mind.

2

All suddenly became quiet. It was a deathly quiet. All of the animals, night sounds, even the swaying of the trees from the wind seemed to settle down after the angel that called himself Greditto had left. Ranyll was burning up from the events that had transpired before him, his face and hands flush. He looked across the clearing at the devastated landscape and scorched earth on which lay the most beautiful and lovely creature he had ever seen and, at that moment, felt pity for it. He was tired as well, feeling as though he could sleep for days. However, he quickly forgot about his pains and rushed to Gabriella's side, hands out, holding her head up from the scorched ground.

Her eyes were closed, lips flecked with blood from the sudden turn. That's the only thing that Ranyll could seem to call it. He saw the angel Greditto come down from the clouds, terror and hate-filled eyes looking upon Gabriella. Then the lightning; so much of it striking her, her soft features now burned from their mortal shell.

He looked down at her face again.

She still held the love, though.

It was inside her, he could still sense it. She was the same caring being that had lain with him only moments earlier. Ranyll was there for her now, until she could recover at least, from the encounter she had.

"I am here for you, Gabriella."

He looked around. It was starting to get light now, but the constant state of quiet remained, almost as if the birth of the morning waited and watched them as well, waiting for something to be done before it began its daily routine.

But what, Ranyll thought to himself.

I don't have the first idea of how to help something like this. A cut, a bruise, even a fractured bone I could do something for; but this. What do I do?

Ranyll looked around and waited for someone else to take charge, someone else to care for this being. Ranyll knew from the first moment after Greditto disappeared into the sky that he couldn't do this on his own, but who could help him? It was himself and only him that was there to do something. And he intended to.

But what? What could he do for a fallen angel, a piece of heaven dropped from above? Where could he take her? Ranyll could hear the beating of his heart in his throat; the dry swallow in his throat holding down his heart, the sweaty palms that always seemed to be a part of responsibility. But he didn't want this responsibility. It wasn't his fault she came down here.

Ranyll laid Gabriella's head on the ground softly and began to get up to leave. He couldn't take this.

Not this kind of responsibility; not now. So many others needed him as well.

Suddenly, Gabriella's eyes flickered open and they were on him. The young man moved to her side. He looked down at her.

"Please help me, Ranyll. I am weak. I must hide for now and gain strength." She coughed and spit up blood, grabbing around his neck with her hand. She pulled him close. Her words were little more than a whisper of pain; the words dripping out like the trickles of blood that trailed down the side of her face.

"Shilinda! Take me to Shilinda! She's at the lake. She will help." Ranyll wiped the blood from her mouth with the sleeve of his tunic and laid her head back down on the earthen floor, her eyes melting back under her eyelids. He stood up and looked around. Telgin was far from any lake. The only lake near here was down the Tirapoor Channel to the Reune Lake.

Shilinda? Does she mean, Shilinda, the witch of the lake?

Ranyll turned to Gabriella but she was already fast asleep, her arms fallen across her chest, her breathing deep and ragged, lips still stained red with blood.

Whatever I do, I need to do it fast or else she'll die.

The youth gripped his sword and slid it in his sheath and, gathering up the angel in his arms, hefted her dark form against his and began to walk out of the forest. It was still early morning, the clouds hiding the waking sun from view. Maybe he could make it to the stables without being noticed. A strange voice suddenly answered him from out of nowhere.

I doubt it. The town is awake, laddy.

Ranyll turned towards the voice. Nothing! The forest was completely deserted except for himself and Gabriella in his arms.

Wrong again, silly human. The voice bit out of the darkness again. It was closer this time. Ranyll began to get agitated.

"How are you doing that? And where . . ."

The voice interrupted. *. . .am I? Is that what you really want to know or is it the first question in which you wish to find out if any of the townspeople will see you sneaking in with an angel in your arms?* Ranyll saw what was speaking his thoughts this time. He turned and almost dropped Gabriella, his mouth hanging open.

Don't drop her, mind you! She's hurt enough already. The Unicorn stepped forward out of the forest; horn appearing first, jutting up into the sky.

The magical beast approached elegantly, as if it were conducting the beginnings of a parade or a show for young Ranyll, who was simply stupefied that the myth he had shot down to his brother earlier was standing, *and talking*, in front of him. The unicorn cocked its' head to one side and leaned its' snout closer to Ranyll's face. It stared for a long time at Ranyll, as if sizing him up.

The unicorn's eyes were a brilliant bright blue, as if the sky had been captured and held by the eyelids that blinked at Ranyll every-so-often while staring. The unicorn's horn spiraled up several hands length above his head, touching lightly the branches of the tree that Ranyll leaned on for support. The enchanted creature was perfect in every aspect. A bright white mane of hair exploded down the mythical creature's neck and tail, which was braided with flowers and vines. The unicorn was definitely nothing like a horse, which many had compared it to.

The legends had been true. Truer than true. The legends didn't even describe in any way how beautiful this creature was.

Why thank you, young man. I greatly appreciate the compliment. The unicorn read his mind again. But, when the unicorn spoke, Ranyll noticed that its mouth did not move. The unicorn's eyes just stared deeply into Ranyll's, watching the young man's face, waiting.

I've been sent to help you, young Ranyll. Shilinda saw this one coming, but she didn't expect it to be this bad. Here, the unicorn backed up and put his front two legs down, *put her on my back. Don't worry; she'll be safe, you can be sure of that. Now lighten your load.*

Ranyll didn't hesitate. Gabriella was mostly dead weight and she was getting heavier to him by the second. Ranyll lifted her up against his shoulders and slid her onto the back of the great myth that stood before him. He reached out to touch it. The unicorn backed away.

Now wait a sec, Ranyll! I'm not a pet. You can't just reach out and take a feel at me that easy. I'm here for Gabriella. That's all. You were just a lucky one to be here. You know what they say about touching a unicorn, don't you?

The unicorn took in a deep breath and held it in, looking stouter than before. The voice that came out this time was an old one, from Ranyll's past. It was his old tutor.

'If you touched the one-horned fantasy, a fantasy it will be and your human eyes can never set forth on it again.'

"How did you do that, unicorn?"

The unicorn's lips stretched and turned into a little smile, showing its' bright white chompers.

I can tap into your mind, young one. It's easy. You just have to have an open mind. And, by the way Ranyll, my name is not unicorn. I do have a name. It's Gwenzel.

"Gwenzel! Where did you get that name from?" Ranyll straightened himself up from the stiffness he had from carrying Gabriella and stretched his limbs.

Gwenzel began walking slowly away from Ranyll with Gabriella on his back, following the trail that led out, away from town.

Shilinda gave it to me when I was born. She loves me very much. That's why I'm here now. She asked me to help Gabriella.

Ranyll followed next to the unicorn, watching Gabriella as she slept, looking back once more at the river town where he grew up.

I have responsibilities there also. My mother will worry and who will take care of my little brother, Tim? The horses wouldn't get fed; the wood wouldn't get chopped in time for winter.

Ranyll could feel the chill upon the wind as it whipped past him. Soon, all would come to a close. Ranyll knew it.

Tim would understand, though. He believed in angels and unicorns.

All of this spun in his mind, stuck hard in his soul every step he took until he could see Telgin no more. It was a long road ahead. He looked over at Gwenzel. The unicorn just stared back; those blue eyes comforting Ranyll, letting him take each step without memories coming to view.

You are a strong lad, Ranyll; strong lad. Gabriella needs your help.

Ranyll quickened his pace, Gwenzel following close behind him, angel in tow.

*   *   *

The human boy and the unicorn carrying the fallen angel walked past, following the trail out of town. For a second, the daemon thought the boy saw him; saw him hiding in the trees not far away. But the boy was looking past the trees, to the cottages and the stables far outside of the forest.

Telgin, that's what they called it. *Yes, Telgin.* The boy was leaving with the Unicorn and taking the precious angel with them.

Take her to Shilinda, the angel that could protect her from harm. But Greditto already knew that was coming, the Daemon thought, *that's why the One sent me. I am to show Gabriella the way.*

The daemon rose from its hiding place in the shadows, darkness burning into the ground that it stepped upon. Shadows, that's all the daemon was; deep, penetrating shadows, as though there were a storm cloud that could take shape and form into a human. And the shadow did. It saw the look of hurt on Ranyll's face, saw the desperation as he fought with his feelings to stay at Telgin, help his mother and younger brother, Tim.

Timothy, the daemon thought, watching as its darkness shifted and changed shape.

The daemon could see Tim in Ranyll's thoughts; see the shape of this boy; his eyes, his face, and the little limbs that reached out for the sky that day. The daemon formed into this being, Tim. It took moments of pain and agony and then a mirror image of Timothy stood in the forest looking for his older brother. Timothy pulled his cloak over his head and tied the string tightly, feeling the wind on his skin.

Little bumps formed on the surface of the skin and the daemon shivered. It was delightful being human. The daemon had done this several times and, every time, learned something new, felt a new feeling that the humans felt. The daemon followed the trail, waiting, looking for the right time to strike. The other daemons followed, six shadows following a lost little daemon boy.

*   *   *

It was hours after the sun came up before Ranyll was pelted with the first raindrop. It was a bright, sunny day, and then all became dreary. Ranyll looked up and saw the storm clouds above, saw them cover the sky, the sun, and what was left of the daylight, casting the three of them into shadows. The first drop hit Ranyll in the forehead. Then the rain came. It came in flashes; sheets after sheets of rain pounded them, the storm making them take cover. They were following the Tirapoor Channel straight down to the Reune Lake, keeping cover in the trees next to it, when the rain hit. They sloshed through the puddles of mud and had to retrace their steps several times because the trees would end up blocking their way southward. Not far ahead, they could see a thicket of trees pushed together they could possibly use for cover. They made their way to it.

Ranyll kept his cloak over Gabriella while Gwenzel pushed through the trees and kneeled down into them. The trees were thick enough to blanket them and give them a makeshift ceiling above them, just a few drops of rain hitting them every-so-often. Gwenzel whinnied and shook the rain off of his coat.

Let's wait here until the rain subsides before moving on. Ranyll nodded in agreement. He felt better in the blanket of trees anyway. He hadn't traveled all that much but he knew you'd have to be a fool to travel in this kind of weather. He looked outside the covering of trees and sighed.

Yep, a fool.

The rain seemed to pour and pour without any hint of ever letting up. Ranyll looked over at Gabriella, who was lying across Gwenzel, and reached for her. Slipping his hands underneath her arms, Ranyll managed to slide her off onto the ground, placing his cloak over the quiet form, drying her face and arms off with the sleeves of his tunic. Ranyll was still dry in places, though his head and shoulders were soaked and dripping. He wiped his face with his hands and squeezed the water out of his hair, shaking his head to get the remaining layer of water off. Ranyll could see the stumps of Gabriella's wings from under her back, the small sinewy bone structures protruding from her now-black strands of hair.

That was all that remained of her wings, Ranyll thought, touching slightly the ends of the wings, his eyes darting back to her face every now and then. Ranyll looked up at Gwenzel, who was looking out into the sheets of rain that poured down around them.

"What can we do for a being such as this, Gwenzel?" Gwenzel did not move from his position at the opening of the trees. He stood, unmoving for a time, the rain trailing down his thick hide, his powerful legs, taking notice of none of his surroundings except for one thing. Ranyll, puzzled, stood up and looked out at what Gwenzel was looking at. Ranyll could not believe it. Not far behind them, back in the trail they had just exited, Ranyll saw him. It was Timothy, his brother! He was wandering around in the rain, his cloak soaked through all the way to his tunic.

What was he doing here, Ranyll wondered, pushing through the trees to make his way out to Timothy, boots sloshing in the mud as he ran to his brother.

Wait! It's dangerous out there! Gwenzel's mind link was ignored as Ranyll pushed on, seeing Timothy reaching out his hands.

Ranyll turned back and answered Gwenzel's call. "Gwenzel, it's my brother." But Gwenzel was too far away to hear, the storm breaking across the sky, the clouds reverberating louder than they had before even when Greditto had been here. Ranyll grabbed Timothy up in his arms and squeezed him tightly to his body.

"Timothy, what are you doing here? How did you find me? Mother is going to be so worried about you." Ranyll began carrying Timothy over to the trees to get his brother dry when he saw Gwenzel standing outside in the rain. The unicorn was blocking them from entering the makeshift shelter.

"This is my brother, Gwenzel. It's okay. Let us through." The Unicorn did not move from its place.

It's not your brother, Ranyll. Just trust me. Let him down. It is a trap. Gwenzel looked from side to side, his eyes darting quickly back and forth, but always keeping to the form of Timothy that lay in Ranyll's arms. But it was already too late, Gwenzel knew. The unicorn bowed his head, his horn glowing a bright blue. Ranyll stepped back. In his arms, his brother writhed in pain, holding his throat, eyes wide with fear.

"What are you doing, Gwenzel? Stop it, you're hurting him!"

But it wasn't Tim at all. In Ranyll's arms, a transformation occurred. Timothy, his sweet little brother, began to melt away into shadows and opened its mouth in protest. What escaped its lips solidified that it was not Ranyll's little brother at all, but something far worse, something that Ranyll could not comprehend in his mind, though it were happening right in front of him. The wail was horrendous.

The human boy's hairs stood up on his arms and legs and, though the rain had made him cold, he began to shiver when images of the pain that the creature had gone through emanated out of its maw that spread across Timothy's young face. Timothy's body collapsed in on itself and began to shift, streaks of black, dark and rough, began to take shape. Soon, all of what Timothy was had gone and, all that was left was a single, dark form half his brother's size that stood in front of them, feeding on the fear that had a hold of Ranyll.

Ranyll was terrified. He stood, motionless, and watched as six shadowy forms melted out of the rainstorm around him. Ranyll reached for his sword, only to find that his sword was gone, along with his belt, which was on the ground now, the shape shifting shadow dragging it away into the woods.

"What is this, Gwenzel? I don't have anything to fight with." The young man tried to catch his breath but couldn't. Then he realized what was happening. He looked over to the unicorn. "They're here to kill us, aren't they?" Ranyll watched as the six, what could only be called daemons approach, razor sharp mandibles clicking together in excitement.

Not if I can help it. Gwenzel charged on the nearest two, his front hooves striking out, bucking one of them in the chest, his horn bursting blue flame at the others. The flames hit their targets and sent searing scorches through the daemons, knocking them back into the muddy earth.

Ranyll took this opportunity and ran for his sword. He knew that he wouldn't be any use to Gwenzel or Gabriella if he couldn't fight, which seemed like, at the moment, was the only thing he could do. The daemons did not look as though they could be reasoned with and seemed to have powers that far outweighed a normal human's.

But not a unicorn's, Ranyll thought, sludging through the mud, his sword not far off now. Above him, two daemons followed behind, bouncing from limb to limb above him, swiping at his head with their razor claws. One struck him, cutting his forehead, the other his left shoulder. Another swipe got the tip of his left ear. He swatted at them with his hands, trying to keep them away and, up ahead, saw the shape shifter daemon dragging his sword and belt. Ranyll reached it and ripped the sword free of his scabbard, swinging wildly.

The tip of the blade cut into a daemon in the trees, dropping it to the wet ground. Ranyll jabbed his sword down into it quickly to stop it in its tracks. It made a howl and then was silent. He looked up into the trees for the other one that had followed him and then down to where the shape shifter had stood and both were gone. Cinching his belt to his waist, he continued on.

The rain pelted at Ranyll's eyes, blurring his vision. He wiped the rain away, sword gripped in both hands, waiting.

Where are they, he thought, moving himself through the tree line precariously, always looking behind him and above him, taking into consideration that they had the ability to do so much more than anything he had ever seen before. Soon, though, he found their hiding place. But, to him, they weren't hiding at all.

An old tree, apparently hollowed out from bugs or wild animals, is where they waited. There, he saw the shape shifter daemon with two other of its kind, staring him down. Ranyll charged, his voice ringing out a battle cry in the rainy afternoon. He swung, cleaving into the tree, again and again, watching as the daemons, almost merrily, bounced away, hanging from the branches above, rain dripping off of their dark forms. They smacked at the tip of his sword playfully as they looked down at him. Two more daemons approached from behind Ranyll, sneaking, fingers raking through the muddy earth underneath their feet. They chortled and made their way toward his legs.

Gwenzel's voice suddenly burst into his mind.

Behind you, Ranyll!

Ranyll spun around just in time to see two daemons charging at his heels. He stabbed down at them, cleaving an arm, severing another's head with a single swipe. The others in the trees took their opportunity and leapt down on him, claws raking into his skin, blood mixing in with the rain. Ranyll screamed out in pain.

"Gwenzel, help me!" Yet, the Unicorn could not be found anywhere. It was storming, the rain covering everything, the two daemons on top of him ripping at his clothes, tearing at the skin beneath. Ranyll flipped his sword in his hands, tossing it hilt-first into the wet ground. The handle of the sword stuck in the muddy loam and Ranyll grabbed at one of the daemons, swinging the creature off of his shoulder and onto the blade, letting it slide down onto his blade as he reached for the other that had a firm hold on his tunic. He reached for it, feeling the daemon's grip loosen. Suddenly, it sprang off his shoulders, high into the air, nearly spinning out of control.

Gwenzel appeared then from out of the trees, horn raised, blue flame streaking into the sky. The flame cut through the air and the rain, finally making its way to the daemon, searing it to death before it landed. It hit the ground with a sizzle and was still.

Ranyll dropped to his knees, sinking into the mud, the several cuts cleansed by the rain, pulling the daemon carcass free from his sword. He pulled his sword out of the ground. Ranyll dipped the blade into a puddle on the ground, cleaning off the dark liquid that oozed down the blade and re-sheathed the sword at his side. The shape-shifting daemon was nowhere to be found.

Gwenzel and Ranyll went back to the safe haven among the trees. The human sat down and watched Gabriella, her breathing a little worse than the last time he had seen her. Gwenzel came in then, rain dripping from his white mane of hair, his nose sniffing the dry air inside the trees. Ranyll ripped a sleeve of his tunic off and took small pieces of cloth to wrap around the several cuts he had.

Ranyll looked up at the unicorn, which had a few cuts himself across his backside. "Do you need me to see to those, Gwenzel?"

No thank you, Ranyll. One good thing about being a unicorn is that our resilience to wounds is very strong. I will heal in time.

"Those daemons were after Gabriella, weren't they?" Ranyll looked at Gwenzel then, watching as the creature's eyes answered him back. There was affirmation in Gwenzel's eyes; but there was doubt and fear as well.

Yes, Ranyll, they were. I hate to say it, but that was just to test our strength. What we have here before us has never happened before; an angel wounded, here on the realm of Ar Solon. She is susceptible to a great many things. It just depends on who gets to her first. You've helped her to live another day, Ranyll. By fighting off Greditto, you've saved Gabriella where she can still have a chance to make it back to the clouds. She still has her powers, but she is just partially human. Once we get to Shilinda, she can give Gabriella enough power to leave here and go back to her home. I'll watch for danger now. Just you rest. Rest now, young hero.

And with that, Ranyll laid beside Gabriella, eyes quickly shutting, dreaming of hope, happiness, and a day that could cover the evil inside his mind that his eyes had seen today. But the dream didn't come. Something else helped him sleep, though; what he had heard Gwenzel say to him. He fell asleep listening to those two words that repeated themselves, echoing in his mind.

Young hero.

3

Gabriella had not stirred once since the battle that had raged between her two protectors and the daemons the night before and Ranyll pushed on sluggishly in the morning light, trying to keep himself from falling asleep. His hands hung limply at his sides, sword almost slipping from them, his eyes blinking the sleep away that continued to beckon to him.

He was exhausted, not just from lack of sleep, but from the battle he and Gwenzel had fought, the rain that poured on them incessantly, and the several meals he had missed since leaving his home in Telgin. Much of his home life seemed to echo in every step he took away from the town, as if he were attached in more than just a fondly sentimental way. It was almost as though he were linked in some way to the small fishing town that, when looking at it for the first time as a newcomer, did not look like anything special at all.

Nevertheless, it had always been cozy to him, Ranyll remembering many a time when the snow had drifted miles from the mountains in the north, covering his small world in blankets of the white splendor for months at a time during the winter season. And he also remembered the summers when he and his brother would pick fruit with his mother at the orchard not far from the border of the town. He also missed his bed, uncomfortable as it was, wishing he could lie in it for days and rest from what he had just endured.

It all seemed so far away now, Ranyll surmised, looking back at the unicorn and who the creature carried on its back.

There's something far greater to worry about than the chores and whether or not my brother gets into bed on time. Yet, Ranyll knew he had to inform his family that he was okay and that he would return; that's why he had agreed with Gwenzel that they should stop at one of the many checkpoints along the Tirapoor Channel, which they followed now, where his uncle lived. Gwenzel had agreed to stay at a distance from the cottage when they arrived, both of them arguing whether Gabriella should stay with the unicorn of with Ranyll while rested with his uncle and the other of his kind.

Gabriella is not welcome there, young Ranyll! She will be noticed when placed among your kind. She will overpower them with her abilities that she still holds within. You do not know of her as I do, the unicorn had said telepathically, trying to get the young human to understand. But Ranyll would have no such misgivings among him and Gwenzel, arguing that Gabriella needed to be properly fed and clothed or she would die of neglect, which what was slowly draining away Ranyll's will at the moment as well.

"Gwenzel, I understand your concern for her, I do. But we need to cloth her so that she can pass for a human and she needs sustenance, something besides the nuts and berries that we've been eating for the last day. She cannot survive, and neither can I, on the forest alone. And if those daemon creatures attack again, I won't be any good to you, Gwenzel."

Gwenzel had come to understand the young human more since traveling a fair distance with him, almost beginning to get used to being around him, yet knew that Ranyll could not be trusted, no matter what. Nevertheless, he knew that Gabriella needed proper rest. She was not accustomed to living on Ar Solon, and in the forest no less, and needed a good rest for the night before continuing on with the remainder of the journey to Reune Lake, which would most likely be more taxing than what they had seen so far. The two agreed and came up with a plan.

Ranyll began. "We can split up within the thick of woods that borders the checkpoint, meeting on the other side in the morning. I can probably get enough supplies to last us for a few days, at least until we get to Reune Lake. I will try to get some clothes for her and some other things that I think we will need for the trip." Gwenzel agreed and they continued on throughout the day.

Gwenzel kept the three of them far from any of the other checkpoints, keeping to the thick of the woods. It took more time, but they kept out of sight from anyone that was passing through the area, the unicorn continuing without a break himself. Several times, Ranyll had asked the unicorn if he would like to rest, but Gwenzel declined. So they continued on.

Soon, the landscape began to change. It occurred over a period of time from Telgin to where they were now; at first, it was simply just the flatland of Telgin fading and turning into thick brush, complete with briar and thicket patches. Trees and brush appeared sporadically now and it slowed their pace down, Gwenzel taking his time with Gabriella on his back. Ranyll had lost most of his strength as well, using much of the landscape around him to support himself.

The sun had kept itself high above them, keeping them warm throughout the day; yet, its form wavered and, after a few more hours of travel and some time with Ranyll foraging for food in the wilderness, the sun dipped into the western landscape and disappeared completely.

It was long after the sun disappeared that the clearing for Ranyll's checkpoint came into view. Gwenzel knelt down, letting Ranyll take the sleeping form of the angel in his arms, shifting the weight of her body against his own as he made his way to the checkpoint cottage.

I shall see you in the morning, Ranyll Tolver. Take good care of Gabriella.

"I will, Gwenzel. You have my word on that." Ranyll made his way out of the woods and into the clearing that lay just outside the checkpoint.

The checkpoint cottage lie only two cottage lengths away from the Channel, several windows in both the first and second stories lit with candles, various shadows moving throughout the cottage, almost making Ranyll stop in his tracks.

Is this the right one, Ranyll questioned, knowing that there were over a dozen of these well-placed cottages down the Channel, trying to remember his best at what his mother had told him about his uncle since he had left Telgin all those years ago. He took careful steps so as not to wake Gabriella, making his way through the brush and onto the trail that led up to the porch. The angel's eyes were shut tightly and she moved only slightly as Ranyll made his way up the steps to the front door. Her face was soft and clean from the rains earlier, which had washed away the layer of ashen hue that had coated her skin after the battle with the other angel.

Ranyll had tucked her into his cloak, covering her torn garments, trying his best to keep her from prying eyes once they entered. Her wings, which were just skeletal fragments of what they had been, were pressed up against Ranyll's arm, the young man holding her tightly to him as he approached the door. The paleness of her skin made her seem almost sickly in the candlelight that spilled out from the checkpoint's windows, Ranyll hearing voices through the doors and windows that lined the front of the building.

He leaned forward to the door and knocked. The noise subsided for a moment inside and footsteps approached the door, a massive lock clicking, the door swinging inward, revealing a stout man behind it. The gentleman wore an apron around his waist and a thick, brown tunic that was stained with various colors. A burly, black beard hugged his thick face, several small braids hanging from it. The man slipped Gabriella a quick, uneasy glance and flashed his eyes up at Ranyll's who, in turn, flashed his own back at the stranger. A resounding voice, barreling out, came from the man, who shifted in his place at the door.

"What can I help you with, son?" The man's gaze turned again to the unconscious form of Gabriella in Ranyll's arms. His eyes returned to Ranyll's, seemingly uncaring about the need or want of any travelers but the ones already inside. Then the big man added, "There will be no medicine here until the morning."

Ranyll countered. "I'm not here for that. I'm here to see Kalir Ranolf. I'm told he is responsible for this checkpoint." The big man now barred the way with his huge body, crossing his arms in recalcitrance at the young man's request.

"And what business do you have with Kalir this time of night?"

"He's my uncle."

"Your uncle!" It seemed to take several moments within this man's mind, then acknowledgement passed through the large man's eyes, his arms uncrossing, the thick limbs suddenly reaching out for Ranyll and the weakened companion in his arms, one arm around the young man's shoulder, the other opening the door the rest of the way, pressing Ranyll inside urgently. The giant man's eyes softened immediately and gave way to the request with but a thought.

"Then you must be Ranyll! I am Dir'grar, the innkeeper, the head cook, and many other things if you come to know me well." He smiled after saying that, his white teeth shining, even underneath his black beard.

"I apologize for the reluctance at the door. It seems that there are many that wish to see harm done to the checkpoint bearers, so security has to be a little tighter these days." He seemed to be uncomfortable speaking on the subject, so continued onto another topic. "But enough about us outcasts here at The Happy Traveler."

The bearded man bellowed and his eyes lit up even more as the entranceway opened up to what the stranger had called his home; The Happy Traveler. Three, thick columns held up the grand two-story establishment, the three comparably sized supports colored with tar, a thick black that seemed to have dried seasons ago yet kept its wet tint, as if still fresh. And, decorated across much of the tar, were scraps of old maps of Kariyl. Many of the maps were in pieces, wrapped around the thickly planked pillars, others still in whole, while a series of charts and several deeds from the old land before The War of the Races hung as well, bringing a rustic atmosphere to an otherwise newly built cottage.

The room itself seemed to capture the past and trap it within its walls, forever holding onto what many could not in the shuffle of generations gone by. Several tables were scattered around the broad room, with a bar and several bartenders located within the middle. Behind them, one of the three pillars had been carved into, several shelves fashioned from it to house the many spirits that were served to nightly patrons and passersby.

The big man lifted his hands proudly at the spacious tavern and, once he saw a nearby barmaid, moved Ranyll in her direction. He smiled and placed his thick hand on the young boy's shoulder. "This is Ranyll. Ranyll, this is Taleena." The barmaid had been serving a table nearby and turned when she heard her named mentioned.

She was a simple young woman, a tan dress with black stripes, a plain white serving smock covering the dress and her shapely form. Her hair was tied up into a bun behind her head, showing the strong tanned shoulders of a river child barren to the eyes of many. Ranyll had heard tales of the Telgin families that had moved from the town and settled upon the Tirapoor Channel, working the ways of the river. They had, over time, developed a dark-tinted skin and become somewhat of outcasts to the townspeople throughout Kariyl. The young man knew now why Dir'grar called his band in The Happy Traveler 'outcasts', for he looked around and noticed many of them were river children that filled the place.

Her smile broke through the pluming smoke nearby and seemed to part the loudness of the bustling tavern as well.

"Kalir has told us so much about you and your mother, not to mention young Timothy," she continued on, only once taking notice of Gabriella, apparently too busy to be concerned with the lives of the multifarious travelers that frequented the inn that had been built above the tavern.

Or not concerned because Dir'grar wasn't, agreed Ranyll, trying to think of a good reason that the whole tavern didn't stop and take notice of the still form of an angel in his tiring arms.

In reality, it was indeed Dir'grar's presence, the apparent head of security, and his ability to calm the atmosphere just with his disposition, Ranyll concluded to himself, moving through the rather crowded room with ease as he followed Dir'grar ahead of him.

The big man seemed proud to know of Kalir's family, beaming with pride through the thick mass of black hair that covered his face. He passed them through the front hallway, which was filled with smoke from cooking fires and pipes of patrons, to another longer hall, which led upstairs to many doors. The big man smiled as he stopped at a nearby door, motioning with his greasy hand to the room.

"I am terribly sorry about that interrogation outside. Again, my name is Dir'grar. I'm the innkeeper and cook of this checkpoint cottage. I look out for any problems that might occur throughout the night. I didn't expect to see anybody this late, to tell you the truth. Nevertheless, I'm sure Kalir will be surprised to see you, as well as many others that know of you here as well. He motioned to the door behind him. "Here's a room you can stay in with your companion while I go get him. Rest, relax. I will be back shortly with your uncle."

Dir'grar pushed open the door to the room and led Ranyll to the bed so he could lighten his load, the big man then swinging back around and out the

door, closing it rather lightly behind him. Ranyll laid Gabriella down and
nodded his thanks to Dir'grar as he left.

The room was lit with a single candle that was covered by a glass funnel
that broke the light across the room into shafts, making the room almost
dream-like, Ranyll's eyes adjusting as best they could, him being so tired. The
contents of the room consisted of a simple cushioned bed with a feather
pillow and two blankets, a table with washing bowl, and a chair and a small
dresser for clothes. Ranyll moved to the chair and leaned into it. In
moments, he had fallen asleep and didn't even hear his uncle enter, the man
moving next to his nephew.

"Well, I can hardly believe it!"

Ranyll awoke with a start, seeing his Uncle Ranolf standing before him.
His uncle was in his early thirties, with a long mane of brown hair that he
kept well maintained in a ponytail that was braided behind his head. He
wore a colorful tunic and a tight fitting vest with a belt that was decorated
with the finest of craftsmanship, showcasing a well-made sword as well that
hung by his left hip. His beard and moustache were neatly trimmed, low and
close to his face, giving him an heir of upper class that many do not see
today, except in the larger cities that bustled with the energy his uncle
apparently held within. Even in the darkness, in the early morning hours, his
uncle dressed for the occasion.

Ranyll had always known Kalir to be extravagant, but things must have
changed for the better since he left Telgin.

Things must have gotten better since he took the position as checkpoint master.

"So, Ranyll, do you like The Happy Traveler? I have been waiting for a
visit from your mother, you know. But I am just as pleased to see you as
well, you know that." The young boy smiled and moved to his uncle's side,
clasping him in an embrace that he had been putting off for years.

This seemed like the proper time to do it, considering all of the help I am about to ask from him at such short notice.

Kalir Ranolf accepted his nephew's embrace gratefully and with a smile, rekindling the affection in seconds that he had missed for the last several summers away from his family on this new charge. He countered the young boy's embrace with his own, trying his best to keep form and not tear up. He had not seen young Ranyll since he was a young boy, no more than seven or eight. Standing here before Kalir, now, was a man. And, from what Dir'grar had said, he had a woman with him and he was brave for such a young man, standing up to Dir'grar without flinching.

Ranyll parted from the embrace and wiped his eyes, which were filled with tears, smiling them away in front of his Uncle Ranolf, knowing that his uncle, of all people, was not afraid of emotions and the ways they worked in the world. If anything, his uncle was the most understanding of many he had met. So much had happened to his poor uncle and Ranyll hated to ask for help, but he knew that Kalir could probably supply him with what he needed.

"I need your help, uncle."

*   *   *

Not only was Kalir glad to help his nephew, but he refrained from asking questions, something he had wanted to do ever since he had walked in the room and seen the pale, young woman lying on the bed and Ranyll passed out in a chair nearby. He brought his nephew and, after the young woman awoke and found out her name, Gabriella down to a small, quiet table that he usually reserved for himself, harboring them within a niche of the fine two-story cottage he had named The Happy Traveler.

Kalir had come across the name in an old tale about a traveler that had been through the hardships of war and lived the rest of his life traveling,

trying to find happiness in a world that had turned his upside down.
Throughout the traveler's life, he had spent most of his time in inns and
taverns, watching the patrons move about and enjoy their time there as they
saw fit.

One morning, an innkeeper found this man had passed on in his bed, a
thick, aged journal within his hands. The innkeeper had read the man's
history, had read of the turmoil of his otherwise simple life and how he had
become, over time, happy within the confines of the cozy inn and tavern.
The tale passed around from innkeeper to innkeeper, finding solace that such
a simple thing as a night's lodging and a fine meal could change such a fixed
man.

Kalir drew from this tale the value of quality, of a place one could stay
and feel welcome. Yet, he did not ignore his duties as a checkpoint guard.
Since the birth of Telgin as a city, the trade routes that traders took on the
Tirapoor Channel were long and arduous. It was on a raft of sorts that these
determined tradesmen traversed, taking several days to pass across the
channels to the Reune Lake, where the drop off would be made and the cycle
would continue over again. It was here and several other places throughout
the channel that checkpoints were built to comfort weary traders and also to
check the channel for debris and any blockage that might complicate the
transporting of goods.

Every day, Kalir would, with several other chosen members, traverse his
portion of the Channel, searching for any problems. Most times, he did not
find anything. But lately, he had found . . . well, that things weren't as they
should be. Something had disturbed the tranquility of the checkpoints. And
Kalir hated to think that his nephew was out traveling during such a
dangerous time, especially trying to take care of this sick, young Gabriella.

But something within Gabriella's eyes told Kalir that she wasn't a girl.
And, within those deep, lost eyes, Kalir knew that Ranyll wasn't just taking

care of her, but was protecting her. From what, Kalir was afraid to ask. His nephew had always been able to take care of himself and was old enough to know what he was getting into.

It must be important, Kalir thought to himself, calling for another serving girl with but a wave of his hand, watching as she placed bowls full of food in front of them, followed by a pint of ale, some of his best.

Nothing less than the best for my nephew. Especially since Kalir knew not when he'd see the poor boy again.

"Anything you need, Ranyll, I can do." Kalir took another drink from his mug, pouring the rest from the pitcher nearby into the almost empty container. He beckoned Ranyll to speak.

"Now tell me how your mother is doing. And Timothy, how is the little one doing as well?" He was eager indeed to hear something of the missing portion of Ranyll's immediate family. However, Kalir was also eager to see if he could get anything about the present situation from what Ranyll would say. Ranyll took another spoonful of soup, already feeling better than he had when he first arrived with Gabriella in his arms, washing it down with the fine wine that Kalir had offered him from his own personal stock. He looked over to Gabriella, who was eating as well, her first meal down on Ar Solon.

She was doing quite well, Ranyll thought to himself, the angel following his lead at first then, once introduced to the different tastes and spices, began to be controlled by the hunger that tore at her very insides. She submitted to the hunger with bowl after bowl of hot soup, which soon became her favorite of all of the dishes that filled the table in front of her.

"Mother is very good. She is working for a head seamstress that sells fine clothing out of her home. She is happy working there. And Timothy, well, he's good. He's such a daydreamer though. The other day, I even caught him looking up into the clouds, off in another world of sorts."

This made Kalir smile. He was glad that they were doing well on their own. Ever since he had left, he worried that they were not doing as well as he thought and he had sent a courier with funds to help them, always getting them returned to him. Rachel was always so proud. As a younger sister, she had grown up with two older brothers harassing her. This, and working at such an early age, made a strong woman out of such a timid girl. She had changed again when her husband had passed on, leaving her and her two children to be tended alone. But Kalir had been there through that difficult time, trying his best to keep them afloat in such a harsh world.

"You came to the right place at the right time, my nephew. You and your lovely friend here shall have what you need for your travels. I shall see to it personally."

And indeed, he did. The garments that he chose for them were of the finest fabric, double-stitched and covered with the most beautiful patterns adorning them. Gabriella, in turn, was given a dark blue tunic with a pair of black breeches, a matching leather belt and a set of high soft boots complimenting them. Ranyll chose from the stock of garments two brown tunics, a gray vest, a set of high, hard boots, a belt, and a satchel to carry supplies and foodstuffs in, along with a new forest cloak, giving Gabriella his older one. Soon, they had their supplies and were back in the room, preparing for sleep. Gabriella had been silent for the duration of his uncle's visit and slid into bed now, her eyes darting around the room curiously. She spoke for the first time since she had fallen. And she remembered the name of the young man who had saved her.

"Ranyll, thank you for everything." Ranyll smiled back at the angelic creature, trying his best to stay awake, for he was exhausted. He sat down in the chair next to the bed.

"I'm not the only one to thank, Gabriella. There is a unicorn that helped as well and, without him, we probably would not have made it here. His name is Gwenzel. He was sent by Shilinda."

Gabriella caught her breath.

Shilinda! Then she knows that I'm here. Then there is a chance to find out why Greditto did this to me. She will be able to communicate to the realm above. "That is good news then, is it not?" Ranyll nodded his head. He knew it to be good news yet didn't know what the journey ahead of them to Reune Lake held.

If it was like anything like what I've already dealt with, Ranyll thought, *then the news is as much bad news as it was good.* But he smiled anyway, looking at Gabriella, now awake, in front of him, a semblance of color coming back to her face from the food she had taken in at his uncle's tavern. Though she had changed tremendously since the fall, she was still enchanting.

"Yes, Gabriella, it is good news. It is good to hear that you have friend's looking out for you down here. Especially since others from above in your realm seem to want you dead." Gabriella knew that this was true. Greditto had meant to kill her at their last meeting, yet had failed to do so because of Ranyll's intervention. He had kept Greditto at bay somewhat, placing himself between the two angels. She owed him her life and much more for the kindness he had done in intervening.

Ranyll took his set of clothes he had received from his uncle and bunched them up on the floor, making a pallet for him to sleep on. He lay on his cloak and closed his eyes. Gabriella leaned over from the side of the bed and tapped him on the shoulder.

"Ranyll, you don't have to sleep there. You are welcome to sleep on the bed with me if you like." Ranyll remembered the dream-like state she had put him in, only days ago, when he had shared an intimate part of himself with her, all the time thinking it was a dream. Now, as she leaned over the bed, he could not look at her, for he had shown his weakness to her and he needed to be strong for her. And he needed to be strong for himself. His feelings would only worsen the pain if something were to happen to her.

But wasn't that why I had come on this journey, to protect her because I have feelings for her? But he couldn't have feelings for an angel, could he? This and many other thoughts traversed through the caverns in his mind, all the while Gabriella's smile numbing the pain he felt inside, bringing him closer to her.

It is happening again, he thought, himself rising slowly up from the floor, his arms moving across the covers, holding them up so he could climb underneath them. As he laid down, Gabriella by his side, he could feel her warmth, so unlike how she felt in the dreaming state that night he had first met her, which seemed like an eternity away since reality burst forth and reared its ugly head.

Ranyll could feel her breath against his neck, one arm across his chest, fingers splayed out over his shoulder. He felt his body ease down into the bed and, soon, his eyes closed and the young man was fast asleep, the fallen angel sleeping peacefully for the first time since her angelic ordeal in the bordering forest of Telgin.

4

"I tell you, Dir'grar, I don't like this one bit! One bit!" Kalir sipped at his mug of morning sweet brew while watching as one of his employees opened the door to the tavern, a small group of dwarves moving inside, the Happy Traveler's first customers of the day. The dwarves closed in on a table not far from Kalir and Dir'grar. The big cook looked over to the dwarves as well, offering a firm but welcoming smile to them then turned his attention back to Kalir, who seemed more perplexed than he had been in some time.

Kalir continued. "I've never seen Ranyll outside of Telgin. And now he's here; and with a young woman no less. Where had his head gone? I bet my sister is worried sick about him."

Dir'grar did his best to console his friend, which wasn't much at all because that sort of thing wasn't really Dir'grar's strong suit. "You must relax, my friend. He seems to have his wits about him from what I've seen last night. Not very many men can confront me like that and have the ability to form words the next day to talk about it. He seems to be a very strong lad, this nephew of yours."

Kalir nodded his head in agreement. "Yes, he is a strong one, Dir'grar. That's what I'm afraid of, though . . . and I believe this Gabriella that he brought with him is something more than just a friend. There's something about her that I can't quite put my finger on. Did you see the way she looked at us earlier, like she had never seen the face of a man before in her life?"

Dir'grar shook his head and gave his long-time friend a reassuring pat on the shoulder as he moved to get up, lifting himself from his chair to serve the dwarves, barely noticing a server had already made her way over to table and began to take their order. Dir'grar looked back to Kalir, who took another sip at his brew, scraping the last bite of food into his mouth with a wooden spoon, pushing the bowl back away from him.

Dir'grar did his best to take the stress of the times off of his friend's shoulders. "Well, Kalir, it seems like we have this checkpoint covered for the moment. If you would like to escort your nephew wherever he is going, I'm sure we could handle it here for a ten day or so. You know I can handle it, Kalir."

The checkpoint captain knew this all too well. Dir'grar was a good man, had been since Kalir had first met him at the tavern in Dradle. Dir'grar had saved him from all too many terrible fates and now, as he looked at the big man, knew he could count on his friend for anything at all, even if it didn't have to do with Dir'grar at all.

Kalir grabbed his pack and walking stick from beside the table and slipped the straps of the pack over his shoulders, looking to the other side of the tavern for his crew. They were all gathered at a table near the corner of the room, talking quietly as they waited for Kalir to finish his meal. Once they saw him stand they followed suit, gathering their things as well, securing what they would need for the morning patrol of the channel. Kalir waved the group on towards the door and turned to his friend before leaving.

"Maybe, if Ranyll will have me, I will help my nephew. But not until he asks for my help." He returned Dir'grar's clap on the big man's shoulder and moved for the door. He looked at his friend one last time before leaving. "You see, Dir'grar, I am learning after all. And you said I was as stubborn as a horse."

Dir'grar was caught off guard by the comment but countered smartly.

"No, my friend, I said you looked like a horse." Both laughed aloud and went their own ways.

For the remainder of the morning, Dir'grar kept busy in his kitchen while Kalir, with his checkpoint crew, approached the channel with the hustle and bustle of men on a mission, filled with enthusiasm and fervor for the unknown. And, with the past few days finds, they had not been disappointed.

The groups had split as they approached the channel, one group taking the northern side, several immediately wading out into the water, while the other group took the southern side, preparing themselves for the crossing over the channel by raft. The northern group kept themselves busy by testing the depths of the water with several long sets of poles, moving them across the bottom of the channel, many taking turns plunging them into the water to remove any debris or rubbish that had collected on the sides or in the middle of the channel where several rocks jutted out into the middle of the steady-moving current.

The southern half of the group made their way to the small raft that was connected to both sides of the channel with a rope, climbing aboard the sturdy vessel to cross to the other side. They made it across with little effort, pressing their wooden poles down into the current, testing for any loose bottoms that would cause the way to be blocked. Once across, they followed the same path the northern side had followed, a lone scribe on each side marking off the daily checks as the rest tested the waters with their devices, using simple sets of nets and gathering equipment to filter the water thoroughly.

Ermoor Tiven moved into the channel until it was waist high, grasping the wading pole at the tips of its handle, the strap secured around his wrist, watching as the others around him did the same, moving as far as they could out into the channel, keeping their heads and arms surfaced above the water, using their poles to reach out into the center of the channel where the commerce vessels traveled frequently. Ermoor didn't notice the others on the northern side, for he was more concerned with his own crew since becoming the new lead crewman under Master Ranolf. He had been an apprentice for many years at another checkpoint but had come here since hearing of new positions opening in the ranks. And this was his chance to show them all back at Telgin.

This is where I am going to change everything. I am going to make a difference here, Ermoor could feel it.

Since changing checkpoints, he had earned the respect among his peers and even some of the elder crewman that had, at first, looked down upon him as not being able to handle the position. But he had indeed showed his abilities when one crewman had been caught in a strong current and pulled into the channel. Quick thinking and an even quicker hand had saved the crewman and Ermoor was accredited hero for the day, which showed him in a new light to Kalir, whom he had much respect for.

Ermoor lifted his pole out of the channel every-so-often, looking at each of the catch holds to see if anything had latched onto them since he had moved his position in the water. Small pieces of driftwood, a dirty rag, and an old fishing net hung on the tips of the nearest catch holds, the young man sliding the pole back within his reach so he could pull off the pieces. He pulled the pieces of rubbish from the poles and gave them to what the group called a collector, a wading crewman that handled all of the refuse they found, and the collector then placed the scraps in a tattered sack, throwing the driftwood onto the land to dry with all of the other pieces of wood that had been floating in the water. Ermoor turned to the channel and placed the collection pole back into the water, letting himself get dragged a little ways out with the current, searching in the crystal blue water once more before continuing on to another location.

The days passed by slowly compared to his old life in Telgin, which had been fraught with pain and hardship. He had followed in his father's footsteps to be a fisherman and, as the years went by, realized that the tradition that had been in his family for three generations was not for him. Ermoor felt that, in some way, he didn't know how though, that he was meant for more. He didn't question the thought either. Several times, before he had left, his father had urged him to stay and give fishing another try.

'I'm not made for that, father. I'm made for something more, can't you see that?' In the end, his father gave in and let him set off from the family, but not without disowning him from the family altogether, making him an outcast among outcasts in the lonely world of Ar Solon.

The lead southern crewman shifted his weight to his right foot now, watching as a piece of debris floated by, arching his collection pole down into the currents to catch it. The debris caught hold on a hook and pulled him a little closer to the middle of the Tirapoor, Ermoor keeping himself steady as he pulled the pole closer to him, his fellow collector closing in behind him to collect. Ermoor reached for the debris with his free hand and turned it over.

It was a pack of sorts from a channel checkpoint nearby, for it had a checkpoint insignia stitched upon it in common lettering. He passed it to his collector and pulled his pole out of the water, moving back toward land to check it with his partner, water dripping off of their clothes as they walked onto solid ground. His collector, Rynen Griff, a younger, inexperienced man yet full of spirit, dropped his sack and used both hands to free the straps off of the pack, opening it. It held the basic supplies of all checkpoint crewman; rope, an extra set of clothes to change after channeling, and some odds and ends for camping in case the crew didn't get back before nightfall. Rynen passed it back to Ermoor who sifted through it as well.

"That's strange. They must have dropped it by accident. We'll have to get it back to them when we meet at the next season meeting, unless, of course, you feel like taking a trip up there with me sometime."

Rynen remembered the trips they used to take when he had started. Nights of entertainment and gambling; they seemed to be cursed with incessant gambling. But Rynen nodded happily, tapping his soggy pouches at his side in response.

"Master Tiven, I don't have any qualms about going as long as you don't get mad again when I win your ten day's wages." Ermoor tapped his wet hand against the young man's shoulder playfully, receiving a slap on the shoulder in return.

"You know I've been practicing, don't you? I've won three straight times at Black Starr against Dir'grar. He'll attest for my skill. You better be careful betting your wages, young one. I don't think you could take the loss as easily as I can." They both snickered in amusement, knowing that today wouldn't be as bad now that the day had begun on good ground for them. They both were slowly admitting to themselves that they were only human, after all, and work was just a precursor to play, as so many had discovered early on in their lives. Ermoor dropped the pack and turned to retrieve his collection pole when he heard a voice call out to him from upstream. It was one of his crewmen.

"I've found something, Master Tiven! I've found something!"

No more than a second had passed when another voice broke through the rush of the channel, alerting Ermoor to move further upstream. After dashing from his position, he soon found the crewman that had first called him, waist deep in the water, pulling at his collection pole to bring the item in. But the debris on the other side of the pole was weighing it down and seemed heavier than the crewman on the other side of the pole.

Soon, a voice further upstream called out, bringing urgency to Ermoor's steps as he neared the crewman. Together, they forced the pole and the debris on its other end out of the current and pulled it closer to shore, the collection hooks holding the debris steady. Another pull brought it almost within their reach, but the hooks slipped on its bounty and upturned it, revealing the corpse of a checkpoint crewman from a checkpoint further upstream.

Both crewmen jumped back and let the pole go instinctively, securing the nearest end of the pole to the ground with the straps and the end of it. Both shook with the chill of the air touching their wet forms as well as the thought that passed through them at that moment. And, again, a voice further upstream called out, requesting assistance to pull in heavy debris.

"The checkpoint crewmen have been killed! I have to alert Kalir immediately!" Ermoor turned to the crewman and gave orders to assist the others as much as possible while he and Rynen made for the raft. But, across the channel, they could already see Kalir looking in confusion at the bodies that had been caught on his side, his hands up in frustration at what was happening. And, as Ermoor climbed onto the raft, counting the heads of his south crewman, he saw something far upstream moving toward them fast. The raft from the checkpoint upstream was flowing with the currents straight towards the rocks next to them, on a collision course that would clog up a good portion of the channel. And, on it, something moved.

Black, hunched forms skittered across the small vessel, bouncing and leaping, several other forms motionless on the deck. As the raft approached, Ermoor ordered all off the boat except for him and Rynen. Rynen was confused, unclear at what they were about to do. The other raft was the same size as theirs yet out of control and moving fast. There wasn't much they could do. But Ermoor had a certain look on his face that showed Rynen what he was about to do. The same look had crossed his face before when he had jumped off his horse to catch the swindler that stole his crewman's supplies from a nearby wagon on one of their excursions, as well as the time he had broken his arm trying to tame a wild horse at the annual carnival. It was the look of fire in his eyes that worried Rynen the most.

He was going to try and stop the raft all by himself. And confront whatever lay on that vessel, all on his own.

Then Ermoor's voice brought Rynen back to the here and now. "Steer this raft, Rynen! We have to reach the middle of the channel before it gets to us so I can jump aboard and take control of it before it hits the rocks."

Rynen, though apprehensive, grabbed the oar onboard and slipped it into the grooves in place on the vessel. He placed it in the water and took a quick look at the other crewmen, who looked at them as though it could be the last time.

It might be, Rynen thought, kicking away from the small dock they were attached to so they were pushed free, drifting faster once the current picked them up, Rynen feeling the oar take hold within the currents that pulled them further out into the middle of Tirapoor Channel.

Kalir rushed from the northern side of the channel, wading into the deep of the water, throwing his gear to his crewman at the shore.

"Ermoor, no!" Kalir could feel the current pull him in quick, using his arms to keep control of his body all the while watching his crewman's raft moving out to meet the other checkpoint's abandoned vessel. He could see creatures occupying the craft and knew that it was something he had seen before. He knew them to be more dangerous than anything he had ever dealt with. Kalir dove into the water, trying to find where the currents stopped underneath and, once he had found it, began to tread water to his crewman's raft.

Ermoor could barely hear Kalir's cries out to him before his captain vanished underneath the water, the southern crew leader pressing on, the checkpoint vessel almost next to their own raft, watching as the unidentified figures took on a substance now that they could see them close up. They were shadows, four of them, moving about the craft nervously, several sets of razor sharp claws clicking wildly as they saw Ermoor's boat approach. The bodies of three crewmen lay motionless on the deck of the raft. Ermoor reached for his sword at his hip and, as he unsheathed it, noticed one of the shadows take notice and move closer to the edge of the boat.

In another second, it was in mid-air, its claws bared, disfigured maw spread open into an evil smile, falling right into the path of Rynen's oar just as it reached Ermoor. It was swatted down in one quick motion and Rynen held it down with the oar as Ermoor drew closer to it. Then the other three cut through the air with a screech and leapt at them both, the two crewmen unprepared for the assault. One landed on Rynen as the other two hit the deck, moving for Ermoor.

Rynen's oar slipped from his hands and his action let the creature he had trapped on the deck free, watching as the one on him unleashed a fury of slashes with its claws. Ermoor saw the escaped creature and brought his sword down upon its head, cleaving its shadowy form almost in two before the other two got to him. The dying shadow let out a howl and hit the deck and then Ermoor felt the raft jerk underneath him, the abandoned checkpoint raft slamming into their own. He saw Rynen lose his balance with the creature on him and go overboard and then all was black shadows.

The forms climbed up Ermoor's legs and were cutting and slashing wildly as they went, fresh wounds breaking upon his skin underneath the wet clothes. He lifted his sword and felt one of the creatures grab at his blade. It almost pulled the sword from his grasp but he held on, trying to steady himself on the tossing craft, swinging his sword out in front of him. The creature that still had hold flew out over him and onto the deck, Ermoor slamming his foot down upon the creature's neck, holding it steady as he delivered the blow that cleaved its head from its shadowy set of shoulders.

Then the raft tossed again as it hit a set of rocks protruding out from the currents and Ermoor felt the waves overtake him and the nightmarish creatures before him, his sword slipping from his grip. Ermoor's blood mingled with the water around him and he could see nothing, save for one of the creatures that came swimming at him.

Kalir broke from the surface of the water, watching as both rafts in front of him collided and Ermoor slipped off the side of the boat and into the water with one of the creatures.

"Damn him for not listening! Damn him!" Kalir soon reached the rushing currents next to the raft and grabbed for a hold just as the rocks came slamming into the other raft, splintering it into several pieces. Luckily for Kalir, the other checkpoint raft had drifted away from the rocks somewhat and he made his way onto the abandoned raft. But, after glancing, he noticed that it wasn't abandoned at all. There were several dead crewmen lying on the deck, cut to pieces and almost undistinguishable in the morning light.

He wasted no time and untied an oar from the cargo sleeves at the side of the raft, trying his best to gain control of the vessel, slamming the oar down into the wild currents. His hands slipped the first several tries but, once locking his fingers together, found that the oars caught between a set of rocks just to his left and the raft locked in place, his own raft soon slamming to the side of the one he stood on. He braced himself and found that holding the oars lessened the impact, looking out at the rushing currents around him for his crewmen.

Kalir left the oars in their places on the boat and moved for the sleeves again, uncoiling a rope from it as fast as he could. He looked again to the currents for any sign of them. He could see Rynen pressed against a nearby set of rocks, his face badly cut and bruised, using his oar to hold himself between two rocks until help arrived. Already, Kalir could see the crewmen on the shore bringing another raft from the Happy Traveler's supplies, tossing it into the water with a heave-ho, men attending to it in haste.

Kalir turned his attention back to the rope, which he had secured one side to the boat, the other side to himself. He made for the space between his boot and leggings, unsheathing the small dagger to cut the end of the rope if need be. He searched the water again. Suddenly, barely yards away, Ermoor erupted from the water, holding his eyes, blood pouring from his face into the water around him. Then another form erupted. It was a daemon, Kalir knew.

Kalir confirmed it when the creature opened its maw wide and went for Ermoor. He had dealt with these things before. He leapt for it, the rope unraveling behind him, the cold water rushing up on him. He felt his shoulder collide with the daemon and he threw his weapon up in defense, cleaving into the daemon deeply, its shadowy form sinking down quickly into the current, trying to escape the dagger and the hand that held it.

"No you don't, you bastard!" Kalir took a deep breath and followed it down. He dove for it, feeling the current take him. Where it took him he did not care, as long as it crossed paths with the daemon's escape route. He felt out in front of him, his fingers tightening around a slippery form, a limb of some sort. He lifted his head up, kicking his legs to make it back to the surface, his captive alive and wild between his fingers. He broke the surface and brought his catch up with him, the daemon screaming in protest. Kalir could feel it slip out of his grasp so he jabbed at it with the dagger, again and again, the watery surface around him filling with a foul-smelling liquid.

I've wounded it. He lifted his weapon in the air above the waves and jabbed it down into the water, bringing the tip of the blade deep into and through the daemon's flesh, the waves silencing its last scream. Kalir took another breath and dove down into the water, resheathing his dagger quickly, making his way further down the way with the current steadily at his back, trying to see within the currents. He came back up from the Tirapoor and saw the rocks just ahead of him, Ermoor resting behind one of them, the currents pulling at him in his weakened state. Kalir, his muscles sore from the struggle with the daemon, used the last of his strength to reach the rocks, grabbing for a hold, the rope around him soon tightening at his waist. He tried to call over the current.

"Ermoor, grab my hand and I'll pull us in." Ermoor, his head lifting up from the watery surface, nodded and reached out a hand, his other hand holding his eyes.

Three long claw marks were dug into his skin across his face and eyes, his hand bloodied from the wounds. Ermoor soon found Kalir's hand and pulled himself closer, wrapping his free arm around Kalir's neck as his captain pulled them in. Kalir could see the raft with his crewmen approach as he finally pulled them both to the abandoned raft, throwing his elbow up onto the deck for a hold. He turned when he heard the shouts from his crewmen on the raft and saw them pointing just as a daemon on deck rushed at him. He turned to see its claws extend out to him. It jumped and was upon him when a flash of metal flew past Kalir and knocked the creature back, the familiar sound of Dir'grar's crossbow ringing out from the nearby raft. The daemon flew back onto the deck and tumbled over the other side, the currents swallowing it up before it could attempt to save its own life.

Dir'grar pulled Ermoor and Kalir to safety on the occupied raft with the others of the crew, soon fishing Rynen from between the set of rocks he had laid against, motionless, waiting for the daemon's to strike again. However, amid the rush of the currents, the Tirapoor Channel was silent, unaware of the battle that had just occurred, save for the wounded crewman of the Happy Traveler. Kalir watched as the shore closed in, several oars bringing them in quickly, hoping to attend to the wounds before they became severe.

And they needed to forewarn the other checkpoints, Kalir reminded himself. *But that would come later.* First, Kalir needed to find out the truth. And there was only one place he could think to start, and he hated it more than ever to think that his nephew was a part of this.

5

It had only been a short passing of time since the incident at the Tirapoor Channel and the checkpoint crew of twelve for the Happy Traveler along with Kalir and his friend Dir'grar had already pressed themselves into Kalir's private cottage, which was just on the outskirts of the Happy Traveler's property, the two close friends looking warily at each, knowing that something was amiss in the land of Kariyl. But they kept it to themselves until they knew exactly what, acting as though they were the victims of an unknown attack; which they, in truth, had truly been, hoping beyond hope that this was to be the only attack.

Nevertheless, they knew that war and Kariyl's history with war had never been like that; that something like this had struck once and only once.

This was a first wave, maybe not even that, Kalir thought, watching the wounded of his crew being placed on the extra beds in one of his many rooms.

"Get the healer, quickly!" Kalir's voice broke the commotion and one of his crew moved from the party and headed for the door, disappearing out into the forest surrounding his cabin. He looked over to his wounded crewmen. Rynen was on a cot, nearly unconscious, his face bruised on the right side, apparently from the run in with the channel's currents and a myriad of rocks that had collected his small frame. The young man smiled weakly when Kalir approached, Kalir clasping his hand around Rynen's cold fingers, placing himself next to the young boy while the others were quick at work on his other crewman, gathering the supplies needed to tend to him.

Rynen winced when he tried to speak, bringing his free hand to his face, feeling the severity of the bruise with the tips of his fingers.

"I suppose Ermoor and I are in trouble now, are we not, Master Ranolf?" Kalir forced a smile through his worry, trying his best to appease the youth and not worry him as well.

"Trouble, Rynen? Why would you think that? You are in anything but trouble, my young crewman." Kalir turned to look at Dir'grar, who was tending to Ermoor, letting others in the crew hold the southern checkpoint leader down while they tried to mend his wounds. Dir'grar shook his head. Kalir turned his attention back to Rynen, who lifted himself up on his elbows, letting Kalir's hand go.

"I heard you calling to us before I fell overboard. I heard you tell Master Tiven to stop." Rynen bowed his head in shame, trying to compose himself among his fellow friends when Ermoor's cries rang out, the young man out of control.

"Stay here, Rynen. I'll be right back." Kalir motioned for the young boy to stay and made his way over to the other cot, pushing through his crewman until he saw Dir'grar pressing a cold rag to Ermoor's wounds on his face. The young man was in a rage. The three cuts had torn straight across his face in three straight lines, one crossing over his left eye, which was now swollen and couldn't be seen. Curses and words of war passed through Ermoor's lips, trying to pull away from his crewmen to cover his face.

"Let me go, you dogs! Do not look! That creature has damned me forever!" He covered his face with a freed hand and closed his undamaged eye, forcing the others away from him with a booted foot. Dir'grar tried to steady Ermoor, but he hesitated, worried that asserting his strength would hurt the man. Dir'grar eased himself back from the young man, letting the man rant and flail, the others watching in amazement as their companion struck out at them.

Within moments, Kalir stepped forward and, with a firm grasp on Ermoor's shoulders, shook him soundly.

"Crew leader Tiven, gather hold of yourself, man! I order you to refrain from this manner at once." The checkpoint master's voice boomed throughout the cottage, silencing Ermoor and any others that may have spoken at that moment. Even Dir'grar held his breath, knowing that Kalir very rarely raised his voice, even since he and Kalir had known each other. Ermoor opened his eye and stared at Kalir for a time before speaking; the next time he spoke, his voice had leveled almost to a soft whisper, and the intensity reminded Kalir of a whimpering dog he had once owned.

"Would you tell the others that I wish to be alone now, Master Ranolf? I have no need of them at this time." Kalir looked down at the man before him, biting his lip as he surveyed the damage the daemon had done to Ermoor's face.

"Fine, Ermoor. I'll have them go. But you must calm yourself." Ermoor nodded, slowly lying his head back down on the cot, reaching for the cold cloth that had fallen from his face. He pressed it onto his wounded eye.

Kalir turned to Dir'grar, who was already dismissing the others, relaying orders that there would be a meeting later and to be available. The only ones left in the room then were Dir'grar, Kalir, and the two wounded crewmen, Kalir watching as the door closed behind the others of his team.

This had been a mighty blow to them on this day, the checkpoint leader thought, taking a look at the two men wounded in front of him. He tried to calm himself, remembering that, so far, his checkpoint and the other one further up north that had been attacked were the only ones that knew of the creatures that scoured the channel.

They were looking for something, Master Ranolf concluded, looking to his long-time friend for any signs of an answer or possibly further concern that could come from this. Kalir moved from Ermoor's side for the moment and motioned Dir'grar closer.

"What do you think, Dir'grar? Is it as bad as I think?"

"That depends on what question you're asking me, my friend. Are we speaking of the daemons or this young man's eyesight?"

"Both." Dir'grar glanced over to the young Ermoor, making sure that he wasn't listening.

"Both are bad. That eye will not be used again. As for the daemons...I have news that you may not be ready for, my friend."

Dir'grar relayed the message that he had received from a carrier at the checkpoint just north of the Happy Traveler, showing him the scroll that he had read moments before making his way, crossbow in hand, down to the checkpoint docks.

"I was hoping to find you before they did. I had no idea that the raft was headed this way. The message had said that the raft had taken another route in the Tirapoor Channel. But then, I had this awful feeling. And that told me that you were in danger, Kalir."

Dir'grar patted his friend's shoulder, watching the crease on Kalir's face form into a small grin.

"And so you decided to save me again, didn't you, Dir'grar?"

"Friends don't come around so easy this part of Kariyl; or at least not to me. Anyways, I must have come at the proper time, because I saw the rescue raft being thrown in to save all of you, and that's when I made my move."

"And a good move you made, my dear Dir'grar." Kalir knew that, without this monster of a man, he would have not lived to see this day and the many others that had passed since their first meeting. The smaller of the two men drew in a breath and was thankful for it, leaning down to slip off his wet boots.

"I must see my nephew. I think he is connected in some way to what has happened here today; him **and** that woman of his."

"You mean young Ranyll? Kalir, are you mad? He's just a young boy in love."

"That's not what I see when I look into his eyes, Dir'grar. Not what I see at all."

Dir'grar watched as Kalir made his way into a nearby room, rummaging through several crates. In no time, Kalir returned dressed in dry garments, sheathing his short sword, its sheath attached to a belt that he had buckled around his waist.

Dir'grar continued. "Then what do you see in his eyes, Kalir?"

"I see fear, my friend. I see fear."

*   *   *

Young Ranyll, we are safe here no longer. They have followed our tracks and are very close now. Awake, young Ranyll, awake!

The sleepy-eyed young man jolted upright from where he laid, his hand blindly reaching for his sword, which was not at his side. He opened his eyes and saw that the morning had passed him by, a small piece of sunlight still lingering within the room yet not the strong rays of the morning sun.

I have slept through the night and some of the morning, too.

Gabriella was standing not far from the bedside, using a cold rag from the basin in their room to clean her arms and legs as well as her feet before she slipped on her full set of garbs. She motioned to Ranyll's sword, which was lying across the small table that held the basin, looking at him closely before speaking.

"You were having a dream, Ranyll. You mumbled much in the course of the night, but most of it I couldn't understand. You're sword is there if you have need of it." Ranyll jumped to his feet, almost startling the angel, grabbing for his sword and the belt that hung limply on it. He slipped it around his waist and tightened it, checking the blade before moving to the rest of supplies.

It was still sharp enough for battle.

He would have to remind himself to get a sharpening stone from his uncle before he left. He turned to Gabriella, sitting back down to slip on his boots, which felt a dozens times better than his older pair, which were worn down to a small piece of leather, many times bruising the bottoms of his feet on rough terrain.

"Gwenzel was calling to me. He says that we're in danger and need to leave at once. I believe the daemons have followed us. We must continue our trek to Reune Lake." Gabriella seemed concerned when he told her of the message that the unicorn had given him, yet she looked a great deal more able to deal with the troubles of the world now that she had gotten some sleep, good food, and clothing that suited her. Still, that didn't ease the conflicting ideas within Ranyll's own mind, which kept going over the battle he had been in over and over.

If there had been anymore of those creatures, then I would have been doomed along with Gwenzel and Gabriella.

The young man watched as Gabriella slipped on her cloak and grabbed her satchel with a change of clothes and other provisions his uncle had given her. The young man knew he would never let the daemons take her while he was still alive and breathing.

He still didn't know what it was between them. He had felt love before, not long ago, remembering the young girl that had moved away without saying goodbye to him. His heart was crushed for a full season, barely able to do his chores, being short with everyone around him. He had felt the pangs of heartache and knew that this was different; that, what he and

Gabriella had was something more than just that. Indeed, they had shared an intimate moment between each, yet that wasn't what propelled Ranyll further and further away from his home in Telgin.

Yes, it was something different completely.

The two of them made their way down to the tavern exit of the Happy Traveler, carrying their supplies, intent on leaving at that moment, when Taleena stopped them short, putting a hand on Ranyll's shoulder.

"Now where do you think the two of you are going? Master Ranolf told me to take care of you two, and that means that I can't let you leave without a full stomach. Kalir would be furious if I let you two leave without feeding you. Now you just have a seat at a nearby table and I'll have some food to you in no time." Ranyll tried to protest but Taleena pressed her strong fingers into his shoulder and pushed him towards a table, motioning for Gabriella to follow as well.

"Shouldn't we be leaving, Ranyll? If Gwenzel has called you, then there is danger approaching. Faeriekind do not lie." Ranyll nodded in agreement.

"I'll just have to tell Taleena that we must be going and are already late, which isn't far from the truth. I'm sure she'll understand." Ranyll rubbed his shoulder from where she had grabbed him and moved from the table they had been seated at, making his way for Taleena, who was now taking an order from a trio of dirty fellows that looked as though they had traveled miles and fallen into their seats from exhaustion.

Ranyll hated to interrupt but did so anyways, thinking it would be in his best interests to leave quickly before Taleena had called the order in to the cook behind the bar. He reached her just as she moved from the table, his hand just missing her shoulder. She turned back to the table and bumped into Ranyll, dropping her serving tray, yet catching it before it hit the ground.

"Ranyll, can I help you? Your order will be out shortly. Now, if you'll have a seat." She nudged him back towards his table with her free hand.

This was beginning to tax Ranyll's nerves. He wasn't a boy, nor should he be treated like one.

"I'm sorry to disappoint you or upset my uncle but I must be leaving now. I cannot wait any longer, no matter how good the food may be." A voice from behind broke Ranyll's focus.

"I'm already upset, Ranyll. Very upset. And you're not going anywhere until we sort this out." Ranyll turned to see his uncle with Dir'grar towering just behind him, arms crossed across his massive chest. Kalir's nostrils were flaring as his eyes glared at his nephew.

The storage room door slammed shut behind them and Ranyll backed into a corner with Gabriella a safe distance away from the other two in front of them. Dir'grar and Kalir had moved the conversation to the storage room, which was connected just past the kitchen door within the cooking area itself.

They've found out my secret, was Ranyll's first fear, turning to look at the frightened Gabriella as she was ushered, along with him, to the back storage rooms of the Happy Traveler.

"Tell me what's going on, Ranyll! And tell me what part she plays in this," pointing at Gabriella, who almost cowered at the tone of his uncle's voice, which had almost broken into a roar, his eyes wild and furious.

"I can't tell you, uncle. It is a secret. Everything's become a secret since I left Telgin. My purpose, my reasoning, even whom I travel with is a secret. And a secret it must stay." He couldn't tell his uncle. He knew it would ruin the bond he had between Gwenzel and he wouldn't be able to see the magical creature again if his uncle got involved. Kalir became enraged and charged for the young man, who drew his sword in response and held it, tip out in front of him.

His uncle was furious. "Ranyll, you have no idea what's going on, do you? There are dangers far beyond your comprehension happening now on Kariyl! I've got two wounded men because of it and the checkpoint northeast of here has casualties! Casualties, Ranyll! There are men dead! And it's the trail of danger you've just walked no more than a night ago! How did you do it, Ranyll? How?"

Kalir, though still mad, seemed to calm himself more than he had been when he first entered the Happy Traveler. Ranyll still held his blade out between him and his uncle, remaining calm though his only connection to his family outside of Telgin had thrown accusations toward the young man, who was defending his honor and a promise.

And what a promise it was.

He looked at Gabriella, comforting her with a reassuring nod and looked back to his uncle, who had now retreated next to Dir'grar. Kalir, knowing he was not to get an answer, nodded to his larger friend. "Show them."

Dir'grar rolled out a sack he had been carrying from behind his back and emptied its contents out onto the floor. Ranyll jumped back as the shadowy body of a daemon hit the floor with a thud and was still.

"This is the secret that follows you, isn't it, Ranyll? Well, the secret no longer wants to remain secret any longer. It attacked a checkpoint crew just a few miles from here and they just attacked my crew. This is the only one we could find after the battle." Kalir paused to let all of it sink in and then continued. "Now you must say something, Ranyll, otherwise I will think you in much more danger than this."

"I am in much more danger than this, uncle. And I travel to try and abate it entirely. I am Gabriella's protector. That is all that I can say." Ranyll had stuck with his promise and received a nod from both Dir'grar and Kalir, though his uncle was still upset, understanding that forces larger than they could imagine were at work here.

"Then, as your friend, I must let you go. But, as your uncle, let me speak to you alone for a moment. Gabriella will be safe here until we get back. Dir'grar will make sure of that." Ranyll didn't know whether to trust his uncle and go or stay with Gabriella and make their passing quicker by leaving that moment. He knew that Gabriella's life as well as his own were in danger no matter where they went. They weren't safe here at the Happy Traveler, and the longer they stayed, the more danger Kalir and his crew were to face. Ranyll had no time to decide.

Kalir slipped past the young man's defenses and disarmed his nephew with a flip of the wrist, prying the sword from his nephew's grip. He resheathed it at Ranyll's side and put an arm around his disoriented nephew, moving them back out into the tavern before Ranyll could protest. Dir'grar gathered the daemon's corpse back into the sack and tied it, tossing it aside, his hands shutting the door behind the two as they left.

Kalir took Ranyll out onto the front deck surrounding the Happy Traveler and further to his cottage just to the west of the checkpoint inn, motioning him in with a firm hand on his shoulder. Ranyll immediately saw the two wounded checkpoint men but was directed upstairs to Kalir's personal room, which consisted of a dresser with small trinkets here and there, a wash basin on a counter like the one in Ranyll's room, and several chests that sat on the floor.

"Since you have been tasked with something of the utmost importance, I must remind myself that it is your duty and not mine. Many times, especially since I've been living here, I've been accused of doing too much. And, when I first saw you here, I thought you needed help from me. And now I know why you are here. Something has brought you here for a reason. And now I know what it is. This." Kalir moved to a chest on the floor and opened it, pulling out a long cloth with an item wrapped in it. He unfolded the cloth from the item and held it out to Ranyll, who stared at it, a puzzled look on his face.

"You may not know of it, but this was your father's sword."

The next few moments seemed like a dream to Ranyll, as if he were a story that was being told to children throughout all of Kariyl before bedtime. The world around him seemed to stop as he felt the handle slide into his grip for the first time, looking down the hilt to the blade that glinted in the candlelit room.

*   *   *

'And for the longest time, the youth stared at the sword that his father had used during the Siege of Terapon, the fabled battle that drove away the evil of the previous world and made way for the new. His mother had told him it was lost amid the chaos of the battle and now, years later, he held it in his hands, surveying the piece of history that had sent his father away, never to return.'

The Chronicler dipped his quill into the inkpot again, moving the worn quill across the page, changing to another parchment quickly, trying to keep up with the story that surged into his mind. He lifted himself from his writing desk and made his way, with the wet piece of parchment, to a section of ropes that had been set up so he could hang each parchment so the ink could dry. He pressed the piece of paper against the small piece of twine while attaching it with a wooden clip, moving back to his desk, quill already in his hand before sitting down. He had written for hours now and was near exhaustion, yet still the story came.

The details were intricate, the faces still burning into his mind. The young boy; his hopes, dreams, all coming to play across the page he now wrote, along with the preceding pages. He knew of the history of Telgin and knew of the glory and fame that the Tolver name had made, yet knew also of the hardships the family had to face losing a husband and a father all at once. Gilden Felves stretched his sore body across his chair for a moment, extending his aching fingers out in front of him.

To think that these are the hands that write histories. A person would be amazed to know that these weak, fragile limbs have yet still further to go.

Gilden leaned forward into his work, looking behind him at the hundreds of pages that hung on the set of ropes, still drying in the early morning hours. The light from outside didn't make it into Gilden's small writing room yet Gilden still knew the time of day from the noises just outside his doors. The scribes were up and serving breakfast, getting ready for the morning's work.

Soon, Gilden thought, *someone will be at my door, waiting for me to take my place at the table. And they will be much displeased when I don't answer*, Gilden concluded to himself, his eyes peering down through the small spectacles on the tip of his nose, looking down at the page as the story came clear to him inside his head.

'The sword had been created by a smith in the great city of Argolis. It had been forged and designed just for the Treaty between the races, not to strike fear in the other races, but to show them it was a sign of a finer time for the world, a time in which peace could reign, yet still hold true with the strength that each race had. But that was not what made the swords famous. It wasn't until The Siege of Terapon that they got use and their respect.

The dwarves had made a set of 30 axes, which were given to the leaders of the council during that time, though none of the original council remained today. The world of the dwarves was always tumultuous and up heaving.

As for the elves, three short swords had been made for the representatives from each elven city that thrived on Kariyl. And the humans, as they began their journey to Fell Whist, left with the finest swords man had ever crafted. Besides the king swords of the old world, the six broadswords that were crafted for the representatives from each city were the most prized pieces in all of Kariyl.

The pommel and hilt were made from the most excellent golden ore, a single blue sapphire stone used as the pommel's centerpiece, the color signifying the town of Telgin. The other towns had colors as well. Ruby, emerald, amethyst, diamond, topaz, and garnet were the other gems that adorned the remaining swords, the broadswords soon finding their owner's hands just before the meeting began in Fell Whist. The blade had been sharpened and shined until every light that touched it glinted off the surface of the finest piece of smithing anyone had seen in ages.

The treaty had been set forth as a pact between the three races to exterminate the remaining threat from the Great War that plagued the small towns on the outskirts of Kariyl. The threats were minor compared to the Knights of the Treaty, which is what those selected had been named after the Great War. They were soon far southeast as the name became known, crossing the Great Bridge Katharsis onto Terapon, a small island just east of the great elven city of Elvinisclar. Then a swarm of the enemy attacked.

A race of goblins, which had been in hiding since the Great War, struck out and surrounded the knights. With swords in hand, the humans were the first wave that faced the amassed liege of creatures. The knights fell quickly and were passed up, the goblins rushing for the elves, the most hated of all the races.

But the dwarves, who were thicker in skin and in numbers as well, moved ahead of the elves and rushed the goblins, which were struck down with powerful blows from the great axes that were forged just for that purpose. The first and last battle the weaponry would ever see again; or so many had thought. Crin Tolver, a human representative from Telgin, had fallen but was not defeated. He had made his way back to the battle, his brother-in-law by his side the whole way, a young Kalir rushing in with him, sword in hand as well. However, Kalir was not a representative from a city but a volunteer, as were many others that fought against the goblins, soon coming to realize that they were outnumbered.

And, as he fought, deep in the back of his mind, he thought of his family back home, safe from harm. And, the one person he thought most of was his sister, Rachel. She had just been married and was expecting a second child on the way. She had sent her brother to ensure her husband's safety on such a dangerous battle.

Crin was not a warrior like Kalir had become over time, nor was he good with a sword. But, what he was good at, many people had discovered, was morale and honor. He was very respected among the town of Telgin and, through that, had been elected as the representative to go and tell of the troubles in the east and offer his services if they were needed. And, amid the rush of battle, his blade rang true and straight as though he had been created for war. Crin's eyes burned with the fire of war, his sword cutting a swath through the enemy. But the story soon ended with the father of the young boy Ranyll falling in battle, Kalir by his side, trying to fend off the enemy until help arrived. The help did arrive, but it wasn't quick enough to save poor Crin's life.'

*   *   *

"Your father wanted you to have this, Ranyll. He put it into my keeping until you would have use of it. And now, I think, is the time." Kalir watched as Ranyll grasped his father's sword in his hands, tears soon streaming down the young man's face.

It was truly my father's sword. He could feel it in each small swing he took with it, almost as if his father was there to help him wield it, pressing his hands tighter against the handle.

"My father's sword." He watched as Kalir extracted a sheath from the chest as well, handing it over to his nephew, watching the young man sheath the great sword for the first time.

"The broadsword was made for sheathing at the shoulder. Your father's sheath was damaged in battle and, when I came back, I had a new one made for it. You'll soon grow accustomed to it, though." Uncle Ranolf unclasped the sheath with Ranyll's sword from the young man's belt, looking into Ranyll's eyes as they sparkled with each thought of his father.

Kalir wished that Crin was here for this moment but he knew that he was probably the best second choice anyone could have, knowing the closeness that Crin and his son had, first hand. Ranyll clasped the sheath around his right shoulder and tied it to his belt to keep it from moving while he traveled. With a few minor adjustments, it fit perfect.

"I think that we can retire this blade of yours, don't you, Ranyll? It looks as though it needs no more action." Kalir moved away with the simple sheathed blade under his arm and placed it into the same chest he had retrieved the great broadsword from, closing the chest back the way it had been. He moved to another, speaking to Ranyll from over his shoulder while he rummaged through another chest not far away.

"I am no stranger to peril, my nephew, I'm sure you already know that. But I, too, have seen the shadowy creatures that follow you in my time and know that they are tricky and deceitful. A man is something with a great blade, which you have now, but he is even more when he is well equipped with another." Kalir lifted himself up from the chest with another blade, yet this one was smaller, the blade thinning to a needle-like point. He handed the sheathed weapon to Ranyll, who unsheathed it slowly until the blade was completely bare to the eye. It was a beautiful creation, all of the blade and the handle including the pommel a magnificent silver sheen. The blade and handle could not be deciphered from one another if they had not been separated by a small, black, hand guard that covered just enough of the handle to stop a glancing blow of a sword or similar weapon.

Kalir smiled when remembering the origins of the weapon.

"That was given to me long ago on Terapon. It is called a war dagger. Only elven warriors used them during the war. These are hard to come by, but I was lucky enough to acquire one. The elves made it to honor the wars that they had fought and only forged the steel that it is made from at night. It is known for its durability and lightness. It has saved me a number of times. I hope that it serves you as well as it has me. Keep it close to you, Ranyll. You'll never know when you'll need it."

Kalir hoped that his young nephew would never have to use a close range weapon at all, *but things always turn out differently somehow*, Kalir remarked to himself, thinking of times gone by, trying to keep good thoughts of his nephew in place of the bad that troubled him every time that he looked at the young man.

"Thank you, uncle. I will keep it close, as you say."

"Good. That's what I like to hear. Well, this can't go on any longer. I know you have to leave. I can only hope that you will be careful once you leave here. I will send word to your mother that you have come here for a while, so she will not worry. Maybe I'll go to Telgin myself and visit. You know it's been a long time since I've seen your brother, Timothy."

Ranyll nodded and sheathed the smaller blade, slipping it into his belt, tying a small bit of cord about it to keep it secure. He hugged his uncle tightly, afraid to let go, fearing that it would be the last time, yet knowing that there was a journey waiting for him just outside the doors of his uncle's cottage. He released his uncle and smiled at him, wiping his face with the hem of his cloak, straightening the broadsword on his back before making his way downstairs. The two wounded of Kalir's crew were asleep now so Kalir and Ranyll moved quietly through the room and out the door, his uncle shutting it slightly behind them.

Dir'grar and Gabriella were waiting just outside the Happy Traveler, the big man looking quickly over to Kalir who nodded in response to his friend's gaze, which was poised on the great sword that Ranyll carried on his back. Ranyll met with Gabriella as Dir'grar took Ranyll's hand in his own two hands, shaking it one last time before the party of two left heading west, the remainder of the day's sunlight following along with them, both forms soon disappearing over a small rolling hill of trees ahead. Dir'grar strolled over to Kalir and patted him on the back, acknowledging the pain that Kalir had felt letting his kin loose into the world now that danger had reared its ugly head.

"You made the right choice, Kalir. You always do. Well, at least, since I've known you." Kalir tried to smile but it was no use. He had sent his oldest nephew out into danger, he had two wounded men to tend to, and the checkpoint still needed to be secured. The entire world seemed to be falling apart around him. The only good thing was that he had Dir'grar by his side, all the way, through thick and thin. The big man looked back at Kalir's cottage and met the man's gaze, which trailed off in the distance where his nephew had disappeared.

"What's next, boss?" Kalir couldn't help but smile. Dir'grar had always called him that when he knew Kalir was down, though Kalir felt that he was far from that title, except when it came to the checkpoint.

"You know I hate it when you call me that, Dir'grar. It makes me feel old."

"Well, you're not getting any younger standing there, Kalir. And I don't have many years left to waste standing in one place, if you know what I mean!" Kalir knew what he meant, knew what he wanted. Kalir took a deep breath.

"I need a meeting at once. First and foremost, though, I need the checkpoint cleared before dark. Double up the remaining members, assign leaders to both sides to take over for now. After that's done, I'll have a plan ready." Dir'grar nodded and went to prepare for a long night when Kalir continued. "And Dir'grar… get a horse and rider to deliver a message to my sister. Make everything sound fine with Ranyll. I don't want her to worry about her oldest. Make up something good. You know, like you always do when telling me awful things. Get him on his way immediately."

Kalir grinned when reminded of the times that had come his way throughout his life. And he grinned even wider when he thought of the hustle and bustle that came his way. Though it had been terrible what had happened to his men and the others they had found, he knew he was one of the better checkpoint guards to deal with it. Kalir's hand then drifted to the hilt of his sword, watching as Dir'grar moved away, the huge shadow following behind him as he made his way to the Happy Traveler, soon disappearing in through the doorway to alert the crew.

Yes, things were coming his way. And he intended on stopping them with every chance he was given.

*   *   *

No sooner had Ranyll and Gabriella left the safety of Dir'grar and Kalir that they saw a form within the woods, moving at a fast pace to intercept them. Ranyll reached for the handle of his father's sword over his shoulder when a familiar voice popped into his mind.

Glad you could make it, young Ranyll. I was beginning to think you weren't coming. Gwenzel broke through the tree line and moved close to Gabriella, who petted him and stroked his soft mane as they walked. Ranyll stared silently for some time, still amazed that such a beautiful creature was so close to him, the sight still entrancing him, his hand moving back away from his sword.

"Yes, we're here, Gwenzel. I had to say goodbye to my uncle. As you can see, he cared for us well while we were there," motioning to the satchels full of supplies and food in both of their packs.

I take it then that it was a good goodbye? Gwenzel made a steady pace next to both Gabriella and Ranyll, looking over the things they had acquired with interest, sniffing Gabriella's attire every now and then while she wasn't looking.

"Yes, Gwenzel, it was." Ranyll felt the weight of his father's sword move against his back in rhythm with his step, pressing his hand against the bottom of the sheath that sat on his left hip from time to time as they made their way to Reune Lake.

It was his now, though, he corrected himself, feeling the weight again to make sure that it wasn't all a dream. It was heavier than that of his previous sword, yet he didn't mind the weight at all, especially knowing where it had come from. He looked up from his thinking and noticed that he was trailing from Gwenzel and Gabriella.

*   *   *

'He moved to catch up, the great broadsword moving with him, the great blade filled with dark memories though, hopefully now in a better place, during a better time than it had seen. But the darkness still held shadows that, even with the brightest of good, were not easily defeated. But time has a way of changing things and, as Ranyll began to keep pace with the other two, he felt a calm that he had never felt before; something that would take years to explain. And he hoped that, after this journey, he would be alive to explain it all. All of this was new to him yet he would never forget it, not until the day he died, however close or far that may be.'

The old scribe lifted the quill from the still wet page, using a handful of drying salts to speed up the process so he could move from that page and continue to the next. It had been three nights and he still had not slept. Every muscle in his body seemed to call out to him in desperation, begging him for sleep. Nevertheless, he knew that he couldn't sleep until the deed had been done. And a deed it was for Gilden Felves, one of the more revered scribes in the guild. He had written all night many times before, several times in fact, and never had it affected him as much as this stint of writing had done him now.

Gilden lifted slowly from his seated position and, grabbing the finished page in front of him carefully with both hands, moved over to the twine line and clipped it so it would dry while he was resting. The muscles in his back began to tighten, either with age or lack of sleep, he could not tell, for they had so intermingled with another that every pain had different reasons and he cared not to spend the time figuring which it was. Gilden straightened himself back up and felt the weariness set upon him now, as it had never done before, his body giving out under him. He collapsed on his bed and sleep overtook him in moments, a quiet, peaceful sleep that calmed the weary muscles, the knotted up hands, and the swollen lids that covered the strained eyes. Gilden was given a proper rest for the first time in a ten day.

6

It was late in the day, one of the prettiest days of the season, when she appeared. It was at Reune Lake, far beyond any of the fishermen or travelers that frequented there. No one could see her with the exception of the faeries. There were dozens of them, the faerie kin, hiding in the shrubs, in the trees, behind the older elms, their branches swaying in celebration when Shilinda appeared.

There was a golden mist, like a sandstorm but calm, the shards of gold floating in the calm afternoon air. She appeared at first as an angelic being, without substance, void of clarity and the only explanation would be to believe that you were dreaming awake. Her angelic wings fluttered and tensed high above her head, then slowly bent themselves back behind her, disappearing from view completely. As her mortal form appeared out of the mist a texture of ages cast itself off of her, taking on the beautiful gracefulness of a queen as she approached the faeries, bare feet touching the soft grass.

She was clothed in a light blue silken gown, a silk scarf tied around her delicate waist, trailing behind her. The Faerie Queen wore no jewelry or fancy ornaments; in fact, she did not have need of any. Small, magikal sparks flew around her head, cascading down her arms, as though it were the life's blood of the magikal world itself. The faerie queen also wore the crown. Full of the same sparks that littered around her shape and followed it, the crown was created for her by the creatures of the forest years ago and she had always worn it afterwards when appearing before them. A mossy veil swept over her hair, a single topaz stone set in the center of the crown so that it was placed on the center of her forehead, facing out to the ones that watched as she approached them. Shilinda smiled at her faerie children and held out her arms. As of late, she rarely came down to see her children; she only came when there were problems that needed to be solving. And, when she came to them, they did not take her appearance lightly.

And, indeed, something was amiss. Shilinda could only hold the smile for so long, and then it dissipated, her eyes sad and filled with tears.

"My children; something has happened in the clouded world above and has brought itself down here upon your world, little ones." Shilinda had never spoken of the realm she had come from. The faeries gasped then quieted down, a few giggles bursting out from the sprites in the trees. All sorts or faeries, pixies, luffes, mixels, sprites, gnomes, and many others scooted close to hear what Shilinda had to say. One in particular yearned to hear.

"Lousy sprites, be quiet! This is important!" Triggle pushed forward among the others of his faerie kind, his fuzzy beard almost getting under his big-booted feet. The Miftle faerie had seen Shilinda before, but never this close. He had to get a better look. Triggle nudged a few Unicorns out of the way, squeezing in between their massive, powerful legs, and sat in between two of them, taking off his dirty green hat. He sighed. Shilinda spoke again.

"We have an enemy. The daemons are on the surface again. I don't know how, but there have been sightings in Telgin." One of the Unicorns spoke, pawing at the ground close to Triggle.

"Isn't that where Gwenzel is at; in Telgin?" Shilinda nodded. The young Unicorn had left over a ten day ago and had yet to return. The Unicorn stomped his front hooves into the ground, almost denting poor Triggle.

"Hey, you enchanted horse, watch where you're getting angry!" wobbling off to somewhere safer.

"Sorry, little Miftle. Didn't mean to cause you discomfort." The unicorn directed his conversation back their queen and to the others of its race; a very few compared to the many other fairies that flourished among them, huffing in unison, trying their best to stay calm with the turmoil in their land that seemed to be brewing. "It's just that Gwenzel is still a young Unicorn." The eldest unicorn looked back to Shilinda.

"How can you put something that serious on his shoulders? Gwenzel's just a baby. He has yet to reach Flossto. Why didn't you send me?"

The elder unicorn grunted, looking among the others of his kind for support. But they were silent, waiting for a response from the faerie queen. The eldest knew that Gwenzel was ill educated compared to the others of his esteemed race, thinking now that that might be the main reason Gwenzel was chosen to go. The eldest knew from the look on Shilinda's face, within those eyes that stared back at the entirety of the faeries that lived in Faerie Homme, that Gwenzel was sent to do something important, though the details of Gwenzel's trip were of no importance at the time. Either that, or they were secret and for the young unicorn alone to know of.

"Gwenzel is young, yes, but he needs to understand that there is a whole world out there that is fierce and harsh and his magik can be of more use than just playing childish pranks on the fishermen." The eldest Unicorn lowered his head in shame. Shilinda continued.

"Yes, I know about his pranks on the fishermen. That is dangerous. If he got caught doing something like that, it would be the end of the faerie folk that live here; the end of the Faerie Homme at Reune Lake. Do you remember what happened with Kira Wells, that little human girl?" The faeries remembered all too well about the little girl, Kira as she was called by her race. It had been twenty summers since that horrid accident had taken place. All fairies tried to forget.

She had befriended some faeries years ago and was given a gift. When the humans found out what she had, there was a hunt for the girl and her magikal friends. The faerie folk had lived near Elvinisclar then, not far from the southern coast of Kariyl. That all changed once Kira Wells came into view.

The Faerie Homme they had there was burnt to the ground and hundreds of faeries had been killed, if not by human hands, then by the flames and trees that entrapped them within their homme.

Shilinda couldn't raise a glimmer of a smile or even look at the faeries now. She had foreseen this at the judging, when Greditto had rushed out of the courtroom, full of anger. She knew he was going to do something, even if it meant disobeying the Creator. But she couldn't let that happen. Intervening was prohibited, even if it was to help someone, which Shilinda was doing right now, but she had to take that chance. Gabriella, if taken over by the dark side of the earthen realm, could destroy them and all the inhabitants before the next season arrived. Shilinda watched the faeries now, some of them standing about, some flying high in the air, waiting for her to speak again.

She needed to send more help to Gwenzel. If not, then the hope would ride on a single faerie folk alone. Shilinda knew how that felt. Her mind suddenly flashed back to her past and the problems that had arisen when she had just been a faerie herself. She knew that the unicorn needed others to complete the task at hand. She searched around the circle of faeries, trying her best to find someone, a team of sorts that could work together and use their powers as one and not separately. The struggle of doing this was incredible.

The rules of the Creator and his angels were simple, basic instructions that helped you to work with another in order to complete any task. But the faeries, though they were her children and she had been raised as one, were free-spirited, went by no rules while living, and did not know now the severity of what was happening. But she looked again at the Unicorns' faces and knew that Gwenzel would not be enough.

"I need someone to meet Gwenzel and help bring the angel here. We need to act fast; the daemons have already attacked once." Shilinda looked over at the unicorns. She knew they worried. She could sense it in their beautiful eyes, saw now the way they pawed the ground with their great hooves.

"But he defeated them," Shilinda added. "However, they will be back. And there will be more. Speaking of more, I have something to tell you about the angel." This was going to come as a surprise to them just as much as everything she had said earlier but it had to be said. Shilinda couldn't risk the future of the races on faeries, as the Creator had done before. The faerie queen needed to forewarn them before they did something drastic.

"She had someone with her. A human boy; Ranyll is his name. He has seen Gwenzel. But he is a good soul."

This was ludicrous. Triggle stood up. In all his years, he had never heard anything like this; a human actually seeing a Unicorn. He had to say something, speak out. But what would he say?

I can't just say I'm displeased, he thought to himself, looking around at the other fairies with displeasure, *even though I do hate these stupid meetings. I need to say something great, something that will stand in the mind of these other faeries and show the true strength of the Miftles, though we have nothing to do with these others.* He couldn't think of anything good at the moment, so he thought of the next best thing, which he regretted as soon as it slipped out of his bearded lips.

"I volunteer." Triggle pushed out into the open, close to Shilinda, raising his dagger that he had plucked out of his belt. "I want to help Gwenzel. I can't stand this any longer. I saw the Faerie Homme in Elvinisclar burn down and I did nothing. I was helpless against it. And now Gwenzel is trying to save this angel by himself? Ludicrous! I can't believe it! I'm on my way now, Shilinda. I won't fail you." He bowed so low that his beard touched the ground. The faerie crowd was in shock.

They were amazed that Triggle, from the race of Miftles in the west, would actually volunteer for something that didn't have to do with him at all. Two sprites then raised their hands, fluttering close to Triggle. One was a red-wing, from the Glor clan, and flew quickly to volunteer, a faerie staff waving in his hand.

"I am Drigno, of the Glor clan, and I will go also." He landed on Triggle's left shoulder, his small faerie chest sticking out in pride.

The other faerie, a blue-winged, from the Sifter clan, landed on Triggle's right shoulder, her long slender arms holding her skirt as she curtseyed.

"And I am Tristle, of the Sifter clan, at your service, my queen."

Shilinda saw the hope in their eyes, saw the speechless expressions on the other faeries, and knew that she had a good task in the grand scheme of things.

"Alright, then. We have volunteers. Gwenzel and the others have already reached the Tirapoor Channel but there is a storm that keeps them there. If you can reach them before they get to the Faerie Pass, then I think they'll be safe. Any questions?"

The crowd behind the team abruptly parted. There was a short, slender animal approaching. Its fur was red, a thick coat covering its entire body, slicked back and smooth to the tip of the tail, which was fluffed up at the ends. Short, brown hair spurted off the top of the creatures head and it had a tail like that of the forest creature the fox and a long jaw that held a row of pearly white fangs. It walked on all fours as it strutted its way past all the other faeries. The fire fox was loud for such a small creature, with a rough voice that echoed through the trees as it spoke.

"You got room for one more?"

7

Shilinda watched as her faerie folk parted and let the group through, the small sprites floating above the Miftle and fire fox, waving goodbye to their fellow clan members, their eyes layered with tears. It would be days before Shilinda would know if they made it in time. She had heard rumors in the west that more daemons had been sent to attain Gabriella, and there were rumors even of a flesh daemon leading them. This frightened Shilinda greatly, knowing that the One had begun to use his own power in order to gain use of Gabriella during her moment of weakness. He had always been obsessed with power, even before he had been banished from the clouded world of Drillidan.

The Queen of Faeries departed from the Faerie Homme without anyone seeing, her eyes focused on something far, farther than that of any elf, human, or dwarf could see. She closed her eyes and concentrated, opening them once again.

He was here.

She could sense him. The One was above on the realm with the inhabitants. He had not done this since the War of the Races, when he had been banished completely, deep into the tunnels of Ar Solon to live the rest of his life out, beneath the world of the inhabitants.

She could see a black outline taking on shape just outside of the Faerie Homme, a human form materializing from within a shadow of trees. He stood there waiting for her.

He looked different than when she had seen him last. His hair was trimmed short and he looked skinny and frail compared to the vision she kept in her mind of him next to the Creator, his strong build and chiseled features that had worked their way into her heart long gone now. But things had changed since then and centuries had passed since their last meeting. She had changed and been given the position as Queen of the Faeries and, once he had fallen, she had never looked for him on Ar Solon, for fear that his crooked vision of the world would misshape hers as well.

He looked almost human now; with small, dark rings around his eyes, his lips thin and resolute, as if he were pondering on something quite important. His dark garb fit close to his frame and blanketed him in black, a small cape hanging around his neck, billowing in the wind like a wild serpent leaping from his shoulders, his hands clasped together in front of him as though he were holding eternity together for her within his grasp.

No one would ever guess that he was the evil that held the world at bay, or that he was the heart of all the pain and suffering that went on. In fact, every twinge of pain the inhabitants had suffered through had been thought of by him, the One's mind calculating and manipulative in so many more ways that the Creator had given him credit for.

So Shilinda tread on unknown ground with him at that moment, making her way closer with caution. She knew that the One only arrived on the surface when something was important to him.

This was a very rare occasion, indeed, Shilinda thought to herself. She held her hand out for him to remain where he was.

"I am surprised to see you above, with your victims, but I am in no way pleased that you have used what power you have to see me."

The One separated his hands and leaned against a nearby tree, peeling the bark from its surface, breaking a sliver into smaller pieces and littering it upon the ground with his fingers. He didn't look at her, just stared at the moist, dew-coated ground, a slight smile forming when he heard her voice.

Shilinda continued. "I know what you are up to, Darien. I know that you search for the fallen angel."

He had not heard that name in such a long time that it caught him off guard.

Darien. The name seemed to call out to him, to things that he had long since forgotten. His love, the ache in his heart as he left, the…his mind trailed off and then he stopped himself.

The One stood, looking at Shilinda for a time, noticing the features that had nearly driven him mad, then countered. "And I know that you have tried to stop me; and failed."

He looked up at her. Shilinda stared at what was in those eyes. His features may have changed tremendously over the centuries, but the burning in his eyes forever remained the same. He continued. "And I know that you sent off a group of your own to save her. Why do you do this to yourself, Shilinda?" The Queen of Faeries was puzzled.

Do what, she thought to herself, trying to decipher what he meant. The One could tell she was confused.

He smiled again. "By trying to help Gabriella, you have also weakened yourself. Your powers are diminishing as we speak. That is the only reason I come to you today; that and to tell you of my plan."

Indeed, Shilinda had felt the weakening of her powers ever since she glided into Faerie Homme; first her ability to return, and then her ability to materialize before her faerie kindred had sapped the remaining strength from her. She still retained her faerie magik that stirred within her soul on Ar Solon, but the powers the Creator had given her were quickly diminishing altogether.

But how did Darien know?

She looked over at him questioningly. His reply came almost immediately.

"I know the angelic pact, Shilinda. Do not forget, I helped write the manuscript the Creator goes by this very day. You all above may call me an outcast, that is all too true, yet I still keep the knowledge of that accursed place locked within. Shilinda, **you** have broken the rules and are being punished; just as I was all those years ago."

Shilinda knew the consequences but also knew that Gabriella, if the tables were turned, would do the same for her. She couldn't abandon the angel in her most desperate time of need. Darien leaned up from the tree and approached Shilinda, his hands at his side. She began to move back, her hands reaching for her pouches. Darien stopped in his place.

"Please, do not take offense. I only approach because I want to tell you I understand what you and everyone else are going through. There are several others that have problems separating themselves from Ar Solon as well. It is a curse that the Creator has given us when making us tend to it like a sheepherder with his sheep. Do not think that you are the only one. In fact, Greditto is coming to see me today."

The name burned the inside of Shilinda's soul. She despised everything about that angel. He had caused all of this, bringing down Gabriella with his own magik, leaving her vulnerable to the world and its perilous ways. The One knew that would get her attention. She spoke up.

"What is this? Do you think just because we love some part of this world that we are like you and should be banished from Drillidan? Just because I am here doesn't mean that I have anything in common with you. We are not the same. We are complete opposites, in reality. That is why you were banished in the first place."

The One stood, silent for a moment, staring at the beautiful Shilinda, his thoughts burning through his lips, poisoning his tongue. Then he shot his hands out at her, capturing her wrists in his hands, swinging her arms behind her back, pressing her close to him. His hands found their familiar place on

her body and tightened. Darien's face was parallel with Shilinda's, his eyes
more ablaze than she had ever seen them.

"The only reason I'm down here is because of **you**. I loved you. We
were to be together forever until he decided to send you down here. You
never understood what I was trying to accomplish by doing what I did. He
cursed me when he made you!"

His face brushed against hers, his hands squeezing hers harder against her
back. Shilinda let out a cry of pain and then released her remaining magik at
him, her hands alive and moving, the emerald fire dancing around her
fingers. The blast carried Darien through the tree he had been leaning
against and sent him slamming into the ground, face down, his cape still on
fire at the edges from the magik.

The flames suddenly went out. The One lifted himself up from the dirt
and brushed his garb off, looking back at her. Shilinda was furious now.
Her nostrils flared and her eyes focused in on Darien. She could feel the last
of her power ebb away inside of her and she watched as The One nodded in
understanding. Her hands slipped to her sides and grabbed at her pouches,
which weren't there. She looked down at her waist. They were gone!
Darien laughed.

"So that's how we are to be towards our old lovers, eh? I came here to
offer you a place by my side but it appears that you want no part. That is
fine. Greditto, I'm sure, wants no part either. That's why, when I see him
later, I'm going to kill him. But, as for you, my love, I will let you live and
see the destruction of the world you so love. All the time we spent building
this place never amounted to anything to the Creator. Why should the
destruction of it matter to him now?" Darien emptied the contents of
Shilinda's pouches on the ground in front of her, discarding the small velvet
pouches once they were emptied. Shilinda moved closer, her hands still up
in defense.

"Darien, you don't love anything anymore. Sometimes I think that you never did. You can try to take Ar Solon, like you tried during the War of the Races, and you'll see the good tear down that evil wall that you've built. We'll never let you take anything from us again!"

The One seemed saddened by this fact, yet he remained solid, his demeanor diminishing all thoughts that he ever did care about anything other than his plans. He pulled out a dagger from his boot. Shilinda recognized it immediately. It was made by the goblins ages ago, when they ruled Abryll, mining the ore for most of their short lives from which the blade was made.

"This will be your downfall, Shilinda; you and your faerie kind. You may know of this dagger, but not of the properties that I've bestowed upon it. You see, my daemons are scouring the land right now, using these as implements of destruction. It won't be long before they arrive here. Then you'll see what I have planned." The One threw the dagger at the fallen tree, watching with fixed eyes as it disfigured and gnarled the tree into a lesser version of itself. He leaned over to retrieve the dagger. That's when Shilinda struck.

"The Creator will never let you do this!" The Queen of Faeries released her magik upon the One, her emerald flames lancing straight at him. He held up the blade. The green fire burst into shards against the blade, exploding into harmless fragments that littered the ground around Darien. He moved forward, the blade in his hand.

"Or on second thought…," trailing off, deflecting another of Shilinda's attacks, the fire separating into pieces all around them. Shilinda backed away, but it was not fast enough to escape Darien's grasp.

Pulling her close to him, he thrust the blade into the soft flesh of her stomach in one, quick movement, dotting her beautiful robes with blood. Her crown slipped from its place on her forehead, the topaz stone dropping aimlessly out of its fitted position. Darien reached for his beloved one last time, his arms about her, and pulled her close to him, her hands hanging loosely at her sides. She tried to resist but, somewhere within the depths of those angelic eyes, knew that it was too late.

"Goodbye, my love." His eyes are a fire, his blackened soul seeping out of them; Darien ripped the dagger from her body as the queen of fairies convulses before lying still in his arms.

"And goodbye to my previous life…forever."

The One lays her down on the grass near the fallen tree and, pulling his burnt cape from his shoulders, lays it over her still form. Without a warning, the ground begins to quake and a small crack opens up at Shilinda's feet, soon overtaking her body and drawing her into it.

The day is quiet. The forest is still. Shilinda's death is silent, somber, peaceful. The One fits the goblin dagger back in its sheath in his boot and leans down to pick up the crown, half of it caught inside the collapsing earth. He notices the topaz on the ground and slips it into a pocket in his black vest, keeping safe.

It will come in use soon, when my plan is coming together. I was merciful with you, Shilinda, because we had loved at one time. That was the old me. It has died with you. That is the only death I will allow to be in that fashion. The others will suffer, just as I have suffered, but they will suffer far worse.

The One watches as the ground closes up over the piece of his past and, staying until late in the evening when the moon is out, feels the power course through his veins. He was weaker now than when he had first entered the earthen realm that morning, but it is of no consequence.

It will all change in the next couple of days. Soon, I will have the ability to harness immeasurable power through Gabriella and will be invincible. But his mind turned to other things, to the present at hand.

Ahh, Greditto. Poor, helpless Greditto. We will see each other soon. And your pain will be much worse than Shilinda's.

"Yes, Greditto. I am on my way. And I cannot wait to see you again."

The One made his way back to his entryway, pressing on the stones that opened the secret entrance, watching them glow as they began to open in front of him. The tunnel opened up before him and he could see the faint glimmer of red in the tunnels. The daemons scurried through the caves, making way for their master, their Creator.

They wait for Greditto as well. The promise of angel flesh was a high promise indeed.

They stared at their master and wondered if he could supply them with it at such ease as he did everything else. Then the tunnel closed and all light died inside the cave, save for the red slits that sparkled to life and hurried down the passage, following their master.

In the forest nearby, the small form of a sprite that had watched all transpire before her glittered away into the trees, tears running down her faerie face. Today, she has seen an end far worse than all that she had read about in the tomes of the past. Today evil conquered against good.

Does this mean that evil has a chance, she thought to herself, trying to wipe away the tears before she entered the Faerie Homme? *How will I tell the others? What will happen now that there is no queen? Would there be a new one?* All of these questions raced through the little faerie's mind as she raced through what could only be the most saddening day of her faerie existence.

To the small sprite, it seemed as though the world was changing into what had been rumor since the beginning of time; that the world was, indeed, going to come to an end. And, if the One's plans continued on much longer, the world would end for sure. However, the question of Ar Solon seemed unimportant at the moment. In fact, the world seemed a foreign and dark place when the little sprite looked at it now.

The trees from afar screamed in agony; but not in pain for their warped, misshapen limbs. They cried for Shilinda, their creator; their mother. And, in its cries, the pangs of the earthen creature, one word in the common tongue of Kariyl could be heard, repeating over and over; vengeance.

8

Far in the west of Kariyl, further than the great city of Argolis, at the edge of the Argolis cliffs, evil dwelt. It dwelt in mass, hundreds of them, daemons; scattering throughout the underground tunnels that stretched underneath almost all of Kariyl. They scattered even faster as Greditto approached, robes wet and clinging to his body as he landed in one of the caves on the cliff side, nearly a two-hundred foot drop below him. He straightened his messed hair and pushed past the daemons without a single thought, swatting them away as if they were just flies and not creatures that could devour his flesh in moments with but a command.

He passed through several of the main tunnels, most of them crudely fashioned out of the rock cliff, then came to a set of different tunnels a hundred feet or so into the caves. There was an eerie glow all over the rock walls, a luminescent glow, as if the sunlight had been captured and held within the thick rock, screaming for an escape. Greditto pressed into the newer caves, those made of thick clay, noticing the writings and designs carved into them over the years. He knew all of the primitive languages, had seen the glyphs and pictures many times before, in the halls up in the clouds, but they seemed darker down here on the earthen realm, inside the rocks that he so wished to be free of.

Then the passageway opened. Long, solid rock pillars jutted up to the ceiling that was over forty feet high, with sconces hanging every ten feet or so, all the way up to the top, forming a concentric circle within several more circles. And, in the middle, was a high-backed stone chair. The chair was carved out of the side of the wall and towered six feet above the rest of the cavern, a makeshift set of stairs dug into the earthen floor just to the right of the chair.

The One was there, facing away from Greditto, leg hanging loosely over one side of the chair, it swinging aimlessly, as if the One was being playful. But the One was never playful. Lives precariously swung in the One's grasp every second of every day. The daemons lowered themselves when passing the One, eyes to the ground out of respect, but mostly out of fear. With one strong gaze, the One could peel the skin from bones, tear into muscle with his smile, and make blood boil with but a laugh. Yes, Greditto had heard many tales of the One, even some songs written about the One.

Days had gone by since he had last spoken to Darien, waiting impatiently for the daemons to ambush the fallen angel and her misfit protectors. But something had gone awry. A unicorn was now involved and there were rumors of another group of faerie kin on their way to meet up with Gabriella.

This had all gone way too far. Greditto wanted Gabriella dead at the feet of the One but, once Shilinda got involved, things seemed a little different, a little bit more dangerous. The angel of song and music now stood in front of the stone chair that held the One, his fingers locked together in front of him, his eyes level with the One's feet. The One spoke first, before Greditto could get anything out. His voice sounded like rusty nails grating down a deep well but never hitting the bottom. The One leaned out over his chair.

"They have failed, Greditto; yes, I know."

"They weren't supposed to! They were supposed to bring her to you so I could see my daughter."

"I chose for them to fail. I sent the weakest group of daemons to Gabriella, to see if we had anything lethal on our hands or not."

"What? Are you crazy? This isn't some kind of game; this is real. We aren't playing here. I've done what you asked of me; now let me see my daughter." The One gazed down at Greditto, a glimmer of a smile leaking out of the corner of his mouth.

"You haven't given me what I asked for, Greditto. I asked for Gabriella here and, until she's here in my protection so I can perform the sacrifice, your daughter will be waiting for you."

Greditto protested. "This isn't right, do you understand me? I risked my livelihood bringing her down to you and you say that's not enough? The Creator would banish me for eternity if he even thought that I would betray him like this and you say my daughter will be waiting? What else is there that you want from me, my soul?" The One lashed out with his right hand and grasped Greditto by the throat.

"Something like that. Oh, poor angel, down here with the rest of us rejects. You will see, Greditto, that there are more than just mortals and faeries down here. There's evil down here so terrible, so unconceivable, you still don't understand why your only love died down here without you. I saw her, Greditto; I saw her scream in agony as those brutes above that call themselves humans rape her soft elven flesh, tearing at her very soul that had, years ago, brought your precious daughter into the world. But where were you, Greditto, to stop these vandals as they tore down the city of Dribbis? Oh, I see, you were up in the clouds above playing your cursed music while half of your family was killed in hatred for their beauty; their beauty, Greditto! That's what they were killed for in that final war that brought this land to its knees. I was there. So was the rest of my rag tag group. We watched them massacre hundreds just to make marks of glory on their leather belts. You don't understand, Greditto." The One's grip tightened. The angel could feel his air supply lessen, could feel the One's fingernails bear into the soft skin on his neck, drawing blood.

The One's grip squeezed hard on Greditto's throat until the angel could taste blood on his tongue. His vision blurred and then he was released, falling to the floor, gasping for breath as he spit out a mouthful of blood.

"I don't think you'll ever understand. You see, I live for pain. I was the strongest I had ever been when that war occurred. I was ready to come out from hiding I was so strong. But some great hero came in and saved the day as always, riding into battle with his head held high, taking away my power with one quick strike. After that, I hadn't felt any power surge through the earth like that, with the exception of Gabriella, of course. So, now she's my power. And you're telling me you're done?"

The One paused and leaned back into his chair. He continued. "Fine! The deal's off, Greditto."

Soon, Greditto thought to himself, hands clenched, standing back up in silent cavern hell, eyes gazing up at the One. *Soon things will turn out for the better and you will get what is coming to you.*

Greditto swallowed to get the dryness out of his throat and spoke. "Fine, then give me my daughter back."

Just then, one of the doors opened on the wall. A daemon skittered out of the opened door and Greditto's daughter appeared behind it. She was dressed in what once was a white gown, but it was tattered and dirty now, her blond curls bouncing around her as the elven girl ran to her father.

"Father, I knew you'd come all along." She wrapped her arms around his neck and hugged him close, her face buried against his chest. He squeezed her closer and backed away from the One.

"All this time I've waited for a chance to bring Gabriella to the surface for you and I did that. But you don't care about that. Now I can see why the Creator banished you from above. Your heart has no place there. You've found a home here just like Gabriella did. That's where you were wrong.

You should have stayed with us, up above. It was paradise there; it still is. Some day you will learn."

Greditto turned to leave, his daughter in his arms. He passed through the clay caves out through the rock tunnels, keeping his daughter close as they passed the hundreds of daemons, Greditto's magik at the ready.

That was too easy, the angel thought, seeing the tunnel opening up ahead. The sunlight poked through the edge of the entrance and slivers of sunlight touched them as they approached the opening to the hidden cave. The One spoke from behind them.

"It was, wasn't it, Greditto?" The angel paused.

"What?"

"Escaping! You didn't think I'd just let you leave without getting **my** prize, do you?" Greditto turned to object but stopped in his tracks when he saw what the One had in his hand. The One bellowed loudly, his voice echoing outside the cliffs, out over the ocean, to places none have ever seen. Greditto looked at his daughter now, reeling back from her as she transformed, bones falling into place, hair dissipating in an instant, soft skin spoiling and turning black, back into the shape of a daemon that smiled at Greditto as it hurried back into the tunnels behind the One.

The One continued. "I decided that, since you didn't have my prize, I'd take what I wanted from yours. Her head will do nicely on my mantle, don't you think, Greditto?" He lifted the head of Greditto's daughter out into the light for Greditto to see.

"You sick creature! Do you realize that you've just made the biggest mistake of your life?" The angel propelled himself forward, hands outstretched at the One.

"No, I made it years ago not killing you when I should have. Goodbye, Greditto." Flames burnt through Greditto's robes before he had a chance to get to the banished creature, blasting him out of the tunnel. The angel spread his wings and lifted into the air, out above the ocean, his hands glowing, blue lightning ready to strike. The flames the One had surprised him with had singed his wings but did no real damage.

But there was something wrong. Greditto could feel it; a rumbling. A long, uneven rumbling, as if thousands of human foot soldiers came for him. From deep inside the darkness of the caverns in the cliffs, a sound could be heard. It was a faint buzzing sound at first, and then a solitary cackle broke through the buzzing. Then another and another piercing cackle sounded out over the others, growing closer. Greditto leaned back against his wings, preparing to make his escape, when they came.

Hundreds of daemons surged out of the cliff walls, flying through the air, razor-sharp claws digging into his skin, pulling him down closer to the ocean, even now with the cave entrance the One stood in. The One lifted the head out to Greditto mockingly, swinging it from one side to the other by its beautiful locks of hair. The laughter in his face was gone now, replaced by a solemn expression as he spoke.

"She died in a lot of pain, Lavena did, you know. It took several ten day before her body gave out on her. Too bad you couldn't be there for her either, Greditto. Doesn't look like you were meant to have a family here on Kariyl. Well, I must be going, my friend."

The daemons continued to pull on Greditto's flesh, more surging out of the tunnels, piling up on him until he could feel the waves against his back, soaking his wings, making it impossible for him to fly. In a desperate attempt to escape, Greditto pushed the last of his power out into the pile of daemons upon him, melting their skin to the rocky shore, his hands erupting out bolts of lightning upon them.

Dozens of black forms were swallowed by the tide, but the numbers doubled on him so quick that Greditto had no time to act. The angel let out a cry of pain that echoed off of the cliffs, trying to reach the other angels in the clouds. But the taste of blood caught in this throat. He stared at the clouds then, knowing, feeling that the end was at hand. He felt his immortality slip away as the tide drank up his blood, sap at his open wounds while the daemons savored it as well, his eyes staring up at the beautiful world one last time before the waves overtook him.

9

The Argolis mountain people were the first ones to hear the cries. When the cries started, it sounded as though it were the warning sirens for the coming of the dragons, those sirens that had been sounded centuries ago, the stories told still lost in the oldest books in their libraries, hidden forever under a pile of aged dust and time.

But it wasn't the sirens of old. It was something worse, far worse than could ever be imagined. It swarmed over the town like a plague of locusts, buzzing in their ears, pounding into the soul of everyone that had the ability to hear. The screaming coursed through the townspeople's veins, made an impression on even the youngest child, their eyes soon dampened from crying. The elders of the town dropped to their knees, begging for forgiveness for a sin unknown to their eyes. But the mercy did not come; the forgiveness was not given.

All that came was the voice of the familiar, the voice that pierced the strongest armor, cracked through the strongest mountain, fought the waves of the world and lost; the broken, crumpled body on the rocky shore below, just miles from the town. Its echoes curved through the wind; screeching, squealing, turning through the air as though it were a bird in flight, trying to find a place to land. But it couldn't land. It was just the wind, just a dream, just a tinge of the past filled with remorse. Soon the sound died down, or so the town thought.

But it did not go away. It traveled. Just like a weary soul, it traveled. Far from the Argolis townspeople, who were now sick with grief and didn't know why, through the crags and crevasses of the mountains and down into

the Brarden Valley near the Reune Lake. It was a spirit of agony and despair.
The coldest darkness followed it, followed close behind, like the tail of a
comet in the sky, freezing and falling, it came.

The soul of Greditto, an intangible and hideous thing, fell into the damp
night air. In an attempt to right what he had done wrong, the angel tried to
find her. Through the thick of woods of the quiet valley below, it came,
sifting through the trees, finally finding the set of trees that shaded the fallen
one, his forgotten angel, the angel called Gabriella.

The forest was wet; moist and thick with moss and vines as though the
forest was truly trying to hide her. Her face was calm, pale, with drops of
rain on her cheeks from the swaying trees surrounding her. Gwenzel and
Ranyll were huddled not far away, sleeping, eyes closed tight, as if to push
out the beginning rays of sunlight peering up over the trees at them. Ranyll
had taken first watch, making a small fire to dry them before they began on
their journey to the other side of Reune Lake, the safe hold that was said to
guard the queen of the faeries.

The flames were out now, just a small pile of cinders burning their last
embers before the day awoke. Gwenzel sat on his hooves, trying to keep
warm, his head bowed and in a deep slumber, yet his ears could hear sounds
Ranyll never thought possible. Gwenzel had taken second watch over the
sleeping Gabriella, huddling near a set of trees closely grown, trying to keep
the morning chill from getting to him.

Then it hit her. It scorched Gabriella almost as bad as the lightning had
done just days ago. Her body bolted upright, face gray and pale, her eyes
wide as if she had seen a revelation of sorts. The scream came with a
quickness that couldn't be seen or heard; it just arrived, like a message on the
wind, twisting and winding its way through the tangled forest. The forest
seemed to come alive that instant. Gwenzel woke first; firm, muscular legs
erupted from underneath his body and he was up in a moment, hooves

digging deeply into the wet ground. The blue flame laced around his horn, his eyes wide and alert.

Awake, young Ranyll! Something is amiss.

Ranyll didn't have time to stand. The echo of the dead angel blew him back into the trees, Gwenzel lowering his head to get some leverage on the ground below. Ranyll covered his ears with his hands, the shriek of the wind almost deafening him. It vanished completely moments later. He looked over to Gabriella. She was awake, eyes wide with fear, hands covering her mouth, tears filling in her clouded, misty eyes. The words she spoke to Ranyll then he would never forget.

"An angel has been killed!" She said it through her hands, her slender fingers trembling as her breath touched them. She looked up at Gwenzel, knowing that the unicorn had felt the same thing, yet she knew which angel had been killed. And she knew who had done the killing. It was no secret. Greditto's soul told her what had transpired. He even spoke of the injustice his secret family of inhabitants had received on this world.

She looked over at Gwenzel, trying her best to keep her composure. But it all came at once. She saw the head of Greditto's elven daughter held up, felt the thousands of sharp, shadowed creatures pulling Greditto to his death.

"Poor Greditto! He did not deserve such a death." Ranyll moved close to Gabriella and wrapped his arms around her tenderly.

"What is it, Gabriella?" Her face became sad, fearful; her eyelids let several tears drop down her face before she spoke again. "Things are happening on your world that is beyond my or any other angel's control. The Creator would not stand for this. Something is wrong." Her eyes focused on him but he didn't say anything. Gabriella looked then over Ranyll's shoulder at the sword and spoke again, this time her words still and calm, like the seas after a storm. She understood now.

"There is a reason you have that sword, Ranyll. It is not by chance that we had to go to Reune Lake and we crossed paths with your uncle. Something is driving us forward."

Ranyll reached out to her. "Gabriella, it's alright. I'm here to help you. He's here to help you, too," pointing at the unicorn that stood paces away, the magical steed pawing at the muddy ground with his hooves. The blue flame was gone now, his hooves sinking into the muddy earth as he padded his way over to the angel. The unicorn used its voice this time to speak to her.

"Yes, Gabriella. Shilinda has sent me to bring you back to her." Gabriella's eyes brightened.

"Shilinda's here; now? Where is she?" Gabriella looked around, hoping to find the Shilinda peeking around a nearby bush or shrub, followed by so many of the faeries' smiling faces that the faerie queen praised in the court halls day after day, high above in the clouds.

But that was not the case. Shilinda was miles away, at the other side of Reune Lake, Gwenzel told her, in the Faerie Homme that was hidden from all humans.

Gabriella looked to the other two as she grabbed her things up and threw her pack on her back. "It's not safe to stay here any longer. If that was an angel dying then he has more power than we can imagine."

Ranyll turned to Gwenzel, a questioning look on his face. "Who has more power?"

Gabriella's face became paler at the thought of it.

The One.

Ages have past and the name had not been spoken in her presence. Angels were forbidden to speak the name. She remembered suddenly what had occurred during the last battle on Kariyl. It was centuries ago, when the towns that now stood were still being built.

The One had somehow gained enough power to amass a daemon army. He almost came to be on the land of Kariyl himself. But one thing stopped him; his lack of power. The One could not conjure up enough hatred from all the battles to stay on the world long enough to rule. He needed to be able to harness and hold the power at bay.

And, if I have the power still within me to bring him upon mortal land, then the One will stop at nothing to claim me.

Gabriella pulled her cloak tightly around her shoulders, feeling the cold cut through the tree line around them. It chilled her to the bone. But it wasn't just the cold that did it. It was the feeling inside the cold; the feeling that someone could take away her power, her entire being, use it to their own advantage, as if she were just a tool for power. That sent shivers down her spine. The question rang again in her ears, bringing her eyes to rest on Ranyll's.

"**Who** has more power, Gabriella?"

"I cannot say his name, Ranyll. I have sworn an oath not to." It was more than a question to Gabriella though, who tried to forget the being that had caused so much harm over the centuries. It struck the chords of thought for Gabriella. But she felt something else in it. There was a reason that his name was never spoken. It was told in stories and books of lore to children that, if his name was spoken he could find you and, that just the mere mention of him could invoke his spirit. In fact, it seemed that he knew when he was being spoken about. It had become a superstition in some of the villages and towns in Kariyl and other continents on Ar Solon. Gabriella turned around suddenly, scanning the forest.

"Gwenzel, do you hear something?"

The unicorn bowed its head to the side, catching it's breath inside its nostrils and holding it. Gwenzel's eyes were closed.

"Yes angel, I hear them. There are too many to count. They are all around us." The unicorn paused, sniffing the air to the left of it one more time. "I hope the faeries know we are near."

Ranyll stood, dumbfounded, his hand shifting up to his sword, hesitant at first to draw.

"What is it? Are there more?" Ranyll could feel the beads of sweat trickle down his forehead. He had hoped it was just the rain but knew that it was something more that filled the forest with silence. The daemons had approached without anyone knowing.

Gwenzel could see from afar a chasm in the ground that had opened up by an unknown force, a mass of daemons surging from its bowels, each of them carrying a dagger that was twisted and misshapen. And it sounded as if there were more than before. The movements seemed scattered yet with purpose, Ranyll drawing his sword for the first time, preparing for battle.

Gabriella stood, motionless, her eyes darting over all the small forms that ran, almost in frenzy, towards her. A lump caught in her throat and she couldn't breath. Her breath caught in her chest and refused to expel. She knew what this was that she was feeling. She had seen the same things happen to the inhabitants on this land, but never thought she would feel this way. She was frozen in fear.

The trees screamed the warning but only Gwenzel could hear it. The trees themselves were crying out in pain. One by one, the dark forms attacked; not the three that were thought to be the sole reason they came, but the dark forms stabbed into the trees with their weapons as they passed, the three watching as the forest began to twist into warped versions of themselves at the hands of the daemons. The trees were soaked to the bark with rain water but a number of dark flames sprang forth from their limbs, several trees now ablaze in the dark fire, the flames hissing and spitting as it touched the fresh bark, as though it hated the taste yet devoured it nonetheless. A darkness seeped into them, rotting them away quickly, black flames licking up at the arms of the wilderness, burning away their skin, leaving a dry husk of death.

Each daemon Ranyll saw approach carried a dagger. It was unlike any dagger Ranyll had ever seen. It had a short handle, the blade sharp like a needle, with no sharp edges, just a point. The blade that protruded out was black; a milky blackness almost like death taking on a form of its own. The twisted metal chilled him to the bone as he looked down at his own weapon, trying to come to terms with what might happen if they got hold of him and wounded him with the blades they carried.

The daemons had spread out all over the forest, jabbing their sharp daggers into the trees, passing one and continuing on to another, letting them wither away and warp in agony. The evil creatures smiled, too. Their clicking sounds they usually made had not been made as they approached. Instead, they repeated a line of incoherent mumblings, their razor-like maws opening and closing in the misty morning light. Ranyll saw no chance for escape. The three of them were surrounded now as they watched the dozens approach from all sides, their death blades pointing straight at their intended victims.

*   *   *

Within the dead and dying forest, not far from the daemons that surrounded the helpless angel and her two protectors, the small group that had set out from Reune Lake began to establish a plan. Triggle, of the faerie-kind Miftle, was the first one to speak.

"I have no idea what to do. They're lost to us now. Look how many there are down there!" The dwarf-sized creature hunkered down beneath the brush, hiding from sight, the group of faeries just above the forest on a rise just above the trees that had fallen when the daemons surged through, hiding a small distance away within the cover of the trees that still lived, watching as the daemons crept ever closer to Gabriella and her companions.

The two sprites flew down from the trees above the Miftle, taking their place on a branch near Triggle and their other partner, the fire fox. The small animal had said nothing since their departure from Shilinda, following closely behind the party the whole way, not even entering into conversation when it came about. This perplexed both the sprites, who relied on conversation, especially now, since every step they took led them deeper and deeper into danger. And, at this moment, danger seemed to stare at them through the dying trees just ahead of them.

Drigno, still a young faerie by faerie standards, lifted his staff in disagreement. "No, they're not, Triggle! They have us to back them up."

Tristle, the Sifter Clan faerie, flew closer, adding her comments to the argument as well. "I think Drigno is right. They have us, not to mention Gwenzel."

The fire fox just shook his head and, without looking back at the group, began to walk down into the dying set of trees just below them. The two faeries and the Miftle stared in disbelief, thinking of a way to stop him until they had come up with a plan.

"What are you doing? We don't even have a plan yet and there are too many down there anyway. What can you possibly do to help them?" They heard the voice of the fire fox for the first time as the creature made its way further down the hill, completely out of sight now.

His voice piped up now, a little bit irritated, but determined.

"Watch me."

The three faerie kin watched as the fire fox maneuvered his way forward without being seen, all the while the three keeping their eyes on Gabriella and her party as well.

Triggle began again with the complaints. "Well, this is great! We've got an independent pet and no plan. This is ludicrous!" Triggle huffed and plopped down on the soft grass, slipping out a pouch from the satchel he carried at his side and took out a handful of berries, shoving them into his mouth one by one. He chewed them hastily and without a sound, yet he continued without a single breath until they were all gone. Drigno left his place on the branch and flew down to Triggle, swinging his staff at the Miftle's thick nose. He missed completely, but Triggle got the point.

"Triggle, this is no time to eat! We have to save Gabriella and the others."

The Miftle countered. "But I can't help it. When I get nervous, I get hungry. And besides, I've been walking for days with nothing but berries and nuts to eat. I can't go on like this." Tristle raised her staff in protest, leaving her place as well on the branch, her eyes darting from the scene down below to the Miftle that was finishing the remainder of his rations, wiping his bearded face on his sleeve, his lips purple from the berries.

"I have a plan. Triggle, you go explore that chasm and try to find a way to close off their escape. Drigno and I will assist the fire fox in the rescue. We will meet back here after we have Gabriella. Agreed?"

Triggle had a slight problem with the plan. "Are you crazy? Did you not just see a dozen daemons dash out of that hole and you're saying you want me to go sniffing around in there?" He gathered his things together and stood up, dusting off his breeches.

Drigno agreed. "Tristle is right! That sounds like a feasible plan if I ever heard one. We should split up, that way we can cover two important areas at once. Come now, we must not waste anymore time. Gabriella could suffer if we delay any longer." The two faeries flew high into the air, their final words still echoing in Triggle's head.

Go check out the chasm? Ludicrous!

                    *   *   *

The daemons surged in closer, daggers within a hand's length away from Gabriella and the others, the black, gnarled shadows contorting and twisting, their red eyes digging deeply into Gabriella's newly acquired soul. The angel had never felt these things called emotions, as Ranyll had called them earlier, her mind surging with ideas and possibilities, with indecision and doubt. She could not control them, could not wipe them from her mind. Gabriella lifted her hands in front of her, waiting for the attack.

The three waited. The attack didn't happen. Gwenzel reared his head back, horn aflame and waiting for them, Ranyll gripping his sword with both hands. The young boy backed up against Gwenzel and held his ground, pressing the angel tightly to his side. The frenzy of daemons that surrounded them did not move from their places. They snarled viciously just a breath away from their soon-to-be victims, all the time swinging their daggers at them threateningly.

The last attack had been random and planned, but now it seemed that they didn't want to attack at all, Ranyll thought, watching the daemons as they stood their ground, still encircling, though their facial expressions looked like they wanted to attack. Then Ranyll found out what they were waiting for. From the far edge of the daemon circle, the frenzy parted, a lone daemon walked closer to Gabriella and her protectors. It was taller in stature, almost more human, less vicious, and carried itself almost like a human, *though he could hardly be called that,* Ranyll thought to himself, watching as it approached ever closer. It was an actual daemon made of flesh, about the height of a dwarf, complete opposite to its brothers that drooled and snarled, their shadow-like forms void of any real parts and their height barely reaching a dwarf's shoulder.

The daemon watched as the crowd of his brethren opened up before him and merged back together behind him, his objective almost complete. He had endured the change, the agonizing pain that comes with a body of flesh. And he had been given a quest with the deal; to find the three innocents and break them apart, returning with only one of them; the angel. As soon as the first pack of daemons the One had sent failed, the daemon was granted his flesh and traveled from the Argolis cliffs through the passageways to where the forest where Gabriella had slept the night before. He did not get to witness the death of the other angel, Greditto, at the hands of his brethren, only heard the screams that echoed forth, as did the rest of Kariyl. He stared at the three now, looking at them one by one.

One, the angel from above the clouds, the fair Gabriella, the sole reason for this journey. Two, the young boy, still innocent, without a flaw upon his human soul, void of any wrongs in his heart. He draws power from the blood of old, thought the daemon, his own soul twisting up in hatred for the blood that coursed through the boy's fragile veins.

Soon, boy, very soon we will be upon you and your line. Then the power that lies within your grasp will be lost.

The daemon turned his black eyes to Gwenzel. *And the third innocent; the unicorn. An undying race of faeries that used their magiks for power. You will get no pleasure from our deaths, young unicorn. We will show you the pain and suffering that we have been through throughout our existence.*

He smiled at the thoughts that ran through his own mind. It had been centuries since the One had bestowed a body upon a daemon. The daemon stroked the power that lay inside of his body, the sheer power that the One had given him when making him his own vessel in which to live and feed. The One never made use of his power unless it was absolutely necessary.

Gabriella must be very important to him, the daemon thought, *even giving me my own name.* The daemon TSeT was now separated from the other daemons in many ways. He and his brother, Test, were given knowledge about things that were to come to pass, knew that their thoughts rested safely in their own mind, knowing that there was no fear of the One knowing their thoughts and peeling their shadowy skin from their forms. His brother daemon Test had yet to attain a flesh body, yet TSeT knew that his brother never had need of one though, preferring to move about and use his changeling ability that the One bestowed only to his best daemons. Though his brother had failed to get Gabriella the first time, TSeT knew that his brother was ordered to do so.

He stopped in front of the three now, his hand out to Gabriella. He approached closer, breaking the circle of daemons. The voice, though it was more than that, as though agony and despair could speak and did so through him, crawled over his black tongue and razor-sharp teeth and out to the pure forms before him.

"Gabriella, fallen angel; come with me. I will take you where you shall be safe. Here, they cannot save you from your fate; but I can. The One has sent me to bring you to his side. You can do so by just taking my hand. If not, we shall have to kill your protectors." TSeT motioned to his brethren and they began to chant inaudible words, unlike any Ranyll had heard before.

But the chant sounded familiar somehow. Maybe it was that the words had no vocal cords in which to travel through or that the daemons did not know speech and how to use its power. Yet, when the words were chanted, Ranyll thought he heard them chanting the word 'Kill'. TSeT held out his gnarled black hand, the misshapen fingers curling out to her. The angel hesitated, looking around as though lost in a world of mazes, trying to find her way out. Then her eyes caught something in the daemon's eyes and hers glimmered. She understood now.

She looked to Ranyll, who was pressing her close against him, separating her from the daemon TSeT and the other daemons.

He was so much of what he should be now that he held that sword. Much of his father in him, Gabriella thought, watching as this young man, this young warrior, held himself steady, even when death stared him in the face. She looked at Gwenzel then, the unicorn bowed and ready to defend, its eyes suddenly catching something in her own. Gwenzel seemed to know what she was going to do. His hooves pawed at the ground near her. It moved closer to her and Ranyll.

Something is amiss, Ranyll. Hold Gabriella close, she..., but Gwenzel didn't get to finish. Gabriella moved away from Ranyll and Gwenzel and toward TSeT.

Ranyll grabbed for her hand and began to pull her back when she stopped him, the urgency strong in her voice.

"This is the only way I'll be safe from them. This daemon dares not harm me. They want me to go with them, Ranyll. I will not be killed." She stopped and looked at the daemon, TSeT, then back to Ranyll, almost dream-like, almost as if she were in a trance.

"Anyway, I have seen something you have not, young Ranyll. I have seen the future of the world. We shall meet again." Ranyll felt himself let go of her arm, watching Gabriella move away from him. Gwenzel's voice called out to Ranyll in his mind.

What is wrong, Ranyll? What is it? Ranyll didn't answer. Ranyll didn't know what to say.

The daemons behind TSeT chattered and hissed, watching as the angel held out her hand, pressing it into TSeT's own, letting her friends live another day. It seemed to both Ranyll and Gwenzel that she was under a spell of some sort, but they knew that they couldn't do anything about it, only fight until they fell in battle.

And a battle it would be.

As the fleshy daemon spoke to Gabriella, Ranyll had time to count the numbers of the daemons he and Gwenzel were up against. It was a high number, eight and twenty. There was no hope of victory, at least not seen through the young boy's eyes.

As long as Gabriella's safe for the moment. That's all that matters, Ranyll thought to himself.

Then the magik began.

From out of the trees and brush to the west of them, a streak of wild flame arched forward, zigzagging its way towards the circle of daemons, growing bigger and bigger the closer it became. The daemons were distracted momentarily, watching it close in on them with ferocious speed. Finally, it exploded, fracturing into shards of flames that stabbed through the daemons' shadowy limbs. They howled in pain, their fury growing as they set themselves upon the two remaining of the party. The lead daemon, seeing this, grasped Gabriella's arm and pulled her away, its voice piercing Ranyll's heart as it screamed orders to its brethren.

"Attack them, daemons! The others from the lake have found us. Guard my escape with the prize. Do not let them pass." With those words, the lone daemon made for his escape, pulling his own blade out and at the ready, soon breaking from the battle that ensued with the angel in tow.

Gwenzel was the first to attack, rushing deep into the mass of daemons, crushing several shadowy forms beneath his hooves as he landed in the deep of them. His horn burst sharp rays of blue light that burnt and tore at the daemons, their red eyes closing in pain as their screams echoed in the dead forest around them. Gwenzel dashed at more with his hind legs, shaking them off of his haunches before they had a chance to use their daggers on his hide.

Ranyll flashed his blade out at the daemons, parrying their daggers, in defense more than anything, fearing the blades and the poison that they carried. He stabbed at one daemon approaching, and then another that tried to rush in on him, keeping them at bay long enough to move out of the way of their daggers.

I can't hold this position very long, he knew this. Then something caught hold of him by the leg. Small, clawed fingers grabbed at his boot first, and then made their way up the outside of his breeches, the small nails of an unknown creature digging into his flesh. He parried a daemon's blade long enough to look down.

It was a fox; but not an ordinary one in the least. It was smaller than a regular fox and had a thin trail of white hair that flowed down its back to its tail. The fox climbed up Ranyll's back and perched itself on his shoulders, wrapping itself around his neck for protection before he had a chance to stop it. It spoke to him.

"Do not fear the daggers, Ranyll. They carry not the power they had before when you saw them. They only poison earthly things made of this world, such as faeries and the world that we helped create. Push through them. Others of my kin are waiting for us." Ranyll nodded.

Another faerie creature. That's the only thing this fox could be to hold the magik of speech. It must be the help that Gwenzel was hoping for. And just in time, too.
Gwenzel's voice pierced into Ranyll's mind.

The daemon is taking Gabriella. We must go after him. We have to break through these creatures. Come, Ranyll, grab onto my neck and let us go from here.

Without another thought, Ranyll slashed at the several dark forms in front of him with renewed purpose and jumped over the remaining that he didn't take down with his sword, grabbing for Gwenzel's neck. His left arm hooked around the broad, white shoulders and he felt Gwenzel's muscles tense beneath his touch. Then they were on their way, leaping over the mass of daemons as quickly as possible, trying to catch up with the lead daemon. Several daemons latched hold to Ranyll's feet at the last moment and now clung to his boots, climbing up his body. He felt their dark claws tearing into his legs, dots of blood soon appearing on his breeches. Ranyll cried out in pain.

"Help me! Someone help me!" He could feel the weight of the daemons on his thighs now, hanging on with their clawed fingers. His left arm was weakening from the strain of holding on and he could feel his grip beginning to loosen on Gwenzel's neck.

"I'm slipping!" The young boy's hands began to slip from Gwenzel's neck even more and he thought for sure that he was doomed at that moment to fall underneath Gwenzel's powerful stride. The magikal fox at his shoulders suddenly released its hold of Ranyll's neck and moved down the boy's side, closer to the daemons. The fox slipped free and, with one quick glance at the daemons, turned into a streak of fire that lanced straight through the two daemons, their shadowy forms falling off of Ranyll and down onto the ground that moved at such a pace they vanished in moments. The daemon's howls were drowned out by the sound of Gwenzel's hooves as they tore up the ground beneath them, Ranyll pulling himself up onto the unicorn's back. The fire fox moved back across Ranyll's back and around his neck again, tucking itself in for the bumpy ride.

The barren, treeless landscape soon revealed the lead daemon just ahead of them, pulling Gabriella further away and, after riding a moment longer, revealed also the daemon's escape plan. A hole had opened up in the ground and the daemon urged Gabriella forward with prompting from his long dagger, pushing her in with his free hand. Gabriella disappeared out of sight and into the crevasse.

"Gabriella!" Ranyll's voice carried to the TSeT, who quickly jumped in himself, sheathing its dagger before it disappeared inside the hole.

Gwenzel quickened his pace, all three watching as the hole began to close. When they had seen it, the hole in the ground was close to thirty hands across. They soon arrived and now it had almost closed completely, with barely a nine-hand space remaining. Ranyll took one glance at the hole and looked back at Gwenzel.

"Goodbye, Gwenzel! If I don't go now, we'll never see her again!" With that said, Ranyll sheathed his sword over his shoulder and jumped into the hole, hands at his side, the fire fox clinging to his cloak as they were swallowed up by the darkness inside.

Gwenzel bowed his head and tried to link with Ranyll's mind. The young man was gone. The link had diminished when the ground closed in about the young boy and the fire fox. The lone unicorn could hear over a dozen skittering forms behind him and knew them to be the remaining daemons nearing him, waiting for their chance to move in and attack. But Gwenzel knew something that they didn't.

From above, the unicorn could see the small outlines of faerie wings as they flapped; shimmering in the morning sun, the two small faeries sent down a magik the daemons knew nothing of. The dust floated in the air for moments, shading the air in sparkles of color and dimensions of light, as though the world could be mirrored in a single shimmer of faerie dust. And, indeed, it could.

Once the dust caught on to the daemons, it burst into flame, searing the shadows and, mingling with their howls were the battle cries of the two clans of faerie kind, raising their weapons in victory. The daemons never made it to Gwenzel. The searing daemons dropped to the ground in the dying forest just before they made it to the unicorn.

As the flames died down, the two faeries approached Gwenzel, greeting him as they did all other faeries, bowing gracefully in mid-air. Gwenzel nodded his still-flaming horn in salutation, pawing at the ground urgently.

"Gabriella has been taken by the daemons. The human boy has followed Gabriella and her captor into the caves underground. He and the fire fox are surely doomed if they do not find a way of escape soon. Those caves will lead him right into the lair of the One and his army of daemons."

The faeries were distraught. They had known this all along as they traveled here, hoping that they would be able to get to the angel before the One had released his army upon the few protectors she had. Now, they had lost the fire fox in the cave with the human and Triggle was nowhere to be found. The Glor clan faerie was the first to speak. He slipped his magik pouch back in place on his belt and ran his fingers through his hair, replacing the small faerie helm back onto his head.

"We know of this also, Gwenzel. We had just come upon you when the fire fox, we know not his name for he hadn't told us, acted on his own. We told him to wait but he refused. We've also lost a Miftle by the name of Triggle. He was here with us before the attack but we know not where he is now. We must find the angel and the others. Are you well enough to continue on?"

Gwenzel nodded. He had several cuts on his legs that raised slight concern among the many other smaller cuts, but they would heal overnight with the magik that coursed within his veins. The unicorn continued.

"Do you know of another way into the caves besides the Argolis Mountains?" Gwenzel knew of the caves but did not know much, for he was still young in the ways of the world. The Sifter clan faerie spoke up, straightening her small cloth cloak around her shoulders as she flew. Both were so young, so full of life. Gwenzel smiled when she spoke, her small voice piping up, almost inaudible over flapping of both their faerie wings.

"The only other way we know is through the Wilden Marsh, the old trading route the humans and dwarves used to use before it was closed, just north of Reune Lake. But Shilinda forbids faeries to go there, and with good reason, too."

Gwenzel had heard the stories since before his horn had grown out. His elders had spoken of the Mist that tore at the very core of magik and could steal away dreams. There was a creature that was known to feed off of magik, a wild faerie that had lived off of humans too long that hid in the mines of the small town of Wilden. Yes, Gwenzel had heard and feared the place greatly, knowing that the mines were no place to go, even when he broke rules and left safe boundaries for unknown territory. Even then, he would never venture into Wilden Marsh on his own. But the situation was different now, he knew.

"So are we going or what?" The small faeries waited for Gwenzel to respond. The unicorn led the way into the unknown, fearing, for seconds only, that what they were walking into was far more dangerous that what he had ever faced before.

10

The darkness rushed in around him, pulling Ranyll in, the small fire fox curling around his neck, both falling into the abyss together. The smells, the sounds; all rushed in on them at once. Ranyll could feel uneven ground give under his feet as he fell, pieces of it rushing down with him as well, his hands grabbing for a hold to slow himself down for the unknown below that was approaching fast.

Soon, he was enveloped in complete darkness, the ground passing him by, his hands finding holds that offered no assistance and crumbled between his fingers. Ranyll began to get worried.

Was this ever going to end? The constant reminder of what he had followed kept echoing in his head. *It was a daemon. They only live in one place. And that's down, down in ….* Then a light suddenly appeared below him. The fire fox was the first to notice.

"Young Ranyll, I believe we are coming to the end of the tunnel. Look!" The light brightened, yet it was only a dull light, for in no way could a blanket of light smother the darkness that covered them. As they grew closer, Ranyll felt his hands catch on something solid. It felt like a piece of rock.

"I found a hold! Hang on!" Ranyll and the fire fox jolted to a stop, his feet digging into the ground underneath him as well, dust and pieces of dirt parading over them, falling still further down into the tunnel. The air was dry and thick, clinging to their skin and hair.

Ranyll felt around, testing the ground around him with the tip of his boots. It was as if he were on a ledge of sorts, on a corner of the tunnel that started to straighten out slowly to slow the abrupt fall. Ranyll then noticed that it gradually straightened out into a tunnel in which you could walk. The fire fox, whom Ranyll still knew nothing about, released its hold, dropping onto the ground as well, taking a corner for his own. It peered down into the rest of the tunnel, looking back at the human every-so-often. The magikal creature turned its attention to what they had been saved by. It climbed up what looked like a pedestal and clawed up to the top of the slab of stone, examining it.

"I wonder what this is! It looks awful old; must be from the elves." The fire fox took his comment back after further inspection. "Maybe of dwarven make. What do you think?"

Ranyll could see a little better, his eyes adjusted to the light as much as they could be. The young man went back and felt at what his feet had caught on moments earlier. It was smooth all except for two jutting edges which one he had caught onto to stop them. He closed in on it and the filtered light in the tunnel caught a face, horns; sharp fangs protruded from a snout-like head.

"It's a statue. It looks dwarven-made to me. But what dwarf would carve something so menacing?"

"Probably a warning to any who enter on what's to come if you go further." The fire fox was quiet for a time, and then spoke again, his small snout looking up at the young boy beside him.

"Young Ranyll, I must speak to you about something, if you don't mind." Ranyll nodded his head for the creature to continue, examining the statue further. "You are the first of your race that I have met in person here on Kariyl and I wish to understand why you go all this way for something you don't understand."

"What, you mean Gabriella? Understand? Is there something I need to know that I don't already? She's in danger. If that's what you're talking about, then there's no need to worry. I go for a promise I made to her. I told her I'd keep her safe and I've broken that by letting that daemon get a hold of her. I can't stop until I find her."

The fire fox nodded in agreement, his little mouth spreading open in the dim light, revealing its tiny fangs in what Ranyll could only decipher as a smile.

"Then the others of my kind are right. You are a human still connected to the world. Ar Solon controls you. You have the grand scheme flowing through your veins. The Creator works through you." The small fox's voice almost squeaked with excitement. Ranyll still didn't understand.

"What's this 'grand scheme' that you speak of? I don't think I've heard of that before." Ranyll had been schooled in religion as a child but much of it drifted away as he labored through the days the last few seasons, trying to help his family earn a living. His schooling had been neglected the last couple of summers and, as the fire fox mentioned something of history, Ranyll perked up, waiting for a detailed answer.

The fire fox was happy to explain but this darkness seemed to be getting to him. His tail was caked in dry clay, his paws were sore from the journey here, and chasing daemons wasn't his favorite past time. But history was. He cleared his small throat.

"The grand scheme is a gift given by the Creator to the inhabitants of the world as a map of sorts in which to live by. Over the years, the scheme has vanished amidst the bloodlines, but there are a few left in Ar Solon that have it. My faerie kin say you are one of them that have it. They say you have a thing called dreams in which you live pieces of your future while you sleep." Ranyll was finished examining the statue and turned to the little fire fox.

"When you speak about dreaming, it sounds as though you don't do it yourself. Do you dream?" The little fox shook his head.

"Faeries don't dream. We don't even sleep. We do a thing you inhabitants call 'rest', but that's after a very long day of doing repetitious things, which us fire foxes do not do anyway!"

"So that's what you are? I wasn't told; too much has happened all at once. I'm afraid we haven't been properly introduced. I don't even know your name." The fire fox stuck out its paw, remembering the manners of the sprites at the meeting earlier. Ranyll leaned down and took it, giving the paw a little shake.

"You are Ranyll, I presume. I was told who you were when I volunteered for this journey. Young Ranyll, my name is D'meir. I am the fourth generation of my race and have lived on Kariyl since a pup. And you, young Ranyll? Where do you live?" Ranyll remembered his family back at home. He could feel the pangs of guilt from leaving them now.

"I live in the town of Telgin, just east of here, with my mother and my younger brother. They don't even know that I'm here. I wonder if they're doing alright."

The last comment was more to himself than to D'meir, who just looked at him, apparently impressed with the idea of leading a search party with a human. The thoughts that lingered in Ranyll's mind after that hit him hard, making him walk faster and, after taking several steps toward the exit, Ranyll noticed something else just steps away that he had apparently missed before.

It was another statue, one of many he realized now, looking down the hallway at similar statues that stood as well, guarding the entrance into the tunnel.

But an entrance to what, Ranyll questioned, his hand jumping to his sword instinctively, his eyes catching the light on several more statues as he made his way down the tunnel. Ranyll soon decided it was best to move his sword to his hip instead of over his shoulder due to the fact that the tunnels were somewhat small and it was quite impossible for him to unsheathe the blade over his head.

The dirt soon faded beneath his boots and was replaced by a bumpy, rock-like surface, the fire fox at his side, just by a step, the tunnel opening up the further and further they went. The light remained the same, his eyes finally beginning to adjust to all that he saw around him.

The statues were all different, yet they all carried the same grotesque face as he passed them. Some were crouched low; others were climbing the walls they were carved from. They resembled the daemons that he had fought but with a more savage look about them. As he passed them, he realized that the further he walked, the more detailed they became. He looked over to the fire fox for any signs of danger, yet the creature looked as if it were strolling through a calm forest and not the deep tunnels there were in, probably coursing with daemons. Then there was a slight turn in the tunnel, veering to the right. There was a change in the statues' appearances at once. The ones that made Ranyll shiver were the ones with victims in their arms.

The first one he passed by was of a daemon with a small child in its claws, raking across the small child's face. Then the one opposite of that was of a group of daemons tearing at a woman's hair as she lay crumpled on the ground, her body a pedestal for the daemons. And, as Ranyll looked closer, he noticed that the victims were all dwarves.

"That's a dwarven child," Ranyll exclaimed, pointing at the one they had just passed and then, motioning in the opposite direction," and that's a dwarven woman." The others were the same; dwarves being attacked by a number of daemons throughout the newer parts of the tunnel. Yet, the one thing that Ranyll noticed that puzzled him was that none of the dwarves had weapons in which they were battling with. He felt something when looking at the statues; something threatening. There was a presence, as if something were watching them. It was eerie, yet something he had felt before.

He remembered the feeling. It was back during the second battle between the daemons. Ranyll felt the same now. His grip tightened on his sword. Soon, the tunnel ahead was in plain sight in front of him. It ended with two similar statues yet they were feet taller, almost his height, their backs turned to him, looking out into the open room that lay ahead. The light that Ranyll and D'meir had been using had come from a number of torches on the wall, scattered throughout the room, in sconces, flickering this way and that, playing with the shadows back and forth against the gray walls. There were more statues, yet these were set all over the middle of the room, not in any particular order. The room was a great hall, an entrance; for what, Ranyll did not know. It seemed as though there was a keeper of the room, for the floors were barren and not filled with the dirt of ages, and the sconces were clean and newly lit.

This didn't seem like the type of place a daemon would inhabit. As Ranyll stepped completely out of the tunnel, D'meir following suit, he noticed what he had not before; the tunnel he had come through had apparently been a newer edition to the great hall, a flaw on its beauty, the hole marring the smooth surface of the wall.

Something made this hole in the wall, Ranyll noticed, seeing the jagged breaks across the smooth stone, thick tears of each stone ripped in several places.

And the feeling was still there, this time stronger. As Ranyll searched around the hall, through the number of statues, he found out why. TSeT came from his hiding place with Gabriella. She was hanging limply over the daemon's shoulder. But the daemon was not alone. From atop the statues, a rank of daemons crawled forth, their eyes beaming red, their claws running over the smooth statue's surface. As they crawled over them, the statues began to bleed. The daemons smiled. Many of the dwarven statues were, in fact, stained red. Now Ranyll pieced it together. And so did D'meir.

"I believe I know what happened to the hall's previous owners, young Ranyll," glancing over to the several statues that bled freely now.

But what did really happen to them, Ranyll questioned, holding his broadsword out in front of him, watching the daemons as they approached, closer by the moment. D'meir growled, a tuft of fur on his back raising in caution.

He growled a warning to Ranyll. "We must get Gabriella back soon, young Ranyll, for the daemons' influence on flesh is great. The truth surrounds us in these statues. There's no telling what will happen to the angel if she remains with them. They outnumber us by many. Do you have a plan?"

Ranyll stared TSeT down, his eyes trying to find the daemon's weakness. Ranyll could take out many of the smaller daemons with ease, but he felt that TSeT would be a problem, and this human couldn't take them all at once, he knew.

Yet that's the way they came, with no rules. He gripped his sword in his hands, staring, trying to think of a way out of the certain death that he faced. TSeT's voice broke the hall's silence.

"Your friends gave us no choice but to break the arrangement." TSeT leered at him, knowing that it was a near impossible task for just the two of them. The daemons were bloodthirsty and it seemed as though it had been decades since the taste of blood had crossed their lips. TSeT felt a surge of excitement course through his body as he called out to the human again.

"You do not know what you face, human. I will enjoy watching my brethren feast upon your flesh." TSeT turned to leave, resheathing its blade in a loose belt that hung at his side, a brutal grimace on his face that glared at Ranyll and then was gone from sight completely amid the statues. Ranyll could not let this happen again.

"Nooooooo!" The young man surged forward, his sword at the ready, watching as the daemons jumped from their places, leaping at him, their claws reaching out for him. He grabbed a sconce from the wall near him and used it as a second weapon to keep the daemons at bay, taking them down one at a time. He swiped one down from atop a statue, and then another that tried for his legs, taking a third with the hilt of his sword to its shadowy skull.

Behind him, D'meir burst into a trail of fire, leaving several daemons in flames, howling in pain. But they came on, quicker than Ranyll had ever seen before. These daemons did not have the daggers that the ones from above had, but they did have a jagged set of teeth and razor-like claws that hung on to him as he darted past one statue then another, trying to find TSeT, swinging his sword in a wild arc. Ranyll could suddenly feel blood pour from his wounds, down his arms and legs, his clothing stained red.

Then he saw it. There was a smaller passageway through a doorway, just ahead, that lead further into the grand hall, TSeT passing through with Gabriella on his shoulder. A handful of daemons blocked his path. Ranyll tossed the sconce into the thick of them, watching them scatter, his sword cutting a swathe through their ranks, taking them out as quick as possible, watching as many others replaced them just as easily. He felt as if, for every one he killed, three more replaced it. But Ranyll pursued anyway. He could hear D'meir calling to him from behind, howling his name. But Ranyll would not stop.

This was his second chance. He didn't know how many more chances he was to have. Another mass of daemons came upon him, appearing from behind another set of statues. They pounced on him, their fingers and teeth tearing at his flesh. He could barely stand from the force the daemons attacked him. The world around him suddenly became a blur. Ranyll could feel his life seep out of his open wounds, feeling the daemons surge on him, one after another, relentlessly. He cried out as the bursts of pain broke into his mind, his body beginning to lose its momentum. He couldn't focus.

Ranyll saw the passageway ahead fill with more daemons that spewed forth from the passageway just behind them. He knew that he had made a grave error.

Ranyll attempted to turn back. Daemons now surrounded him on all sides. He saw why D'meir had called him. The fire fox was in the hands of the daemons, shaking back and forth violently. They had him by the tail, smacking at him with their sharp claws playfully.

Ranyll tried to stop them. His body had weakened severely and, as he took his next step, he felt his knees give way under him. The world spun around him as he hit the floor, his hand loosening its grip on his sword. The clatter of the steel on the cold gray marble brought him to his senses long enough to see the daemons close in, their dark claws clicking wildly, their jaws open and waiting for their kill to take its final breath.

There was no one to save him, no one to help him on his quest this time. His world was about to end, finally, in this great hall. He thought of it as a fitting place for him to go.

The world rushed in on him without warning. A blur of images shot into his mind along with the pain. Flames, red-hot, tore through the daemons that were upon him and the pain was driven away with a touch from the fire fox that stood on him now, its body taken on the form of a flame. The flame's surged around Ranyll's body and in through his wounds, the magik the fox had taking on a new shape and color all its own, sealing many of the wounds from the inside out. The yellow flames poured through Ranyll's torn frame and filled him with a surge of energy.

D'meir, however, warned him.

"It will not last long, my friend. Hurry, before they regroup and attack." Ranyll lifted his head up to see the daemons waver in their attack, watching as the small creature took on a new form; a fierce, determined form of a protector. Faint trickles of life surged within Ranyll's limbs again and D'meir moved off of him, plowing into the nearest pile of daemons, searing a path through them. His voice echoed off of the statues.

"Ranyll, we must take refuge! Follow, I have found a place to hide." His arms trembled as he lifted himself off the floor, staring down at the smears of blood his body had made on the marble floors. He was still weak, he knew this, but many of his wounds had closed. The young man picked up his sword and gripped it in an aching hand, trying his best to keep it out in front of him. As he turned to follow, Ranyll saw what D'meir had done. There was a path of burning daemons forming a trail that turned close to a nearby statue. The screaming forms of the daemons writhed in pain and, as the magikal flames covered them, they grew silent and dropped to the floor in front of him.

Then Ranyll saw **him**.

The fire fox was on the head of a statue, his tail fluffed in anger, his small fox-like ears down against the back of his head. And **someone** was there with him. Hunkered against another statue across from D'meir, there was a dwarf. His thick, short body slipped past several nearby statues, closing in, an axe in one hand and a great hammer in the other, his eyes hidden by the edge of a helm that lay seated upon his brow. His mouth opened and from it came a war cry that Ranyll would never forget.

"Revenge!"

The dwarf uttered it only once and then fell upon the daemons with such ferocity that all the young human could do was watch in awe, the small bulk of a dwarf smashing and tearing through them with his hammer before the echoes of his cry had dissipated. His axe flashed in the faint torchlight and, with a heave, he flung it into a cluster of daemons, taking off limbs, cleaving into a skittering form, dropping it and many others to the floor in one swing. The dwarf grabbed Ranyll with his free hand, throwing the weak boy's arm over his thick shoulder.

"Come with me, human. Your animal friend is waiting for you." The dwarf rushed back out of the circle of daemons with a swing of his hammer, slamming the head of it into slithering bodies, smashing a way through the darkness that closed in on them quickly. The dwarf stopped at a far wall and pressed his hand against it, the thick wall moving inward and away as he called back to the fire fox.

But D'meir was at his side in an instant, darting in past him. The wall was pressed again from the other side and a sound of grating stone penetrated Ranyll's ears, the youth watching as the daemons surged forward, only inches away, then the stone slab was in place and again, Ranyll and his friend D'meir were in darkness, this time with a guide.

11

The rest of the darkness seemed to rush by him as though time went by through thoughts, thousands every second, colliding all at once in Ranyll's mind. He felt the dwarf's firm grip on his forearm and knew that he was being pulled. He could even feel the fire fox at his side from time to time, the furry tail rubbing against his barren leg, a flap of his breeches hanging lazily off of his knee. It had been torn open from a daemon.

He could feel the dried blood caked on the hair's on his leg and could still feel the pain that the other attacks had done on him in his mind, though they weren't on his body now. It was all confusing to him. He was exhausted, had been for the last many hours that he pushed on, but he had no choice. Or did he?

Well, he felt as though there was no choice in the matter. He would have never been able to leave Gabriella there for the angel to dispose of, no matter if he didn't know her or not.

It wasn't right, he told himself, being dragged down further into the darkness, his mind and body a puddle of mush. He stumbled several times, trying to find the step in front of him, his knees taking the impact, the dwarf continuing to drag the human though he had hit the ground. He heard the dwarf whisper to him several times.

"Keep up, human! Keep moving! No time to slow down. They'll catch us if we slow down." It sounded as if it were almost a threat. And, in a way, it was. There was no way that Ranyll could face the daemons again, not now. He held onto his pain without complaint, taking more of a beating as the tunnel narrowed, his head knocking against the lowered ceiling, the youth having to bend down, his knees almost touching his chest, his hands out in front of him, trying to catch the next lowered ceiling. But there were no more. The walking had gone on fine, except for the fact that there was no light, that there was just complete darkness, and that he was going away from Gabriella, which hadn't been his plan when he had leapt down into that hole to follow the daemons and their leader, TSeT.

He needed to know some questions before going any further. He yanked his arm away from the dwarf's firm grip. It took several tries but he was soon loose and took a few steps back, startling the fire fox behind and the dwarf ahead, both at the same time.

"Where are we going, dwarf? I need to know because I have a promise to keep." The dwarf turned and stopped in front of him, Ranyll could tell, because the heavy scuffling feet had stopped and the dwarf's thick breath hung in front of him. His breath smelled of blood and sweat, intermingled with a smell Ranyll could not decipher but, if he had to put a name on it, it would be rage. The dwarves are known for having much more of a temper than the other races and have been known to go into a fit of sorts where their anger gets the best of them. Ranyll sensed that this dwarf was still in it.

The dwarf turned and, without hesitating, strode up until he was even with Ranyll's head, which was lower than normal due to the ceilings, so now they were face to face.

"Listen here, human! I don't care if you had a promise or not. Don't you realize that I saved you from that mess out there? Maybe there are others besides you that have promises as well. So, if you want to go back, you know the way. If not, give me your hand and keep quiet. You don't realize right yet where we are. If you did, you'd have the sense to keep your trap shut!" Ranyll silenced immediately and handed out his arm, being led again, this time, faster. The tunnel was easier than the ones before it, a lot wider, yet still a little too short for him in height for a human. He could feel the fire fox by his side now, its tail shaking against his leg with each stride he took.

Then the pathway opened up ahead. There was a dim light and the young human's eyes squinted at it, trying to get his surroundings in focus. The pathway opened and made a little entryway that split into three ways, with a light in the center, just lighting the paths enough so each way could be seen. In each path, there was nothing to be seen. The dwarf stopped here and let go of Ranyll's arm, dropping it as he leaned against the stone wall. Ranyll now noticed what the light was. He hadn't smelled oil when they approached and noticed that it wasn't a lamp, but a stone, the shape of a rounded rock, lit with a blue tint that emanated out onto them. It was as if it were powered by magik. The dwarf caught him looking and smiled.

"Oh, that's right. You humans have never seen this before. Well, magik's not dead here. We have plenty of it. But it's not what you think. This has been here since the first dwarves built these caves centuries ago. It's called a sephic stone; it was a stone that was used by the masons who made these caverns. Ahead and through the left passageway are more of them, in many numbers as well, lighting up whole rooms. It's quite beautiful. If we had time, I would give you a tour. But, as you said, you have a promise. And so do I, young human." The dwarf's voice had calmed since the last time he had spoken, his gruff voice now almost a whisper, yet still out of breath.

Small beads of sweat rolled down his waxy forehead and into his thick, graying beard, his face and beard tinted in blue light that gave his features an almost statuesque appearance.

He looked like one of the dwarven statues in the previous room, Ranyll thought to himself, trying not to give himself away by his actions. The dwarf seemed to notice this though, and commenced to slide himself down into a seated position upon the floor. He reached behind him and pulled out a water skin, offering it to Ranyll, who drink heartily, almost too much, he noticed, taking deep gulps to quench the thirst that had been building inside of him since entering the caves which seemed like almost a full day ago. Nevertheless, he was sure it had only been hours. He took another long gulp of the water and was handing it back to the dwarf when he felt a small paw on his leg, scratching lightly. D'meir bared his teeth in a menacing smile.

"Fire foxes get thirsty, too, y'know! I'd be grateful if you could hold some in your hands so that I could drink." Ranyll almost laughed at the thought and then, once noticing the seriousness in the small animal's face, held his hands out to the dwarf, who poured a considerable amount into them. D'meir drank gratefully, his tongue lapping at the water until there were only drops in the cracks of the young man's fingers. D'meir licked his lips and backed against a nearby wall across from the two, curling up into a ball, his eyes alive and darting between the two as they exchanged words.

"I know that there is much that you yearn to understand, young human, and you will in time. In time, you will know too much and you will wish to give much of it back. So, before you follow me into the next passageway, you must be prepared. You must know that this is how it is right now with us dwarves and that, for us, it is the end. We do our best to protect our own. It will be hard to protect you from the daemons. They do not know our hideouts and we do not feel like they should know anytime soon. So, once you pass the threshold, you must follow with me until the end, or you are on your own, do you understand? All will be safe if you just do as you're told."

Ranyll did not know how to react to this. It was almost as bad in the tunnels as it had been up above it seemed. Was this how the world was all the time? Were there always battles amongst the races of the world and the daemons?

No, that couldn't be right, he concluded, reminding himself that there was no history of these sorts of things written in the great books in the library. Ranyll knew that he was sheltered having lived in only Telgin for the small amount of time referred to as his life, but he knew that this wasn't supposed to be happening. There had to be a reason for it. He looked over to the dwarf for answers.

"Why is this happening; the daemons? Why are they attacking everyone?" The dwarf's eyebrows arched quizzically. He threw back the water skin and drank the remainder, recorking it and placing it back on his belt at his side. He slipped another hand into a thick pouch by his hip and pulled out some dried strips of beef, which Ranyll and D'meir accepted gratefully.

"You mean that the daemons are attacking the surface as well?" This seemed like a surprise for the dwarf. Apparently the dwarf had thought that the dwarves were the only ones.

"Yes, they attacked me and my party before we were separated. Then I followed Gabriella here and the daemons led me and my friend into a trap." The dwarf looked over at the fire fox who had just finished a small strip of beef and was working on a larger piece that Ranyll had given him. The dwarf smiled, as if greeting an old friend.

"What do you think of this, D'meir? Do you think this is all over one thing, or is there something bigger at stake?" Ranyll was awestruck that the dwarf knew the fire foxes' name. He looked questioningly at the dwarf.

"Do you know D'meir?"

The dwarf chuckled through his beard. "You could say that, couldn't you D'meir, that we are acquainted?" D'meir had just finished the last of his meal and commenced to clean himself. He answered every several licks.

"Yes, we are. Yes, we are. I think Oagthor here is the only friend I have in this part of Kariyl. And, as for your question, my old friend, I think that there is something brewing within the land that has an effect on us all, above and below. I have yet to find out what it is, but Gabriella is at the center of this puzzle, I assure you."

"Gabriella? You don't mean Gabriella the angel… noo!" The end of the dwarf's sentence drifted away into his beard as his eyes stared out into nothing, a blank gaze that lay lingering on the floor, his shoulders showing his understanding, slumping forward, his hammer dropping out of his hands. D'meir looked concerned for his friend. He stood up, stretched his legs, and walked closer to the dwarf.

"What is it, Oagthor?" Oagthor's answer seemed to echo what has happened since the beginning of Ranyll's journey with Gabriella.

"That is what they spoke of when they came; so many. There was a flesh daemon with them; a leader. I heard it speak of a fallen one that he was searching for. As they passed through the tunnels and my party after them, they disappeared. But that was days ago. Was that the same team that came through that you two were battling before I came in?" D'meir nodded his head. The dwarf jumped up quickly and pulled himself to his feet, grabbing his hammer from the ground. He motioned them forward.

"Then we still have time to catch them before they reach the exit! They have to come through the last town in order to get to their caves. Come, quickly!"

Oagthor slipped into the right passageway, the two others following suit, and led them silently through the lower passageways, his eyes darting quickly down the tunnel for any signs of life ahead. A light suddenly appeared ahead not long after and there was yet another blue sephic stone that was attached to the wall. Oagthor crept slowly past and signaled for silence, his hammer gripped tightly in his hand. He turned to Ranyll and looked at the young boy, his face the same statue-colored coldness it had been before.

"Here's your chance, human. You can still turn back." Ranyll had thought hard on the decision earlier as he traversed through the passages with the two companions ahead of him as they spoke about times past, his mind always wandering back to his home, to Telgin and his brother and mother. He wondered why they almost seemed to haunt him, calling out to him to return home. But he couldn't think about that now. His word, his promise to Gabriella, could not go undone. He had to pursue this flesh daemon and its party. Most of all, he wanted Gabriella safe and near him again. It was almost as if he and the angel had a bond of some sort. It was strange, but he couldn't think of anything stranger than where and why he was now, so why couldn't that happen as well?

He looked over at the dwarf, the one D'meir called Oagthor, and tried to understand what he was going through as well, what hardships he had faced. Maybe one of those statues that bled had been one of Oagthor's friends or family and he had made a vow as well to avenge them. Ranyll wasn't about to back down now. He wouldn't have it. He pulled his sword free of the scabbard and nodded his head.

"I want to go with you, Oagthor; with you and D'meir. I will have to face the world someday, why shouldn't I face it with you two?" D'meir smiled at this comment, looking over at the dwarf. Oagthor nodded at the fire fox. There seemed to be a past between the two as though they had faced challenges far greater than this and understood the seriousness of this. Yes, they were the seasoned veterans and Ranyll was but a novice in this area of the world.

That seemed to change by the second, Ranyll thought to himself, watching as the dwarf hefted a boulder ahead of them to the side, letting the light from the town in on the three of them.

The world Ranyll had known for all of his life seemed to catch in his throat and die. He knew that, through his eyes, he would look at things differently until his death, which he didn't know when would come. But, as he walked out of the passageway and into the dwarven city ahead, he thought that his time might be up. Oagthor had said it had only been like this for a short time but the world around him looked as though it was in agony all of it's life. The city was in flames, had been in flames, and seemed to burn from a forever fire that tore at the fabric of Kariyl and all of Ar Solon as well.

12

The three faerie kin made their way just to the outskirts of the Wilden Marsh and looked back in the direction that they had come from, not seeing even a glimmer of the Reune Lake or the towns they had passed in their three days travel. It had taken them longer than expected, moving in the cover of brush all the way there, almost being seen by several caravans of travelers. They followed the abandoned trade routes to Wilden, thinking that no one passed through there; but they had been wrong. There were many that frequented the trails, yet they had grown more and sparse as the three fairies grew closer to the town and the marsh that seemed to creep over every bit of land for miles around.

At first, the trees began to become less dense, and then the foliage disappeared altogether on the second day, leaving them with only a small stream in which to drink from. Now, with the marsh in front of them and miles behind them, they looked for any sign of an entrance into the mist and murkiness.

The two sprites lifted off the back of the Unicorn's shoulders and searched through the wasteland they meant to traverse through, seeing only the tips of withered trees in the distance. The dirt beneath the unicorn's hooves had become less and less stable and, as Gwenzel trotted ahead, his hooves sank into the green mass of earth and it made him wrinkle his nose in disgust as the surface of the ground beneath him broke open and the most rotten smell permeated the air around them. Tristle waved away the smell with her small hand.

"What foul odor comes from this place? This is worse than I have ever heard of it being! Just the smell alone is enough to drive a sprite to pull off their own wings!" Drigno nodded, bringing his hand to his small nose as well. He looked over to Gwenzel, who had stopped momentarily to look at something off in the distance.

The sprite continued to wave his hand in front of him, grabbing something from one of his pouches to try and curb the awful smell.

"I agree with you completely, Tristle. If this place reflects the owner, I would hate to meet them. Wouldn't you agree, Gwenzel? Gwenzel?"

But Gwenzel was lost in his thoughts. Both sprites looked in the direction he was looking in and, after a time, the gray mists that veiled the way in front of them opened in a path just a few feet away. They could see the ground's surface bubble and harden right in front of them. The area that the mists covered was marsh, but the open pathway in front of them had somehow turned solid, as though someone were expecting them. Gwenzel nodded them forward.

"It looks like someone has been watching us from afar. I see no signs of life for miles, yet the mist seems to be controlled in some way. We were looking for a way in. I believe we found it, my sprites." Drigno flew in front of him and blocked the unicorn's way.

"Gwenzel, sir, if I may speak. How do we know that it's not a trap? We have heard the rumors of this marsh. How do we know that it is not alive and it is leading us into the bowels of itself to have us for lunch, or worse, for breakfast?" Gwenzel had thought of this as well, watching the mists as they swirled through the air now, shaping and colliding together, reshaping and starting the whole process all over again. He decided if they had wanted to trap them, whosoever could have done it with ease, with the power that the marsh and whoever inside the city of Wilden held.

But the unicorn answered his questions with care, carrying the weight of his answer as not to offend the two sprites. "We don't know that at all, Drigno. All we know is that the fate of an angel is in the hands of a powerful daemon and his rag-tag army and Shilinda has entrusted us with her keeping. So far, I have failed miserably at the attempt at being a protector. But I can feel, from afar, that our little fire fox and the human have not. They are pursuing her just as we are. But I feel that they are closer to her than we, so we must quit waiting and carry on, for there is much yet still to be done before we reach the other side of Wilden, where the mines are. So, if you don't mind…" Gwenzel nodded his head forward, softly nudging the flying faerie in front of him to the side. Tristle lifted her weapon in front of her and flew by Drigno, her hand out to him, her eyes on the unicorn that led the way into the unknown.

Drigno grasped the other sprite's hand and both made their way into the marsh, watching as the mists came up from both sides, both heads turning in unison to see the trail they had just entered disappear and turn back into marshy land in the blink of an eye. They looked to Gwenzel in front of him but he was already gone.

The sprites' hearts skipped a beat. They looked from side to side, scanning the marsh, watching it close in on them, the bubbling land below pitching and swaying, small forms breaking the surface and sinking back down into the stagnant waters. They were invaded on all sides by the odor and presence of the marsh around them, tugging at their strengths that had gotten them this far.

We can't stop now, not without finding Gwenzel. Drigno broke the stillness of the marsh by calling out to the unicorn. His voice was weak, wavering, and unsure that it could penetrate through what magik had them cornered.

"Gwenzel! Gwenzel, where are you? We've lost sight of you. Gwenzel!"

The unicorn's presence could be felt but the mists hid him from them. They had heard his hooves clomping on the solid surface they had been following just moments before, his mane shimmering in the pale light; still a splendid sight in such an awful place, though he had been through much in the last several days and hadn't groomed himself since meeting Gabriella and the boy, Ranyll. They heard his hooves through the mists in front of them now, not far. It seemed as though he were getting closer. Tristle brightened up when she heard him, tugging at the other sprite to follow. She pulled him ahead through the mist, calling out the unicorn's name.

"Gwenzel! Gwenzel, it's us. Can you see us? We can hear you. We're following your hoof falls. We're on our way."

Then, just ahead, the mists parted. Drigno stopped in mid-air, watching as the form ahead materialized before them. It hadn't been Gwenzel's footfalls at all. Both sprites turned to retreat but saw the mists around them grow darker. The form in front of them approached closer, a deep growl rumbling within its throat. The deep grating broke through its maw and the creature's breath nearly made the two sprites swoon with disgust. Its breath smelled like that of a rotting corpse. It spoke.

"You have entered Wilden Marsh, faeries. You have made a grave mistake and will pay. But first, the master wishes to see you. Follow me." The mists grew closer until the tips of the sprite's wings grew cold and stiff and they fluttered forward, following the unknown beast through the marsh and into the city of Wilden.

Gwenzel turned to the others of his party and watched as they disappeared behind him into the mist. He turned to follow but the mist clouded thicker and all was suddenly shut into darkness.

"Drigno? Tristle? Can you hear me?" His horn glowed in response, blasting into the mist, tearing through it as though it were nothing. But, as he did so, the surrounding mist filled in the broken spaces and looked as though it had never been attacked by the unicorn at all. Gwenzel went into a rage. His magik arced into the mists again and again, his voice rising after every strike.

"Drigno… Tristle! I am coming for you! I am here. Can you hear me?" But it was no use. The mists seemed to multiply just as fast as he attacked them, filling back in, taking place of the shifting mists that he shot through. His muscular frame was shiny from a layer of sweat that had formed and he snorted in disgust as his horn's blue light faded and he caught his breath. He snorted again.

This isn't getting me anywhere. I need to think if I'm going to get out of this, Gwenzel told himself, watching the mist swirl in different shapes and designs in front of him, all around him in fact; even above him, blotting out the sun, hiding the surface of the marsh from any light.

The surface! Gwenzel looked down and noticed that the ground wasn't as firm as it had been when he had entered. In fact, his hooves had sunk without him noticing, almost covering the tops of each hoof now. He pulled his two front hooves out first and went to pull his back hooves out when he felt something slither past them. He looked down. Creatures of all different sizes: large, small, different shades of black, sharp, spindly-legged masses, climbed up onto his sinking legs, moving up closer to his chest. Gwenzel attempted a buck but felt his legs sink in deeper and he began to panic. He could feel the creatures on his haunches now as well, Gwenzel swinging his snout to push them off as best as he could. Several flew back into the marsh but more came, apparently enticed by Gwenzel's inability to fight them off.

Take this.

He turned his head down at his feet and the blue fire coiled around his horn, erupting into the marshy bottom below him, sending several creatures into the air in all directions. Several of the creatures still above the marsh were on fire with blue flame, squealing high-pitched about their pain as the fire tore through their black forms. The creatures had stopped climbing on him but still they came. He shot another blue flame into the marsh and the creatures scattered away, apparently knowing that the creature they came after had more of the magik where the first attack had come from.

Soon, they disappeared completely into the bog around him. Gwenzel braced his front legs on the bottom of the marsh and pulled his hind legs up out of the marsh. His legs were coated with a slimy substance that dripped off them, several small bite marks scattered across his hooves and up his hind quarters. He blew a sign of relief from his nostrils, continuing on towards the city of Wilden, knowing now that something didn't want him here, that something was afraid.

You better be afraid, Gwenzel thought, his mind now focused, determined not only to find Gabriella and the two that searched for her, but also to find the two sprites that were probably in danger as well.

It seemed like a tall order to fill, Gwenzel remarked to himself, his blue magik cutting through the mist just enough that he could make his way forward, *but there's nothing that can be done about that now.*

The town of Wilden had been, as the rumors of old had said, a mining town. The ore from the Agnar Mountains had been separated at the entrance of the mines and carted down in mining cars to the edge of town where it was melted into weapons, coined money, and raw materials that was shipped to the human towns, miles away. It was primarily manned by humans due to the fact that they had the tools to mine the tunnels yet, when called for, dwarves were hired for their ability to see in the darkness, and it was the dwarven race that pushed on to construct a means far easier than the human's original way.

They had fashioned weapons from the ore in the mines and used them against the mines themselves, cutting the time of work down by almost half the time. The town of Wilden had become one of the most prosperous towns in all of Kariyl very rapidly. In less than ten summers, it had tripled the worth that Goletta would ever make in its history as a town in shipping goods, Wilden making a name for itself among the great towns in all of Ar Solon. Many thought that it had become too powerful a town and that its downfall was approaching soon. That's why, when the town mysteriously broke contact with the rest of Kariyl, it came as no surprise. The other towns had concluded that the mountains were dry from being mined all those years and the trade had stopped without a warning at all.

But what had happened was far different from what anyone had conjured up in their minds. Wilden miners had been mining only the southern tip of the Agnar, just scraping the surface, when they came upon a surface of mineral they had never seen before. No human mining tool could break through the ore surface that they had found. But, since the dwarves had the upper hand, they used their skills as craftsman to break through the surface and, soon, the outer layer of the mineral had been broken and what lay beneath was unearthed.

A mist rolled in almost immediately, draping the town in a veil from the rest of Kariyl. The land became soft and the mining tracks sank into the ground, the girders from the inside of the mines collapsing from the weight and lack of a solidly-braced floor. The buildings cracked from lack of foundation and collapsed in on their owners. The mineral they had broken into had been a layer of acidic liquid that was made after the splitting of the continents during the beginning of civilization and it had lain dormant since then.

But, as the first dwarf slammed down his mining tool, a liquid broke through and flooded all of the mining caves and the town, soon along with several surrounding miles as well. All of the trees and plants died around Wilden. The water supply became contaminated and many died from that, as well as the livestock. The human and dwarven miners rushed to escape but were trapped within the mists, choking on the fumes that had been released by the error of their ways.

The town lay empty until now. But there were always rumors of something within the mists that had escaped and it thrived now on the soil of Kariyl, extending its borders further and further every summer. It was as though something ancient from the beginning of creation had slipped out of the cracks made in the mountains and roamed free within its own personal dwelling, the now abandoned, broken down Wilden Marsh of the Agnar Mountains. Dwarven travelers from the Upper Agnar speak of creatures emerging from the marsh to attack lonely passerbys, dragging them into the marsh to feed upon their flesh. Many have even spoken of flying creatures that now nest within the upper mountain chain where few inhabitants have ever tread, waiting for caravans to pass within the mountains to fly down and attack. But these are all unconfirmed stories by travelers from afar, not truth like that are written in the great books in the libraries of Goletta and in the elven towers of Elvinisclar.

Many say that the miners are still there, within the mines, trapped in a vicious cycle within the very mists themselves, struggling to escape, fighting for their lives and then dying, only to be resurrected again and again to repeat the same mistakes over and over, the magikal properties of the marsh taking hold of their lost souls as they wander wearily through the abyss that is the town of Wilden.

Gwenzel stood at the edge of the town now, the surface still soggy but a little more firm than the outer edges that he had come across had been. It seemed as though it had been a full day since he had entered the marsh with

Drigno and Tristle, passing into the mists unknowingly, losing them just as quickly as he had first met them when TSeT and his daemons attacked. But it had just been a few hours, for he could still see the glimmer of the sun in the morning sky. The night had gone and was replaced by a waxy ball of yellow up high in the sky, though the unicorn could barely make it out in the gray, shifting mist. He shifted from one leg to the other, trying to relieve the cramps he had obtained while making his way slowly through the muck, the muscles throughout his body sore, aching. He needed to rest somewhere before continuing on, he knew. He could faintly make out shapes ahead of him in the mist, small square shapes just a bit taller than himself.

As he approached, he noticed that they were the remains of the buildings that had been Wilden, sunken almost to the thatched roofs that were just pieces of broken and splintered wood held together with the help of a nail or plank attached to it. He found several sunken tracks and mining cars flipped over along what used to be the main road of the town, wagons and carts full of rusted, rotted supplies still packed up, just as if they had been ready to move out, finishing up the packing before departing for another town nearby.

All of this gave Gwenzel the creeps; a long, thin layer of hair fraying up on his mane. He could feel the presence of the people that had been here with his magik, could feel the suffering just by looking at the mess that had been left in their hurry to leave. And, once he began to see the bodies lying in the marsh, arms jutting out from the misty bog, heads floating up from the sunken depths, he knew that the town of Wilden was, indeed, cursed.

Gwenzel needed to find a safe haven and rest as quick as possible; then he would have to find the way into the caverns that connected with the dwarven caves, where Drigno and Tristle said they could meet up with Ranyll and the fire fox. But, as he looked around, he could see no place that seemed safe at all. The deceased miners that he passed on the path deeper into the town made him more edgy, his horn lighting slightly, eyes scanning the edges of the town that he could see through the dense fog. The air was tepid and more foul the further he went, making him on the guard even more now that the smell was in his nostrils.

Then he saw the entrance to the mines. It was different from what he had pictured. There were mining tracks that could be barely seen through the muddy bottom, but there were also other trinkets and wares tossed upon the ground, as if they had been dropped hastily.

That seemed perfectly normal, Gwenzel thought, closing in on the opening, the mouth to the cave twice as big as the unicorn himself. But there were other things that lay closer to the cave, things that sounded off an alarm in his mind, making him take several steps back and examine them.

They were weapons. No mining tools, no buckets or barrels; weapons. There were rusted swords, broken axes, dented shields; all of this had been devoured by the marsh now, but had been fresh the day they were used, as if the Wilden townspeople had fought something….something **at** the cave. Gwenzel looked now into the depths of the dark cave and wondered what creature had come from the ancient world and what it wanted. Most of all, Gwenzel wondered if Ranyll had met it…and survived. The unicorn hurried into the entrance, his purpose masked in his features, his faerie powers lit and at the ready. He knew what his task was at this moment; to save the day. He would not let his friends down this time.

13

The faeries at Faerie Homme could see the glimmer of hope fade in their fellow faeries' eyes as she told them what had just transpired on the outskirts of the Faerie Homme earlier. The sprite was Timber Fey of the Glor Clan, her features more rigid and expressionless than that of the Sifter Clan, yet her telling had broken the mask of pride she had always worn and now a sparkling river of tears flowed from her doe-like eyes. Many of the Glor Clan sprites had found her wandering through the forest, trying her best to fly straight, her vision blurry and face filled with sadness. They tried to discover what was wrong. She spoke in between uncontrolled sobs.

"It was horrible! Shilinda, she's…she's….gone." At first, many of the faeries gathered around her took this as a sign that she had left mysteriously, as she had always done once what she needed to say was told to them. Thinking this young sprite Timber had just had never known of the queen's frequent appearances and disappearances, they dismissed her with a pat on the back, nudging her to fly back to her nestling place high in the great trees that surrounded the Reune Lake. But she turned and, though the sprite was small and her voice only a whisper when she spoke again, a thunderclap of shock struck the faeries that blanketed the forest in a deathly quiet.

"I saw Shilinda die! She was swallowed up by the ground and her killer walked away free."

When the details of the battle and conversation between the two finally came out of young Timber, the fairies stood afloat, almost to the point of disbelief. But deep down inside of them, inside each heart of fire that burned within their breast, they knew she was true to her words. In fact, the

Faerie Homme seemed more like a cemetery than a home now, they began to notice, watching as the leaves on the trees had stopped their swaying though the wind blew fiercely through the great forest. They all stood now at a great precipice where something had to be done, something had to be righted from this great wrong. The sprites from the Sifter and Glor Clans were the first to begin putting on their armor and gathering their spears and swords. They strapped on their magikal pouches, securing the last of the things they would need for their journey.

The rest of the faeries did the same; the unicorns said a silent prayer, the last remaining seven of them bowing onto their front legs, their thick, powerful muscles holding them inches from the ground. They called for strength, for power beyond their control to wield to make the wrongs right again in their time of need.

The tree phumps stretched the sleep from their long legs and pulled themselves down from the treetops, feeling the earth for the first time after years of guarding the life source of the Faerie Homme.

There was no need to guard it now, all of them thought in unison, using their ability to mind-speak and prepare themselves as well, pulling their sting sacs from several holes within the hollow set of trees nearby. They had been the first to see Shilinda appear, remembering to themselves how she had seemed so beautiful in the beginning and became almost a dream-like apparition after that, a ghostly mother to them all since that day.

The sloags and drenights slipped on their ceremonial garb and watched as hundreds of sprites flew over them, preparing for what was ahead. The sprites were on their way to the Argolis Mountains to call on the other faeries that hid from the dwarves. The sloags and drenights turned from the sprites above and continued on their task quietly, moving their large tails behind them, watching as the bipedal creatures followed, some riding forest creatures, others walking single file.

All of this was an unspoken language between the faeries and they did what was needed of them without question, watching the others of their kind with intense expressions that had never before been shown on the visages of a single faerie. Rage had never passed the ageless faces before; never did the enchanted faerie kind have a reason for these feelings that stirred uncontrollably in their blazing hearts.

They rest of them made their way to the same place; the mining caves in the Wilden Marsh. It would take them days to make the trip, some longer than others, but they knew the daemons would be waiting for them. Nevertheless, they had a surprise for the daemons. The faeries were going to wipe out the daemons completely. They would not leave anything black and slithering alive in the deep caves that ran through most of the Djup Sleel Pass, including much of the Agnar Mountains. It was true that the faeries had let the daemons retreat in the Great War, when they had won the last of the battles that raged on Kariyl, watching as the many scuddling forms sunk into the cracks that had become the scars upon the earth now.

Many of them had escaped. But that wouldn't be the case this time. The daemons would pay. And so would their master, The One. He would pay the most. There was no need to conceal their presence now. The faeries had lost their only link to the clouded world above and that had broken any pact made for concealment from the other races that they had known once Shilinda's body had sunk into the ground to be forever lost to her children. Timber Fey floated above the faerie army, looking down at her brothers and sisters as they flew just below her.

Her children, Timber thought to herself. *Shilinda had called us that so many times in the years that seemed to pass like the wind in the trees of Faerie Homme.*

Many of the faeries kept to themselves as they continued on, harboring the sudden hatred they were feeling.

They would need that hatred to face the things that dwell below, Timber continued, always having heard of the grotesque creatures beneath Ar Solon, slithering in caves, the faeries trying their best to gather what courage they could and use it to their advantage. However, many knew that this journey would probably be the last journey they made before sealing their fate in the caves of the Djup Sleel Pass.

The thought of Shilinda's death tore at all of their minds, the image of her enchanting form fighting for its last breath as it came out in a gasp as she died, killed by her former lover, Darien. But Darien had slipped into the form of The One since he had been banished to Ar Solon, forever spending his immortal life confined to the caves that smelled of the ancients that had constructed the earth.

The faeries knew that the end was coming, knew it all too well, but had no way of stopping it. Of course, they had started the process all on their own, ever since the beginning; they knew that. They had, after that, forever vowed to hide from the races that populated the now-separated Ar Solon they had once enjoyed as the inhabitants did now. But they had known since the birth of the inhabitants that they were different from the rest, that the faeries were a special race created out of the spirit of the Creator, that he had made them special among the rest.

And so it was to pass that the first of those born on Ar Solon made their way to their own execution blocks, following the wagon trails of the other races that knew nothing of them, watching as the sun raised itself in the pale morning sky, blanketing them in sunlight, a thing that many would not see again. They relished in it, watching as it broke over the great Agnar mountains in midday, finally to set just past the Argolis Mountains in the west, sinking into the Alvanus Sea until the next morning. It happened like this two more times and then the forest that they had made their way through throughout the trip disappeared behind them, the mist of the Wilden

Marsh rising up in front of them to block their path. But they would not be blocked; not hidden from view. Not now, not ever again.

The seven unicorns stood at the edge of the mist, watching it swirl and take form, swirl and become a gray shadow over and over again, almost making a pattern, but not enough for them to take notice. All seven lowered their heads and their horns flared to life, their combined magiks breaking through the mist, the other faeries reeling back in surprise, hearing the mist shriek in pain. The ground beneath the mist came to life and hundreds of creatures broke out of the murky bog, squealing in pain, burning for moments then lying still on the barren ground in front of the faeries.

The unicorns continued forward, their hooves breaking through the ground below them as they charged forward, blue arcs flowing wildly ahead. The mists began to retreat, passing fallen buildings, carts, wagons, corpses captured in the muck that had held them for decades. Still, the unicorns continued their assault. It wasn't until they saw the caves ahead that their hooves dug into the soggy ground, standing firm in their positions, watching at the mist took shape in front of them. The mist lowered itself to the ground, the outside thickening, forming a hide of sorts, hiding from view the insides of the mist, massing into a long, snaking, serpentine body. The mist formed into scales; a cold, ashy gray, the tip of the mist slanting and spilling forward a long, forked tongue that slipped out of a hooked jaw and lapped at its misty jaws eagerly. The unicorns still did not back down.

It reared back to strike at them.

*   *   *

Devver Tollins had the most calming sleep for the first time in weeks. Maybe it was because of all the stirring of the town he lived in, the bustling shipping town of Goletta. But it had always bustled with newcomers from all over Ar Solon and he had never been bothered before. He agreed that it must be because of the recent events in the other towns, miles away that bothered him most. He had heard rumors that a library had been burned down; one of the greater ones at that. He had always worried that there would be someone after him and his guild, threatening to destroy all that they had worked so hard to build.

But that was just in his mind. He had deemed himself a peaceful man and, though he was a human and still had desires for the outside world, Devver Tollins had pushed them away when the chance to be head scribe in Goletta had come his way. This had been a dream of his; to run an establishment that held such magik, such spirit inside of its walls. And, when he first came to work here, almost thirty years ago, he had never thought he would be the head scribe and have such power in such a peaceful town.

Of course, Goletta had seen its share of problems. But then again, all towns had seen their share of troubles, especially since all were still recovering from the War of the Races. It had only been a few decades earlier that this land trembled with booted feet, all running towards their death eagerly, the corpses behind them forgotten for a time, each warring race building mountains of dead upon the battlefield.

Devver stirred in his sleep.

But that had all ended, the books had said, storing away the bad memories within the musty library, The Great Tomb of the Dead, many younger scribes had begun to call it, referring to all of the dead that awoke to life within the pages. Head Scribe Tollins had read nearly all of them, with the exception of the much older ones and the newest few that were written, many scribes still coming in from all over the land with their own volumes of lore. It would take a full season to collect all the information and get it written, date it, and bind it into a tome to rest until needed again. But Head Scribe Tollins had someone to do that for him.

The head scribe woke that night to a firm tapping on his door, the firm taps from the knuckles of one of his younger scribes, Scribe Jildens, his robed head poking inside the chamber, a dim light breaking into the otherwise dark room. He had a look of worry that broke through his placid features, telling the head scribe that something was amiss. Indeed, something was.

"Master Tollins. There is a problem in the master writing chamber. Come quickly."

The head scribe opened his mouth to speak but stopped short when he heard the screaming that echoed through the hallway outside and into his chamber. Scribe Jildens turned back into the hallway and the light soon disappeared, the screams loud and unmistakable this time.

It was that old man again, Head Scribe Tollins told himself. He knew by the sound. His someone was going mad.

The old man stood in the master writing chamber, his hands in the air, bloody and ink-stained, his fingers outstretched to the ceiling above him. He looked around the room every so often, watching as the other scribes crowded around him, trying to calm him. But he couldn't be calmed. Something had stirred inside of him again and he had begun to write. But this time, it would not let him stop. He had been writing secretly for three days in his room, claiming sickness to the others in his guild, trying his best to stay awake. He had circles under his eyes, his brown eyes now wide and fierce, fists clenching and unclenching. He paced the floor in front of his usual writing desk.

He had had enough of a candle to burn for the last few hours but it had ran out in the middle of the night. But that did not stop the urge. He could feel it pull him into the room, make his hands grab his writing tools; half-filled tome, ink and inkwell, his bare feet shuffling against the cold stone to his regular daily copying room. He had lit the candle by his desk and sat down to continue when it came to him; the vision, the words; all of it at once. He couldn't stand seeing it again; he wouldn't. He wouldn't watch it, he swore to himself, yet he couldn't stop it from happening.

It was the boy! The boy was in trouble! He could sense it, could feel the words form on the page in front of him every time he wrote them.

The old man screamed at the others in front of him.

"I will not write any longer! I will not! He can't make me!" All of the scribes looked around at each other, trying to figure out who he was talking about. In moments, the double doors opened again and Head Scribe Tollins entered, watching as all the faces turned to him. He had heard the old man's tantrums from outside in the hallway. He made his way closer to him, watching closely the quill pen that his master copier had in his bloody hand.

"Calm down, Gilden! Calm down! Now tell me what's wrong." He signaled for the other scribes to back away and give Gilden room, to let him breathe a little. They moved against the bookshelves that held their newest tomes that were finished, watching as their head scribe closed in on the older man. Gilden screamed at the approaching head scribe, slamming his bloody fist down on the table in front of him, pointing at the book that he had been writing on for three days straight.

"I will not let this happen! I will not allow it! I thought he loved us! I thought he loved us. He can't let this happen!" He looked up to the ceiling again. "Do you hear me? Why are you doing this to us? Why do I have to write this if it doesn't matter in the end?"

Suddenly, Gilden's eyes rolled back into his head and he crumpled to the floor, dropping the quill in the process. Head Scribe Tollins rushed to his side, calling to the others.

"My word, scribes, he's delirious! Get me some wet rags. You and you," pointing at the two nearest to him, "help me take him to his chambers. He needs rest and fluids. It looks as though he's starved himself." The two he had called upon and the head scribe lifted Gilden up off the floor and took them to his chambers, appointing a guard to watch him throughout the night until he woke again.

He would need to be replaced longer now, Devver thought, trying to think of someone who could write with such neatness and accuracy as Gilden had the last several years he had been employed at the Writing Guild.

It would be difficult, he concluded, making his way back to the room they had transported Gilden from. It was empty now, all except for a few scribes cleaning up the mess the old man had made. One of the fellow scribes saw Head Scribe Tollins enter and rushed over to his side, grasping at his elder's elbow. He pulled him toward the writing desk.

"There's something we think you should see, Master Tollins. It's something that Gilden's been writing on." Head Scribe Tollins looked down at the tome that Gilden had been pointing to and saw that it was partially full, with footnotes and textual references in it, quoting from the ancient texts that he had learned from in writing school. And he saw something else in the writing. There were faeries and daemons fighting each other. In every sentence, there was an intense battle that filled pages and pages, the Head Scribe flipping back several pages, trying to decipher what Gilden had been writing about. Then a name appeared that brought Devver back from the nightmare-like landscape that filled half of the tome in front of him.

The One.

He stumbled through the pages and read other names, other stories, finding finally the threat that seemed to be waged on all of Kariyl itself. And one name was written over and over again, dotting the pages throughout the book. It was as though the word were a plague that, at first, dotted a page or so, but as Gilden's writing became more feverish and haphazard, the name blanketed every page. Devver motioned for one of the scribes, pressing his fingers against the name that sparked his interest and the scribe followed his wrinkled finger to the letters.

"Find this person. And find him quickly. I feel that Gilden is writing this for a reason. We must help this person as much as we can." The scribe stifled a laugh, being caught off guard by the seriousness of his master's actions. No one ever took Gilden's writing serious. He was famed for being a little far from sane, yet he could wield a pen though it was a sword and he was a knight fair and true. They had even given Gilden a knightly name, as a joke; The Chronicler. No one ever took it serious, though. Nonetheless, the scribe stifled his laughs when he saw the stern look on his master's face.

"I don't ask much out of life. Just do it, scribe! Now!" The scribe hurried away and slipped out of the master copying room, his footfalls heard echoing down the hallway. Head Scribe Tollins pushed the rest out of the room with a wave of his hand, half of the room still in shambles, his hands now on the book in front of him. He sat down.

What else is there that you haven't been telling us, Gilden? He flipped the book back over to the front and began on the first page. It was written in shorthand but he could read Gilden's handwriting well.

Far in the west of Kariyl, further than the great city of Argolis, at the edge of the Argolis cliffs, evil dwelt. It dwelt in mass, hundreds of them, daemons … … … He continued to read on.

14

"I shouldn't have taken the shortcut, I knew it!" Triggle slumped over when he saw the same set of dwarven statues ahead, knowing that he had circled around to the same position he had started in when coming through the hole in the wall just steps away. It was impossible to tell if the others would be coming in or not, yet he hoped they were, otherwise he would be stuck in here by himself. He looked at the statues, with their realistic wrinkles of pain on their faces, and shivered within his dusty clothes.

"Boy, I shouldn't have come in here in the first place! I'm lost and now I'm hungry. That's two things you don't want to be at the same time; lost and hungry. I'll have to write that down when I get back home." He tried to keep the admirable quote within his head so he could sit and write it down sometime, but it skittered away like everything else did in his mind when he was hungry. He just couldn't concentrate. And he especially couldn't find his way through this maze of halls that seemed to go on forever.

He had already been through two passageways that led him back to the same hall and now he looked down the hall at the dozens of passageways that were lit by the sconces on the wall. Who lit the sconces, he had yet to find out, for there was nothing here except for the statues that drew on what he had left of his courage, making him regret his every step further into the unknown ahead.

His life had never been this jumbled before now. He remembered well when he had left his faerie folk in Shinol, a small city just south of Reune Lake, and come here to find out the truth behind all of the strange happenings that seemed to plague the land almost overnight. There had been problems before with things in the land, but nothing like this.

And the dreams; he hated to think of them. All of his folk had been having the strangest dreams. He remembered them well now as he walked into the next passageway, his fingers twitching nervously as he made his way into the darkness.

Here it goes again. The light from the sconces had not been able to penetrate through the passageway's darkness and so he had to traverse through the darkness many times, reaching his hands out to feel for a hold to steady himself. He had done this in the other two passageways and hated it every step of the way, nearly biting his lower lip off in stark terror.

But now was different. This passage seemed even worse than the others, the small hairs on the back of his neck jumping up in warning. He rubbed them back down with a sweaty palm and padded quietly through the passageway, his hands waving out in front of him, making sure he didn't slam into a wall or tumble into a handful of daemons waiting for him in the darkness.

He had always felt that he got the bad end of the deal ever since birth in the faerie lands. He had no special abilities, none that he could tell yet, and he had never had the chance to dine on any of the fine cuisines that he had always stared at through the rough glass of the small homes that laid on the outskirts of the town. Several times, he had been discovered and a shrill scream would echo through the cottage, moments later a young boy or a man would come running out, some implement of destruction in their hands.

And all for what? All I wanted was a piece of the pie. A piece of flanriggin pie! Can't us Miftles get some pie around here? All we do is eat from the earth, the crummy forest. Sure, there's enough to survive on, but you can never put it on a plate in front of you and serve it as an actual meal.

Triggle thought on this and all the other fine delicacies that he was missing out on being an outcast from the city life, not even having a real chance of becoming a true outcast, for the faerie promise had been kept by his family name and he had upheld it since being able to speak.

The Miftle walked on for a time in the darkness, making his way the best he could in the darkness, his little hands out in front of him, always waiting to bump into something dreadful, yet never seeming to do so. He was relieved when he finally saw a light appear ahead of him, his arms tired; his short, stumpy legs as well, dragging himself closer, yet carefully, to what gave off the light.

He slipped his small dagger out from its place at his belt and kept it at his side, watching as the well-lit passageway grew closer and closer, his eyes making out the scene ahead. The light radiating from the passage was lit by a single torch on the wall in a sconce, the flames flickering left and right as he approached closer, his shadow casting itself across the wall in front of him, creating what looked like to him an evil, one-horned beast.

He laughed and thought about Gwenzel and the other unicorns at that moment, remembering when, on the last meeting a few summers ago, Gwenzel had lit his horn up in the darkness so every faerie could see as they told stories late into the night. It was a grand event, for Triggle hardly ever came to visit the Homme since his faerie kind had moved away to Shinol permanently.

The Miftle made it to the torch and peeked cautiously into the passage, which was made just as crudely as the original entrance he had come through, broken through to make a short cut into another passage.

But for what, Triggle wondered, trying his best to see into the passage without revealing himself completely within the strange entrance. It was dug into the wall and curved up toward the ceiling, his view only catching the half finished walls within the simple tunnel.

He began to make his way into it when something moved ahead of him. He didn't have time to think. The answer to his question was moving in the passage just as he had made his way in, the Miftle watching nervously as the shadowy forms ahead of him made their way to the end of the tunnel. They were the same creatures as those he had seen on the surface not long before he moved into the hole in the ground. They were the ones that had come for Gabriella. Their claws clicked wildly and they moved ever closer to the terrified Triggle.

I'm dead for sure now, exclaimed Triggle, pressing himself against the wall of the cave, moving back towards the exit, trying to make it into the shadows before the daemons could see him.

But could the daemons see me within the shadows, he questioned, wondering in sheer horror if he could even hide from these creatures that were made of the darkness itself. The Miftle moved back into the original passageway without alerting the daemons that carried on as if he wasn't even there. He even made it through the mouth of the cave and past the lit torch on the wall, taking a last look behind him before darting into the shadows.

Triggle could feel his heart beat in his chest, almost bursting out of his brown tunic, small beads of sweat dripping down from his forehead into his beard. He could scarcely see the passage around him he was so terrified, maybe that was why he didn't notice the uneven ground of the tunnel ahead until his foot caught on a jutting rock and he fell, face first, into the darkened passage, the very same one he had come through earlier. He was still in the light of the torch and his shadows bounced off the walls, making his shadow look almost like it was dancing. As he hit the ground, his dagger slipped from his sweaty grip and scraped against the darkness ahead of him, breaking the silence and sending him into further danger.

His heart seemed to burst when he heard the grumblings from behind him of the two daemons now outside the corridor, in the clear light of the torch. His mind fumbled for an idea, his blood raced through his veins. His breathing came in gasps, his hands and feet trying in unison to bring himself back up from the floor, his eyes darting from the daemons to his missing dagger in the darkness ahead. Then, as if all that transpired before him wasn't enough, the daemon nearest the torch, noticing that Triggle was looking for something, sent the torch flying with a wild swing from its clawed hand, hoping to extinguish the flame in one fatal swipe. But, as the torch flew from its sconce on the wall, it bounced off the wall and landed right in front of the terrified Miftle. This was Triggle's chance.

The Miftle leapt for the torch just as the two daemons surged at him, grabbing it tightly in one hand, his other holding a lone daemon at bay long enough to set the daemon's flesh ablaze with the flame from his newly-made weapon. It howled in pain and scurried back several paces, taking an evil glance at the daemon that had hit the torch aside and gave their victim a fighting chance. Triggle backed into the passage slowly, watching as the two daemons followed close behind, the Miftle taking a look back every so often to see where his blade had landed.

The daemons grinned from ear to ear, closing in on him as he took his eyes away from them, Triggle soon seeing the tip of the handle appear in the torchlight he now commanded. He closed in on it, watching the daemons take their turn closing in on him as well. He waved the flames at them.

"Come on, you grubby little bottom feeders! Come and get me! You think you got what it takes to take on a Miftle? Let's just see." Triggle made a false jump at one of them and they both backed away in fear of the flames, the wounded one howling in defiance at the accursed flame, its claws scraping madly at the ground beneath its feet.

Triggle leaned down and soon felt the handle of his trusty dagger, changing hands with the torch, setting the sword in his right hand with the torch in his left. The torch still had much left to burn from its base and he was no longer in fear of the two daemons that trailed behind him, soon taking quicker steps to make haste, trying to find an exit or an entrance, which ever took him away from the daemons and the possibility of death.

And somewhere that has food, his stomach reminded him, rumbling softly through his tunic, urging him that he had only so many steps left on him before he would drop of hunger and fatigue. But that wasn't the only thing that rumbled within the passage. All around him, the rumbling seemed to get louder and louder every step he took. The daemons behind him became more excited as well, clicking their claws together, moving in and out of the torchlight, making it hard for Triggle to see them from time to time.

"Confounded daemons! Think you can outsmart me, do ya? Well, I still have a few tricks up my sleeve, you shadowy turds!"

With that said, Triggle slipped his dagger into his belt and rummaged through the satchel at his hip, looking for his stash that he kept hidden from the world, all except his closest friends, of course. The daemons couldn't be seen now as they stayed far from the torchlight, Triggle hearing them close in even faster now that he didn't know their location in the passage.

He lifted the flask from his satchel and uncorked it with his fingers, taking a long drink from it. He swallowed the first gulp, feeling the surge of the fine spirits come alive within his cold, clammy shell of a body, and lifted it again to his lips, this time, keeping the liquid in his mouth. He brought the torch up a little closer and waited to hear the clicking steps of the daemons. Once he did, he spat out the spirits, a bright yellow flame surging forward, wounding one of the daemons in the flame's path. Triggle chuckled aloud.

"How about that, you spunkett? You think you got the best of me, do ya? Well, think again. Ha Ha!"

The Miftle watched as the blazing daemon rolled around on the passage floor, trying to put itself out, wailing aloud, the other daemon scuttling away from its companion. Then the rumbling grew louder as the flaming daemon started to wail. Triggle looked around, trying to discern from whence the rumbling came, moving the torch this way and that, until he came upon the reason for the rumbling.

Above him, throughout the passage, hundreds of daemons lay huddled in sleep, curled together on the ceiling, their demonic red eyes shut from the harsh light of the world. But the flaming daemon brought them awake, its fierce screams echoing throughout the cavern, breaking the silence of their nesting ground.

That's why there was an opening made in the wall, so they could rest far away from the traffic of their home. Triggle wished now that he would have taken the two daemons on barehanded, watching the daemons above him move from their place, eyes popping open, staring down at the lonely Miftle, staring deep into his soul.

Triggle didn't think twice and ran for the exit.

If they take me, it won't be here, Triggle declared, tearing his dagger from his belt, the torch wavering back and forth from the speed that the Miftle moved, his short legs taking the longest strides possible in his exhausted state. He could hear the wild clicking moving closer on the ceiling, the floors and the wall, and saw soon the passage up ahead.

He wished he had another trick up his sleeve but he didn't, feeling his chest tighten in exhaustion, the pain from so much exertion almost too much for the faerie creature. He felt his legs giving out on him and his pace began to slow, the daemons closing in on him. He saw their red eyes now as they broke into his torchlight, their claws digging into the stones in the wall and the ceiling. He didn't know what else to do.

Triggle took the last swig from the flask and slipped the container back in his satchel, swallowing hard, knowing that he would need it far more than a few of the daemons that would surge around his dead corpse once he had fallen. He was terrified inside but was determined not to let the daemons know, for he knew the stories he had been told all those years ago.

They lived off of fear. I must stand tall in the face of death, must remain strong until the end.

But somewhere, some place deep inside of the Miftle named Triggle, he suddenly felt sorrow that the end had to come so quick, and a single tear dropped down his dirty cheek, mingling with the sweat that lay heavy on his face. He gripped his dagger tightly in his hands and prepared for the worst.

*   *   *

Fisherman Falwen Sanse lifted his nets up out of the water, taking a look at what the tide had brought him on this fine day for fishing. He counted seventeen; pretty impressive for only the first of twelve casts that he usually did on his morning route across the Argolis shore. It took him most of the morning to traverse down the cliff side, following the old trading routes that the early settling boats used to use to bring in supplies and riches from the shore to the town of Simmer Lo, a small city just south of Argolis, dragging his nets behind him, arms full of lines and sinkers attached to the ends of the nets.

He didn't mind though, not in the least, almost happy to take the brisk morning walk down from Simmer Lo, its hustle and bustle almost too much for this simple fisherman who had learned the trade from his father as his father did from his father as well, an age of tradition that made Simmer Lo and the neighboring town Goletta what it is today.

Strongly knit communities and a family to back an idea was all one needed to get along in the western cities, Falwen told himself, though it was hard to see it from looking at the booming towns as they expanded closer and closer to the coasts, Goletta finally building several docks that branched out past the shore just summers ago, taking the next step in what would hopefully be a growing and thriving lifestyle.

Indeed, thought Sanse, *the land of Kariyl seemed to be taking to a rise of population and wealth*, something that Sanse never thought possible.

The fisherman chewed on the tip of his pipe as he pulled in the nets, using his smaller net to grab the energetic fish as they bounced off the rocks into his net, taking one after another to his storage net not far away; a shallow pool in which he stored his catch of the day until he was ready to leave. His count so far had been fifty, which took a toll on him when he made his way back up the cliffs, but they were certainly worth it once he sold them to the Argolis vendors that came for miles to collect fine fish from Simmer Lo.

He set his nets back in place and pulled them in slowly, trying not to catch them on a sharp rock, which sometimes happened when he wasn't paying attention. He whistled a tune while he worked, thinking how happy his wife would be to see all that he had caught, helping him to clean and cut them into slices, ready to be sold. He puffed on the tip of his pipe as he pulled the nets in, throwing them over his shoulder, leaving puffs of smoke behind him as he made his way to the next fishing area on his route he knew well to be full at this time of the day. The nets dragged behind him, catching small crabs and seaweed in its pull, which would have to be shaken out once put it the water, but wouldn't be hard at all for this seasoned fisherman, his mind steady and full of purpose.

A small handful of vessels could be seen out on the coast, leaving from the small ports that Argolis had set up for trade between them and Goletta, the vessels catching the fresh salty wind up in their sails, pressing on through the white clouds and matching blue sky, the sun beating down on their fresh, white sails.

It was stunning to see that kind of beauty, Sanse thought, remembering when he had taken the up the job of sailing all those years ago.

Aye, but it wasn't for me, he had decided, almost twenty years ago, keeping to the shores, making that his happy in-between for this former sailor turned family man. He loved it that he was so close to both things that he loved; his family and the sea. His two boys would see this scene years from now as they grew up and became fisherman as well. But, as he already knew, times were changing and the land of Kariyl, gathering so much wealth in such a small amount of time, left demand in so many areas that the population could not grow fast enough to incorporate the amount of inhabitants needed for the skills required.

So, Sanse reminded himself, *they might leave fishing for something more suitable to the times*. He feared sometimes that he would be the last of his name to fish the shores, while his children went off to bigger things that were being created in the world of inhabitants.

He soon found his next fishing spot and turned around, unfastening the clasps that held his nets together, bringing them in front of him so he could get a could casting. He grasped the corners of the netting and was turning to swing it out into the water when he noticed something near the shore, caught against the rocks, the waves lapping back and forth against it.

It was a body.

The clothes it wore were bloodied and torn, covered in seaweed, the robes barely discernable from the distance that Falwen stood away from it. He dropped his netting and grabbed his spear from behind his back, sliding it out of its leather wrap, his hands shaking as he moved forward. The figure was floating on its stomach, a head full of wavy brown hair moving in time with the waves that continued as Sanse decided what to do. From a distance, it looked as though the form were alive but, as the fisherman approached closer, Sanse saw the blood that colored the water around the body and knew that it was already dead.

"What in all of Kariyl!" Then Sanse noticed the most terrible thing; something that made him uneasy as he realized, with horror, the only thing that it could be. Things began to come together inside of his mind, making him shake even more, the spear almost dropping out of his aged hands. He knew that, only days ago, an occurrence had brought the town of Argolis to a halt, something that couldn't be explained. All of the townspeople were in shock, some of them still trying their best to recover from the unknown ailment. Older townspeople had even died, the smaller children in tears until they cried themselves to sleep. It was such an uncontrollable happening. Many believed it to be the Creator sending a warning to all of the inhabitants of Kariyl.

Truly, Sanse remarked, *this was a sign.* As he turned the body over, using the shaft end of his spear as a lever against the rocky shore and the stiff body, the terror grasped his very being, making him stumble back. He lost his grip on the spear, the aged man landing hard against the rocks, tears streaking his tanned face.

The angel on the shore had been torn to pieces, by what the fisherman did not know, a look of anguish forever etched upon the otherworldly face. The beings' skin was torn in several places; the face marred the most of all, the torso ripped open and exposed. Falwen turned his gaze away to the sea, trying his best to compose himself, sobbing uncontrollably.

"Who.… Who… would… do such a thing?" He called forth the question, posing it to the skies above, to the clouds that had seemed so innocent to him until now. He ran his fingers through his graying hair, trying to keep from thinking about such wrongs in Ar Solon.

Something is awry, terribly awry. For such things to happen, Ar Solon must be forgotten by its Creator.

He wiped the trail of tears from his eyes and lifted himself up slowly, turning back to the scene of the angel on the shore, a mar upon Kariyl if ever he had seen one. His spear was sitting against the rocks, caught in between two uneven stones on the ground. He grabbed for the spear and almost stumbled to the ground again in surprise when the body moved.

From underneath the corpse, a dark form slipped free of its holdings, prying itself from the dead angel's hands, clawing upon the rocks, freeing itself from the watery hole in which the angel lay floating. It coughed and hacked up water, trying to free its throat of the sea it had swallowed, its red eyes not even noticing the fisherman standing next to it. After it had caught its breath, it took notice of the fisherman. It spread its dark maw wide open, revealing a bloody set of teeth, its clawed hands clicking wildly.

Falwen turned and began to run. This excited the creature, who, in turn, lunged at the frightened fisherman from across the rocks. Falwen jumped away from the creature, watching as it took a deep breath, apparently still exhausted from the battle with the raging waters. It looked at him again, its claws clicking faster than before. Falwen turned and began to run. The creature kept a considerable pace against the aged fisherman, the creature digging its claws into the sandy shore, soon catching up to Falwen. Only moments earlier, the old man's heart had sunk down into his stomach; now it seemed to jump out of his chest and almost burst.

Falwen turned to see what could only be called a daemon, something from myth that seemed to come to life before him, swiping at his heels with a clawed hand, almost on top of him now. Falwen was at the sheer face of the wall of the Argolis cliffs and knew that he had nowhere to run. He also knew that, if he tried to climb the face of the cliff, the daemon would catch up to him and get him for sure. He was out of breath and knew that he couldn't spear this creature without stopping completely to take aim. He had to think of something, and quick.

He ran towards the oncoming face of the cliff, watching as the daemon followed quickly after, its stride beginning to lessen the space between them by only a hands breadth away. Falwen saw the cliff face approach, just three strides away, and turned sharp, almost all the way around, the daemon in mid-spring slamming against the cliff face, the fisherman turning, fumbling back the way he had come.

However, this only made the daemon go into a fury. The dark form bounded off the cliff face and leapt forward at the fisherman, catching onto Falwen's leather wrap that held his spear, cleaving into the fisherman's shoulder.

"Aaarghhh!" The pain spread through the Falwen's arm and soon blood began to flow steadily down to his forearm, running across his left palm. Soon, it began to drip on the ground. The daemon leapt at him. With one broad sweep of his right hand, Falwen slammed the handle of the spear into the daemon's head, knocking it off its path to him and onto the sand, Falwen trying to dress his wound before it became worse.

It would continue to bleed until it clotted, the fisherman noted, soon approaching the area where he had found the fallen angel. He threw his spear into the ground in front of him and grabbed for his empty netting on the ground, waiting for the daemon.

The daemon surged forward, flailing in the air, not noticing the net spread out before it, already too far in its gait at the fisherman to turn back. Falwen threw out the net and watched as the daemon flailed about within it, its claws trying to cut the nets. Falwen tied the ends of the straps closed on each end and began moving it towards the rocky shore. The fisherman lifted the net above his head and began spinning it slowly, feeling the pain in his arm surge to life even more.

This must be quick!

He could hear a cry issue forth from the daemon, the creature seeming to know what the fisherman was going to do, Falwen soon reaching the rocky edge of the water. He made one last swing and brought the netting down onto the rocks, the daemon colliding with the jagged surface of the rocks, its body going limp on impact. Fisherman Sanse watched the still form a moment longer, making sure it was not teasing him with a victory and, once acknowledging that the creature was still, moved for his spear. His wounded arm had gone numb now and he raised the spear high above his head, aiming.

Suddenly, with the last of its strength, the daemon jerked away inside the netting and lunged for Falwen, only to find the tip of a spear waiting for him, plunging deep into its chest, its last utterance on the shore a gurgling bellow, the dark form finally dropping to its death within the netting.

Falwen pulled the spear from the carcass and washed it in the tide, cleaning his wound as well, dressing it as best he could with a strip of torn cloth from his vestment. He winced in pain as he tightened the cloth and looked to the sea, trying to focus and not collapse from exhaustion.

"This has not been a good fishing day!" He looked at the dead pair that lay at the shore next to him and thought on what he should do.

Now, if I bring these two to Argolis, there will be an outbreak and panic will turn everything into disorder and nothing will get accomplished. But, what if I find someone knowledgeable in this area and get them to help me? Then we might have a chance figuring this conundrum out and make sense of this madness.

He decided on the following course of action: the scribes at Goletta might know what to do but, of course, that is a good ways away and he would have to acquire a wagon in order to transport the bodies to the scribe's guild, one of the Great Libraries in Ar Solon, the second constructed on Kariyl in his time. The other was in the east, far from here and no help to Falwen at the moment.

Yes, that sounds reasonable. A trip to the scribes in Goletta is needed.

He slipped his spear back in its leather wrap and moved the daemon in the netting to an overhang in the rock face, pushing it with his foot into the space until he felt that it was hidden well enough for the moment. Next, he looked at the angel, which was a massive being altogether. He needed a plan to pull this being from the water's edge, making sure that it wouldn't get caught in the tides later that day while Falwen went off to find transportation. He looked around, trying to find something that could help him, when Falwen caught sight of a man approaching off to the eastern part of the shore.

The man was enormous, garbed in a thick brown robe that set off his red beard that hung down to the ties that were around his waist. He was within speaking range in the blink of an eye, looking over at the form floating on his back in the water, then at Falwen, who was at a loss for words. Falwen could only think of one thing to say.

"I found him like that! I don't know what happened to him." Falwen could feel the sadness well up inside of him, almost bringing him to the point of tears in front of this stranger. The man approached, almost a foot taller than he, pressing his hand to the fisherman's wounded shoulder. Falwen winced in pain and dropped to his knees, looking up at the stranger in defeat. He had no energy left to fight. The huge man smiled softly, though his size made him almost menacing, and moved his hand across Falwen's wound, speaking in ethereal tongue at the distraught fisherman. After he was finished, he spoke in common tongue.

"I understand, Falwen. You have done well, human. You have made many of us proud of your race. However, this is not your battle to be fought. The battle is waged upon the surface of this land, your thoughts aim true, fisherman, yet this deserted battlefield you tread upon was a mistake that will be corrected in time. That is all it takes to make things right; time."

The pain in Falwen's shoulder lessened the longer the man kept his hand pressed near it, the aged fisherman feeling a breath of life flow into him as he stared at the being in front of him, knowing well who it was. He had studied the histories of the world while traveling on his voyages when he had become a shipmate, reading about the great beings that sometimes walked the face of Ar Solon whenever they were needed. He remembered the description of several of them, but one the most, for it told of honor and justice, something a young boy thrived to know as he became a man. He looked into the angel's eyes and smiled.

"When I was a young boy, booking passage on one of my first vessels, I knew you personally, Divlo. I traveled the seas with you at my side, never fearing what may lie ahead of me, for I knew that you would protect me. And here you are, doing just that."

Falwen shed his tears now, trying to come to terms with what was happening before him. "I thought I lost you somewhere down the road in my adventures."

Divlo smiled, this time it was true and good, something the angel hadn't done in a long time. He hadn't been down to the surface of Kaiyl in over a hundred years, yet remained other places; watching, guarding the inhabitants he had been tasked to, noticing the change in all of Ar Solon. The angel released his hold on Falwen, the fisherman's wound now healed, and patted him softly on the shoulder, easing the pain that Falwen now felt, yet the pain originated not from the wound, but from within his soul.

"You are here to bring peace, not death Falwen, so I must take this angel from you and send you on your way. The creature, on the other hand, deserves to spend his death rotting among the carcasses in the sea. I have a task for you, if you think you are up to it." The fisherman nodded his head in understanding. Divlo, the angel of honor and justice, helped the fisherman back up to his feet.

"Then you must prepare, Falwen! There is little time in this world you know. I will give you what you need for your task; simply a name. And that name will guide you further than you ever thought possible." Divlo reached over to the fisherman and whispered the name into his ear then turned to leave, making his way to the other of his kind at the water's edge.

The angel reached down into the water and lifted the still form of Greditto easily into his arms. Water poured from the body and Divlo looked down into Greditto's blank stare. He stifled a sob, biting his teeth together. The angel whispered into his long-time friend's ear, the silent Greditto taking it in.

"Poor fellow! We will have you as right as rain, my friend. There will be no more pain to suffer through." Divlo made his way back the way he came, his robes parting on each side of his back, a set of feathery wings branching out behind him. Falwen moved to catch up, still weak from the battle with the daemon. He caught his breath.

"Divlo, what is this task you want from me?" The angel turned back to the fisherman, tears streaking his now saddened face. He smiled to the fisherman, but now it was a sad smile, one of endings and of things still left to be said. Falwen Sanse knew the world was going to end when he looked into the angelic depths of Divlo's eyes, yet the human did not know when. He didn't care when it ended, for he knew now that there was purpose in every step he took from this point on. He was ready for death whenever it took him.

"You will know when the time comes, my friend. You will know. And you will not fail, for the future is set and you are one of mine. You are strong. Find the man that bears that name and his way will guide yours as well."

The angel then turned and lifted himself and the fallen Greditto from the shores of Argolis high into the air, the land of Kariyl soon clouding over,

Divlo and his passenger slipping into the clouded world above. The angel would return, he knew this, but it would be to lend his hand when it was needed. And now, he couldn't help in anyway, for he had many things to do. He looked down at his friend's shell of a body, trying his best to remain calm.

Yes, many things to do.

15

Oagthor led Ranyll and D'meir closer into the city, watching as the remnants of the townspeople sifted through the wreckage of their homes, trying to find pieces of their past that were still able to be salvaged. Ranyll watched in horror as a world he had never known crumbled before him. Though he had no connection to the people that passed him and the other two in his party, the eyes, the faces, and the blank stares that all of them gave him as he passed made his heart go out to them. He could only imagine that pain he would feel if the same happened to him and his small town of Telgin. It would be unbearable.

Yet, through the ashes of several buildings and shelters, the dwarven townspeople survived. However, the flames that tore at the dwarven city of Dardist tore at the townspeople as well.

Though the common flame was known for never being able to burn stone, these flames, which were several tints of gray instead of the colorful yellow and orange, were doing just that. As Ranyll, D'meir, and their dwarven guide Oagthor, passed through the streets of Dardist, the young human took notice of the fine dwarven architecture that, though it had been attacked, still stood the test of time when the cities built by human hands would have crumbled to the ground. Ranyll was awestruck as he looked skyward to the great stone canopy that arched from one side to the other, blanketing the city with a sky of skilled stonework. The young man had come upon the great dwarven craftsmen and smiths of the caverns while studying the history of Kariyl. But to see them in all of their glory was another thing all together.

However, here the stones of Dardist were scorched with burn marks; large, black, ashen whelps that started at the ceiling of the domed canopy and slowly crept their way down to the homes made within the stones. All of the city's townspeople had apparently been evacuated and sent to a sanctuary within the caves, for there was no one upon the stone streets ahead of the three travelers. D'meir moved up in between Ranyll and Oagthor, trying to keep pace with their long strides as they moved further into the abandoned city with every step they took.

Suddenly, Oagthor stopped and the two next to him prepared for the worst. Oagthor's thick voice came out through his thick, bearded lips, a twinge of fear breaking through his otherwise unwavering voice.

"Ranyll, you must follow closely now, for the way is more treacherous than you'll ever know!" Oagthor motioned for Ranyll and D'meir to follow, hefting his axe in one hand while taking his hammer out from its sling over his back where he kept it. Ranyll followed the gesture, unsheathing his sword in the deserted city of Dardist, unknowing that it would come to good use ahead.

As they continued on, the fires began to disappear and what took their place were small, smoldering buildings, *or what was left of them*, Ranyll noticed, keeping his father's sword close to his body. From time to time, there would be movement ahead and a small party of dwarves would cross the path in front of them, making their way to the other side of the city, Ranyll guessed, noticing their eyes on him and D'meir the whole time they moved until they were finally out of sight.

"Oagthor, don't they trust you?" Ranyll couldn't help but ask for, even with a dwarven guide, he felt unsafe, as if he were moving into more danger than being out in the open portion of the city. At least he would know when an attack was coming.

But, with the shadows moving across the ground and the fires far behind, only darkness surrounded them now, with the exception of a small set of torches set at various intervals as they passed. Ranyll was doing good just to remain standing. Walking, well that was another story. He reached for Oagthor's shoulder with his free hand and grabbed onto the chain mail suit the dwarf wore, the dwarf turning for a moment to realize that he had forgotten that Ranyll was not accustomed to the darkness as his own race was. He patted the young man's hand understandingly and continued on, at a slower pace than he had been going earlier.

"Well, that would be the case, Ranyll, but things have changed to the point where the dwarves have no one else left to trust except for their own kind. If the other races cared, they would have already been here to help us and Dardist would not have fallen. It's a dark time down here, Ranyll; a dark time."

D'meir's voice piped up in the darkness.   "Not to fear, Oagthor! Ranyll is our savior and has come to help." Ranyll and Oagthor laughed together in response to the fire fox's response, stopping for a moment to catch their breath and wait for the fire fox to catch up with them. The fire fox was quiet for a moment but then spoke up again, this time there was more resolution in his voice.

"I didn't say anything that was humorous, did I?" Oagthor stopped himself short from laughing and cleared his throat, trying to break the tension that had been placed into the air around the three with more of his words, which comforted Ranyll as he spoke them.

"I don't disagree with you, D'meir. It's just that Ranyll is so young and, well, he couldn't even find his way out of these caves by himself. And he knows it." There was a silence and Ranyll felt the dwarf's eyes on him, then Oagthor continued.

"But there must be something special about him, I can agree with that, because I haven't seen anyone around here in a few ten day, let alone a stranger to the mountains who hasn't been taken by the daemons."

They continued on for a time, Ranyll watching as the city disappeared and became a set of well constructed caves which opened up before them. Oagthor selected the way in which to go without a thought and had placed his hammer back into its sheath at his back when there was a noise ahead in the passageway before them. The dwarf moved Ranyll against the passageway and D'meir followed suit, pressing himself against the back of Ranyll's boots, the small snout peering out into the darkness.

"What is it, Oagthor?" Ranyll could not hide the fear in his voice. He could not deny it. The darkness scared him. But it was more than that. Knowing that those daemons were out in the darkness made his body shudder, just imagining what could be staring at him from the dark recesses ahead. He then thought of Kalir and the creature that he had killed at the channel checkpoint.

How had Kalir known about the daemons before this? Were there other attacks that Ranyll wasn't aware of? Everything that could pulse through Ranyll's excited mind forced its way through, a mixture of fears and hopes, of beginnings and endings. He tried to control it but the darkness began to seep inside his mind. Then he was brought back by the sound of Oagthor's voice.

"It's a party of dwarves! It must be the nightly patrol. Boy, I didn't think I had been out that long! I'm beginning to go crazy, Ranyll. I'm losing track of time. It's been two full nights since I've been out!" The fear that had washed over Ranyll was suddenly gone and he nodded his head, trying to smile, though he didn't even know if Oagthor could see the expression on his tired face.

Most of the dwarves that the trio had seen earlier were just small remnants from the city, darting from one location to the next, carrying what they could to small wagons, trying to make away with what they could find in the ruins of their great city. None had taken notice of the trio until this patrol approached. Ranyll watched as torchlight broke through the darkness around them and several shadows cast upon the walls just ahead. Soon, there were voices that followed the movement and light, still difficult for Oagthor to decipher what they were saying.

Five dwarves, roughly the same size as Oagthor yet in different attire, approached, weapons in hand. They moved to intercept the only dwarf in the party; Oagthor.

"Halt dwarf! Who goes there with you?" A dirty dwarf moved within eyesight of the trio then stepped back when he recognized Oagthor, wiping a layer of dirt and sweat from his own brow to clear his eyes.

He had a great, black beard that was mussed up, yet the tips of his beard had several little beads attached to them, all of the beads a dark coal color that were contrasted with the bright, almost marble set of beads that sat atop the black beads. He held a small hand axe limply in his right hand, his left arm bandaged tightly from the elbow up to his shoulder. He was clad in a thick set of chain mail that covered his chest and shoulders and cut off quickly just below the belt, as were the other of his team. They looked the part of a scouting party; however they did not seem to be protecting anything worth saving. There were several thick sets of wrinkles that broke through the dirt on his face that showed his age, though he moved with the quickness of a young human. He stopped just in front of Oagthor and motioned with his good arm for the others of his crew to stop as well. He looked hard into the dwarf's eyes in front of him and it was long moments before he spoke again.

"Oagthor? Oagthor Axeblade? It is you!" The burly dwarf surged forward and swung his arm around Oagthor's thick shoulder, giving him a great bear hug with one arm, taking care to keep his bandaged arm from harm. Oagthor returned the embrace and pulled away, apparently perplexed at who this black-bearded dwarf was. Ranyll knew that it had been several days since he had returned from patrolling the caverns, just by taking account of Oagthor's provisions he had been able to guess that. Oagthor's face looked as though he had tasted a fine drought and still had trouble deciphering what it was.

But then came the smile that Ranyll didn't expect. The smile cracked through the dirty beard and again the two dwarves embraced, this time Oagthor starting it.

"Rathor! I can't believe it! But I thought you were in Argolis, taking care of unfinished business." Rathor pulled away from him and smiled at the others behind him, the four other dwarves letting their weapons relax in their hands, their eyes still eagerly taking in everything the other two said as they continued.

"The business is no longer unfinished. I found him and what was lost is now safe. Let it be said and done at that, my friend. I see troubles far worse are upon you and yours. We must take care of this and quick." Oagthor smiled again when he looked at Rathor, grasping the back of his friend's neck, pulling him to his side. Oagthor turned to Ranyll and D'meir and motioned for them to follow.

"We shall do introductions somewhere safe, away from the flames and smoke of the town, away from these caverns that echo our movements. Once we come to safety, we shall rest and gather fresh supplies. We will not and cannot stop until then." Oagthor finished with that, turning his attention back to his friend, which he practically had in a headlock. Rathor was soon released by his friends iron grip and separated his patrol into two groups, one set of two in the rear of the party, the other in the front, taking the lead as the eight of them moved quickly out of the light and back into the shadows. They soon moved into another set of caverns, the light from their torches being extinguished on the ground before they continued. D'meir rushed up Ranyll's leg and perched himself on the human's shoulder, speaking to him as they walked.

"I hope you don't mind, Ranyll. But I am having trouble keeping up with the dwarves' fast pace. If you wouldn't mind I…" The creature's voice broke off and Ranyll felt the fire fox's body tighten against him, a low but strong growl emanating from inside D'meir's chest. Ranyll unsheathed his sword, listening to the sound that came from just a few passageways ahead.

*   *   *

The torchlight brought many daemon faces into view for the small Miftle, his eyes darting from one set of eyes to the other. He could feel the evil and knew that it surrounded him as well as blocked both possible exits.

This is it, Triggle thought, taking his stand in the dank hallway, the daemons surging forward at him. He closed his eyes and began swinging the dagger and the torch with full momentum behind them, waiting, fully expecting to make contact with something before he fell. He touched no daemon. In fact, they had stopped their movement around him. Triggle slowly opened his eyes to see what had happened, not expecting almost to be blinded in the process.

Two lights, brighter than any he had ever seen, were lit and shining in front of him, making him turn his gaze away immediately, trying his best to make out what was there before him. Soon, once his eyes became adjusted to the brightness, he turned his bearded face and let his eyes fall on the light, which… were his hands. He dropped his torch and dagger in shock and no sooner had the items hit the ground when he heard the intense clicking again and felt the air around him become tense and thick, Triggle waving his hands around trying to figure out what was going on.

"What kind of mumbo jumbo is this? Did I drink too much?" But no answer came, none except for a surge of daemons that fell upon him, though they had no idea of the power they had just encountered. Claws tore at Triggle's clothes, several behind him as well, tearing through his pack, the Miftle now feeling the surge of what was taking him over fully.

He could feel a magik, *his magik*, flowing through his veins, Triggle's hands reaching out for the daemons. Once he took hold of one of their shadowy forms, Triggle could feel the surge of magik release and, from the light surrounding his hands, a great ball of white flame erupted.

The flames slammed into the daemons, engulfing several in front of him, clearing a small way in which he could now move. The other daemons wavered for a moment, taking in what the little creature had just done to the others that still burnt with a white flame. They weren't moving after him out of either fear or from amazement and Triggle jumped at his chance, gathering his thick fingers into fists. The Miftle took wild swings at the ones that were on him, watching as they howled in pain as they were set on fire, dropping to the floor and rolling in pain. The Miftle fought as though untamed as he drove the daemons back; trying his best to find a way out of the situation he was in.

Sure, this magik was working, but only for the time being.

Slowly, Triggle could feel the surge of power within him begin to fade and he knew that whatever this was that was happening would only continue for moments longer. He had to do something and he had to do it now. The daemons had broken their circle and were scattered about the passage, some hidden in the darkness while others stayed upon the ceiling, watching with malicious intent the creature that tore at their brethren.

Triggle held one of his glowing hands out at the daemons while grabbing for his dagger with another on the ground, sheathing it quickly at his side. He then reached for his torch, which still had a flicker of life within its tip. As he closed his fingers around the torch, he could begin to feel the magik within him subside and his hands dimmed slightly.

"Just my luck!" Triggle moved past the broken circle of daemons and lifted his torch up above his head to get a view of the tunnel ahead. It was the same tunnel as before. He had seen it many times in the last few hours and, still, he was happy to see something besides the menacing stares of the daemons, which tread upon his heels. He did not dare turn around for he knew that they were waiting for him to falter. So far, the only luck he had had just run out and sheer will to not be devoured seemed to lead the small set of legs forward, propelling the terrified Miftle deeper into the darkness, yet further from the daemon's nesting grounds.

Triggle broke into the main hallway with all the energy he could still spare and turned his exhausted body left down the main hallway, the large dwarven columns coming into view as his torch broke through the darkness. Triggle was still trying to break from the daemons, hoping that there was some way to prolong what seemed to be the inevitable.

But on they came, scores of them, one after another, getting closer by the second. Then, many of the daemons broke from the pack, moving across the columns into the darkness where Triggle couldn't see them. His legs were aching, his chest felt as if it would collapse in on itself if he ran another second. He could hear the daemons surround him again, this time the Miftle knowing that he wouldn't escape.

From out of the corner of Triggle's firelight, a daemon leapt for the Miftle. Triggle lifted up his dagger to defend but it was too late. The daemon was upon him. The Miftle slammed into the ground, a small cloud of dust rising around him as the daemon collided with him. The daemons' clawed fingers tore into his shoulders and he could see the small pack on his back fly into pieces around him. His free arm was pinned beneath him and the only thing he had left was the torch, which he couldn't let go of. He had to get the daemon off of him before the others joined in and he was turned into a quick meal. Triggle thrust the lit torch into the daemons chest, watching as it writhed in pain and launched itself back into the air and landed on all fours just behind him.

Triggle pushed himself off the floor quickly and regained his footing, swinging his dagger out at any of the daemons that moved within his fading torchlight just paces away. The torch sputtered and was now just a few cinders that lit a foot or two in front of him. He tried blowing on the cinders in desperation, but that didn't work at all. The cinders flew off the torch and dissipated once into the air, leaving Triggle in complete darkness.

But it wasn't darkness, Triggle thought, looking around at the columns, finally seeing that two of the further most columns were lit and glowing with a soft light. The daemons were even lit with the light; their hideous forms now clear and easily discernible. They moved away from the light at first then, once noticing that it did not harm them, began to approach their prey again, moving closer. Triggle turned towards the light and was almost blinded, trying to focus the best he could on the two columns that glowed more fiercely than before.

Then, from between them and all outlying areas, the main hallway began to take on the shape of milky, white wall. It was almost translucent yet was fringed with ripples of the white substance that seemed to flow like water. This all happened in a matter of seconds in front of the faerie, his eyes soon adjusting. The wall seemed to be charging up, gaining power from some unknown source. The only thing that Triggle could think of was that this was magikal.

But no race has use of this much magik, Triggle thought, his eyes taking in the milky wall as it gobbled up the darkness behind it. Triggle came back to his senses and realized he was still in danger.

Soon, Triggle feared, *it would gain all the power that was needed and form completely, trapping me with the demon hoard that had chased me for what seemed like miles through the dark tunnels.*

He made a dash for the magikal wall, his legs carrying him closer. As he started, he became winded at once, still not fully recovered from the last chase moments before. The wall was becoming more solid and less transparent and, for a moment, Triggle feared that it was too late. The daemons behind him cried out in fury as they came closer to their prey and one took a wild leap from the pack, landing across Triggle's back, almost knocking him down. Triggle stumbled but kept his balance, the claws of the daemon soon alive and wild.

Triggle began to slow as he approached the wall, trying to fling the creature off of him. He thrust at the daemon but it deflected the jabs of his dagger with its claw-like fingers. Triggle felt himself stumble again, this time dropping to one knee. He could hear the clicking of the hundreds behind him yet the squeals of victory of the daemon riding on his back drowned out any other sounds, Triggle looking back to see the wild, red eyes staring down at him as it licked the blood off of its fingers. For a moment, Triggle seemed to notice a wicked grin form across the creature's face as it waited for its companions, keeping him at bay with jabs of pain in his shoulders and back.

"You damned creature! Get off my back!" With the last of his strength, Triggle brought his blade over his shoulder with both hands, the tip of the blade piercing the daemon's flesh for the first time. He left his blade buried deep in the daemon and lifted himself back up to his feet. The daemon howled in pain and released its hold for a moment. That was all that Triggle needed. The faerie closed his eyes and dove at the magikal white wall with the daemon still astride.

The magikal wall swallowed the Miftle whole and white sparks flew as the daemon atop him hit the barrier, a white flame erupting as it caught the daemon on fire, the wall spitting Triggle out through the other side. The daemons followed after the Miftle through the wall, unknowing of its magikal power.

The daemons writhed in pain as it tore at their dark forms, setting them ablaze. The milky wall did just what the Miftle had thought it would do. Somehow, the dwarves had acquired the ability to control magik and used it as a force against the daemons.

Triggle landed flat on the other side and watched now as hundreds of daemons tried to make it through the wall, which was becoming brighter by the second, the daemons slamming helplessly against the white brilliance that saved Triggle for the moment.

Every time the daemons leapt for the Miftle, they could not break the plane of the white wall and were jolted backwards, their black bodies making ripples across the surface. The ripples increased as the bodies of the daemons came in contact with the wall, dark forms slamming against the pearl white of the cascading magik field that kept Triggle from harm.

"What a creation!" the Miftle exclaimed, reaching out his dirty fingers to the wall and, once touching it, felt warmth coalesce in the tips of each finger and then run down to his elbow. He could barely see the daemons through the wall now, only noticing the blurs that moved from the other side. He tried to pull himself up from the position in which he had landed but he was too sore and exhausted from his last effort. The Miftle leaned back against his elbows and soon felt fatigue take hold of him, his eyes closing, collapsing onto the floor in an exhaustive sleep.

16

The town of Argolis had begun to settle down from the sudden occurrence that had swept across its inhabitants days ago. Now, the event was just another story told by the local patrons at taverns and small-town folk that desired to remember the world that went by them, day by day. Traders and crewmen from random vessels pulling into harbor heard of the tales and laughed and carried on, some of them even considering the ideas to be possible truths. But not a one really believed in that sort of thing; not anymore. The inhabitants of the world slowly slipped into their routines that took them away from their homes from early into the morning where they finally returned as the sun sank into the Alvanus Sea, a thing of beauty to all that beheld it.

Not far from the city, in the town of Simmer Lo, Falwen Sanse stared out the thick-paned window and admired the last glimpse of the sun until the next morning, looking back to his meal of cooked fish and vegetables along with a fresh loaf of bread that had been picked up by his children earlier in the day. His wife had mended the shirt he had torn and praised him for the catches he had made that day, but she still had yet to hear what went on in her husband's head. Falwen's mind was at work now, not thinking at all of eating or fishing or any of what he used to take pleasure in. This and the way he greeted her earlier made her cautious, watching his every move to try and decipher the problem.

Falwen wanted to know what his purpose was. He needed to know. The old fisherman looked back at his life now and realized that he was being selfish with his thoughts. Throughout his marriage with his wife, he had always told her how he felt. But now, as he looked at the aging beauty at his side along with his children at the table, sadness penetrated his heart. He was worried that danger was coming to threaten his content life and the lives of the others around him.

Falwen looked over at his children as they ate. Both of the boys looked at their father from time to time and smiled, mouths full of fish as they gobbled down one of their mother's great dishes. She always had a knack at preparing some of the finest meals. And the things she could make with fish. Falwen, though he had grown nearly tired of fish, was always delighted when his wife had put forth the effort to please his palette as well as her own.

She smiled at him as their eyes made contact. She had the most beautiful eyes. It wasn't the crystal blue of her eyes that stared back at him that made them beautiful, but was more of the shape of them. They almost looked as if they were elven, with a slight hint of mischief in them. And Falwen knew that his wife, no matter how old she became, could cause mischief. He smiled when he remembered how their two children came about. *Mischief indeed*, thought Falwen, smiling back at his wife as she seated herself at the table.

"So, Falwen, what is on your mind tonight? You've been awfully quiet for someone who usually has much to say during the meal. Is everything alright?"

She reached out her soft hands and cradled his rough fingers within hers. This had always been her remedy for prying any information from her husband. Each gentle caress from Larissa would break down Falwen's defenses ever so slightly until he would finally give in. But tonight was different. Falwen couldn't let the ideas that plagued his mind free out into the open for discussion as he usually did.

Tonight would be different. He could feel it within him. Something was happening and he was afraid things would change forever.

Maybe, if I don't say anything, it won't happen and we could be happy the rest of our lives and pretend that this war business is not going on at all.

But deep down inside Falwen knew his duties lie somewhere else other than to his family, which made his heart almost stop completely. He couldn't let Larissa see that in his eyes. He turned to her and smiled.

"I was just thinking that it would be a good idea to go into Goletta tomorrow with the rest of the traders and sell the remainder of the catch instead of sell it to the locals. It would take a good while before they need all that I caught."

Larissa nodded in agreement. "That sounds like a great idea, Falwen. I think we should get out to Goletta for a day or so. It would be good to get out, especially since that terrible occurrence here a few days ago. We could find out if anyone else was affected by it outside of Argolis."

Falwen had a sinking feeling inside that everyone on Kariyl had felt the death of the angel and knew that something more was to come, this being only the beginning of a great number of things.

Falwen lifted a piece of fish into his mouth, washing it down with the water from the cup near his plate. He looked at his two sons and then to his wife.

"I think I'll go it alone this time. Anyways, there are some things I need to do in Goletta, some information I need to get." Larissa tilted her head to the side, scanning her husband's face. Falwen knew his plan wasn't going to work. His only choices were to lie or to tell her, which would probably make her think he was lying.

"Falwen, dear, is something wrong?" Falwen finished another bite of fish and wiped off his mouth with a small kerchief he kept in his pocket. He slipped the kerchief back into his side pocket and looked back to his two sons.

"Boys, me and your mother need to talk alone. Go on and take your meals into your room. Your mother will call you back when we're finished." The two boys did not hesitate, glancing at each other with puzzled expressions, both grabbing their plates and cups and slipping away silently, the door behind them closing. Larissa looked to her husband for the answers. She had no idea what he was about to say and knew that was unlike her Falwen.

"What is this all about, Falwen?" She lifted herself from her place at his side, beginning to clean up after their two children, who had left small crumbs on the table. She reached for the bowl of muffins in the center of the table. Falwen's hand caught hers before she could take it away.

"Dear, please sit down! What I have to tell you is important." Larissa felt Falwen's light touch on her hand and she sat back down in her chair, attentive and ready.

"Something's happened to me. Something's happened to us all, to tell you the truth, and I'm afraid I can't tell you what it is right now. I know we've been together and have shared everything from the start, but there's something that's far beyond us and everything we are, and it's asked me for help. I have to go and help it."

Falwen was trying to keep the tears inside that had been building up since he walked in the door that night, trying to remain strong in front of his children, but now they slipped down his wrinkled face and he did not attempt to wipe them away.

"Falwen, dear, what's wrong? I don't understand this. If it's that important to you, then we'll all go with you. I'm sure we can help." Falwen looked into the eyes of his wife of so many years, the one who had been with him through hard times and through the good times, showed the spirit that he had been drawn to since he had met her, and smiled, placing his palm against her face.

"It's something I have to do alone, Larissa. It's dangerous and even I don't know what to expect. I don't know how long I'll be gone, but you must tell the boys that everything's fine. Use the money we have been saving for a boat until I return. I have to leave tonight."

All of this came too sudden for Larissa, who wasn't expecting what her husband had just told her. Falwen lifted himself up from the table and reached for his wife, who cradled herself into his arms, her face hidden in the folds of his tunic. She began to cry softly. Larissa had never been much of an emotional woman throughout Falwen's knowing her. She had been practical, down-to-earth, yet kind and understanding.

He could feel the pain in her cries at not knowing what was happening. Yet Falwen, too, felt out of control, not really knowing what was happening. In fact, he didn't even know where to start once he got to Goletta. The only thing he did know is that he couldn't just sit here and let the world fall apart around him and not doing anything to stop it.

The aged fisherman pulled his wife closer and kissed her lightly on the mouth, squeezing her one last time before letting her go. He moved for the closet and grabbed his old fishing pack, filling it with things that he might need on his journey. After tying his pack, he reached back into the closet and pulled out a long object tied up neatly in a thick cloth. He untied the knots in the twine and slipped the cloth off of it, his eyes taking in the sword he hadn't seen in years. It had been almost two decades since he had reached for his sword and, now that it was in his hands, he knew why he had put it up all these years. It didn't fit him.

Falwen had become a fisherman instead of a warrior or a fighter for the sheer fact that the he didn't seem to fit into the role of a fighter. By no means was he a barbarian and knew that his swordplay was only as good as his own small children, for he had stopped practicing to focus on his skill with the nets and the spear.

He strapped the sword and scabbard around his waist with a belt he found in the closet and grabbed his spear by the door, tossing the full pack onto his back. He looked to his wife, who had already gathered some food from the cupboards and tied it into a small sack for him to carry as well. She threw her arms around him and nuzzled her face into his neck.

"I love you, Falwen. I always have and always will." Larissa gathered her composure and drew away from Falwen, drying her eyes on her apron.

"If it's something you have to do, I understand. The children and I will be fine. Just come back to us in one piece, Falwen. That's all I ask. You know, there are things in the world we can't explain. Maybe once you're back, we can spend the rest of our lives together trying to figure them out." She smiled at him and reached past to open the door, noticing that his hands were full with items.

Falwen returned her smile and leaned over, kissing her on the forehead.

"I'd like that very much, Larissa. That sounds fine to me." Falwen did not say goodbye, knew that he didn't need to because he knew that he would be coming back, just as his wife had requested and just as he had promised himself as well. He would help until he could help no longer and come back to his home only then.

The cool night air cut through his tunic and gave him the chills as he watched his wife shut the door behind him, his eyes on the sky and the moon that lit the path to the town of Goletta, a place full of business and trade.

And answers, Falwen hoped to himself, using his spear as a walking stick, his boots echoing off of the tiny pebbles on the ground, the moon lighting his way through the south side of town.

He could faintly hear the waves of the sea as they broke against the rocks on the very cliffs where he had found the angel and one of its killers that morning, the event that had changed his view on his creation forever. Falwen looked ahead at the trail before him and knew that every footstep he took from this moment on was a path unknown to him. He only hoped that, at the end of the path, there would be something that would help him with his task. The fisherman continued on.

*   *   *

The young unicorn traversed through the mines for what seemed like hours, though he seemed to make little distance within them, always finding himself going in circles, a pattern of his own hoof prints merging together on the soggy ground. The soil was much more firm within the mines though, since neglected, Gwenzel had to cut a swath through thick reeds and vines with his horn. Several times, the unicorn had called out the two sprites names within the mines, only to listen for long moments without a sound coming back to him. Not even his own echo was heard for the thick and permeating fog that seemed to seep in from the Wilden Marsh and cover the mines in mist as well.

This isn't what I had in mind when I began this quest, Gwenzel thought to himself, shaking off a number of vines and debris that had collected on his back as he pushed forward, his hooves breaking through a thick layer of muck on the bottom of the floor. Ahead, several passageways opened up before him, one curving to the left, another to the right, and one straight ahead, which seemed to keep with the general direction of the tunnel he was already in. In this fork in the Mines of Wilden, several skeletons, dwarven and human, lay scattered against the walls, each of them contorted in ghastly poses, their forms huddled close to the walls.

It seems as though they were trying to escape from something, Gwenzel noticed, his bright eyes growing wider as he saw more bodies splayed out before him in the passage just ahead. The unicorn lifted his hooves and began the tedious task of crossing the river of bodies without disturbing their rest, each hoof resting on the floor of the mine or on great slabs of rock they had been mined when the great accident occurred all those years ago.

Gwenzel could feel his hooves slip a bit on the moss-covered rocks, almost colliding with a set of fallen dwarven skeletons. Then his hind hooves dug into solid ground and he stopped himself. For a moment, he thought he saw a flicker of movement from the bodies, and then thought better of it, continuing on through the tunnel until he reached a clear path where bodies no longer littered the tunnel.

Here, the tunnel opened up into a large cave which was lit by faint traces of light breaking through a twenty foot ceiling, patch-worked with large timbers supporting the ceiling, which were only two or three solid pieces of rock. It was in this tunnel that Gwenzel noticed there were no bodies, only a number of tools and broken mining cars. The ground was solid more here than it had been in the previous path and, as Gwenzel walked further into the cave, his footfalls echoed into the many passages just ahead of him on the other side of the immense cave.

All around him, small caverns had been dug, some from all sides of the room and many were even on the ceiling. There were a total of twenty or so tunnels through the cave, though many of them were no larger than a few feet in size. However, there was one main entrance that followed with the mining car tracks. This one was filled halfway up with fallen rubble and supports beams, Gwenzel trying to look through to the other side. Within the darkness, the unicorn could see several other caves that were bigger than the many that were in this cave.

That's just where I need to get and can't, Gwenzel thought to himself, the unicorn looking around for another way out of the cavern. That's when he noticed the mist that came in from all sides. At first, the mist seemed to come only from the small holes that littered the cavern walls. Then, as

Gwenzel turned, he noticed the way he had come also seemed blocked by the swirling mist creeping in from outside.

He was trapped; he knew it. It was a trap from the beginning. There were many things this unicorn did not know, which he admitted freely. But, when it came to being defeated, Gwenzel seemed to go into a fury with rage at the idea.

The unicorn dug his feet into the ground beneath him and jerked his body upright, turning back to the blocked passageway behind him. There were a dozen or so large rocks and there seemed to be no way to move them. The unicorn tried nudging one with his snout. It didn't move. Again, the mists began to swirl closer, nearing Gwenzel's hind legs. He brought his front hooves down against a set of rocks, smashing them into smaller pieces. But still, that was not enough to fit him through.

I have to try, though, Gwenzel decided, climbing up the small layer of rocks the best he could until he reached the gap between the rock pile and the ceiling of the cave. Gwenzel sat down on his haunches and placed his front hooves in, attempting to scoot in, his horn blazing its blue light through the darkness. He began to make his way the best he could through the passage, the growing mist behind him closer now, his way out nothing more than an empty crack in a world full of tunnels.

His front legs now through, he craned his neck down, putting all of his weight on his hind legs, his hooves pressing down against the rocks underneath him, slowly but surely lifting and pushing himself through the passage, his front legs dangling over the edge of the other side. Once partially through, Gwenzel looked back and saw the mist on him. It broke through the passage, snaking its way around him, the lower half of his body completely enveloped by the swirling enemy. He pulled with his front legs one last time before the mist swallowed him whole. Gwenzel felt the darkness surround him.

17

The Miftle woke to find himself not at all where he had last remembered himself being, which perplexed him greatly to no end. After escaping the army of daemons that had nearly torn him to pieces, he had sworn that the last place he had been was on the floor of the great dwarven halls. But he was here now, in a bed, resting nicely. All of his wounds had been mended and were bandaged and he felt rested for the first time since he had taken his long journey from home. Even Faerie Homme had not offered him this good of a sleep that he had just woken from. The Miftle looked around and took in all that he could see in the muted light.

The room was dimly lit by means of a lantern hanging from the ceiling, the metal shutters on it half closed, blanketing most of the room in shadows. The Miftle lifted himself off the bed and threw the covers aside.

I'm naked! Triggle grabbed for the covers and pulled them back over his barren self, covering his furry little body with the sheet from the bed.

He was in a room that seemed to fit his size nicely, complete with a washbasin, a small dresser and a plate of food. His eyes darted immediately to the food on the dresser. A loaf of fine, dwarven country bread, a leg of some undistinguishable animal and a bowl of hot, steaming what looked like stew, sat on a rough, metal tray. There was a door as well, but Triggle had no time for that.

Whoever had captured me sure knew how to treat their hostages!

Gathering up the bed sheet, the Miftle covered himself and made for the food tray just a few feet away. He grabbed it up with his free hand and brought it back to the bed, sitting it down in front of him.

"Now this is what I call service! Ask and Triggle shall receive." The Miftle leaned over the tray and took the sweet smells in, his hands suddenly on everything at once. He dipped the bread in the stew, which was delicious, not too spicy, then tore into the leg of meat, which had to be Gradsplid, the small desert animal of the surrounding parts of the area, Triggle knowing the smell all too well. He devoured the bread in moments and was finishing off the leg of the Gradsplid when the door to the room opened, a woman's voice stopping the Miftle in mid chew.

"Ahh, I see you're awake. And finished the meal I made for you as well." The woman came into the light of the lantern and Triggle almost choked on his food. She was a dwarf; and she was beautiful!

Her long, auburn hair was braided into a bun on the back of her head, several small strands escaping to dwindle onto her fine, rosy cheeks. She wore a plain white tunic that stopped at her elbow and a black leather jerkin that fit snuggly around her waist. Her light, red dress shuffled across the floor with her as she approached Triggle.

"It looks as though your wounds are doing nicely. My, you *were* hungry. I'm sure you are parched from thirst as well. I brought this for you." The dwarven beauty took the empty tray from Triggle and sat it on the dresser, handing him a full water skin. He uncorked and, in an instant, was drinking from the engorged container, licking his lips at the taste that washed away the dust from the dwarven caves as well as the meal he had just devoured in no time. The water was sweet, not dry and hard as he half expected, him being in a cave and all.

The young dwarven lady returned and sat on the bed beside Triggle who, in turn, scooted back further on the bed. The dwarf scooted closer again and looked strangely at Triggle.

"It's okay. I'm only going to check the wounds. What's your name anyway, stranger?" Triggle loosened up a little and let her check the dressings on his wounds that he had received from the daemons.

"It's Triggle, milady." That was enough. He wasn't supposed to be here, not naked either, and not with any inhabitant poking around at him. Miftles had the same rules just as the other races of faeries did. He was still in awe that the dwarven lady had not found him out and ran away screaming. But there was something about her.

The look in her eyes, maybe, he finished to himself, holding his arm out to her to check his bandages, his eyes following each move she made until she was finished. He didn't know what, but she didn't seem afraid of him at all. It was true, he didn't look too much different than any other dwarf, but down here, maybe in the dim lighting, not many could tell the difference.

"Triggle, is it? Well, Triggle, you're awfully lucky to be alive, I'll tell you that much. The guards were just finishing up their patrol when they found you by the shield barrier. They first thought you had died trying to get through. Once they brought you here, we knew you would be alright."

"That thing you have, the magikal thing, it's a barrier?" The lady finished her survey of his wounds and stood up.

"Yes, it is. It's our only line of defense against the daemons that have been attacking since the seasons changed. We can't find out where they're coming from but know that they have been living in our main hall for some time now. We haven't seen anyone pass through here in a three ten days time."

"When you say we, you mean….."

"I do apologize. I didn't introduce myself. My name is Ilthen Lendure. I, and the we I speak of, are the remnants of Dardist, the only dwarven city that has not fallen to the daemons that roam throughout these caverns."

Triggle wiped his bearded mouth with his hand and pulled his bed sheet up closer to himself.

Only one found in over three ten days? That can't be possible! There must be some mistake. He looked over to Ilthen, who was at the dresser nearby, pulling some things out from the top drawer. She handed Triggle some clothes and a belt. They were not his own, but they were close to his size.

"When the guards found you, most of your clothes were ruined. We kept them if you would like them, but I brought you some new garb that you might like." Triggle took them gratefully.

Being clothed for a change would be good, the Miftle thought, slipping the clothes underneath the sheet with him, slipping the breeches on as he spoke.

"You said there haven't been any visitors in the last three ten days. Is that true? Has there been no one else?" The Miftle slipped on a close-fitting tunic, taking care not to pull at the bandages on his shoulders, and tied the strings at his neck and wrists, pulling on a fine leather jerkin as well. He fastened the straps and planted his feet on the floor, standing up.

Ilthen was not much taller than he, Triggle noticed, the dwarven lady handing him his boots.

"They say there have been travelers, but no word has come from the guard on the other side of Dardist yet. We think that there is an attack that has severed the ties that we had to the remaining Dardisians. Why? Is there someone that you seek?"

With a full belly and clean clothes, Triggle felt a dozen times better. After tying his boots, he moved over to the washbasin and rinsed his face, drying his face and beard off with a towel.

"I seek the companions I came with. They are hunted by daemons as well, many of them. I was looking for them when I came upon those unearthly spawns. They cut me off from searching for them." Triggle found the items he had been carrying in the second drawer of the dresser. He slipped the pouches into his belt and began looking for his dagger when he remembered where he had left it. Ilthen seemed to notice Triggle searching.

"We have a supply of items here at the post that we can give you. We will not send you out to the daemons without proper provisions, Master Triggle." Ilthen reached for the metal tray and placed it between her and the Miftle.

"The checkpoint guards should be in soon. They have their nightly meetings not far from here. I am tasked to take you to the armory and then show you the way to the main checkpoint myself."

"Your people have been most kind, Mistress Ilthen, especially to a complete stranger such as myself."

Ilthen seemed hesitant at first and then stopped them both before they left the room.

"Do not take my own kindness for that of my people. They are distrusting of everyone. It is I who took you into my care. Expect a thorough questioning from the guards once we reach them. It is not over yet, Master Triggle."

Ilthen moved to leave and Triggle reached out his hand to her, placing it on her arm.

"Then why are you so kind to me? You do not know me, lady. I could be working for the daemons. I could be a spy."

The dwarf leaned in close to Triggle, moving the tray. The scent of fine Dandell petals and sweet mead filled the Miftle's nostrils. She whispered in his ear.

"Fear not, Master Triggle. I bear the same mark as you. You are not the only Miftle in this dwarven sanctuary." Ilthen lifted up the sleeve of her tunic and showed Triggle the mark of the Faerie, the small, ancient markings that were born on the skin since the beginning of time when Ar Solon had been created. Triggle almost fell over with surprise.

"You mean…?" Triggle couldn't finish his words. Ilthen finished them for him.

"Yes, Triggle! And there are many more besides me, fighting with the dwarves."

Triggle met Ilthen's gaze and knew that it was true; that what he had seen when he first looked into her eyes didn't deceive him after all. He was with one of his kind and felt the magikal presence all along yet he had denied it.

"Why with the dwarves? Why don't you come back home where you belong?" Ilthen looked at the Miftle as though he had much more to learn. Indeed, Triggle knew little of the dwarves' troubles and even of any other troubles besides that of the faeries. It had been years since he had been out of his homeland and, now that he had the chance to travel, everything seemed new and unfamiliar. Ilthen opened the door and prepared herself to leave.

"Much of that will be explained when you hear of the troubles of the dwarves. And that will be soon enough. Come now. Let us get you some supplies. And let us leave this conversation in this room, my fair Miftle, if you value your life." What Ilthen said was not a threat, Triggle knew, once he looked into her eyes, but was a warning. The Miftle knew all too well about the inhabitants and their reaction to a faerie of any kind, no matter how much they looked like other races or not. That was why he was in all this mess in the first place.

Gabriella! I cannot forget my task. Cannot forget it, indeed! Triggle straightened up in his new attire and followed Ilthen out of his temporary sanctuary and into what the Miftle could only call the Great Caves, for he had seen nothing like it in all of his life.

Ilthen led him through several lit hallways with doors similar to the one they had just left, each hallway lit with several lanterns on each side of them. Ilthen stopped short of a hallway and lifted one of the lanterns off its hook from the ceiling, which was just a foot or so above them, and held it dangling in front of her. Triggle knew little of dwarven culture, but he did know that they were skilled artisans in the ways of the earth and molding it to their ways. But he knew nothing of the workmanship that was suddenly shown to him. Miles and miles of catacombs lay ahead of him, each cavern filled with the history of the dwarves on Kariyl, the ancient dwarven script going on and on for what seemed to be forever across the walls.

The walls had been separated into what they called 'fractions', Ilthen explained to him later, small sections broken down to identify a certain important date or occurrence in time. The rock that was carved into was a gray ash color, with small flecks of silver and copper dotting the writing every-so-often, some script almost glittering when the torchlight struck it. Ilthen looked back at Triggle, her face smiling, the light from the lantern lighting only the left side. She smiled again when she saw the sparkle in Triggle's eyes. She knew what he was thinking.

"Impressive to the eye, is it? That's what I thought when I first saw them. But nothing can really prepare you for it." She waved the lantern ahead to the upper right corner of the hallway that ended in front of them.

"Each catacomb has a simple marking that can be seen above every entrance and exit, a collection of symbols that stands for the way the path leads or to its location. We are traveling to the checkpoint station, which are only a few paths ahead. If you look very close, the script ends here, which is the last documented piece of work we have. It was carved over ten years ago."

Triggle touched the last of the markings with his fingers, watching as the walls around him became barren as they continued.

"Why wait so long to continue?" Triggle knew that the daemons weren't the reason just because there had been no record of daemons lasting for over a decade, though they had popped up throughout the previous century several times. Ilthen stopped, looking back at Triggle.

"You sure ask a lot of questions."

"I do apologize if I've offended you. Just making small talk. We can stop if you'd like."

"For now, please. We're at the supply post. You can get the things you need here."

The female Miftle glanced back at Triggle who, in turn, tried his best smile, it being a long while since he had to use it. It seemed to work just fine. Ilthen answered back with a glorious smile of her own.

The passageway ahead seemed to light up around them, both Miftles soon approaching a large door that ended the passageway completely. The double doors were wood though there were many other parts as well, mostly metal, that dabbled across the wood grain's fine surface. The doors towered over both that wished entrance by a good six feet, measuring almost a full ten feet in height. The hinges that connected the door to the wall were carved and sat in hinges made from the very wall itself, a stone set connected to a metal set, a full set of three securing the double doors.

The artistry of the doors, though, is what drew Triggle closer. Battles depicting dwarves fighting against dwarves, dwarves fighting other races, and even dwarves fighting grotesque creatures from the abyss were shown here, all of the battles separated by a chain of jewels that were fastened into the wood with small, metal clamps. Triggle touched the doors, his fingers moving across the still form of a dwarf, though the dwarf's face seemed to be alive. Triggle looked at Ilthen in amazement, befuddled.

"These doors, they're beautiful! The figures look as though they are locked in battle forever. They look almost real. And the jewels…" Triggle traced his finger around the jewels that lined the reliefs, noticing that many of the brilliant black jewels were missing.

"Why are some of them missing?" Ilthen lifted a hand to her vest pocket, extracting a small key. The Miftle approached the door and, moving her hand across the raised surface of the door, stopped after a moment and pressed the key into a dwarven figure, a depiction of some great and honorable figure. There was a click sound and the two doors slowly moved outward toward the two, Ilthen holding a door in her hand as Triggle followed her lead and did the same.

"Years ago, the dwarves invited a party of humans here. Later that night, after the party had left, the jewels were missing. That was the last of the humans to ever visit here. They stole what is missing. Or so the story goes, at least that's how it was told to me. But that's been a while now. I've been here and have yet to see a season pass me by. It seems as though I never age or never feel as though the time passes when I'm down here in the caverns."

"Were they sure it was the humans? Couldn't it have been someone else?"

An unknown voice broke out through the inner doorway.

"What they say is that, if it were someone, say another dwarf, it would have gotten out by now and the jewels would be found and placed back into the doors. But there have been no stories or legends or even a hint to where the jewels have gone." The doors were completely open now and a party of dwarves entered through, a dwarf leading the group.

"Of course, I could be wrong. It's been a while since I've read the dwarven histories. When I was younger, perhaps, I could have told you more. Ilthen, it's good to see you again. And your friend, we have heard so much about you."

The lead dwarf parted from the others and walked into the firelight. This is where the scruff voice had come from. A redheaded dwarf moved into the light, his beard and eyebrows matching that of his long, red mane. He wore his beard braided into three thick braids that hung halfway down his chest and it was neatly trimmed. He was well dressed also; a tight fitting suit of chain mail across his chest and forearms, much of it dangling down past his waist. Over it he wore a set of leather straps that held what seemed to be a weapon on his back, along with a matching pair of thick, leather gloves.

One of his leather gloves reached out to Triggle. Triggle looked into the dwarf's dark, brown eyes and completed the greeting with his own hand, feeling the dwarf's grip tighten on his.

"I'm Arntheer HammerHeld the Third. I'm supply captain here in Dardist. And who might you be, my little friend?" Though Arntheer stood almost a head higher than Triggle, they were both considerably the same size when it came to thickness. Triggle straightened himself up and spat out his name.

"I am Triggle the First, a traveler from beyond Reune Lake who searches for his friends." Arntheer erupted into laughter.

"Friends, you say! That's a good one. We haven't seen anyone for over several ten days. You are the first, unless there's been some mistake and we haven't received word. Did they come the way you did, through the Dwarven Halls?"

"Not exactly. We were following a group of daemons through to…"

Arntheer interrupted again, a bolt of laughter breaking the silence. By this time, the doors had been closed behind them all, a thick door bolt sliding across the two doors, Triggle being led further into the supply post tunnels.

"Ah, that's a good one, too! Quite a wit you have there! Around here, we don't chase daemons; they chase you. Just face it, my friend; you've got yourself a problem."

Ilthen interrupted.

"I hate to break the mood here, but Triggle is here for supplies and that's all, Arntheer. He doesn't need any additional questioning. He'll get enough of that with the Guard." Ilthen pressed past Arntheer with a turn of her shoulder, motioning for Triggle to follow, which he did, watching as the rest of the dwarves swarmed around him with questions.

"Where did you come from," one dwarf said.

"Any word from the outside," another voice broke through.

"Does anyone know that the daemons have begun their attack," was the last question Triggle could make out, coming from behind the other dwarves.

A barrage of questions came at Triggle all at once, none of which he could accurately answer. He knew that many of the faeries knew about the daemon attacks, but he didn't know if any of the inhabitants knew at all.

Maybe they didn't know or didn't even care. None except for the boy, Ranyll, of course. But, then again, Triggle didn't know who this Ranyll really was in the first place. Triggle just looked ahead and followed Ilthen until they reached another door, this one smaller than the first and only a single door. It was less intricate and more simplistic than the one they had went through as well, looking like it had been added recently and not centuries earlier. Ilthen opened the door and passed through a small hallway with Triggle, Arntheer following them as well, closing the door behind them, completely silencing the rest of the dwarves that were intrigued by the new visitor.

Arntheer spoke ahead to the two that moved at a fast pace. "Don't take offense, my friend. It has just been hard times for us here and we've been waiting for some sign of an end to this battle. It's been almost a season and we haven't heard any word back from our scouts that we sent out." Ilthen stopped him short, turning around.

"Stop it, Arntheer! He is not here for that. He came in looking for his friends, that is all. Now leave him be. He's had a hard road!"

Arntheer closed in on Ilthen, his face puffing out, his fists clenching at his sides. He seemed to be holding himself together by sheer will.

"So have we all down here, Ilthen! Maybe you forget that! You should go out and see what the daemons have done to our city. They've torn it apart!"

Triggle felt the tension between the two, watching as they stood face to face. He had to do something.

But what, he questioned, trying his best to think of something and quick. He didn't know how to talk to others; he didn't want to meddle in the affairs of the inhabitants as so many other faeries had done. But, then again, his kin were at fault for most of the changes across the world. He had to admit that the world would be a lot better if the first faeries had not stepped in and meddled with the world and left it as they had originally made it; perfect, unchanged. But he could not let suffering go on if he could help it, not here, not now while he was able to stop it. He stepped next to Arntheer and placed his hand on the dwarf's shoulder.

"My friend, it is not the same on the surface as it is down here. There are no daemons, well, not until a few days ago. They have just begun to surface. Apparently, the fight that the dwarves have been continuing since the beginning has prevented them from escaping almost completely. I must say, I do not know if your messengers made it out of the caves, but I do know that there are others, my friends, that are doing their best to combat this evil that you so desperately fight. The battle is not lost yet, Arntheer. And you are not alone."

Arntheer's muscles suddenly relaxed under Triggle's hand and the fire in his eyes grew calm and steady. He seemed to take comfort in knowing something instead of being left in the dark, which seemed to have been happening for a time now, Triggle noticed, the Miftle releasing his hand from Arntheer's shoulder. The dwarf nodded his head and refrained from looking into Ilthen's eyes, turning back to the door behind him and departing silently back to where the other dwarves sat and waited. Triggle turned back to follow Ilthen.

Ilthen stood, unmoving, staring at the Miftle in disbelief.

"You have a way with words, Master Triggle. You were wise in your speech. It has been a time since Arntheer has been able to compose himself as he just did in front of us. I thank you." The female Miftle bowed her head in thanks and continued on, not waiting for a response from Triggle and apparently not wanting one, the two Miftles soon approaching a fork in the tunnel. Ilthen took Triggle left through a tunnel that almost double-backed, soon turning right and then left, several doors appearing throughout the hallway. She stopped in front of one of them, eyeing Triggle's expression in the darkness.

"This is where we store most of our inventory. Be careful what you say when you go in, many of the dwarves here are not as kind as Arntheer was." Triggle nodded in the darkness and expected to have to speak in agreement, but Ilthen must have seen his silent nod, for she reached out to the door and opened it without another word. As the door opened, there were shards of light that shot out from the corner of the door, making Triggle squint, the Miftle adjusting his eyes to the sudden transition from complete and utter darkness to the immediacy in which the light seemed to escape.

As the two stepped inside the room, Triggle noticed the source of the light; two sconces were lit at both sides of the door as well as several torches in sconces lit ahead of them. The room was blanketed in shadows; nevertheless Triggle could clearly see what the room held.

Swords, axes, hammers of all sizes, small shields, and full-length war shields from decades ago lined the walls, many of them stacked on top of each other, but most placed in barrels for sorting the size and quality. By no means was there a low-quality item in the entire room, seeing as how all the weapons that Triggle eyed were made by the hands of dwarven smiths throughout the ages of time. Triggle followed next to Ilthen as they passed dozens and dozens of boxes and barrels full of weapons, passing through a small, well-dug passage just behind a few barrels.

Ilthen began to walk through the passage when she stopped next to a barrel and opened it. The torchlight around them was not enough to bring to light what was in the barrel, but Ilthen didn't seem to mind, reaching her hand down and into the barrel, bringing out from it a short sword with a silver handle.

The female Miftle's eyes locked in on Triggle, who stared at what she held out to him, a look of amazement on his face. Triggle extended one of his hands out and took it by its sheath, looking back to Ilthen questioningly. Ilthen smiled at him and let go of the sword, letting him feel the weight.

"This is of our finer stock. The dwarves down here spend a lot of time on such things, so don't let go of it as easily as you did your own."

Triggle reached with his other hand and pulled the blade free of its scabbard and noticed the fine dwarven carvings on the hilt as well as the foremost of the blade, his eyes following the single-sided blade to the tip and back again, admiring the blacksmith's work. In moments, he had the sheath in place on his left hip and looked the gift over once more before putting it away. Ilthen moved on to the next few barrels, her lantern lighting a dozen barrels up in front of her.

"I thought you said that I was to be interrogated by others. I don't see any others."

Ilthen stopped in mid-step and looked about, popping open another barrel with her free hand. She set the lantern on a barrel next to her and rummaged through an assortment of items, pulling out a hooded lantern for Triggle and some length of rope bundled up.

"Good point. Someone's supposed to be here guarding the rest of this, but I don't see anyone, do you?"

"Not yet." Triggle took the supplies as well as a shoulder satchel from a peg on the wall and began filling it with the supplies Ilthen found for him.

"Well, I'm sure someone will be along to check this place out soon enough. There are four or five posts ahead of us that we have to go through before we reach the main checkpoint where you were picked up. I'm sure, once there, we can pick up some things for you to eat on your way back and maybe even an escort until you reach a…safe…." Ilthen stopped short suddenly. Her eyes grew wide with fear and she looked to Triggle, who was still packing up his things. When he was finished, he looked up and the smile he had vanished from his face.

"Ilthen, what is it?" At first it was faint; a slight break in the silence around them and then, ever so softly, a weak sound echoed through the room, carelessly at first, then grew louder. Then the room was silent again. For moments afterwards, Ilthen had moved her finger to her mouth asking for silence from him, her ears picking up the sound again. It was a bell being rung over and over again.

Ilthen grabbed a weapon in a nearby barrel and pulled free one of the swords, grabbing up a shield from the wall as well. She handed the shield to Triggle and grabbed one for herself. The fear had vanished from her eyes, soon replaced with a fire Triggle had never seen since he had met the other Miftle.

"The daemons have broken through one of the points ahead! Those are the warning bells. They couldn't hold them off any longer, Triggle! That means they'll be coming this way if they've broken through all the checkpoints. But that's impossible! We must hurry to the first checkpoint to see if they've broken through." Triggle nodded in agreement, though the thought of confronting more daemons so soon after his close call didn't give him a warm feeling inside.

However, he knew that he couldn't just lie in hiding, *for that fate lay for another, not me and not any of my race,* Triggle suddenly decided, straightening himself up, trying to kindle the same fire inside of him that he saw in Ilthen.

At least I'll be with one of my own kind if I fall to those insufferable creatures, Triggle thought to himself, following the flickering torchlight ahead of him, Ilthen passing several empty tunnels as they moved closer to the drumming sound.

As they turned a sharp corner, walking into a new corridor, the sound grew louder, a constant rhythm now, the silence around them broken, Triggle's hands growing damp with sweat, his forehead beginning to moisten in the darkened caverns.

I know what it is, Triggle thought to himself, his hand squeezing tightly around the new sword that had been given to him, the shield pressing against his left shoulder, his eyes darting to the shadows in front of him for any sign of movement.

All was still. Nothing stirred in the shadows save for the dirt that their booted feet stirred underneath them, Ilthen leading them ahead, the beating sound growing louder and louder as the cavern tunnel began to slope upward, Triggle feeling his legs beginning to ache. They were going up a slight rise now, Triggle noticed, small, carved steps slowly forming under his feet. He had no problem getting used to them, for it took his mind off of the drumming sound that echoed in the tunnels ahead of and behind him.

Suddenly, the drums stopped and, with that, Ilthen stopped as well. Triggle almost ran into her but stopped himself short, holding onto the tunnel for support. The sudden stop shook the lantern light, shooting slivers of light back and forth until Ilthen steadied it with the hilt of her sword. Her breathing was labored and Triggle could see small beads of sweat running down the back of her neck.

She was nervous, too, he thought.

Her voice started him. "I think something's wrong."

"Just because the beating stopped?" Triggle questioned, trying to calm himself by leaning against the tunnel wall for a brief rest.

She turned to him, her face dabbled with sweat, her lips quivering yet her stare hard and set as if it were carved from stone.

"No. Something's wrong because of **them**." Ahead, not far past where the lantern light reached, several blood-red pairs of eyes grew wide with excitement and broke from their still, guarding positions, eyes darting over the top of the tunnels, eyes bouncing across the walls, several more pairs of eyes using the stairs to quicken towards the two lit by the lantern light. Ilthen and Triggle knew that they didn't have time to retreat or time to formulate a plan. Soon, the faces that held those eyes came into view of the lantern light.

Triggle, gathering up the same strength that had kept him alive during the last attack, decided he must take a stand now and pushed Ilthen to the side, holding his shield out in front of him, his sword canted over the edge of the shield.

He charged the rushing daemons.

18

Falwen saw the city borders of Goletta appear over a small rise just before sunrise, his legs aching from such a long hike without stopping. Nonetheless, Falwen knew that, once he arrived here, he could get some proper sleep at his favorite inn not far from the North Entrance where he was only a few hundred steps from now. Goletta had four entrances, though one could not really be considered an entrance by any traveler who didn't have a shipping vessel. The North, East, and South Entrances were a set of well-guarded towers with two iron gates and a wooden reinforcement in case of an emergency.

This fourth entrance, however, was the Western Entrance where all of the ships docked and paid their shipping fees, unloaded supplies, and traded straight off the boats to the marketers that waited for the ships to come in. Many sailors only used this Western Entrance and Eastern Entrance and never knew of the North and South Entrances, though they were still widely used by traders from all over Kariyl. Falwen used the North Entrance just due to the route he took and for the splendid hospitality he had been offered time and again. The Fisherman's Quarrel, though not the most respected inn and tavern in Goletta, held a high place in Falwen's heart because he had always been welcomed there since he was a young boy.

He had cleared the Northern Entrance tower easily, nodding to the guards that watched the points, one of them pulling on the level that operated the gate to let travelers in, the pulley system that Goletta had built lifting the gate in front of Falwen. The fisherman entered into the town of Goletta, something he had never tired of in all of his long life.

The Fisherman's Quarrel sign came into view just as he passed the Northern Gate, Falwen taking slower strides now that he had passed the rise, his aching feet begging him for a rest.

And that is what I shall give you, Falwen agreed, looking up at the large carving of a man carrying a fish two times his size. He pushed the door open and stepped inside. Since it was still early morning, no one had awakened and it was still early for anyone to be in. A familiar face popped up from sleeping on a nearby table and mumbled out a greeting.

"Welcome to the Fisherman's Quarrel, best sleep by the sea. We're not open now, but…" The sleepy-eyed tavern owner rubbed his eyes and finally took notice of his first customer of the day, a weary Falwen Sanse walking in with his spear in hand.

"Aye, Falwen! It is good to see you, though I didn't expect you to be in here so soon, being it the best of your fishing season and all. Nothing biting lately?"

Falwen reached out and embraced the older man lightly, who was almost a foot and half shorter than him, the odor of the unwashed man overwhelming him with unwanted smells. Falwen pulled away and waved a hand in front of his face, wrinkling up his nose.

"My goodness Darder, when was the last time you bathed?" Darder lifted his arm up and sniffed himself.

"It has been a little while. I've been too busy to get to it. You know how business is, always booming on the North Side." Darder spun around on one foot and walked over to a small set of keys hanging on the wall by a simple hook and took them off the wall, leading Falwen up the stairs and down the hall without a word until he reached a door.

"Luck has it that your room was vacant last night, believe it or not."

Falwen nodded to his long-time friend and reached down to his pouch. Darder shook his head.

"Falwen, don't worry about it, my friend. Your family can use the money more than I can right now. Anyways, I'd like a fine set of fish from your special casting spot whenever you have the time to bring me some." Falwen smiled to the shorter man and unslung the small pack from over his shoulder, reaching inside, his fingers grabbing the small fishing line and, wrapping his fingers around it, pulled the remainder of the catch he had made the morning before, still fresh as if they had come out of the water. Falwen handed the line to Darder who, in turn, took it and nodded in pleasure.

"This is more than enough, Falwen. How about a meal and a nice warm bath served up when you wake? That should about cover the fish, wouldn't you say?"

Falwen nodded sleepily. He knew that he needed sleep, but the food and bath sounded good as well. He agreed with Darder, who was about to leave when the fisherman stopped him.

"I also need some information, Darder. I need to know if anything strange has been happening in the east, any stories or any tales that would seem a bit odd. Can you do that for me?"

Darder looked at his friend questioningly, a little concerned about the request that his fisherman friend would ask him. After all, Falwen was a simple man, not bound up with society as many others were. That question seemed to be reserved for others, not of Falwen's upbringing and social standing.

Darder knew that something was amiss but knew also that it was in his best interest to comply and get the information, for Falwen had been an honored customer for some time now and continued to be good to Darder and his crew at the Fisherman's Quarrel. Many times it was Falwen and his family that had brought a stock of fish they had been saving and offered them up for a few nights stay, resuscitating the employed at the Fisherman's

Quarrel with fine fish that not a fisherman in Goletta could catch and not a buyer in Goletta could purchase without reaching heavily into their purse. Falwen always had the finest fish when he came into town and was all too generous to give them out.

Yes, Darder thought, *this information must be important to the old fisherman.* Darder would have no trouble finding information of that kind out there in the wilds of the town of Goletta. He smiled back at his friend.

"That should be no problem at all, Falwen. I'll have something for ya by the time you wake then; good enough my friend?"

They both nodded the other a goodbye and Falwen went into his room, shutting the door behind him. Darder retraced his way back downstairs and went into a small door past the front counter, passing through the cooking area and into the sleeping quarters. The sleeping quarters were located near the rear of the inn and were used mainly for workers and any late night drunkards that were regulars at the tavern. The innkeeper passed by several cots and stopped at the foot of a cot, trying to see through the darkness and underneath the covers at who was sleeping. Darder laid a hand on the covers and shook them violently.

Underneath, a form moved, slowly at first, then recognized Darder and jolted up in the bed. It was a young boy, maybe eleven summers at the most, wiping the sleep from his eyes. He tried to straighten his messy auburn hair but it seemed to win the battle he fought and soon he quit altogether, looking up at the innkeeper for further instructions.

"I have a job for you, my boy! I need you to make your rounds a little earlier than usual." The young boy nodded in reply and slipped himself out of his cot, quickly tying his breeches and slipping on a loose-fitting tunic while slipping his feet into a dirty, brown pair of short boots. He lifted himself off of his cot once finished and slipped on a small knit hat, tucking his hair underneath it. Darder handed him the fish.

"Wake the cook and tell him to prepare these for dinner. Falwen has made his rounds early. It looks like we'll be eating like kings tonight."

The young boy smiled a little wider and grabbed the fishing line with the fish attached, rushing past the innkeeper and back through the cooking area, disappearing into the main hallway in mere moments. Darder smiled and turned back around, following the scent of fresh fish back out into the main entrance area where he opened the doors for the start of the business day. He wiped his hands on his dirty tunic and sat back down in his chair to wait for customers. It was starting out to be a good day.

The afternoon sun woke Falwen Sanse, the fisherman staring up at the window in which light crept through, covering his eyes with his hands to keep the light out. He yawned and stretched out on the cot, the soreness he had walked in with earlier now gone, his eyes still adjusting to the intensity of the light. He lifted himself up from the bed slowly and stretched until he was good and ready to continue on with the morning, gathering his things to meet with Darder downstairs. He stopped by the washbasin in his room and splashed some cold water on his face, helping to wake himself. Falwen threw his satchel over his back and shut the door behind him. As he looked down the hallway, there was no movement, but sounds could be heard; a general hustle and bustle of scores of travelers taking a room for the rest of the night, a number of patrons down at the tavern which had opened just shortly after Falwen had fallen asleep, and the cooks and servers weaving through the mess of crowd that were their everyday throng.

Falwen had become accustomed to this and many other things, not surprised in the least when the sights matched the sounds as everything came quickly into view. The regulars were there in their tables in the corner and Darder had left Falwen's special table empty just for the fisherman, Falwen

taking a seat just as Darder approached with a pitcher of water and an empty
glass.

"Now, don't you look a mite better, Falwen! I wanted to wake you a little
while ago, but it just got so busy."

Indeed, Falwen noticed, *it was busier than it had been in a long time.* Every table
was taken and many were standing around the less occupied tables. It
seemed as if business had sprung in a matter of hours.

Darder sat down the glass in front of Falwen and poured him some fresh
water, sitting down the pitcher as well.

"And I suppose I owe it to you and your catch you brought me this
morning. As soon as we slapped them on the grill, every Golettan this side
of Kariyl was in here. We've sold out of almost everything thanks to you. I
had to send an errand boy to get us some more stock of fine meats and mead
to last the night through until my vending cart arrives tomorrow."

Falwen knew the approving look of Darder, had seen it many times, and
this was one of those times. Darder looked around the room, his shoulders
slightly higher than they had been this morning. He even tried to suck in his
enormous belly, which could be seen jutting out of his tunic like a pregnant
woman. To Falwen's surprise, Darder had even bathed and wore a strong
scent that covered up any bad smells that Falwen had smelled this morning
when he arrived.

The sun was still in the sky behind them through the windows of the
tavern and several of Darder's servants began loosening the candle chandelier
from its place to prepare for the evening that approached, lighting them with
a hooded lantern they carried. Soon, the tavern was lit brightly, plumed with
smoke from pipes that were wielded by older patrons, giving the air around
the tavern a thick, rich smell.

Perfect mood for dining, thought Falwen, watching as Darder moved away
from the table for several moments, attending to his other duties around The

Fisherman's Quarrel. He returned with a smile on his face, though it was different than the other he had shown his friend the fisherman, this one barely noticeable when he approached closer and sat a plate of food down.

"Here is your meal, as promised, my fine friend. And the bathwater is being drawn up as we speak. I'm giving you use of my own personal bathtub tonight. We are far too busy for you to be shacked up with the likes of the strangers that bath in the other public tubs. And about that information you asked for; funny thing. My errand boy came back with some things, some bizarre things that just might fit your inquiry."

Darder took a seat at the table, motioning for one of his servers. The small girl nodded her head in understanding and, in moments, had walked through the crowd of patrons and brought Darder a small pitcher of mead with two clean mugs, setting them down and carrying on with her duties. Darder poured himself a drink and did the same for Falwen, taking a long pull off his own before continuing.

"Rumor has it that there have been some attacks across the Tirapoor Channel. Some of the local checkpoints have been…compromised." Darder looked around to make sure no one else was listening and looked back at Falwen, who had pushed aside his meal and was listening intently. After all, if he couldn't find something soon, his journey all the way here would have been for nothing.

He countered with common sense, his patience beginning to grow thin. "What else? Is there anything else? It could just be local bandits. It's happened before."

Darder grew flustered. "I'm getting to that, Falwen. Calm yourself. That's just what I said to the boy that came back with the information; however he was very clear in telling me who the culprits were; **Daemons**! He said that the checkpoints were being destroyed by **daemons**." Darder leaned back in his chair, pouring himself another glass of mead. He took a small sip of it and waited for Falwen to react.

Falwen looked away for the moment. The roar of the crowds around him died down, the long stare from his friend in front of him could not be felt. The meal prepared for him didn't seem needed or wanted, for everything seemed to halt once Darder spoke that word. That word conjured up the figure that had attacked him at the shore, the black, shadowy creature hiding underneath the body of the angel this simple fisherman had found. Falwen could feel the weight of the sword at his side; he could hear the wail of the creature as he had killed it, the throaty gurgle as it breathed its last.

Falwen suddenly felt a hand on him and Darder was at his side, the sounds and smells coming back to the fisherman, his mind slowly tracing its way back to the present, his friend chuckling softly to himself amid the clamor of the tavern.

"Are you alright, my friend? I didn't mean to frighten you with the story. It's probably just some hoax, you know, to keep children up at night or something. You know how those river children are, telling stories like that. Truth be told, I heard one the other day about someone seeing a band of faeries northeast of here, but…." Darder's voice trailed off, noticing the look of concern on his friend's face.

"Falwen, I didn't know it would upset you that bad. You told me you wanted information of strange happenings east of here and I found you something strange. Of course, it can't be taken seriously because of the person that the boy I sent got it from."

Falwen looked around the tavern. The room was even more crowded since the sun had begun to set and the room holding the occupants had become filled with the smells of food being prepared in the cooking area just a room away.

Pipes were lit and the plucking of a stringed instrument had begun in the corner of the room, a small crowd gathering around a local minstrel. The world seemed to crumble before the fisherman. This had happened before, when he had encountered the daemon the first time. He knew that there were daemons on Kariyl, knew that they were close. He had even fought one. Nonetheless, hearing of sightings frightened him to the core. He was able to face off with one daemon just barely, but a whole number of them able to take an entire Tirapoor Checkpoint? This journey was pointless. He would just end up getting himself killed trying to fight those things off.

Falwen returned back to his meal, which had began to get cold sitting off to the side while he had contemplated in what to do so long. He also noticed that Darder had left him for the moment to assist in the kitchen.

Falwen knew he must do something. If there were daemons attacking the checkpoint, there must be some reason for it and he was going to find out, even if it meant death. The fisherman tried to focus on the words that the angel Divlo had told him.

There is a reason for you to be here, a purpose. All of that will come to you in time.

None of it made sense to him right now, but hopefully it would if he followed the path he thought was right. And this path seemed just as good as any.

I should follow the sightings; look for the man that bears this name there.

Darder soon returned and refilled his mug with mead, taking Falwen's empty plate and returning with a fresh hot piece of pie from the cooking area.

"So, what is your plan my friend? I hear that the washing area is ready whenever you are and one of my cooks just finished making this pie among others if you are still hungry. Stay for a while, we'd love to have you here. You know you are always welcome here, as well as the rest of your family."

Falwen finished the rest of his mug of mead and took a small slice of pie, devouring the moist, flaky crust filled with hot, sliced apples. He nodded to Darder once he was finished and picked up his things.

"It was a grand meal, Darder. I do wish that I could stay longer; I just have things to do right now. If you could direct me to your washing area, I would love to take advantage of that bath. Again, your kindness is greatly appreciated."

Darder hesitated but eventually led Falwen up to the washing area, an estranged look upon his rugged face. They stopped at a door on the third floor.

"It may not be any of my business, Falwen, but I hope you're not doing what I think you're doing. I hope you're not going after trouble. That would not be a wise thing to do." Darder extracted a key from a pouch at his hip and slipped it into the keyhole in the door, pushing the door open wide. Inside, there was a washbasin on a cupboard and a large tub the size of one of the dining tables downstairs, filled with hot water. Several towels lay across the side of the tub and a change of clothes had been set out to the size.

Falwen patted his friend on the shoulder, trying best to alleviate the tavern owner's fears.

"I don't think what I'm doing is wise right now, but it is something that I have to do, Darder. I don't have time to wait for something to find me. I must find the threat that is upon this land and do everything I can to fight it."

Darder walked inside the room and turned on his heels to face Falwen, a stern look upon his otherwise complacent features.

"Maybe I don't know everything that is going on, that's true, but I don't understand what any of what I told you have to do with you or your family. When you first came in, I knew there was something the matter with you because you were wearing your sword. You never wear your sword, Falwen! Has something happened to bring all of this onto your shoulders? We've been friends for years now; you can talk to me Falwen."

Falwen dropped his bags in the room and unbuckled his belt, letting his sword drop to the floor. He sat on the floor and unlaced his boots, slipping each one off carefully. His feet were sore and, though he had rested, they were still aching from the long walk from Simmer Lo. He looked up to his friend now, trying to gain a little more perspective, trying to understand the reasoning behind his own actions himself.

"Darder, we have been friends for years, but that does not change what I have to do now. I was called upon by something greater than myself, something that showed me that I have a purpose in life."

"And what is that purpose, Falwen, to die and leave your family alone because of some foolish adventure?"

"I don't expect you to understand, Darder."

"You are right. I don't understand, my friend."

Darder walked back to the door, giving Falwen his privacy, knowing now that he couldn't pry any information from his friend or change Falwen's mind until they had talked it through, which didn't seem to be a possibility at the moment.

Darder shut the door behind him and Falwen slipped off the rest of his garments, letting himself sink into the soothing water.

It had been a time since Falwen had let himself relax in a bath and this seemed to cure all of his ailments at once; there were knots in his shoulders from carrying his bags and his legs still ached from his long trek to Goletta; this felt as though it were the first time he relaxed since first encountering what could only be construed as a war between the heavens and the world below. Everything seemed to drown in the tranquility of the hot water.

His wife and his children's faces slid in and out of his mind, small flashes of their smiles and whispers of their laughs coming through to him as he closed his eyes and relaxed himself further, small rivulets of steam rising in the air around him. Falwen could feel his bad knee from many years ago loosen and, as the heat soaked into his aching bones, it slowly broke down the soreness in his otherwise exhausted limbs.

Falwen gradually lifted himself out of the comfortable bath and dried himself off, putting his garments back on, when there was a tap at the door. The old fisherman smiled, knowing that Darder had never given up that easy and prepared for another round of verbal battering when the unexpected happened.

A young voice barely broke through the surface of the door.

"Master Sanse. Master Sanse, are you in there?" Falwen pulled the rest of his garments on as quickly as possible and called back to the softer voice.

"Yes. Yes, I'm here. Please enter." The door rattled and the lever lifted, a young boy only eleven or twelve summers spying into the room to make sure he was allowed in. He wore a simple peasant's garb and held his small hands behind his back, a gesture of respect among the simple folk in the west. He bowed his head.

"Master Sanse, your wagon is waiting for your downstairs, sir."

Falwen finished tying up his laces and lifted himself up from the floor, looking back at the young man questioningly. "Wagon? I don't remember asking for a wagon."

"That's true, sir. Darder told me to tell you that you are to leave immediately if you are to follow your path. He has booked you passage with a supply wagon. A man by the name of Treese is waiting for you down in the tavern. He will take you where you need to go."

Falwen strapped on his belt and adjusted the scabbard to his left side, throwing his bags over his shoulder.

"Did Darder say where this Treese is going?" The boy shook his head.

"No, sir, he didn't. He only said that you should be on that wagon if you want to follow the path you told him about."

"He did, did he? Well, young man, show me to this Treese."

In all the years that Falwen had known Darder, he had never known him to give this easy. It had to be a ploy, a joke, a trick to get Falwen to stay right where he was. Any moment now, he was going to be introduced to a complete stranger and the joke would be on him.

Falwen followed the boy down the stairs and into the tavern, which seemed to be busier since he had gone upstairs. There were no rooms at the tables and many patrons just stood near the bar, ordering drink after drink. The boy cut through the crowd and Falwen soon became lost in the crowd, his pack catching on an occupied chair nearby. The patron dismissed the disturbance with a slight nod of his head and Falwen carried on, the little boy leading him, stopping near the exit. The boy began speaking with a man at a seat near the door. Falwen squinted through the pipe smoke and surmised that this must be the Treese that the boy spoke of.

Falwen guessed Treese to be a little younger than himself yet he carried with him a considerable amount of weight. He had a thick brown tuft of messy hair atop his head and was clothed in simple garb marred with small patches of dirt and wear on them. His eyes were close together and the brown in his eyes was closer to black than brown, the man called Treese almost in a perpetual state of disagreement, his face covered with lines of age and unhappiness. Falwen had hoped for more of a companion for the long journey but he supposed that this Treese fellow would have to do, especially since it seemed that Darder had gone out of his way to find his friend transportation.

By the time Falwen had reached Treeses' table, the disgruntled man had already gotten up and finished his drink. He motioned to Falwen's' bags on his shoulder and waited. Falwen shook his head and held out his hand, stating that he needed no help carrying his things. Treese nodded and turned his thick body towards the door and walked out it. Falwen looked down at the little boy, who just shook his head. The little boy spoke.

"Don't worry, sir. That's just how Treese is. He's awful quiet these days. A lot has happened to him the last few summers. You'll be safe with him, I promise. Darder wouldn't let one of his best customers go out with a stranger."

This said, the boy nodded his head of thick hair at Falwen and pushed his way back into the crowd of patrons around them, disappearing from sight a moment later. Falwen opened the door and went to retrieve his new guide, the man the boy had called Treese, who seemed to be having problems of his own as well.

The night sky was blanketed with stars and, throughout the well-lit streets, the only sounds that could be heard were the bustling taverns on the corners of each street. The Fisherman's Quarrel seemed to be taking on several more patrons this night than the other taverns not far from the center square of Goletta, the small taverns on the corners having extinguished their lights for the night.

Falwen could see the outline of Treese not far from the entrance to the tavern, making his way onto a small wagon, two horses hitched to the front of it, both full-grown brown mares, greater of a breed than the fisherman had seen in a long time. He had become accustomed to walking from place to place and, once seeing these great horses, he knew that he would enjoy the ride, for the owner of these horses had taste. Falwen approached the wagon and patted the closest horse on the side, feeling the horse lean into his affections.

Treese spoke up. "That's ones name is Tartoll and the other's name is Finrass. They are sisters and are inseparable, have been since they were born."

Falwen smiled at Treese, stroking Tartoll once more before climbing onto the wagon. Behind him, Treeses' wagon was covered with a white tarp, several ropes tying the material down, flattening the bed of the wagon completely. Treese had a small hooded lantern hooked onto a pole out in front of him and a sword underneath his seat, as well as a small crossbow with several long steel bolts for protection. He lifted up a small pouch to Falwen and smiled.

"Dried beef? We've got a long way to go. Might as well take advantage of the hospitality."

Falwen accepted a small portion of the dried beef in the bag though he was full from the meal earlier, taking a small bite off of it while storing the rest in the sack on his back. Treese picked up the reins and snapped them lightly, Tartoll and Finrass starting up, their hooves clicking on the stone walks of Goletta, the hooded lantern swaying slightly as they began their trip together east.

The chilly Golettan night seemed to creep through the simple garb of both Treese and Falwen, both of them sitting in silence as the darkened pathway on the outskirts of Goletta lit up in front of them, dark shadows surrounded by an even darker night. Falwen had not seen the eastern forest outside of Goletta for years since his travels before he had children and, as they traveled through it now, it seemed darker than he remembered. The old man could feel his skin crawl and the small hairs on the base of his neck stick out as he watched the shadows in the forest, remembering the creature he had beaten down on the shore.

It's face; that's what he remembered most. Falwen needed something to take his mind off of that so he looked out in front of him at the great mares pulling them forward. Falwen had taken an immediate interest in Tartoll and Finrass, Treeses' fine horses, and began to ask questions about them.

"I got them from a horse dealer in Dradle a few summers ago. It seemed like the right thing to do at the time. I had just won at a game of cards and my luck had been bad before that for such a long time that I knew I had to do something that would bring me joy."

Treese didn't seem to have a problem speaking about his horses that was for sure, Falwen thought, watching as the two great animals moved the wagon and its contents with ease, keeping a steady pace throughout the ride.

"So, you don't regret getting them, then? Aren't they a lot of upkeep?" Falwen grabbed in his bag and pulled out a piece of dried beef, stuffing a few slices in his mouth. He had begun to like this stuff as well. Falwen was so used to eating fish; he had forgotten what he was missing with other meats.

"Well, at first, I did have a problem caring for them. In the beginning, I had to work them a little to get the money to build them a stable. But that's all in the past now. It's been years since I've had them and, believe me; they are well worth the trouble. They have seen me through quite a fix more times than I like to remember." Treese smiled after saying this, bringing to his lips a flask that he had pulled from a compartment underneath his seat, taking a long pull from it, then handing it to Falwen. Falwen shook his head and declined the offer.

"Thank you, but I only drink on special occasions."

"Special occasions! What are those?" Treese corked his flask back after taking a second sip, slipping it back from where he got it, wiping his mouth with the back of his hand.

"Oh, you know. Birthdays, celebrations; things like that. After all, I have a family to look after and, from my experiences, drinking has never helped me in that area at all." Treese smiled back at Falwen and nodded respectfully.

"I don't claim to know the first thing about marriage or all those other rituals involving commitment and devotion, but I respect you for taking hold of your life and your duties, yes sir. I may be young, but I'm not ignorant. I understand that there are commitments far greater than what we see in this world."

Falwen felt himself wanting to say what commitment he had been tasked to do, what grand scheme had been set forth upon him by none other than an angel, but he looked at Treese and knew he couldn't say anything on the topic to his guide. He would have to continue his secret until….well, he didn't know if he'd ever get to say anything to another human, elf, or dwarf on the face of Ar Solon about what he had experienced no more than a day ago.

It all seemed so dream-like; the findings on the shore, the battle between the daemon; everything, including the angel coming down to task him with what he knew he had to do no matter what. Everything seemed as though he had dreamt it all, yet he had complete recollection of everything as if it were engraved upon his mind, at the forefront of his thoughts until he accomplished his task.

He knew of the stories, sure; of the grand scheme that was to be instilled upon every race from the first day of creation. It was one of the most widely told stories passed from generation to generation ever told. However, now, when Falwen thought of it, of the grand scheme, it wasn't so ridiculous a story and, in reality, it wasn't a story at all. He had just been given his grand scheme a little bit late.

That's what it was. That's what it had to be.

Suddenly, Treese stopped the wagon. Falwen was brought back to his senses and he looked out into the darkness.

"What is it, Treese?" The driver lifted himself up and pointed to something out in the road.

"It looks like a tree fell. It's blocking the road. We'll have to get out and move it before we can move on."

Falwen felt an overwhelming sense of danger and looked around the dark edges of the lantern light as Treese climbed off the wagon. Treese noticed the look on Falwen's face and chuckled, moving closer to the fallen tree, setting the lantern down by the tree.

"I know what you're thinking, Falwen. You're not from around the city. You're a simple man from the country. There's nothing to be afraid of. It's just a fallen tree on the path."

Falwen caught a glimpse of the red eyes in the lantern light just a few paces away from Treese. Falwen pulled out his blade and cried out to Treese.

"It's a trap, Treese!" But it was too late. In moments, the daemons leapt out, taking the driver down in one fell swoop. In another, the horses began to whine with nervousness and what just happened and Falwen jumped off the wagon before it took off, the wagon veering straight in the direction of the daemons.

The only thing Falwen could do was run; run far away from the wagon, from the lantern light and from the screams of the horses that penetrated through the darkness. Falwen ran into the woods and tried to find a place to hide from the daemons.

19

Ranyll could feel his blood grow cold instantly. He knew why D'meir had growled, why the creature had tensed up. Behind the party of dwarves and their new companions, there grew a slight hum throughout the cave and then there was a brilliant light. The light splashed across the rocks of the cave, bathing each of them in radiance. The dwarves covered their eyes yet D'meir and Ranyll stood, glaring into the light, trying to find the reason for it. Ranyll had never heard anything like that before. It was as if hundreds of bees had been caught and harnessed into a cage, all of them buzzing at once. However, it sounded like something he had heard not too long ago as well.

He remembered the angel Gabriella when she had called Greditto down from the clouds and he had harnessed the power of lightning, bringing it down upon Gabriella, time and again, until she was almost nothing before the young man. The humming sound, which was almost unbearable to Ranyll now, sounded like lightning being shot through a glass tube over and over again.

Oagthor grabbed Ranyll by the arm and shook him soundly to get his attention. Ranyll could barely hear the dwarf over the humming sound.

"Ranyll, it is okay. It is the force shield. It just cut on all of a sudden. Do not fear it. I will show you the origins of the shield when we get there." And that was all the dwarf said to him. The dwarf dropped his hand to his side and met back up with his friend Rathor, the two dwarves ahead of them continuing on, Ranyll trying to gather his thoughts together to continue. The two dwarves leading the party nodded Ranyll and D'meir forward, both of them still on edge yet a little more calmed now that they knew there was nothing to fear. D'meir soon crawled down off Ranyll's shoulder and buried his head underneath Ranyll's arm, keeping its ears covered from the humming noise. Soon, the noise Ranyll had been hearing became a part of the cave around him and, as he followed the torchlight of the dwarves ahead, he saw that, indeed, it seemed that there was nothing to fear.

The humming grew louder every step he took, but he had become accustomed to the sound, felt it vibrate through is limbs, making his teeth chatter, forcing him to bite down on his lip to keep his entire jaw from vibrating. The cavern they were in broke off into several caves, the dwarves ahead of them taking a smaller passage than the others, disappearing into the passage ahead. Ranyll followed and, for a moment, felt as helpless as could be in between all of these dwarves. He felt he didn't really know what he was getting into, hadn't known from the start what he had actually started by stopping Greditto from crippling Gabriella.

All he knew is that she was an angel and, for a moment, had been generous enough to give him a part of her that he would never forget. He had never been close with a woman before, never had a chance to and, as he looked around him, didn't know if he would ever again. He didn't know what Ar Solon had in store for him at this moment. He just knew that he needed to find Gabriella at any cost, before it was too late.

The party ahead of Ranyll came to a halt and Oagthor approached the human, leaning close to him to speak to both him and D'meir. The dwarf stroked the fire fox's mane slightly, D'meir poking his head out from underneath Ranyll's arm. Oagthor continued.

"We're coming close now to our exit point. What you'll see coming up may surprise you, I'll assure you of that, but you must keep your eyes on the path ahead of you. If you don't, there will be trouble. Follow the path, that's all I ask."

Ranyll nodded his head in understanding, detecting something different in Oagthor's voice, though he didn't know what. D'meir looked up at Ranyll and then burrowed his head back underneath Ranyll's arm, Ranyll almost carrying the fire fox with his free hand. He sheathed his sword and situated D'meir where he was almost cradling him in his arms and continued on.

The cave they were traveling through was shorter than those they had traversed through and it soon came to an end, opening up before them on the right side into an enormous cavern. Ranyll gasped and suddenly realized where they were. He was still within the cavern entrance and saw the opening down below him. He stopped in place, his body suddenly refusing to move.

He had read about this in books; he knew what lay beyond the opening of the cave. He could see the straight pathway ahead of him as it disappeared left, curving around the face of the cavern cliff, the great opening to his right a sheer drop that did not know an end.

The Dwarven Crag.

It had been known to swallow up entire cities as well as all sound and light that came near it. The two dwarves behind Ranyll motioned for him to continue, not a worry on their grubby faces, their eyes shiny balls of white staring through the darkness. Ranyll turned back to the exit of the cave, watching as the light from the torch continued further, blanketing him and his surroundings in darkness. The dwarves behind him could see, so it did not bother them that the light was gone. Terror kept Ranyll in place, yet it was terror that flung him forward, knowing that, without proper lighting to see the path ahead, he would plummet into the Crag for sure.

He took a step forward, then another, soon entering into the most enormous cavern he had ever seen and would probably ever see in his entire life. The cavern stretched up above him until the darkness swallowed it, the same going for the open area just to the right of him, draping the open area with what looked like night to Ranyll; but he knew it was much more than that.

An age of darkness lay down in the crag, not being disturbed since the beginning of time. Ranyll could smell something ancient, dust-ridden, resting within the world that he had not known or feared to know. The books he had learned from never gave any insight, nothing more than just a vague description of what lay in the crag, though his mind, at this moment, could come up with a hundred things.

Behemoths, winged creatures that can see in the dark and hunt for food, great beasts that can only be killed with magik of the old ages; Ranyll knew that something was down there in the crag. He felt ashamed to be there, sensing that, if the crag itself had emotions, would know that he should not be looking in on it as he was. Ranyll looked ahead at the small pathway ahead of him, a sheer wall on his left that continued on and sloped slowly around the cliff, and a sheer drop just a few paces from him on the right, nothing but open space and the Dwarven Crag waiting for him.

The light from the torch began to fade again so he quickened his steps, one after another, never taking his eyes away from the pathway to look down into obscurity, fearing that he would see something that he didn't want to see at all. But, most of all, he feared that something would see him. Ranyll brought the fire fox closer to his chest and leaned his left shoulder on the wall next to him as he walked, trying to keep away from the crag as much as possible.

The torchlight ahead had grown as he caught up with the rest of the party, now able to see the lip of the precipice as well as a little bit down, where before he had only seen the shadow of a path ahead of him, just enough to follow. The light almost made things worse. For a moment, he thought he could see things moving down in the crag, things that flowed through the darkness as though it were water. He dismissed the thought of that possibility altogether as he continued on, but then felt the fire fox tense up in his arms.

D'meir lifted his head out and looked out into the dim light, down into the crag. The torchlight ahead stopped and the four dwarves ahead of him stood motionless for a time. Ranyll was exhausted from moving through the caves, wanted to rest, and hoped that the stopping point was close. His eyes ached from having to strain them in the dim light, but he knew for sure he saw something in that Crag below. He did not know if the Crag had a bottom and, from the histories he had learned and the stories told by the bards in his town, knew it to be a bottomless cavern. But, as he strained to see down into the Crag, his hands clinging to D'meir as the fire fox looked as well, he swore that he saw something move down below, could almost hear the faint sounds of a shuffling or scrambling about.

For a second, he thought he heard….*clicking*.

His mind reeled and he went to lean back against the wall when he realized he wasn't at all near it and that, somehow he had been drawn to the edge of the precipice and he fell backwards, almost dropping the fire fox as he tried to scramble up to regain his footing. He soon felt the cold wall behind him, his pack pressing against it, a layer of sweat coating his skin.

As he came to his senses, Ranyll noticed that he was covered in sweat, his tunic soaked through, the young man looking around to see if the dwarves around him had noticed what he had just done. If they had seen him, they took no notice now, all of them looking around them in the darkness. Ranyll lifted himself up off the ground and followed the wall to Oagthor, making sure he did not get near the edge of the pathway. The path as well as a good portion of the wall next to him was lit up from the torches that the first two dwarves held, casting their huge shadows across the blank wall, their shadows flickering from the torchlight.

Oagthor looked over at Ranyll, who was next to him, D'meir still tense in his arms. The dwarf spoke as loud as he could over the humming noise, which Ranyll suddenly took into account was still there, this time noticing it was louder than before when he had been in the smaller passageway.

"Our stopping point is just a half-days journey, Ranyll, through some gates far ahead. After that, we'll rest for awhile and regain our strength." The dwarf stroked the fluffed fur of the fire fox and leaned forward, scratching its head.

"Everything okay, D'meir?" The fire fox relaxed a little in Ranyll's arms when it heard Oagthor's firm voice, D'meir repositioning himself in the young man's arms.

"As good as I can be in a place like this!"

D'meir lifted himself with his legs, as a cat does when stretching, and let himself down from Ranyll's arms. The fire fox licked its lips and stretched out on the pathway, following Oagthor as he made his way back to the three dwarves waiting in the torchlight. Rathor shot his friend a glance and Oagthor nodded, Rathor motioning to the other two ahead of him to continue. They lifted their torches and moved forward on the pathway, keeping close to the wall until it began to open up ahead of them.

Soon, Ranyll could feel the darkness of the Dwarven Crag subside around him and a wall replaced the emptiness that had been there, this time the left wall beginning to fall away as he continued on. As soon as the left wall faded into darkness, a faint light could be seen ahead. It looked as though it were a door made of light, but Ranyll knew that such a thing did not exist. As the party drew closer, the two dwarves extinguished their torches, letting the light from the object ahead bathe them in its white radiance. Ranyll looked back at the dwarves who were leading up the party and saw a slight smile on their otherwise placid faces. They nodded their heads in understanding and Ranyll continued to look on as the great object approached. D'meir was in awe as well, his paws padding lightly on the ground as they stopped in front of what could only be a wall of magik.

This is where the humming had been coming from all along, Ranyll thought to himself, trying to see through the milky white sheet of magik as it radiated out at them. Ranyll's entire body was bathed in its brilliance and the young man watched as one of the dwarves approached the wall. The dwarf squinted in the light, reaching his hand out in front of him to touch the wall's surface. Once his fingers made contact with the wall, the dwarf pressed his whole hand against magik field, pushing his entire body through it slowly until he was no longer there. The other dwarf did the same as well as Oagthor's friend, Rathor. Oagthor did not look back at Ranyll before he passed through the wall and D'meir darted forward after motioning for Ranyll to follow, the fire fox's little fuzzy body disappearing through the white curtain of light as well.

Ranyll watched as the two dwarves behind him continued forward, passing through the white curtain of light as well. Ranyll stood by himself now. For the first time since the journey, Ranyll was alone. He looked around him to see if anyone or anything was looking at him and he reached out his hand to the wall as he approached it. He felt his hand grow warm as he touched the wall, passing his hand through it one time before letting himself be engulfed in it. His body grew warm and he closed his eyes as he walked through, coming out on the other side of the wall in moments, the droning sound gone completely now as he looked around at his surroundings.

Oagthor grabbed him by the arm and moved him forward a little, letting Ranyll rest and adjust his eyes to the light on the other side of the tunnel. "It's another half-day's journey to the safe hold from here. Will you be alright to continue, or do you want to stop?"

Ranyll shook his head. "Let's not stop now. I don't feel right so close to the crag."

The dwarf nodded his head in agreement. "I know what you mean. We'll try to make it there as quick as possible. All of us are tired, Ranyll. Just hold on and we'll be to a place where we can rest and resupply."

Oagthor hefted Ranyll back up off the wall, watching as D'meir passed by them both, moving lightly forward on his paw pads, his steps not even heard in the dimly lit dwarven passage ways.

The half-day went by without interruption. The party stopped twice to rest and eat, telling of the tales that got them to this present place. Ranyll just listened but was silent about his own story. The dwarves took no notice of this; either because they knew he had different reasons for being there and they didn't want to pry or they didn't care at all; which one it was, Ranyll could not tell.

Soon, they were upon the last of the passageways and more markings began showing up on the walls. And, in a few more steps, they stood in front of a great set of double doors carved out of the cavern rock. Oagthor did the honors and knocked on the thick door with his hammer, the echo reverberating throughout the entire door and around the cave, Ranyll listening behind him as the echo disappeared down the passage ways they had just come through. The great doors soon opened with the assistance of great chain pulleys on the other side and the group walked in.

They were in a courtyard, or what Ranyll would call a courtyard. It was well lit by a number of lanterns hanging from hooks on the walls of the courtyard. Oagthor approached Ranyll, taking him by the arm. He led him forward.

"This is our fortification, our last safe hold. That barrier you saw has been around even before the race of dwarves began inhabiting the caves in the mountains. We just recently learned how to use it."

Ranyll noticed that the dwarves that they came with were nowhere to be found. Neither was D'meir. Ranyll looked around and soon noticed that they were not alone. All around them, dwarves looked out at the two that passed by them. There were several small cooking fires made and dwarves crouched down by them, preparing food for their party. Ranyll could smell a stew boiling in a pot nearby. Someone even had fresh bread that they were baking somewhere within the encampment. The young man felt his stomach growl at this and he tried his best to qualm it with some water from his water skins.

At the cooking fire closest to them the party of dwarves sat, D'meir resting comfortably on a bedroll. Oagthor directed Ranyll to an empty bedroll next to D'meir and Ranyll unloaded himself of pack and sword, collapsing down on the bedroll. D'meir did not move, as he was already fast asleep and snoring slightly. The dwarves in the party were preparing a meal and they passed around a water skin, taking a long drink from it before passing it to the next.

The dwarf next to him finished a long swig from the skin and handed it to Ranyll, who took his turn, a strong, warm fluid breaking past his lips to his mouth. He took a long pull from the skin and handed it to the next dwarf, who finished the water skin off, placing it down next to him. Ranyll could feel the warm, dwarven brew take its toll on his tired body and, in moments he was asleep, his aching body subsiding into a deep sleep. He could not hear the roar of the dwarves' laughter or smell the fine meal they had made.

Oagthor and the others continued on throughout the night and caught up on present times with his old friend, Rathor, every now and then looking over at the sleeping form of the human boy, this so-called Ranyll, *the savior* D'meir had called him earlier on. He caught the tail end of his friend's conversation and he was passed another full water skin. Taking it in his hands, he drew from its contents, feeling the dwarven brew work its own magik, loosening his aching legs, taking the cold away from his bones that he had gotten from passing the Crag. He looked over to Rathor now, who had cleaned his face at a nearby washbasin, his features more prominent than before, yet still shadowed by the firelight.

"It was the first time that I saw him afraid, believe it or not, Oagthor. It surprises me to this day that....Oagthor? Are you even listening?"

Oagthor shook his head and broke from his concentration, looking over to his old friend of so many years. He smiled at him and passed the water skin to him.

"Sorry, my friend. I was thinking about something D'meir said earlier before you and I met up in the caves." Oagthor had peeked Rathor's interest. It wasn't every day that he got to hear what a faerie creature thought. Rathor quieted the rest of his party and leaned in closer, within earshot of his old companion.

"What did the fire fox say, Oagthor? It must be pretty important stuff to get you thinking the way you just were. I haven't seen you this intense since, well....it has been a while."

Rathor closed the top on his water skin and sat it in his lap, his hands reaching for a piece of firewood to add to the fire. He grabbed a small log and tossed it into the already burning cooking fire, cinders and sparks popping up and out into the air in front of them.

Across from them, the fire fox jumped at the loud noise, its little ears plastered down on top of its head, eyes still closed, small wrinkles creasing in between its eyes. In another moment, the creature relaxed and the creases disappeared, its ears returning to their raised position. Oagthor looked into the flames and seemed to fall into them for a moment, deep in thought.

Then he looked at Rathor and, with the most intense and sincere gaze, he said, "D'meir said Ranyll is some sort of savior. He said that Ranyll is here to save us and his other faerie friends are looking for Ranyll and an angel, Gabriella, he told me her name was."

Rathor drew in his breath and leaned back into his bedroll, lying back on his elbows. He stretched out his short legs, his unshod feet gaining warmth from the fire.

"What do you think about it, Oagthor? You've known D'meir since we first met him at Drolgar. Do you think he's serious?"

Oagthor nodded his head. "I'm pretty sure about what he says. He wouldn't just up and tell stories like that, especially after what we've been through together. The only thing is…" Oagthor trailed off.

Rathor shifted a bit in his place. The brew had begun to take hold of him and his senses seemed to be tingling as they always did when he drank the brew. He looked to his friend from across the fire that kept many of their party's attention, smiling to Oagthor.

"What is it, Oagthor? Something that little fuzz ball says getting to you?"

Oagthor took a passing water skin and drained much of its contents into his mouth in one long pull, swallowing down its quenching sweetness. "D'meir said that Shilinda told him about Ranyll. Do you remember what D'meir first told us when we met him at Drolgar?" Oagthor didn't give Rathor a chance to speak. He continued. "He told us that his kind was from the continent of Dree and we refused to believe him."

One of Rathor's men spoke up. He leaned forward into the firelight, his face still dirty, his beard wet from drinking the brew that had been passed around throughout the night. "You mean to tell me that this boy, this Ranyll, is going to save us from all this that's happening? You are kidding, right?" His name was Dennil Brighttooth and he wasn't known for being the smartest dwarf around; but he was good with an axe. Rathor lifted himself back up and tucked his feet under him.

"Listen, Dennil! If Oagthor says it's true, then it's true!" Rathor nodded to Oagthor who, in turn, looked over at Dennil, who was taking another swig of brew from a water skin.

"Wait a minute, fellas. I didn't say that he was **our** savior. I don't know what D'meir means by savior. It could mean anything. I don't know what it means. All I know is that this human was still alive when I found him, which makes me think that there's more to him than what I've seen."

Oagthor left the conversation at that. He didn't know what else to say. He also didn't want to give the dwarves around him false hope or lead them to believe as he did at that moment; that Ranyll **was** the answer to his call. The boy wasn't an army, Oagthor knew that, but the boy came through fear and knowledge that he could die at any moment and still he came. That had to mean something. Oagthor had known humans all his life and few have ever impressed him as much as this boy did now.

Soon, the fire began to die down and, by the time the last ember burned away and died, the dwarven party was fast asleep.

<h1 align="center">20</h1>

Head Scribe Devver Tollins looked out onto the tranquil city streets of Goletta as he passed them by, the lolling back and forth of his plush carriage almost putting him to sleep. In no time, Devver had read through much of Gilden's secret writings and deduced that this matter could no longer go unwarranted and that he should do something immediately. If the writings were right, this boy, Ranyll, did not have much time in which to save this angelic creature from the unknown realm.

Devver almost laughed when he thought of the ridiculous ploy that an angelic creature was down among the inhabitants, for he had, to date, never seen one, and was more apt to believe in dragons or some other sort of faerie creature from the histories than messengers from the Creator. In the years that he had been a scribe, he had come to know the reality of the world around him and that, though hope and faith were two things that were very dear to others, were not very dear to him.

He looked now over to the scribe he had brought with him, Scribe Henzell, a young man of only fourteen or so summers, his eagerness to go out on his first real chronicling expedition coming out in his facial expressions. The boy had a round face, slightly plump, though the fullness would probably wear away once manhood approached, which was only a summer or so away. The auburn hair that he had come to the guild with had been shorn from his head; only a small clump of hair remained, a nest of wavy locks perched atop his youthful head.

Devver had, over the years, decided to shave his head entirely, a thick guild hood covering his aging features, shadowing his face completely. He reached out of the carriage and rung the bell just outside his door. The carriage stopped and the driver leaned over the edge in response.

"Yes, Master Tollins? Is there something wrong?" The coachman almost lost his cap but pushed it further down on his head, waiting for Head Scribe Tollins to respond in his regular, feverish jargon.

"I should say so, Jennings! We have yet to get our supplies that we need for our journey. I have arranged for us to meet with Minsel, the shopkeeper not far from the square. Let us away to his locale and do not dally! We are in a hurry!" Coachman Jennings tipped his cap in response and, with a crack of the reins, the three-horse carriage was moving again, off to shopkeeper Minsels, only a few buildings from the library.

In no time at all, Coachman Jennings had received and strapped the proper supplies onto the roof of the carriage and, taking a last look at the knots he had made, hopped back onto the front and snapped the reins again, the horse's hooves the only noise in the empty streets of Goletta. The lanterns had been all but burnt out for the night and Jennings had lit one and hooked it just ahead of him on a lengthy piece of metal, the streets ahead slowly coming into view piece by piece, cobble by cobble. It was slow moving within the city, but Coachman Jennings knew the ways well and, once out into the open dirt roads, could make ample time to their appointed destination.

It had been years since Head Scribe Tollins had traveled. He had, in fact, even cancelled his yearly trips to the Master Library, sending another to deliver the historical copies of the tomes they had written every season, the middle-aged man wrinkling his nose at traveling, for he had known much of it and wanted little to nothing to do with it now.

Even carrying weapons, like the two resting in his lap, had become cumbersome and pointless. He had grown accustomed to the library and its calming books, the safe walls around him, keeping him from the cruel world that seemed to eat up the poor, helpless and wretched of the town's people. He, at one time, had been one of those, poor, helpless, wretched beings and knew what it felt like to be lost and wandering most of one's life. Devver looked over at Scribe Henzell now, remembering when he had been that young, when that spark had glimmered in his eyes just as it did in Henzells now.

It had all been so easy, so simple back then. There was no war, no pain, no loss to learn of and life seemed to take you by the hand and show you the world and what it could be for you.

Now, Devver thought, *life seems to grab me by my aching wrists, pulling me deeper and deeper into old age, trying to find the weaknesses in my body and expose them, one by one.*

It had been years since he had thought about his family and his pain hidden deep inside, but he knew that those were the things that his drive used as a reason to propel him to where he was today. He let his thoughts wander until he noticed the trees outside the carriage cast their lengthy shadows across the dirt road they traveled. He turned his attention to Scribe Henzell.

"Scribe Henzell, I have something for you." He withdrew the soft cloth that covered the two short swords lying across his lap, both of them complete with leather scabbards and matching belts. The young scribe's eyes grew wide and it looked as though he could hardly contain his excitement. Devver picked up one of the swords and unsheathed it.

"This is a brutal weapon. It is called a Golettan short sword. The merchants had supplied our guild with many of them in case there was an attack on the town and we had to defend ourselves. Usually, a scribe, even when going on an expedition, is not allowed to carry a weapon because it demeans his whole purpose as a scribe. There is a message to deliver or details to attain and a weapon deters one from being a complete person. The reason I say this to you now is because this weapon is not to be spoken of to anyone back at the library."

"We are on an expedition to get any information on the towns that we can get. You have heard the scenario many times and I feel that I do not need to tell it again. All that I have told you thus far has been a lie until now. What I am about to tell you now is the truth and cannot go outside of this carriage, is that understood, Scribe?"

Scribe Henzell nodded his nearly bald head, his gaze still transfixed on the short sword sitting on Devver's lap.

The young scribe looked up at Head Scribe Tollins. "I knew that there was something wrong in the look that you gave the others and how quiet you were when you spoke with me about taking me as your novice. I would just like to say that I am honored and I agree to help in any way possible to further this expedition and see that it gets done, whatever it may be."

The years of knowledge did not play on the young man's face as it did in his speech. He was wiser, wiser than most his age, and that is why Devver had chosen him. His dedication to the Order of Scribes was a strong one at that and Devver knew that a secret told to any scribe was a safe secret indeed. It was not every day that a scribe gets to be part of scandal and adventure. Most of the time, they just write about others portraying that role. It was a different experience for young Scribe Henzell, indeed.

Devver continued. "Thank you for being so understanding during these trying times, Scribe Henzell. I shall continue on with my story, so that you may see the urgency of this task and why we have left everything we know and have known to set out and do what we do now."

Head Scribe Tollins relayed the better part of the story of the fallen angel and her young hero Ranyll to the younger scribe, Scribe Henzell's eyes wide with interest, his hands in his lap, the hood from his robes pulled over his head to keep the night wind from getting to him completely. Head Scribe

Tollins did the same, sitting across from the youth, his story, detail after detail, pouring out until he came to their appointed tasks.

"I feel that, unless Ranyll is assisted by others in this task, he will fail, and that will be the end of creation as we know it. I don't mean to put a damper on things, Scribe Henzell, but I believe that Scribe Felves is writing what is transpiring before us on Kariyl and all of Ar Solon. I have not had the chance to look at his other tomes, but I believe they are just the same, except they cannot be stopped because they are finished."

With that said Devver resheathed the short sword in his lap and handed it to Scribe Henzell. The scribe took it up in his hands and ran his fingers over the leather scabbard, loosening the belt to fit the scabbard at his waist.

He looked back to Head Scribe Tollins. "Thank you, Master Tollins. I have never been given such a grand gift before."

Devver waved away the compliment. "Young man, the sword is not a gift for giving. It is something that shall keep you alive in time of absolute peril, which we are about to embark upon traveling this very road. And, please, Scribe Henzell, call me Devver. If we are to be on this journey together, I would prefer it if we are friends, not teacher and student as we have been up until this point." Devver extended his hand to Scribe Henzell, who took it, shaking it lightly.

"Fine, Master Tol… I mean Devver. That is fine. My name is Laram." Laram sat back down in his plush seat and admired the sword a little longer as they traveled, watching also as Devver unsheathed his sword and began telling about a book that he had read, not too long ago, about swordplay and the rules that it involved. Many questions were asked by Laram, who knew much of the history of the weapon, but not of its use. After a few brief but effective examples by Devver, Laram felt better qualified to wield the Golletan blade without dishonoring it.

Much of the remainder of the night passed this way; a brief conversation about Devver's other journeys as a young scribe years ago, a few stories about the tomes and other things that he had read prior that might relate to the situation they were about to be entering into, several other things clarified before the conversation died down and there was a quiet that hung inside the carriage until they were into the thick of the forest, no shadows breaking across the road now. The moon that had given light to most of the journey outside of Goletta had suddenly been extinguished, the only light being the swinging hooded lantern outside the carriage. Devver decided that they should take a brief nap while they had the chance, his hand almost blindly finding the shades to the carriage windows and pulling the strings. Soon, both Devver and Laram were rocked asleep by the swaying of the carriage and felt the pressures of today's events slowly melt away.

A sudden stop woke Devver from his sleep, his eyes blinking several times before he realized he was still in the dark. Once his eyes became adjusted, he reached for the shade pull string and lifted up the shade, sticking his head out.

"What has happened, Jennings? Why has the carriage stopped?" The coachman's head appeared over the side of the carriage, his hat slipping from his head this time, dropping to the ground below before he could swipe it out of the air.

"I'm sorry, Master Tollins, but I think we have a situation here. It seems someone left their cart in the middle of the road." Coachman Jennings slipped down from his perch atop the carriage and retrieved his hat, dusting it off before slapping it on his messed up pile of hair. Devver noticed Laram begin to stir and his eyes opened, looking over to Devver questioningly. Devver replied back to Jennings.

"Well, can you not just move it from the road and let it be at that?" Devver stretched the sleepiness from his tired muscles and yawned.

Laram did the same and leaned forward. "What is it, Devver?"

Devver lifted himself up from his seat, straightening his robes. He had to duck for a moment because of the limited standing room in the carriage, and then he opened the carriage door and stepped out.

"It seems there is a wagon of some kind blocking our path onward. It won't be but a moment. I will assist Jennings and then we will be on our way." Devver grabbed the lantern inside the carriage and opened the glass casing around it, handing it to Jennings to light from his own. Jennings walked to the front of the carriage and climbed up, lighting the second lantern for Devver.

"Can I come along and help, Devver?"

Devver shook his head. "No, I don't think we all need to be dawdling with this all evening. Besides, it's far too cold for one of your age to be out in this. If you caught cold, I would blame myself for it. I'll be right back, Laram."

Devver disappeared from view and Laram could feel the carriage rock to one side when Jennings stepped off from his place up front.

Devver and Jennings approached the wagon with both lanterns, lighting up the rear of the cart so they could see if anyone was hurt or needed assistance.

Devver called out.

"Hello! Is anyone there? Do you need assistance with your wagon? We are just trying to pass through and we saw that you had stalled."

There was no response. They both approached closer and soon saw the back wheels of the wagon and noticed that the right wheel was tangled up in something. Upon closer inspection, they noticed that a little sapling had gotten caught between the right wheel and the wagon, the small limbs wrapping up into the spokes of the wheel itself. Jennings freed the wheel easily and urged himself to the front of the wagon to push the wagon back when he stopped in mid-stride.

He turned to Devver, who moved up next to him, his eyes catching a glimpse of what had stopped the wagon. The two horses that had been pulling the cart were lying on the ground, harnessed to the wagon still by only a few straps of leather and some metal bolts and joints. Jennings motioned to the marks on the ground by the horse's feet. They were two great mares, or had been during their life, and were torn to pieces by something, not much of them left with the exception of their skeletal frames and a mess of bloody footprints left by several somethings. The footprints looked like that of an animal, yet there were so many and the tracks were smeared across the ground and led into the woods.

"They were trying to get away but were caught up by the wagon. Look at the marks they made trying to escape. Something got ahold of them, alright."

Devver pulled out his short sword, looking around the tree line for any signs of movement. Jennings looked down at the sword and back up to the Head Scribe, who had never brandished a weapon until now.

"What is it, Master Tollins?" A look of fear had crossed the Head Scribe's face and Jennings began to feel a little on edge. Devver moved closer to the horses' remains and cut the harnesses from their torn bodies, freeing the wagon altogether. He sheathed his sword and sat the lantern down on the ground.

"Say nothing of this to Scribe Henzell. He does not need to know. Come help me with the wagon. We must quicken our pace now. Something is awry."

Jennings nodded his head and decided not to question Master Tollins decision, placing his lantern on the ground as well to help free the wagon completely from the sapling that had ensnared the horses, having kept them from any attempt at escape. They moved the wagon into the brush and went back to their lanterns, walking briskly to the carriage, Devver hopping into the back while Jennings slapped the reins and continued on. Laram, though looking concerned, smiled at Devver as the older man sat down in front of him.

"So I take it everything is fine now, Devver?" The youth looked out at him underneath his hooded robe.

Devver nodded his head and bit his lip, looking across at the innocent youth, his stern visage turning suddenly to the look a father might have when realizing his son will be hurt while in the world.

"Everything's fine now. Let us get back to sleep. We have a few more hours before sunrise, and then we'll be at a village we can stop at for the morning and water the horses." Devver tried to hide his nervousness by burying himself back into his hood, motioning for Laram to do the same.

Laram leaned back into his cowl as well, closing his eyes, drifting back to sleep in no time, Devver silently watching the young man as he slept.

Devver listened to the carriage as it passed the wagon and the fallen horses, continuing on through the forest, though Devver was fearful of finding ahead what had massacred those horses waiting to feed on them next. Devver would use the last breath in his body to stop that from happening.

21

Ermoor Tiven had been up all day and could feel his muscles ache as he walked further on with his checkpoint guard Rynen Griff. He had bandaged up the left side of his face and, though Kalir fought him on it, decided to continue on with his guard duties, still intent on finding one of those daemons to take his aggression out on. Since earlier that morning, Kalir had tasked additional areas of the Tirapoor Channel to his qualified guards as well as other volunteers from the checkpoint station. Some were hunters in a traveling party with their families; others were vendors and shopkeepers from the small towns that dotted the Channel, just on their way to drop off another shipment of supplies; while others were mere patrons that had heard the call of duty and were set out with what weapons they had and a lantern, scouring the channel side for anything out of the ordinary.

Since mid-morning, none had come across anything that could be considered out of the ordinary or even had a trace of the daemons that had attacked the checkpoint further north. Ermoor hefted his sword back into its sheath, leaning against a tree as he straightened his boots, a newer pair that he had to change into after his dealings with the daemons in the channel.

Rynen tried his best to smile at his friend yet, every time he looked at him, he could see the slight traces of the claw marks beginning underneath the bandages over his friend's left eye, making Rynen himself wince just thinking about it.

"Listen, Ermoor. We've swept this area three times now. Everyone else is back at the checkpoint fires at the Channel. They'll be looking for us soon if we don't check in. We can try again in the morning. I'm sure we'll find something when it's lighter." But Ermoor wouldn't hear of it. His bottom lip was trapped underneath his teeth, his eyes alight with a raging fire inside that Rynen had never seen before. Sure, he had seen Ermoor angry before, but nothing like this.

"I don't care about the others at the checkpoint! I'm going to find those daemons, and I'm going to find them tonight! Kalir said they came from the north, so I say we head further north." Rynen didn't disagree with him, for he knew that it was no use. He had told the others of his party to keep an eye out for them both and he would take care of the wounded Ermoor himself, though the wounds on the inside seemed far more dangerous than the ones everyone had seen on the outside.

After a moment of rest, they continued on, Ermoor in the lead, holding out the lantern to watch as the shapes appeared before him; trees, hedges, a small trail in front of them that disappeared past some brush. They had followed this trail several times before; it was the trail that took them to Telgin. The checkpoint guards made it a habit of going there when they had the chance because it was a little more occupied than the smaller towns spread out across the Tirapoor Channel.

In fact, Ermoor thought, *that's where I bought these boots. It was strange though,* Ermoor continued, *because Kalir never went there. We all even knew he had family living there, but he never went. I wonder why that was?*

Ermoor knew that Kalir kept to himself and managed his own affairs without anyone ever knowing about them, yet he also knew that everyone, at some time, went home to their families for their stretch of vacation once they were finished protecting the checkpoint and the next rotation came in. However, Kalir never went to see his sister and nephews.

Ermoor was a little bit calmer as he walked ahead, the channel's distant rippling waters soon melting away, replaced by the soft scuffling of leaves from the wind. It was a cool night; the sun had fallen away early on and left the crescent moon hanging upon the skyline, weary yet content with its surrounding stars placed here and there across the dazzling blue sky. His eye still ached, but the salve that Kalir had put on it numbed most of the pain that he had felt when he was first brought into Kalir's cabin. He shifted the lantern from his left hand to his right and looked back at Rynen.

"Hey, Rynen. Sorry about the acting out earlier. But I'm not sorry for dragging you out here like this. It's just that nothing makes sense unless I have a sword in my hand. And, right then, at the Channel, I felt like I knew what I wanted to do with my life. I don't expect you to understand because you've got everything already planned out, but..."

Rynen interrupted him. "I understand more than you know. Just because my father has decided for me to become a checkpoint guard doesn't mean that's what I want to do, Ermoor."

Rynen stopped walking and turned to face Ermoor, who stopped in turn as well. "And I was out there on the Channel with you, Ermoor. You **are** a fighter. You were made to be. You don't have to have your life planned out for you to realize that. This is what you were made for." Ermoor smiled at his friend and patted him on the shoulder, turning both of them back around.

"Thank you for being my friend, Rynen. And thank you for dealing with me even though I can be a menace sometimes."

"Sometimes, are you kidding me; all the time. You snore, you know!"

Rynen had become accustomed to Ermoor's eating and sleeping habits since having to share the same room once their checkpoint rotation began.

Ermoor started them back on their way to the Channel. They had gone far beyond their patrol area and could not see the checkpoint fires near the channel itself. It looked to be a long walk back and Ermoor was glad now that he had decided to head back because he could feel his energy waning as they continued on. The toll his body had taken at the Channel this morning had drained him of nearly everything except his rage, and that was the only thing that kept him going to get back to safety before the night covered in about them and kept them until morning.

"Come on. We need to get back before they send a rescue team after us again. I hope they still have some stew left in the pot because I'm starving."

They continued back on the path and were about to break onto the path connecting to the Channel when Rynen caught something out of the corner of his eye. He stopped short and Ermoor continued only for a moment, soon turning to watch as his friend scanned the eastern side of the forest.

"What is it, Rynen?"

Rynen stood motionless for a moment and then drew his sword slowly out of its sheath. "I saw something move out there in the woods."

Ermoor dismissed the idea completely. "Come on, Rynen. It was probably an animal or something. You probably scared it away by now."

But Rynen shook his head. "Is there any animal around here that stands on two legs?"

Ermoor reached for his sword as well.

*   *   *

The Happy Traveler had closed early for the night and, as the last few stragglers left out of the front doors, several more checkpoint guards came in, Dir'grar closing and bolting the door behind them. The huge man nodded his head to them as they moved past him, his eyes on the two tables that had been placed together in the middle of the tavern. He and his friend Kalir had spent the last few hours bringing a proper plan together to keep any daemons from the lands and, as the sun broke across the Tirapoor Channel and began to set, Kalir had all of his checkpoint guards called and, by nightfall, every one of them had come, with the exception of the few that had been sent off to assist in guarding the northern checkpoint that had been attacked earlier that day.

That totaled the checkpoint guards numbers to almost forty, which wasn't much when compared with an army of daemons, if that's what they were faced with, Kalir thought to himself. *Well, that would have to do for now.*

Kalir pointed now to the map he had on the table. "**This** is where I think they are coming from. From the reports of the town east of here and the reports we've received from the messengers at the northern checkpoints, they are moving south, apparently scouring this whole area. We must do the same. Now, we already have the checkpoint guards on duty covering the surrounding areas, but tomorrow we need to be even more thorough." Kalir was hesitant to continue but knew that it had to be said and every one had to know what they were up against.

"Now, for some of you, you already know what we are up against, but for others, let me just say this: we fight something that is not a race from this world. These creatures are bred from darkness and they live in darkness. If you see them, you must kill them immediately or you will be killed. Because, when you see one daemon, be prepared for a second and a third. They fight in packs, like animals, but they are worse than any animal you could imagine. But gentlemen, they can be killed; killed like anything else."

The crowd of guards began to move from their place a bit, a little uneasy from what they had just heard. Some of them finished their drinks while others took a seat around the table.

One guard spoke up. "So, what you're saying is that there is some kind of army of creatures running down through the channel, maiming and killing at random?"

Kalir countered. "They are not just creatures. They are **daemons**!" A silent hush fell over the guards.

The same guard stopped for a moment, looked around the room, and continued with his questions.

"How are we supposed to fight against daemons? They are said to have no soul and they have no remorse in their killings."

Kalir slipped his sword free of its sheath and slammed the blade down into the map and the table under it as well. The tip of the blade was buried deep.

"These daemons can be killed and I have killed many of them myself. This world, the world you live in, has secrets and stories that many of you have never heard and would cower in your mother's arms if you heard any of them. I have brought you all here today to face this evil because that is what you have taken an oath to do. All of you were deemed worthy to wear the garb of the checkpoint guards because you knew what responsibility was and how to handle it."

Kalir continued.

"Show me now how you handle yourselves in the face of adversity! Show me what you have been holding back for so long since the human kingdoms have fallen and there is no more knighthood of old! This world is being pulled apart and we have been tasked to hold it together. Now, I have already sent messengers to the other towns for support and we are to meet with many of them in the morning. Am I to go alone? Now, you all know the plan, know what you fight; make your decision." Kalir freed his sword from the table and the others made an opening for him, Kalir and his friend Dir'grar passing through and out of the tavern.

The cool night air caught Kalir off guard and he shivered, tightening his vest with a couple of loose strings, pulling his cloak over his shoulders as well.

"What of the checkpoint guards that I have scouting, Dir'grar? Any news?" Kalir resheathed his sword and looked over at the big man, who was gathering several small satchels of supplies up onto his shoulders. He turned and smiled at his friend.

"Nothing so far, Kalir. Not one patrol has found anything out of the ordinary."

"They've all checked in by now, Dir'grar, right? They were supposed to check in by nightfall and wait for my command to do anything else."

"All but Ermoor and Rynen have checked in, Kalir." The smaller man almost leapt up in place he was so furious. He knew he shouldn't have let Ermoor go back out so soon.

"I told them to come right back! I told them to! Let's go. Get others assembled and tell them to bring the barrels." Both moved from the front of The Happy Traveler and traveled along the Channel, not paying attention to the dozens that filed out and followed behind them.

Apparently, the speech had worked, Kalir concluded, his lean form bounding down towards the Channel and the checkpoint fires on the eastern shore.

The guards on the shore stood up when they saw Kalir approach, their leader passing them by, his hands sweating furiously, his throat dry and parched. Suddenly, he could feel the chill in the air and it didn't seem to be from the cold at all, but from what he felt deep down in his gut. He knew something was wrong. Kalir leapt into a transport boat and Dir'grar climbed in as well. All of the checkpoint guards were assembled and looked at their leader as though he were in another world of his own. He smiled back at them.

"We have a task to finish before we start our journey. We must find two of our crew that may be lost. Follow me."

*   *   *

Rynen climbed through the bushes, moving off the trail from where they had started their search. The checkpoint fires still could not be seen and Rynen urged Ermoor to follow, needing the additional light to see clearly. He had stepped into a thick of briars at the moment and was trying to get out without hurting himself.

"Ermoor, would you help me here? I seem to be stuck. I think it's my cloak. I think it's stuck on this briar patch behind me." Ermoor began to chuckle a little to himself and moved off the path to find his friend out in the woods. He lifted his lantern out ahead of him and, almost immediately, he had found his friend stuck in a thick patch of thorns. He lifted his sword to strike when he stopped, his mouth dropping open in awe. Rynen took his friend's reaction as horseplay and he shook his fist at Ermoor.

"Come on, Ermoor, quit playing around! These patches of thorns are tearing me apart." Ermoor pointed out in front of him to a spot not far from the briars and the complaints of his friend in need. Rynen stopped his squirming and looked ahead.

Rynen could hear his friend's voice die to a soft whisper.

"I see what you are talking about. It's over there. I think it saw us, too. Here, let me help and then we'll go see what it is." Ermoor gently brushed his blade across the thorns and moved them away from Rynen's path, holding them down with his foot until his friend had cleared himself of the accursed thorns and was away from it before letting them go again.

Ermoor stepped around them, using the lantern to follow an animal trail nearby, slightly covered by the fallen leaves from the trees around them. Rynen and Ermoor stood side by side now, both looking at the shadow not far from them move slightly and regain its cover back in the brush.

"Rynen, I'll go to the left, you go to the right. When I say now, we rush both sides and trap it in." Rynen and Ermoor had been on several hunting expeditions and knew the best ways to trap an animal. But they weren't so sure that this was an animal. After all, they had seen it on two legs moments before.

Ermoor continued forward and Rynen moved around to the right, making sure as to keep a constant visual on the thing that was between them. In no time, Ermoor was on the other side of it and Rynen was ready as well. Ermoor gripped his sword tightly and moved in.

"Now!"

No sooner had Ermoor leapt forward when a figure stood from out of the brush, milky white skin the color of the moon's evening rays and long, streaming blond hair that covered much of her bare body, her elbows and knees covered in dirt. The young girl wore a simple rag that covered only her torso, the garment in near tatters. She held up her hands in surrender, trying to cover her exposed self as best she could.

What the two thought was a creature was just a young girl, not quite into adulthood yet. She was probably a season or so younger than the two before her, yet she held them with rapt attention, Ermoor and Rynen in awe at seeing such a beauty at such an hour. Rynen tried to speak but nothing came out, trying his best to clear his throat to speak. This only frightened the girl further.

The voice that piped out of her was tinged with fear.

"Please, help me! I don't know where I am and I can't find a way out of the forest!"

Ermoor gathered what he had left of his courage, for she had nearly scared him to death, and pulled off his cloak to give to her covering from the cold night air. Ermoor sheathed his sword and lowered his lantern, ushering for Rynen to do the same. Rynen complied and sheathed his sword as well, coming up next to the young girl, helping to drape the cloak completely around the girl's shoulders and tied it so it would hold in place.

Rynen tried his best to console her but once he saw the tearstains on her cheeks, it was hard for him to keep from tearing up himself.

"It's alright, milady. Everything's going to be okay, you'll see. What brought you out here so far in the woods by yourself anyway?"

The girl's gaze fell on Rynen, her eyes still glazed over from crying, her face littered with small cuts and bruises from the foliage.

"I'm not alone. I was looking for my sister. She's lost, too. And she's only five years old."

Ermoor could feel the sense of uneasiness come over him as he heard her words. Something was definitely awry in these woods. He didn't know how this young lady got to be out in such a state, let alone her younger sister, too. Ermoor looked about for any signs of life, but there seemed to be nothing out there but the three of them at the moment. He knew that during desperate hours such as this, and with those daemons running around out in the open, it was best for them to find the young girl's sister and quickly make for the safety of the channel where there were plenty of guards to protect them.

However, Rynen seemed confused.

"What do we do, Ermoor?" Ermoor tried to comfort the young girl as well, looking back to Rynen, his gaze more determined than before, as if he had gained new energy from some place unknown.

"You take this girl to the checkpoint and I'll find her little sister," Ermoor looked to the young girl, who was shaking in Rynen's arms, "What's her name, miss?" The young girl was huddled far into the cloak now and she had dried her tears. When she heard that she was to be taken from the forest and not able to look for her sister she began to weep.

"Sir Ermoor, my little sister, Allanna is her name; she is very quiet. She won't come to anyone but me. She will think you a stranger and will run and that will frighten her even more."

Rynen nodded his head in agreement, looking back to Ermoor for guidance. Ermoor was trying his best, yet he did not want to stay in the woods, especially since the threat of daemons had become so apparent with the attack this morning. And, with the oncoming night, he knew this would be the most probable time they would come about to hunt. Of course, he had no idea what they truly were other than beasts, and he drew only from the experience he had this morning with the few that had attacked the checkpoint guards. He was resolute this time in his decision.

"I apologize for thinking of leaving the poor child out here alone like that miss, but I was just looking out for your safety as well. How about all three of us look around for her and see if we can find her? For only a short while, though; we will have to be going because there will be others looking for us as well."

The young girl nodded her head and pulled the hood of the cloak up over her head for warmth. Soon, there was a glimmer of a smile on her face. She seemed more comfortable with them.

"It will not take long. I'm sure Allanna is around here somewhere." She glided ahead with Rynen at her side and Ermoor leading the way. The three soon passed the checkpoint guards stopping point and then moved further past that, coming onto a nearby wagon trail that was much wider than what they had been traveling on. The young girl seemed much more relaxed than she had been when they first encountered her.

It must've been the thought of being alone that frightened her, Rynen thought, watching as they encountered a small rise in the road up ahead that leaned eastward and south. Ermoor was the first to climb up over the rise and he stopped in his tracks when he caught a glimpse of something ahead in his lantern light. It was a small wagon. And it was missing a wheel on one side.

"Is this where you came from, miss," Ermoor asked the young girl with them, watching as her eyes lit up with what could only be classified as joy.

She held the cloak tightly across her chest and watched as they continued forward, the lantern light bringing other details into view. Ermoor stopped again and grew ill immediately, a small child on the road ahead of them, just underneath the cart. Ermoor knew that the child had to be Allanna, and he knew that Allanna was already dead; her eyes staring back at them blankly in the lantern light. Ermoor stopped the young girl and Rynen and began looking around; keeping his sword out to guard against anything unexpected that may jump out at him.

The young girl suddenly jumped up and down excitely once she saw the still form under the wagon, both guards stepping aside, watching as the girl chanted in a shrill-pitched voice.

"Allanna, Allanna, Allanna!" Then the girl stopped jumping up and down. Her eyes were wide and staring, both guards following her intense gaze to the still form of her sister near the wagon. From underneath the cart, several sets of black, sinewy arms reached out for the lifeless form of the child, dragging her underneath into the darkness, the shadow form the cart concealing what transpired underneath.

Ermoor and Rynen pressed the girl back behind them but she pushed forward and raced to her sister's side. Ermoor, knowing it was too late for her sister, reached for her to pull her back and caught ahold of the cloak she wore, ripping it from her naked body.

"Young miss, don't go any closer! Those are daemons that have taken Allanna." She ignored Ermoor's protests and raced forward to the wagon. When she spoke again, it was with a voice like none the two checkpoint guards had ever heard.

It seemed made from the voices of thousands of souls crying out at once. "Silly fools! Allanna is not the name of my sister. Allanna is, in the daemon tongue, what we call **death**."

And, with that spoken, the smooth, silky shape of the young woman broke apart in front of them. What once was beautiful and streaming became a horrid piecemeal of daemons standing atop one another, one by one breaking the pearly white flesh into sharp edges of coal darkness. The arms and legs of the marble-skinned beauty soon became a writhing black daemon and the torso became three huddled together as well, dropping off the legs as they became several more daemons, the daemons intent on watching the horror as it flashed in their victim's eyes.

Both Ermoor and Rynen wanted to close their eyes and never see the lovely image shatter into so much hatred and disgust, yet they were afraid that the world around them would dissipate if they gave it a chance to. And, from all shadows around the old wagon, daemons spread forth, maws a bloody red from feasting on the small child.

It was a trap! Ermoor lifted his lantern as high as he could to see the breadth and width of the daemon army that had led them knee deep into a trap, yet his light did not touch that far. From the edge of his lantern light and beyond the daemons seemed to reach, the two guards apparently walking into a nest of them, the daemons eagerly waiting for their next victims.

Ermoor could feel the pain in his eye surge to life as his good eye found each daemon that smiled menacingly at him. He pointed to each of them with the tip of his sword.

"Each and every one of you will taste this blade before the night is through! Come and see me honor my promise, daemon seeds!"

The daemons did not hiss at him or charge as he expected them to do. Instead, Ermoor noticed, they crowded around the two of them in a semi-circle, waiting for the human's next move.

Rynen lifted his sword up at the daemons in front of him, though he didn't see the point anymore, noting his count had already surpassed the thirties, knowing that he couldn't take that many just with him and Ermoor present. He wished now that he had pulled Ermoor back with him when he had wanted to go. The presence of the daemons made a chill run up his spine and back down into his stomach, Rynen almost getting ill from having seen the small child being taken by the daemons. He had seen the daemons up close this morning, but the night did things to them, horrible things, and it seemed that they were in their own environment; it was Ermoor and Rynen who were at the disadvantage this time. And, indeed, they were; both of them slowly began to retreat back as far as they were allowed to go, watching as the daemons did not move from their positions near the wagon.

Why aren't they attacking us, Ermoor questioned to himself, holding his weapon between himself and the daemons in front of him, the lantern light slowly sinking back away from the wagon and the daemons perched around it. Ermoor looked over at Rynen and he seemed to have the same questioning look on his face as young Ermoor did at the moment.

"Do they know something that we don't?" In an instant, one of them from the pack leapt, trying for Ermoor's bad left side due to his injury. Rynen yelled out and Ermoor struck the creature down with a quick swipe, finishing it off with a strike across the head as it lay on the ground. The other daemons grew weary, yet they did not waver.

Instead, their maws opened and they let out little hisses, their small claws beginning to click wildly, almost in unison. Ermoor leaned closer to Rynen and spoke.

"Let's go…. now!"

"Sounds good to me!" Both turned and began to move away from the wagon when they saw that, behind them as well, was blocked with fragments of daemons scattered throughout the woods, their small, slithery forms moving away from the light as it bounced across the naked trunks of the trees, scattering the red-eyed creatures throughout the forest even further. A daemon from the wagon slipped from its hiding place and moved across the ground near them. Rynen held his sword out at the daemon, trying to stay within the firelight to keep safe. He knew that once he stepped out of the lantern light it was over.

The lantern light, that's it. If it was a fight they wanted, then it was a fight they are going to get, Rynen decided, clenching his teeth tightly together, determination setting in to hold him steady for the oncoming wave of daemons. Before the daemon had a chance to pounce on its intended victim, Rynen ripped the lantern free from Ermoor's hand, slamming it into the daemon in front of him. The oil cylinder shattered against the daemon and oil splashed out everywhere around them, the daemon lighting up in flames, a sudden panic startling the daemons around them.

The group of them seemed to waver in their decision. The ground around the two checkpoint guards lit up as well and the daemon squealed and hissed its disapproval, the blaze burning the shadow from its body, an empty sizzling carcass smoking on the ground near them.

Rynen pulled out the dagger from his boot and launched it into the pile of daemons behind him, knocking one to the ground. As he did this, Ermoor took this as a signal and swung out into the crowd of daemons, delivering a fatal blow to the nearest to him with one wide arc, sending another flailing back into its own, a bloody jumble of limbs thrashing about.

The daemons went into a fury. They half expected the two humans to cower before the mass of daemons surrounding them, yet the humans continued on with a ferocity that was almost maddening. Rynen finished off the one he had dropped with his dagger, retrieving his blade from its lifeless body, keeping the daemons that were coming at him at bay with both blades. Ermoor was soon at his back, both of them circling together, watching as the daemons closed in on them.

They watched as another surge of daemons came at them, this time more than before. With the fire between them and the section of daemons at the wagon, it made it easier to track the other section of daemons. The blazing fire from the lantern's light was still going, yet the intensity had burnt itself down once the daemon had burnt to cinders, giving them only a little light to work with within the wooded darkness.

For every daemon they struck down, another would take its place in the ranks from the other side, giving them no chance of escape. They had made their own trap; they knew this, yet they had decided that they were going to take down as many of these daemons as they could before they fell under those clicking claws.

"This is it, Ermoor! I enjoyed working with you." Rynen was almost in tears, jabbing back and forth into the oncoming daemon mass, taking out one with his sword while holding back another with his dagger.

Ermoor was beginning to tire quickly. He already noticed his side of the ranks of daemons had closed in on him quicker than Rynen's. There was nothing further that he could do about it. He looked to Rynen for help.

"I, too, enjoyed fighting next to you. If I were given a choice who to die next to in battle, it would be you, my friend. I am losing my strength." Ermoor felt his arm drop suddenly to his side and the daemons around him saw this. They lunged. Rynen was there to meet them. Giving up his own position, he pressed in front of Ermoor, tossing his dagger into the fray, his sword holding back two daemons as he reached out for his friend's sword.

"Get behind me, Ermoor!" Ermoor held out his blade to Rynen who took it, pressing himself in between the daemons and his friend, watching as the last of the burning lantern light faded into the darkness. All he could see was the red slits now in the moonlight, yet the wild clicking of their claws increased. He could barely make out the shifting shadows around him, though he could still see Ermoor's form behind him, trying his best to keep close yet stay out of Rynen's wide arcing movements he made with both swords.

Rynen could feel the sword in his right arm slip in his hand and he knew that the battle was taking toll on his sword arm. His left arm still had some swing left in it, but his right was beginning to give just as Ermoor's had. Rynen jabbed with his left into the writhing mass of shadows in front of him and swung widely with his right, trying to clear a path in which to move. Now that the fire had died down behind them, the daemons were forming a circle around the two, which was impossible for Rynen to defend against on his own.

From a distance, Ermoor could see the daemons making progress; he could feel the icy cold stares of the creatures as their eyes bored through him into his flesh. He knew that the two of them were going to fall, he could sense it in each move he took, as though it were his last. In the moments he had given in to the weakness of his body, he had time to regain his strength a bit and, if he was to fall at this moment, he wanted a sword in his hand. He closed in on Rynen, who nearly jumped at Ermoor's presence next to him, honed in as he was on the daemons that were almost upon them.

Ermoor reached for his sword in Rynen's hand, ready to continue on as he had. Rynen took a wild swipe out at the daemon's to keep them back and then released the sword to his friend, who turned around just in time to thrust his sword into a rushing daemon. Ermoor yelled out to Rynen, the last of his strength ebbing away quickly.

"We have once chance to do this. When I turn next to you, I want you to give them everything that you've got and rush them. We'll try and break out of this circle they've managed to trap us in. Ready?" Rynen pumped his legs to make sure they could still be used, for he had stood in one place for so long he didn't know if he could surge forward without falling. He nodded to his friend who seemed on the verge of collapsing at that very moment. Ermoor nodded and took a wide arc behind them, turning to stand next to Rynen.

"Go!" Both Ermoor and Rynen dove into the oncoming daemon ranks, a desperate battle cry echoing from their throats, slamming into the second rank with full force. They jabbed their swords into the masses of shadows before them and felt the cold stabs of pain as the daemons finally found the weakness in their defenses and began to tear at them.

Rynen surged forward and ripped through the shadowy forms, watching as Ermoor fell amid the mass of forms around them. Fear suddenly ran through Rynen's veins, his heart about to burst with fear; fear of being alone as well as fear that his friend had fallen and would not surface from the darkness again.

He made his way back to where Ermoor had fallen when he suddenly saw a light ahead of him. Kalir and the others had found him, a long line of torches scattered across the forest just a dozen footsteps or so away. He saw Kalir draw his bow back and release. A flaming arrow whizzed past Rynen and struck an airborne daemon, knocking it into the swarm of daemons that rushed forward to meet Rynen and his fallen companion.

Rynen began swinging wildly with a renewed strength, with hope that he could be saved, cutting a swath to Ermoor the best he could. Another flaming arrow launched into the daemons; another, then another, the entire forest around him soon lit by burning arrows around him. Rynen thrust one hand out at Ermoor, grabbing his tunic, trying his best to drag him up by his clothes. He felt Ermoor writhe in his hands and he tried his best to stand, his body almost collapsing as he put his hands out to brace himself on Rynen.

Dir'grar approached now, shooting a bolt into a daemon nearby, dropping the crossbow to his side as he took a swipe with the broadsword in his left hand, several daemons flying away from him. He reached both guards within moments and hefted Ermoor up onto his shoulder, grabbing Rynen underneath his sword arm as a mass of checkpoint guards came surging through the woods, a row of flaming arrows launching into the fray, driving the daemon army back.

Rynen could feel his body go limp with exhaustion and he knew that he was badly wounded, for he could feel that his tunic was sticking to him, blood-soaked. Kalir was soon by his side, grabbing him from underneath Dir'grar's arm, carrying the wounded guard in his arms. He looked over to his friend Dir'grar and motioned to the others in the guard.

"Tell them to bring the barrels and clear the nest out now while they have a chance!" Dir'grar nodded and moved ahead of Kalir, the checkpoint leader giving his attention back to the guard in his arms.

Rynen smiled through bloodstained lips. "I knew you'd come, Kalir! I didn't lose hope. I knew you'd save us!" Kalir felt the boy's body go limp and Rynen's sword dropped to the ground as Kalir made his way to the boats.

"Don't lose hope now, boy! Don't lose hope now! You're among friends that can help." Kalir lifted Rynen's chest to his ear, listening for a heartbeat.

Indeed, there was a faint beating. The boy had just passed out. Kalir continued on down to the path and reached the boats, rushing past the remaining guards, Kalir climbing into a boat with Rynen in his arms.

Up on the rise where the checkpoint guards had found the two guards, a bright light could be seen, the burning fires of the daemon's nesting grounds, one of the many that Kalir would have to personally see to in order to assure each checkpoint's safety. He laid Rynen on the floor of the boat and helped Dir'grar with Ermoor, who seemed to be worse off than Rynen. They quickly pulled the anchor ropes in and pushed off, two guards paddling the boat across to the Happy Traveler, the first of the many battles begun, Kalir feared. Kalir just hoped that the battles, when waged, would be more in their favor than it had been tonight, though that would be asking for a lot.

The early morning sun began to rise as they made their way inside Kalir's cottage, sending for a healer to mend the wounds from the night before. It had been a long night and Kalir would soon find rest waiting for his two wounded guards to awaken from their exhaustive sleep.

Kalir looked to Dir'grar then to the two checkpoint guards who were again on the mending tables. "These boys are fools for glory, Dir'grar. They are fools, you know this, right?"

Dir'grar simply stared back and smiled. "Yes, my friend, I do. After all, look who their leader is."

Kalir had no response. He simply watched as the healers came into the room and began tending the wounds.

"We must prepare better for this if the daemons are coming at this rate, Dir'grar. We must use all that we have. We cannot hold back this time."

Dir'grar simply nodded as they both watched Ermoor and Rynen get bandaged up.

Kalir continued. "Did you see the sheer numbers of the army that was upon them, Dir'grar? This is no small battle. It cannot be anymore. We must hit them with everything that this checkpoint has, do you understand me?"

Dir'grar looked over at the windows as the early morning light began to show through the thick curtains that hung above the windowsill. "So I shall supply them all, then?"

"Do what you must, my friend. We move out when the two wake and have been questioned."

Dir'grar nodded silently and left Kalir's side, leaving the mending room and the building completely. Kalir knew where he was going but he couldn't be concerned with that right now. The checkpoint leader stood over the two wounded guards and, for a moment, felt as if he were reliving a moment that he had tried to forget years ago, remembering the day that Ranyll's father had died in front of him on the same mending table.

I will not let this happen again. Not again, not ever again. Ranyll, I am coming for you. Do not lose hope, even in the darkest time. You are not alone.

22

The two Miftles saw the darkness in front of them shift in their torchlight, several dozen more sets of eyes pushing ahead to see who they had blocked inside the cavern path. Triggle took a well-placed swipe out at the daemons and watched as one of them reeled back in response, its body engulfed in a sea of darkness. In moments, Triggle's victim was gone, replaced by another dark, unflinching daemon form. Triggle lifted up to take another swipe, hoping to clear a way through them before they surged upon the two and were overwhelmed, when Ilthen's hand stayed his swing.

"Wait! They're not attacking us!"

Triggle was befuddled. "Good! Now's my chance to get even with those grimy spawns of darkness." Again he went to swing and, again, Ilthen stayed his hand.

"Something's happening, Triggle. There's something they're keeping from us; something important."

"More likely something's keeping them from us," decided the flustered Miftle. Triggle lowered his weapon and stepped back from the wall of daemons that blocked their passage ahead. Red, daemon eyes stared back at them but the creatures did not move from their position. In fact, the tunnels were almost completely quiet. The daemons had even stopped the passing of the wind from one tunnel to the next. Both Miftles lifted their heads and listened for a moment. Then Triggle looked at Ilthen.

"So, what do we do now?"

"We go back and find another way through."

"Through to where?"

"To wherever creatures are preventing us from getting." The two Miftles looked one last time at the wall of daemons, Triggle wanting so badly to take them on yet, at the same time, was terrified at what they were doing, for he had never seen this before either.

They were watching, just sitting and watching. But for what, the Miftle thought, watching as the last pair of red eyes disappeared down the corridor now behind him, passing through the familiar territory that Ilthen had just led him into.

*   *   *

Gilden Felves knew what the little Miftle was questioning about, had known that it would happen this way for years though now, just as he watched his aged hand glide across the blank page in front of him, the worn-tipped quill gripped in his hand, he knew they were all too late. The head scribe, the youth with him, Kalir, and all of the checkpoint guards for that matter that were scouring the Tirapoor Channel at this moment; if only they knew what lay behind the old scribe's eyes at this moment.

Gilden looked over at the tome he had finished and back to the one that he wrote in now, his hand dipping the worn quill into the inkwell every line or so with the least bit of effort, his eyes closing for a single moment to break away from the reality looming before him. But it did not go away. Not in his restless sleeps, not in his breaks for food and frequent walks in the gardens at the center of the scribe's building, though he couldn't remember the last time he had taken one of those walks. Not even a moment of solace in a single blink of an eye without seeing what was to come.

Fates would be made within the next few sunsets, he knew. He saw the rains coming; the Wilden Marsh, the Dwarven Crag, the fate of the angel and her young protector.

Gilden looked down and saw his writing hand begin to shake, his arm soon following the action, his mind suddenly seizing up for an instant. Gilden watched as the tip of the quill snapped under the full weight of his hand and then he saw the pages rush in on him. His chest fell across the half-written tome, his white beard smearing across the wet ink. The old man could feel his entire body tighten with the pain in his chest, his breath caught in his lungs. He could feel the heat move through his chest and up into his throat. His body shook with such force Gilden's legs slipped out from under him. His small frame slipped out from under him and he came tumbling down to the floor, knocking the breath out of him as he landed.

His body seemed to question why this was happening; in response, a small trickle of blood escaped the old man's dry lips, dribbling down onto the floor, a little red puddle soon forming. However, inside Gilden's mind, he knew. His body seemed numb for the moment but he could now breathe, which was good. He could continue to live.

Or what was called living, Gilden thought. The blurring of his vision that had come with the seizing of his limbs would pass as well. He knew it would, for this had happened before. It seemed though, in his mind, almost a full hundred years had passed since he had this all too familiar feeling, but he would never forget it. It was fresh on his mind now, as he sat there, letting the pain have its way with his body.

Soon, movement came back to his limbs as well as his senses, a throbbing strong in his head where he had struck the floor. He lifted himself slowly to his knees and wiped the blood from his mouth, grabbing a cloth from one of the pockets of his robe to clean the small spot on the floor. Gilden could feel a knot forming over the right side of his temple and he swayed a little from dizziness as he righted himself back into his writing chair.

"I accept the penalty." He felt a twinge of pain in his writing hand from the initial tenseness and began to rub it out with his other hand. He looked around and found a small box that had fallen onto the floor. Leaning over ever so slightly, he reached the box and brought it up onto the table in front of him. He opened it and retrieved a new quill in which to write with. After cleaning up the smear he had made across the page, he began a new line.

'The world was beginning to fall apart and the Wilden Marsh is where it had decided to begin…'

*   *   *

The faerie kind that had traveled from Reune Lake to Wilden Marsh now knew where their fates lay. Within the ancient mining caverns of the town of Wilden, the darkness of an old abandoned world had slept. The stories say that it had been trapped under a mountain, unable to escape its enormous prison. It was meant to stay buried, meant not to see the light of day or breathe in the smell of air. The world and its inhabitants were to pass it by without flinching and that was to be that. But, as most historians say, that was not how it happened at all.

With the coming of war between the races of Kariyl, the dwarves had begun mining for ore to make weapons and, as the season passed by, the dwarves dug too deep. The sealed mountain broke and, for several days, a stagnant, grey mist rolled out of the fissure the dwarves had created, blanketing the town of Wilden and several miles around it in a thick fog. The dwarves saw this as a bad omen and many began leaving.

However, many did not make it out of Wilden. Once the mists stopped rolling from the mining caves, something more than just mist began to occupy the town. Legend has it that great beasts came from the caverns and devoured the dwarven survivors. But that was not true. The mists were the plague of Wilden; the mists were the monsters, the mists were the death of the dwarven miners, come to claim their souls and all who lived above in peace and tranquility.

And now, as the faeries stood at the entrance to the mining caves, they knew what they saw before them. The ancient evil that had been trapped for so long hungered for death, for revenge, and for the time that it had lost waiting beneath the mountain.

Immediately, the unicorns assumed the front ranks, their horns glowing in unison the magikal blue fire. The mist attempted to ensnare the faeries with the blue fire, to smother them by letting the mist rise up underneath them. However, the sprites stopped this attempt quickly. As the mists began to rise, the sprites released handfuls of dust, the small creatures within the mists crying out in pain. The dust settled and, in moments, was ablaze and spreading across the swampy ground. The mist began to slip back to its owner, the great mist beat that, now, seemed to waver in its duty.

The unicorns, seeing this, began to push forward, their arcs merging slowly together. And in another moment, the creature dissipated back into the cave. The faeries surged forward, unicorns in the lead, the mist rolling quickly back into the place behind them as they disappeared into the mining caverns.

*   *   *

Gwenzel awoke to the presence of something new around him. Before, he could only feel the two sprites' magikal force across from him; but now, as the mists swirled around him, he knew that something was headed this way. And the mists knew this as well. The hold that it had before this was tight, but now it was almost too much. His legs had grown cold and his chest was pressed in as far as it could go. Gwenzel took small breaths through his nostrils and let a little out at a time, trying his best to keep his chest expanded as much as possible. He had tried to channel the magik within his horn and all it caused him was pain. The mist had somewhat of a magikal hold over him as well as the sprites across from him.

The unicorn looked at them now and, through the mist, it looked as though they were in a reflection of water, their faces and garb blurred by the mist. They did not move, either.

It seems that they are stuck in the same situation, thought Gwenzel, trying his best to look through the haze at the rest of his surroundings. It was no use. The mist had spread across what he thought were walls and throughout the tunnels around him, the unicorn finally giving in and letting his eyes close. All he could do was rest until a moment presented itself. So, at the present, this unicorn would have a chance to catch up on his sleep.

*   *   *

No sooner had the two Miftle faeries left from the wall of motionless daemons then they heard a clicking from that very tunnel. The sounds increased and, as they did, both Triggle and Ilthen began to increase their pace.

"What do you think is going on," Triggle asked, his feet almost stumbling over themselves as the sounds broke through the silence.

"I think they've done their share of waiting and decided upon killing us instead."

Triggle unsheathed his sword. "I knew I should have taken them out when I had the chance!"

"Now's not the best time, Triggle. Look!" And, if things couldn't get any worse, Triggle saw that, from the other tunnels, more daemons approached. The clicking grew intensely loud and it became harder and harder for Triggle to focus on what he was doing. Soon, he dropped his sword and stopped running altogether. Ilthen continued running and turned only when she didn't see Triggle at her side. She looked back and saw Triggle standing in the intersection, red slits lighting up all around him in the tunnels connecting.

"Triggle!" However, the Miftle she called to did not hear her for the clicking that surrounded him.

Triggle could feel the waves of darkness coming towards him, threatening to swallow him up. The Miftle knew there were far too many to fight on his own this time. However, he wasn't on his own; he knew.

He looked at Ilthen and knew that the magikal presence he had felt earlier wasn't her at all. Of course, some of the magik that he had felt was from her, but the bulk of it, what he felt now, was **them**. And Triggle knew what they felt like; had known for years. But Ilthen; she didn't know. Sure, she knew a Miftle when she saw a Miftle, that's one thing. But, her being so far away from her true home, the Homme she had been borne from, Triggle doubted that she knew what an entire army of faeries felt like as they approached. But, for Triggle, it was one of the greatest feelings in the world.

Triggle stared harder at Ilthen, the lone Miftle, her eyes doubting, and reached his hand out to her. The surge of daemons seemed to waiver, to hesitate within the tunnels, watching as the two Miftle creatures reached for one another. The daemons had seen this occurrence many times before as they had devoured their victims. However, there was something different, something that didn't smell right in the milky black nostrils of the daemon ranks. Their hesitation was just that; their waver unchallenged, they continued on and were almost upon the two when they realized what was missing; the fear. The daemons did not smell the fear from the two in front of them.

Ilthen fell into Triggle's arms then, not knowing why, only trusting her fellow Miftle just as she had the dwarven kind she had lived with for most of her life. She looked up into Triggle's face and, through the thick, brown beard, could see a faint smile at the corners of his mouth. Then the world exploded around her. The darkness came at them but a brilliant white light surrounded them, Triggle's hand blazing a blue fire that turned suddenly white. The daemons had ceased their ceremonious clicking and were trying to pull away from then light when it suddenly seemed to multiply, the tunnels around them filling with it as well.

Then Ilthen felt it. The presence seemed to take hold of her and she turned away from Triggle, her gaze on the other shafts of light throughout the tunnels. It was then that the presence emerged.

First, were the unicorns. The tunnels, though small, let the unicorns through, their shoulders just missing the tight fit. The creatures were illuminated by their magical horns, which were alive with a blue fire similar to that of Triggle's, who stood in front of her now, watching, too, as the daemon army fell to pieces underneath the power of the faeries. The female Miftle was at a loss for words. Ilthen had not remembered her past but, as she looked on the unicorns now and more faerie kind that pressed themselves closer into the tunnels, she knew that the part she had always felt was missing had suddenly become whole.

Triggle's magik faded away in his hands and he released Ilthen, who stood now facing the lead unicorn.

The unicorn leaned down to her and touched her head with its horn. The Miftle could hear the unicorn's voice echo inside her mind.

What once was lost is now found.

Ilthen wiped the tears of joy from her eyes and embraced the great creature in front of her. "I always knew you'd come!"

The lead unicorn nuzzled its head against hers, sniffing deeply of the lone faerie that had spent most of its life with the dwarves. Then the unicorn sneezed. Its sneeze made all the faeries jump nervously in unison, the lead unicorn shaking its head.

My child, you have lived long with the race of dwarves and taken on their distinct odor.

"It's something I've learned to deal with over time." Ilthen giggled. The unicorn nodded and Triggle smiled.

"Everybody, this is Ilthen. Ilthen, this is… everybody!"

The unicorns behind the lead began to move closer, pressing in on the two Miftles. One of them spoke up.

Triggle is right; we have no time for long introductions. We have come here with a single purpose.

Triggle spoke up. "Gabriella?"

Yes, my young Miftle. We now know the One's plan behind his actions. There are many things that have happened since we last saw another, Triggle.

"You're telling me!"

We must go now if we are to find the angel before it is too late.

Ilthen looked confused. "Angel? What angel?" She looked to Triggle for the answers.

Triggle just shook his head. "It's a long story. I'll tell you on the way."

Soon, the faerie kind had moved on and went deeper into the chasms that held the answers to the questions that young Ilthen began asking, intent to wonder if it was too late or if hope had any part to play in making a difference in these turn of events that her friend Triggle rambled on, at a pace so fast she could hardly keep up.

*   *   *

The one person that knew the outcome sat at his writing desk deep into the night, his ink well never running dry, his eyelids never closing completely even though sleep threatened to overtake him. He had felt the sleep come and go many times, though he could never say that he had control of it.

"Much like most of my life," he said to himself, dipping the quill in the inkwell again, the old man finishing the last sentence on the paragraph.

The aged eyes seemed deep in thought and, as he wrote on, the world that he had seen earlier was nowhere near as dark as he had thought it to be.

The darkness is always cleared away by the light. Gilden had seen this happen many times, though the outcomes were always different. He tried to smile, to think of the happiness that still lay within the world, but he knew of what was to come.

The old man continued on until the early morning hours. The small sliver of sunlight broke through the windowpanes into the dimly lit room, Gilden finally lifting his wiry frame from his writings, scooting his feet across the thick stone floors until he reached his bed. His mind hazy once again, this time from exhaustion, he fell unevenly across the bed and looked at the framed map he had gotten as a gift all those years ago. He had moved it many times, from wall to wall, finally resting it on the wall next to his bed.

Fitting, he thought, *Kariyl is always within sight during my sleeping and waking hours.* Gilden, for a time, stared at the map, following the thick lines of the Tirapoor Channel down to Reune Lake and back again, his eyes resting on the marsh just north where the army of faerie kin had entered to end the rule of the One once and for all.

It will not be so easy, faerie kin. Gilden closed his eyes for a moment and opened them again. He now looked to the mountains above the marsh.

That is where the answers lie; with the dwarves. But something else lies there as well. And it will not give up its time here so easily.

Many will be lost. Many will never see the light of day again.

The old scribe was nearing sleep. He could feel it overtake him slowly, feel his limbs begin to relax gradually, his eyes moving across to the east, finally resting on the small city of Telgin.

This time he spoke out loud.

"What about you, Ranyll? Do you miss your family as much as they miss you? I have written about them, too. Your mother cries at night, wondering where you are, little one. She thinks you are lost to her."

The old man blinked one last time and his head finally sank onto the pillow, his hands resting at his sides. He spoke once more before finally drifting off to sleep.

"But you're not lost, are you? You know just where you're going."

23

Arntheer was not fearless, he knew that. '*But dwarves do not admit things so easily*', his mother had told him once, when asking about his father. He had never known his father, nor did he want to, he admitted, hearing of the limited patience his father had regarding other people and their needs. So Arntheer had hardened himself on his own, leaving it to the great dwarven heroes of the past to raise him.

He had read the War of the Races Chronicles and the ponderings of Darbin Longbeard and his meddlings in the affairs of others. Arntheer had read more than any dwarf alive and had yet to hear of the stories of daemons. These creatures continued to plague Dardist and the surrounding dwarven towns within the mountains and no one knew why.

The dwarf adjusted his helm a bit and looked out into the darkness, trying to count the sets of red eyes that looked back at him and his dwarves; it wasn't possible. There were just too many to count. Arntheer and his garrison of fifteen had been assigned to check post three, one of the closer posts to the daemon "attacking grounds" as the dwarves began to call them. Arntheer had fought daemons easily enough and, now that he stood a good ten feet above the floor of the cave entrance, he even had an advantage over them. But, looking out over the waves of daemons that sat atop one another, silently staring back at him, he knew there was no way his garrison alone could defeat them.

He had sent one of his own dwarves back with word for reinforcements, but it had been a time ago since then and Arntheer wondered now if his messenger had made it.

"What are they waiting for, sir," one from his garrison asked, moments before he had sent the messenger. Arntheer did not know what to say then, but, as he looked out at the creatures waiting silently in the shadows, he felt he knew the answer to that question now.

"They're waiting for us." Arntheer's voice startled his men, most of them blankly staring out at the solid wall of daemons covering their only way out of the caverns. Behind them, through the small set of double doors, was the tunnel that led to their outpost where the rest of the surviving members of Dardist took refuge. Arntheer had sworn an oath to protect them with his last breath and that was what he intended to do.

One of his dwarves looked at him. "Sir?"

"They're waiting for our move."

"What **is** our move, Arntheer?"

It took no time for the dwarven garrison to gather the supplies that their commander had requested and, by the time they had all the supplies together, they all knew what he had planned.

"Tharnin, roll these reserve oil casks out at the daemons. Geldif, you grab a torch. The rest of you ready your crossbows. These daemons have been here too long at our check post."

The garrison cheered behind their commander, Tharnin climbing down the ladder, watching gradually as one after another of the oil barrels were lowered by rope down to him. Once all four of them were lowered, Tharnin began rolling them forward, closer to the horde of daemons that sat atop one another, watching the dwarves every move. Finally, Tharnin came to the last barrel and rolled it over to the others, leaving it on its side and removing the cork. The clear oil gushed out of the opening, pouring all around the other barrels, Tharnin starting his way back.

Once up the ladder, Tharnin pulled it up behind him, looking over at the daemons again. "They move yet?"

The dwarves shook their heads and watched in silence as the rest of the oil emptied onto the stone floor dozens of paces in front of them.

Arntheer lifted his crossbow, the rest of the garrison taking aim as well.

"Make it count, dwarves!"

Tharnin lifted up his crossbow as well and Geldif began lighting the tips of them.

"Fire!" The bolts hit the tunnel ahead of them and many flew into the wall of daemons, several dark forms disappearing, soon to be replaced by more forms just as quickly as they had fallen. Several bolts slid across the oil and immediately lit up in front of the check point; the other casks exploding out onto the wall of daemons as dozens of them fell upon their own, catching fire to one another. The firelight made the dwarves turn away for a moment and then they began to reload, expecting a rush of daemons to follow the attack.

But none came. The garrison looked out beyond the blaze and saw what was left of the wall of daemons, but there were very few left alive. Arntheer released another volley of bolts, taking down one daemon after another and yet they still remained fixed in one place. The dwarf had his men reload the crossbows one more time and was about to give the order to fire when he looked out at the stone flooring as it burned with the remaining oil.

There were no daemons to be found. Nothing stirred. The daemon threat that he had sent word about was no longer a threat. The carcasses of the daemons burning began to fill the tunnel with smoke and Arntheer tasked two from his garrison to put the fire out with buckets of water that they had stowed inside the armory supply room just inside the door. Then one dwarf pointed out into the smoke.

"Look, there's one now!"

The daemon must have been the only survivor of the fire. It skittered this way and that, trying to see through the smoke without getting any closer to the fires. It looked around a little more and then found the dwarves up on their outpost. It shrieked in defiance when it saw them and headed towards them. Tharnin lifted his crossbow and took aim.

Thunk! The arrow cut through the smoke and embedded itself into the daemon's chest, knocking it to the ground. It squealed in pain. Within the smoke, another shriek answered, a daemon stepping out through the smoke; then another. Two more daemons showed their red eyes, then another after that. Soon, the dwarves were trying to choose which target to shoot at. The smoke was in their eyes and they were out of oil. The oil fire itself was beginning to die down now and that opened more space for daemons to move through.

Which they did, Arntheer noticed, the creatures clawing over the dead, smoking bodies of their former brethren, using their own dead as a bridge over the remaining fire to get closer to the check post.

The garrison fired another volley of bolts at Arntheer's command and loaded for another when the daemons began climbing the walls up to the walkway they stood on.

Arntheer took aim and shot. A daemon dropped off the walkway and another took its place. He waved to his garrison.

"Fall back into the tunnels! We can't let them get inside."

The garrison nodded to one another and began moving towards the door. The daemons noticed this and moved even quicker than before. Arntheer saw one of his dwarves fall and then another, the commander staying at the door as long as possible, trying his best to call over the clicking that came from the cavern ahead, the tunnel alive with movement.

"Fall back, now!" Two dwarves moved in past him and then the daemons became too many to count. Arntheer moved into the doorway and helped two others push the heavy set of double doors, watching as number of daemons began pushing their limbs and heads into the small passageway to hold the doors open.

Arntheer reached behind him and felt the handle of his double axe in his palm. In two tugs with his thick arm, he felt the double axe free itself and he swung the weapon in an arc against the crack of the door, cleaving hands, arms, fingers of daemons as they tried to block the door open. Howls and screeches of pain crept into his ears and Arntheer gripped the double axe with both hands this time, watching as the daemons began pushing at the door.

"Hold that door, dwarves! Hold it just a moment longer!"

Red, daemon eyes looked in through the crack in between the doors, Arntheer watching as the sheer weight of the daemons began to press the doors open. The dwarven commander felt his anger take hold of him and he began swinging his axe into the crack of the door, again watching as daemons dropped before him. The red slits disappeared with another swing, then another, the dwarf's axe hitting the mark every time, the dwarf watching as his men finally pushed the door closed with one, final push. Once closed, they could still hear the clicking through the doors and felt the daemons surged against the door. Then a voice suddenly cried out in panic.

"I think there's one in here!"

The remaining garrison of dwarves crowded together and one of them began to shine a torch taken from the wall around the hallway, panning it across the walls and ceiling as well as the floor. The dwarf suddenly stopped and pointed into the hallway in front of them. Indeed, he had seen a small glimmer of movement ahead on the floor.

"What is it?" Arntheer squinted his eyes, which is odd for a dwarf due to the fact that they can see in the dark. But the dwarf wasn't squinting to see. He actually couldn't believe his own eyes.

A dog-like creature with a long, fluffy tail was sitting in the middle of the hallway. It was red all over, like the dwarven forging fires with the exception of its white chest and the tip of its tail. The creature looked from dwarf to dwarf, eyeing them all, almost seeming to face off with each of them. Then it seemed to smile and, to the garrison's amazement, it spoke.

"Are you lost, because we sure are?" From behind the little creature, several dwarves emerge from the darkness and a young human boy as well. One of the unknown dwarves smiled through his beard when he saw his friend.

"Arntheer, you made it!"

And thus began the conversation that explained Oagthor's situation to the recently attacked garrison of dwarves, the human's situation in this and of the small fire fox named D'meir that met a party of frightened dwarves with such ease.

With a little coaxing, the surviving six checkpoint guards including their commander followed the motley crew of dwarves with their strange friends and continued on until they could no longer hear the scratching of daemons at the door and continued west back towards where Oagthor had entered the caverns.

It was a little while later that they stopped and, amid the excitement of some of the dwarves seeing old friends, Oagthor, Rathor, and Arntheer began to formulate a plan. Oagthor was the first one to speak.

"How I see it is like this: the daemons have rounded us dwarves up into a little group so as to keep us from interfering with the One's plan to meet with Gabriella. If he has his way, the daemons would take her further west, towards the Argolis Mountains."

Arntheer spoke up. "That means they would have to pass by the Crag."

"Not by it, **in** it, Arntheer. What we do know now is that's where they're coming from. A scouting dwarf found a jagged set of stairs that they have made almost all the way up. He saw a line of red slits moving and he watched them until they got to the edge. The stairs end and, for ten hands or so, they climb the face of the crag to the lip.”

“Well, I’ll be a toad!” Tharnin put his face in his hands. He had been listening to the whole conversation just behind his commander’s shoulder. He chimed in. “There’s no way we can secure that area. It encompasses the whole of the cavern.”

“We can if we collapse the ceiling,” Rathor interrupted. “By pulling in the columns that hold the ceiling up, we can collapse almost the entire mountain down on them. But let us not worry about that until we make it there.”

Arntheer looked at Rathor then to his friend Oagthor, trying to get an estimate on how serious the dwarf was by the look on his face. Then he looked to his rag-tag remains of his garrison who were exhausted and to Oagthor’s dwarven party, who didn’t look too much better.

Arntheer just shook his head, wiping the sweat and dirt from his brow with a rag from one of his pouches. “I admire your courage, Oagthor, but that is insane.”

Oagthor smiled back at his friend.

So much history between us and he still doubts me.

“What? Insane….like a handful of check post guards fighting off an entire army of daemons?”

“Hey, you’ve got to start somewhere,” Arntheer concluded, cleaning the blood off of his axe with the same rag. He looked to his garrison and they all nodded their heads. They seemed to want something to be done. Arntheer stretched his aching back and pulled another cloth from his pouch and tied it around a cut on his arm, pulling it tight with his teeth.

“This better work, Oagthor! I’m not going to let myself and my men get killed for nothing!”

Oagthor shook his head and took Arntheer up to the front of the line as Rathor followed behind, the rest of the garrison falling into place as they began walking back the way they came.

And so, the two parties of dwarves, the human boy Ranyll and the faerie creature D'meir began their arduous task of retracing their steps back to the Dwarven Crag. Ranyll was not so excited about the decision, still knowing that there was something more than just daemons inside the Crag; he could feel its presence. The air in and around the crag was thick with it. It smelled of mold and of dust that sat too long and never stirred; *or never had a reason to until now*, thought the young man, his eyes darting back behind him every so often, looking for the red sets of eyes to be following him. However, they weren't following. Apparently, the door was holding them back.

Maybe they found another way in. But it didn't matter, Ranyll concluded. *We're going straight into their lair now.* His hand went to the handle of his sword now, his fingers touching the handle ever so slightly.

Father, wherever you may be, give me the strength to face what lay in the crag. I can sense its strength. There's something down there, calling me. I can feel it pressing into my mind. I felt it when I was there the first time; I'm sure that the second time will be absolute terror.

It wasn't long before something answered back. Ranyll could hear it; faint traces of a voice that he had not heard in several days, echoing in his mind.

The young man tightened his grip on the sword, pulling the blade out a little. The dwarves around him took notice and signaled to Oagthor, who was up at the front of the party discussing the plans further with Arntheer and Rathor. Oagthor closed in on Ranyll, his eyebrows tightening in around his eyes, his forehead covered with a light sheen of sweat.

"What is it, Ranyll?" Oagthor put his hand on Ranyll's sword arm and Ranyll's eyes suddenly opened wider, a look of panic sweeping across his face. The young human responded quickly and in short breaths.

"I can hear him!" Ranyll's face turned ashen white.

Flee, Ranyll, it's a trap!

Ranyll heard it again and was about to pull his sword free when Oagthor shoved the blade back down into the sheath, grasping the young man's hand, which was ice cold.

"Hear who, Ranyll?" The dwarf began to worry. Ranyll's gaze shifted across to the rest of the dwarves and landed on D'meir, who was at Oagthor's feet.

"Gwenzel! It's Gwenzel! He's in trouble, D'meir!"

The fire fox pricked its ears up when it heard the unicorn's name, rushing over to Ranyll's side. D'meir climbed up onto Ranyll's pack and leaned over the human's shoulder.

"Where is he, Ranyll?"

"What is all this about," Arntheer questioned. "Who's Gwenzel?" The dwarf had not heard of this person and didn't think it had anything to do with them and the Dwarven Crag.

D'meir tightened up on Ranyll's shoulder. He swept his eyes back over at Arntheer. "Quiet! This is important. A friend is in danger!"

Ranyll jerked to one side suddenly and grabbed for the wall, his legs buckling under him.

"It won't let them go, D'meir. There are others. There are others trapped and it won't let them go."

D'meir leaned in and looked into Ranyll's eyes, slowly feeling the human slipping away from him. "What won't let them go, Ranyll?"

"The mists!" Ranyll fell under a sudden incredible weight, collapsing into Oagthor's waiting arms. The young man began to breathe heavy, his breath cutting in and out as if he were being choked.

The fire fox jumped onto Oagthor's shoulder and looked down at Ranyll, who as white as a sheet and getting more pale by the second. D'meir's eyes grew wide and it arched its fur high on its back.

Arntheer looked at D'meir and then back to Ranyll then to Oagthor. "Will someone tell me what's going on?"

D'meir shifted from his spot on Oagthor's shoulder, dropping down on all fours next to the fallen Ranyll. The fire fox looked up at Oagthor.

"Something's gotten a hold over him, Oagthor! It came through Gwenzel and has seized the boy's mind for its own!"

Before Oagthor could speak, D'meir leapt onto Ranyll, its ears flattened back against its head. Suddenly, the room lit up around the dwarves, the fire fox burning within its own protective flame. Instead of the great yellow and orange flames that D'meir had struck at the daemons with, a light, blue flame encircled the creature now. The flames did not harm Ranyll but hovered just above his ashen form, D'meir staring down into Ranyll's half-closed eyes.

Ranyll watched through a sudden blurriness that clouded his vision as D'meir leapt on top of him, flaring to life as he had done before when Ranyll had been near death. The human could sense that something was wrong inside of him, that Gwenzel's link inside of his mind had been forced, almost as if it had been controlled in some way by another. Ranyll couldn't tell, though, for he had never heard another voice but his own in his head.

Nevertheless, somewhere inside of him screamed out a warning. But it was too late. The blurriness was now turning into a thick fog that rolled over and over in his mind, clouding all thoughts and feelings from him completely. And that's when Ranyll saw D'meir in the darkness. The darkness enfolded around D'meir as well but was burned away by the magik fire that surrounded his small little frame. Suddenly, the world that had dimmed for those moments grew brighter and the fog lifted, pulling itself free of Ranyll's mind.

*   *   *

Oagthor watched as D'meir clung to Ranyll, the young man wriggling underneath the fire fox, the small creature grabbing hold of Ranyll's garb for purchase. Inside Ranyll, D'meir could sense the presence. He had felt it following along with them, almost hanging in the air, but now it took form. The great eyes that materialized in the fog set its sights on the small fire fox and burned with a white fire at the magikal being, trying its best to snatch Ranyll away for its own. The darkened slits that were eyes in the mist glowed bright white, different from what D'meir had seen since inside the caves. But the fire fox was well taught for his kind. He knew once he had felt the presence that it was not the One at all or any of his minions, but was what had spilled out of the mountains all of those years ago and killed those dwarves in the town of Wilden.

Yes, D'meir knew of this being, had known well since the beginning of time when it had been created.

24

In the times of the faeries before inhabitants had been created to fill the world, there was a being that controlled the darkness and the light. He had been given the responsibility to oversee the world as it was created and watch the faerie folk as they made the natural world, a living breathing organism of green flesh and bark-like bone that protruded up from the world. Before the One had put doubt into the minds of the inhabitants and clouded the grand scheme in each of them, he had confided in **this** being on how to do it. And Scarwol had helped him.

Blanketing the world in darkness, Scarwol hid himself and the One from prying eyes and showed him the great caves beneath the world, caves that Scarwol had created over the ages; in them the One harbored the darkness that he had stolen for himself. And, once he had been trapped under the world of the inhabitant's, the One used it to create his daemons. All of this and more Scarwol watched and helped. All of this and more Scarwol had become more of a servant of the One, harboring great power but only being allowed to use it for the purposes of blinding the inhabitants in their grand scheme.

*   *   *

Scarwol shifted his from his place in the chamber, looking around him, peering back down into the shifting mass of mist in front of him that was Gwenzel. The unicorn moved inside the thick mist that threatened to smother him. The unicorn had tried its best to stop the mist from entering his mind but was nearly smothered to death until he opened his mind up to use his magik; that's when Scarwol let himself in. Half faerie, half elemental, Scarwol had cursed himself when tampering with the elements in his youth. When the Creator had found out about the One, he knew that the only creature that could help Darien would be Scarwol.

After sending Darien down to Ar Solon, the Creator had let the rogue faerie creature Scarwol have his way and soon it had found itself trapped in its own cave where it had hidden the darkness ages before. And, in that darkness, for thousands of years, the darkness played with the faerie elemental, soon warping him into a shadow of its former self. He was never again able to form into a solid mass, only able to take shape as different things that he saw within his mind.

Gwenzel could see all of this in a glimmer of a second as Scarwol passed through the faerie's mind. Scarwol lifted himself from his place in the chamber, moving from the entrance of the once great Faerie Hall, floating down the steps past the great stone columns, looking into the mists at the unicorn.

Scarwol took on the shape of the young man in Gwenzel's mind. Soon, Gwenzel looked out onto a misty form of Ranyll staring back at him. Ranyll gritted his teeth and a rage came over him that Gwenzel had never seen. He reached into the mist at Gwenzel.

"Why are you here, unicorn? And why is this boy in your mind? You're not supposed to have any contact with humans yet the last few days are full of this boy. Answer me!" The evil Ranyll wrapped his fingers around Gwenzel's neck and squeezed. Gwenzel could feel the cold, misty hands tighten, a sharp, icy chill shooting through the unicorn's body. The faerie felt pain lance through its legs and back, the creature sinking into the mist around it, the mist covering over his snout and eyes. Gwenzel tried to steady himself.

You will never break me. I am Shilinda's child and she has taught me well. Do what you will.

"Don't worry, unicorn; I intend to." The evil Ranyll's eyes lit a brilliant, piercing white and the hands tightened around Gwenzel even more, suddenly turning to mist and forcing itself through Gwenzel's body; and into the young man's, this so-called Ranyll's mind. The evil Ranyll faded and the ancient faerie-elemental focused his attention on this boy. Scarwol searched and soon found the fear within Ranyll, the fear that lies within every inhabitant. Scarwol used it to his sick pleasure, watching through the young human's eyes as he dropped to the ground, frozen in fear.

Scarwol's form shifted again to his true form, trying to reach further into Ranyll to find more that he could use, when suddenly a magik appeared.

It was a faerie, no doubt, he thought to himself, waving his hand across the mist in front of him to get a better view. Gwenzel writhed in pain as the mist swirled about him and Scarwol's grip again tightened. The image of the creature was clearer and Scarwol could now see what was at Ranyll's side. The fire fox bared its teeth into Ranyll's eyes and came alive with its magikal fire.

"So, young Ranyll, you have a protector. Indeed, you must be important for the faerie folk to show themselves so openly to your kind. Of course, it has been a long time since the way of things, but I think that rule still applies to faerie kin, does it not, Gwenzel?" Scarwol drifted from his seat in the chamber and closed in on the unicorn, his misty fingers reaching out to touch the unicorn on the back. Gwenzel whinnied and tried to pull away but that only drew Scarwol in closer. The faerie elemental looked into the trapped unicorn's eyes and asked again, this time a bit more specific.

"Why are you protecting the boy, Gwenzel?" The unicorn dared not open his mind anymore, for he could still feel the mist swirling inside of him. So, instead, the unicorn spoke.

"It's too late, Scarwol. He's already upon you and your fate has been sealed. It says so in the Great Books."

Scarwol pulled away and looked at the unicorn, his form changing back to the young human.

"The Great Books are a lie; they have been for centuries! The Chronicler has no power and cannot change the fate of the world. You know that. Look at Gabriella! Look what has happened to her; and Greditto! Did the books mention Greditto's death? Of course the books have not; because the world hasn't been planned out by that old man and his visions. He sees what the Creator lets him see, that's all."

Scarwol then turned to the others that had been brought before him. The two sprites floated in mid-air, a thick mist holding them in place. They, too, had shut all things out around them, knowing that the mist could get to them. But Scarwol knew that, as faeries, their weakness was curiosity, as was the rest of their kind. They had seen too much and always strived for more. In the beginning, the Creator had never instilled a sense of purpose inside of them and, to this day, they always kept their eyes open and barely slept, thinking that they would miss their purpose if they were not always looking for it. So, the sprites opened their eyes when they heard Scarwol call their names. Then they saw him.

"Hello, little ones. Why are you here, in my domain, an army of faeries following your very path?"

They needed not to speak at all. Scarwol soon found a way through the defenses and into their minds and found the answer he was looking for. Scarwol was not happy in the least.

"Damn you, Darien! This is not my battle; this is yours!"

Scarwol, unlike The One, was content living down below in the mountains, further away from the races of the world and further from any trouble that could affect him. But now it seemed that the One had brought it to his doorstep. And now, just like before, the One seemed to unofficially ask for assistance of some kind.

Scarwol looked across his great chamber at the mists guarding his entryway. They took no form at this moment but, as he thought longer on the entire legion of faeries that, at this very moment, traipsed freely through his domain, the mists took shape.

First, a head formed and then a snout; soon, the form of a body took shape and it became almost feline, like the domesticated cat, yet fierce and forever a shifting grey. The sets of eyes appeared on each of the creatures on either side of the chamber doors and stared out at the chamber that held their master and his three prisoners. The two forms climbed down from their perches. In another moment, the doors dissipated as well and Scarwol looked out over his prisoners at the mist creatures that waited for his command.

"Kill this human boy they call Ranyll!" The mist creatures turned and left their master, the door reappearing back into place as soon as they disappeared down the hallway.

"That should take care of our little problem, don't you think?" Scarwol looked at the still forms of his former faerie kin and felt the anger raging in their minds, trying to break his hold.

Indeed, it looks as though it will. Scarwol's shape of Ranyll managed a smile.

*   *   *

Ranyll lifted his head and could see the faint outlines of the dwarves through the fog in his mind as it lifted slowly away, D'meir forcing it out with the power that surged through the little creature, his small, beady eyes glowing the same bright blue that encompassed its furry flame.

Oagthor and Rathor were both by the human's side, their water skins out and at the ready. Ranyll watched as D'meir's magik died down around him, Ranyll slowly lifting himself up on his elbows. The pale, gaunt figure that Oagthor had seen earlier was now replaced with the young man he had first met in the catacombs only days prior. Ranyll looked weak then, too, as he did now. The young man reached for Oagthor's water skin and, taking it in a free hand, poured a little on his face and then the rest into his waiting mouth, which had suddenly become dry and parched. Ranyll handed the water skin back and looked over at D'meir, who was lying down next to him.

"What was that thing, D'meir; those eyes?"

"It's a faerie from long ago."

Ranyll then lifted himself up and was about to get up when Oagthor stopped him.

"Hold it there, Ranyll! I think we should stop for a time and let you gather your strength before we go back to the crag."

D'meir interjected. "Ranyll's thinking is right, Oagthor. Scarwol knows we're here now and he knows I'm here, which means he'll send his minions after us. We can't stay here any longer. We must keep moving forward."

Rathor could see that Oagthor was not pleased but nodded his head respectfully to his faerie friend, offering Ranyll an outstretched hand. The young man regained his footing and soon felt D'meir by his side, climbing onto the back of the Ranyll's pack as he lifted it up and onto his shoulders. The rest of the dwarven party just stared at him as they passed, most of them still a little surprised at what had just transpired before them.

D'meir closed in on Ranyll's ear and began to speak quietly as they set off again to the Dwarven Crag.

"Ranyll, there is something I must tell you." Ranyll nodded his head solemnly and continued on, watching the lantern light ahead of him cast shadows upon the wall.

D'meir, for some reason, began to look worried. A small little patch of fur furrowed over his eyes, his fuzzy lids almost closing as he spoke.

"I may have saved you, but there are consequences to what occurred."

Ranyll knew this, knew now that the party must be leaving, moving on to another place.

But what else could there be, Ranyll thought, his hand moving slowly to the pommel of his sword that rested easily at his hip.

"No, it is not danger, Ranyll. That will come in time."

Ranyll relaxed his hand and let his palm rest against the handle of his sword. The young man felt comforted for the moment, but the way that D'meir put it didn't rest too well inside of him.

D'meir continued. "The way of magik is strange, Ranyll, very strange. It is a world that, though I have been around for a long time, is still new to me. Magik is simple, yet at the same time, very complex. When I saved you, I ended up changing you as well. I only say this because I feel it in you now. The same thing that resides in me resides in you."

"What are you saying, D'meir? That I'm a faerie now?" Ranyll couldn't believe what he was hearing. D'meir could sense the panic in the human's voice and continued, doing his best to calm the buildup of emotions that he felt inside Ranyll.

"You are human, Ranyll, and nothing can change that; ever. But there is something that resides within you now. Before, when I healed you, I only used my magik on the surface, not within your mind. But when I battled Scarwol for control of you, your mind used my magik to keep him at bay. I was only the supplier of the magik, Ranyll; you were the user. Did you not feel that when Scarwol left? He left because now you have it, too!"

D'meir said it so matter-of-factly that Ranyll had no way of denying it. In fact, the young man had remembered something special about the way the retreat had occurred. Ranyll could feel it now, whatever it was, stir to life inside of him. Things around him looked somewhat different, almost brighter, the darkness around him almost easier to see into, almost able to be seen through. He looked over at D'meir, who stared straight ahead at Oagthor and the others. There were two dwarves covering the rear of the party and Ranyll could see them far behind, even without the lantern light.

"So, what do I do now, D'meir?"

The fire fox just smiled.

25

That night, Gabriella dreamed. She had had glimmers and pieces of what she would call dreams, but one who knows what a dream is would simply call them memories. Any inhabitant would know that. However, Gabriella had not inhabited anything at the present moment. The dreams took shape as a gritty, smoky image of Ranyll and her other protectors as they attempted to find her. Ranyll was walking with a dwarven party in the darkness and suddenly the darkness swallowed them up. The small bits and pieces after that were nothing that could be connected. There were horse hooves, a thick tome being filled with words, and an old kingdom in the surface of a rock wall.

It meant nothing to her at the moment, but she knew somehow that it connected to everything that was happening. Then, finally, there was an old man in a desert looking for answers. She didn't know if any of this would pass or not but, as she woke in the darkness, she knew it was more than just a dream. She just wished that she would get a chance to decipher them further.

Moving from place to place, dodging certain doom had been her existence for the majority of her time here on Ar Solon. It was only when Ranyll and Kalir had sat down to eat at the inn; that seemed to be the only time that there was actual rest.

However, now, the rest was forced on her. After the parting from her protectors with the daemon TSeT, they had passed through a number of pathways and corridors underneath the world above that Gabriella knew of so well, rushing through a number of chambers marked with the ancient languages of the inhabitants. Gabriella had soon become exhausted and she stumbled several times before falling for good on the dusty cavern floor, curses and gargles from TSeT the only thing she could hear in the impending darkness. No light had been given; no light had been needed for the daemon leader and his crew. Gabriella was to fend for herself, feeling in the dark with her hands for the ceiling, the walls, making sure she was passing through without harming herself further.

Already, cuts and bruises had surfaced on her forehead due to a low cavern ceiling she had not been warned about.

My mistake, she thought to herself, trying her best to breathe and remain calm in complete darkness when there was nothing but the enemy surrounding her.

"Angel, we leave now!" The guttural voice of TSeT spat out the words.

"I can't," she said, defeated somewhat, hoping that TSeT would be understanding, though knowing he wouldn't.

He wasn't.

The cord suddenly became taut and Gabriella felt the makeshift collar tighten around her neck, pulling her up from her seated position.

Her arms and hands touched on the darkened forms of the huddling masses of daemons in the corners of the tunnels, the red eye slits opening up before her. Their clicking claws flickered to life around her. Gabriella shivered and grabbed for the cord connected to her, using it as a guide to stay away from the others.

"Master commands it," was all TSeT gave as a reason behind his purpose. She agreed to it, though.

I have no room to disagree, she concluded, hoping, at least, that she wouldn't come in contact with another daemon in her path; that cold, distant, far away feeling was something that made her mind go reeling out of control. Every good feeling that she had melted away at the daemon's slightest touch, at the daemon's closeness, at her seeming to be the only light in that darkened tunnel of hate and despair.

In the short time she had been on Ar Solon as a mortal being, she had grown accustomed to the warmth and the light as a part of life. It wasn't until she was down in the tunnels without it that she really appreciated it. She could see how an inhabitant could lose hope without the grand scheme and the many other things that seemed to be needed in order to thrive.

Suddenly, there was a dampness that clung to the walls around her. It hung thick in the air, making it hard for her to take a deep breath. The walls seemed to be sweating and there were small puddles at her feet that she splashed through in her boots.

We must be close to a waterway, she thought, listening around her as the daemons scampered past, clicking their claws wildly in excitement.

Gabriella was right. No sooner had she said that she began to hear the muffled sounds of water splashing against the rocks, a small glimmer of light leaking through into the tunnel way ahead of her. She could feel the light spray of water against her face and it brought a thirst that she had forgotten ever since she had been in the caverns with TSeT and the other daemon minions.

There was also another sound; a constant thumping back and forth as the force of the waves caught something in its tight grip between the cavern floor and the edge of the water. Gabriella watched as the tunnel opened up into the dim shafts of light to see a cavern waterfall forming a deep inlet at her feet several feet across. Just to the corner of the cavern wall, the water had pushed a small man-made vessel into a corner, continually knocking it against the wall. A number of daemons skittered past her and disregarded the vessel completely, apparently more engaged in something else. Gabriella watched as they moved quickly towards the side of the waterfall that they could get access to, Gabriella finally seeing what had caught their eye. It was a young girl! She hung from a ledge that stuck out just past the waterfall.

Apparently she had saved herself from falling to her death by reaching out for a hold as the vessel got sucked into the cave by the tide. Gabriella gasped; she could see the young girl's hold slipping slightly, her fingers wet and losing their grip.

Gabriella could see the fear in the girl's eyes, watched her as she panicked, watching the daemon crowd down below her feet, eagerly waiting for her to drop.

Each of them climbed over the other in an attempt to reach out and pull the girl down. The girl's eyes grew wide and she began to slip. In that instant, Gabriella could feel all the hope inside of her begin to die as the young girl was caught by the daemons. She never hit the cavern floor.

Gabriella turned away from the sight but could not escape the screams that slipped out of the girl's mouth as she was devoured by the daemons. TSeT stood by just outside the tunnel, watching his brethren play with the girl's corpse as they fed. He looked over to Gabriella.

"You not like how we feed, angel? We are made to suffer so why should we not let others suffer, too?"

"You destroyed the only hope she had." Gabriella began to move further way from the feeding grounds.

"Master says there is no hope for the inhabitants. There is only death. That is the way of things. Your Creator know more than death?"

Gabriella stopped in her tracks. What was the grand scheme for the inhabitants? It seemed to slip from her mind. Gabriella had known it, but now....

*   *   *

"Not another! No!" Gilden got up from his writing desk, crossing over to the drying area with a wet page in his hand. He attached the page to the maze of strings tied to the corners of the room, looking at the dozens of pages that he had written only hours before.

"This cannot happen; it simply can't! An angel always knows the grand scheme. To say that she doesn't know… she can't. This can't be!"

Gilden could no longer contain it. He could feel the anger well up within him, the bruise on his head aching even more now. The wave of anxiety began to wash over him. He knew his body couldn't take much more. He grasped for his chair and stumbled, accidentally pushing things off his writing desk to regain his footing.

To the garden, he thought. He scanned the room for his thick walking robe and cane and made his way for them both, taking great care not to pull down the drying pages that floated like phantoms of the future throughout his room. Gilden grabbed his robe and draped it over his shoulders, tapping the cane down on the hard, stone floor. It echoed in his room and down the hallway repeatedly as he disappeared down the dimly lit corridors to the meditation gardens.

The gardens had been created 50 years earlier simply as a place for the scribes to grow their own fruits and vegetables, scoffing at the high and sometimes ridiculous prices of the vending markets just outside the library doors at the marketplace. Since becoming somewhat more private of a guild, the garden had been perfected, soon taking up less space, several walkways and pathways created between each section of garden with, finally, a rock and sand garden created as the centermost point of the garden; a place for the scribes to go to meditate and clear their thoughts. There were a dozen or so large rocks placed concentrically in a diagonal line across the sand, several rippling patterns created around the rocks with hand-made plowing tools that the scribes had made as well.

All of the fruits, vegetables, and spices had been moved into four sets of L-shaped gardens placed at each corner of the newly-constructed meditation gardens. There were a large number of scribes that took great care in nurturing and tending the garden, taking the fruit and vegetables from the garden, extracting the herbs and spices from each place, and trimming the overgrowth to ensure that it was a well-manicured area whenever any entered. It had soon become a proud landmark in the city and many of the city's representatives had come to see it on the days that it was being tended to see how well the scribes took care of their grounds.

There were sets of long benches and short benches spaced out around the stone and rock garden and each side of the garden had long, padded boards attached to the edges of the rock garden for meditation. There was enough room for at least fifteen on the east and west sides of the rock garden and thirty scribes on the north and south ends of the rock garden. However, not all scribes attended at the same time.

Since the library was so extensive and incorporated so many things into the daily functions of the library, an outsider that would come in would only see ten or twelve scribes at a time. Everyone ran on a schedule. In fact, the life of a scribe was already written out for them every day. The inhabitants of the town might find this somewhat tiresome and boring, but the scribes thrived on the idea of structure.

Gilden found, among the many padded seats on the meditation boards, that his seat was available. Pulling the hem of his robes up above his knees, he placed his cane on the vacant seat next to him and sat in the formal meditative position of all of the scribes. Gilden draped his robes over his crossed legs and closed his eyes. At once, his immediate concerns flooded his mind. He let himself fall back and allow the questions to take over, a technique the scribes had used for years.

Why would you let Gabriella, one of your angels, lose her grand scheme? Do you care for your own? Why not just end it all right now? The world is not that bad. I see hope in all things the inhabitants do. Where are your angels to protect and instill the grand scheme into your children? There is something very wrong going on in your world and it will not stop until a power beyond your inhabitants stop it. Where is this power? Will I ever see it?

In the midst of these questions, Gilden could hear pairs of footsteps coming closer behind him. They soon stopped beside him and did not sit down in a padded seat. The Chronicler straightened up and slowly opened his eyes. He turned to see a young scribe with an unknown visitor. The visitor was an older man, in his fifties, with a grizzled white beard cropped somewhat close to the face, with very tan skin and a fisherman's garb on. His arms and face had small cuts and bruises his clothes were disheveled and torn in several places.

When Gilden Felves looked into the old man's eyes, he knew all of his questions would be answered very soon.

Falwen Sanse reached out his hand to the old man, Gilden Felves he was called, and felt the scribe's hand shaking excitedly in his own calloused hand. What he saw in this scribe's eyes chilled him to the bone.

"Hello, Gilden, my name is…"

"I know who you are. It *is* you."

The Chronicler smiled one last time before his eyes rolled back into his head and he collapsed into the sand garden, breathing his last breath into the calming sands underneath him, the seconds and hours in the hourglass of his life dropping away *forever*.

The Chronicler Gilden Felves was finally at peace.

*   *   *

"This cave seems to go on *forever!*" Kalir hung suspended in the massive cave, looking up at Dir'grar and the others as he spun himself around in the makeshift harness, watching as the light from his torch reflected against the walls of the cavern. Small tidbits of a rock surface glimmered and twisted about in the torchlight, Kalir trying to see how deep the daemon cavern went.

"Lower me further down, Dir'grar. I want to see how far this thing goes."

Dir'grar hesitated. He looked behind him at the others that had a good portion of the rope and shook his head, looking back down into the cavern they had found at Kalir. "Just drop the torch, Master Ranolf. We have enough trouble as is, we don't need to lose you in the process of all this mess."

*There were messes, then there was **this** mess,* Kalir thought to himself, trying his best to stay sane in such an insane time, he concluded, shifting himself in the harness a bit so he could put most of his weight on his hip and not the ropes that tightened around his waist and thighs every moment he hung there. It was true that he and his companion Dir'grar had been in messes of these sorts before, but something felt different about this predicament; something wasn't right. It was as if a piece of the puzzle were missing, as if the whole truth had not come out yet and he and the others just had to sit and wait for something awful to come upon them.

He shook his head at this thought. Kalir knew that he would never allow this to happen. In any time of hardship, Kalir had been there, fighting the good fight, by someone's side or leading the way, as he did now. Nevertheless, there had always been hope. There was always hope.

Kalir smiled and tugged on the rope. The torchlight broke into pieces across the wall, showing him scattered fragments of old carvings from long ago; worn statues as old idols during the last war and, finally, scratches. Thick, deep scratches marred the surface of the walls of the cavern from top to bottom, Kalir trying to lean closer to the walls to see the specifics. He looked down at the darkness below. He thought he heard light clicking sounds. Kalir felt a shiver crawl up the backs of his legs to his spine, all the way up to his neck. He shook it off and looked above him to make sure the light still shone in the opening.

Reluctantly, he called up to Dir'grar.

"For once, I agree. However, I have another plan. Pull me up. We've got to do this quickly." Dir'grar nodded to the men behind him, Ermoor and Rynen as well as seven others just behind him, all tightening their grip on the rope. Dir'grar pulled once, the rest of the party pulling just after him, Kalir soon poking his head up out of the cavern, his hands reaching for a hold on the ground. Once up, Kalir looked around their surroundings. His eyes caught on the tipped over wagon that had hidden the hole from sight, his eyes scanning around him. He looked then at Dir'grar, who nodded in understanding.

Dir'grar knew what needed to be done. Without a word, Dir'grar ordered the others to break apart the wagon, tearing the tarp from the top of the wagon into long shreds that were then wrapped around each piece of wood and tied tightly. Dir'grar had seen Kalir's 'tricks' done before, many since they had been together. The big man knew that there were things down there that waited. He knew that those things would wait in the darkness for them or wait until darkness came to come after them all; and there wasn't anything that anyone could do about it once that happened. And that's where Kalir's 'tricks' came into play.

Since knowing Kalir for so many years, Dir'grar knew that his friend would never allow Ranyll to leave without offering some assistance. Of course, he knew of the assistance of the supplies and weapons that Kalir had given the boy and his traveling companion, but Kalir had sent scouts out to all the checkpoints to clear the way for any traveler on the road to ensure Ranyll's safe passage through to Reune Lake or wherever he needed to go. After that, Kalir sent a messenger to each nearby town asking for them to keep guards on double watch for anything out of the ordinary, making sure that the towns didn't allow things or goings on slip through and let something terrible happen; which, of course, could happen, Kalir looking back at Rynen and Ermoor's situation that occurred in a matter of moments; twice, as well.

If that weren't enough to cause him caution, Dir'grar knew it would be one more thing. And it was. The finding of a cave this big and this dangerous was something Kalir would not allow; not on his checkpoint anyway. Dir'grar began piling up the wood with the cloth ties in a stack by the cavern entrance, watching as the rest of the checkpoint crewmembers left to get the rest of their supplies and a number of other items that Kalir now required. Kalir walked up next to Dir'grar, dropping several planks of wood down onto the pile.

Kalir looked at his old friend of so many years. "You know we're all going down, right?"

Dir'grar simply nodded. "I knew we were going as soon as I saw the hole. You didn't have to go crawling around in there by yourself for me to know that. Just as long as you know that I go in first!"

Kalir turned to his friend, now suddenly a little more interested in the conversation than before. In fact, he was intrigued.

"Really?"

Dir'grar felt as if his insides were going to be pushed out of his mouth, watching as the darkness grew closer and closer, soon almost completely surrounding him, the makeshift torches dropped down into the cavern not really working as good as they should be.

"Kalir, these torches you made don't work worth anything! Great job!"

In fact, Dir'grar couldn't see his feet as they dangled down below him, his eyes trying to focus on the depth the torches had dropped before they made contact with the ground below. He still couldn't make out the shapes of the torches. All the big man could see were little glimmers of light in a sloppy circle. They had all dropped one down into the cavern with hopes that they would make a circle of sorts to clear a path. With his own torch, Dir'grar couldn't see that circle, but he could see faint flickers of light and….. something else. And that something else looked like darkness taking shape below him. He waved his torch up above them, the hole a small dot in the darkened cavern.

"They're down there, alright! I can see them moving."

Kalir's shout could barely be heard in the cavern. "We'll get you a little closer, then we'll drop'em."   Dir'grar waved his torch in an easterly then westerly direction, looking down at the approaching darkness. Below him, he could hear the clicks that Kalir had described. They were moving quite furious, almost as if they were excited at what was about to happen.

It's not what you think, Dir'grar thought, shifting a bit more so that he could see the ground below him and the dot above him. He tugged on the rope twice. Soon, he stopped moving completely, hanging in mid-air.

He could hear Kalir's voice again, just barely this time.

"Here they come, Dir'grar. Watch your head!" Soon, Dir'grar could feel a shaking on the rope he was tied to and, as he looked up, he could see the water skin pouches sliding down, bulging at the seams. Dir'grar held his torch out at his side and placed his hand on the rope up above him, stopping all of the water skins from colliding with him on the rope. He then let them slide down into his lap, where the rope was tied. Quickly, he untied them from his rope and kept them in his lap. He uncorked one of the water skins, pouring it down onto the flames below him. Suddenly, the flames took on a shape below him and burst alive, bringing into its light hundreds of waiting daemons below.

Dir'grar did not hesitate to pour the others out as well. The remaining torches below were splashed over with a water skin of oil, Dir'grar raining down the liquid, watching as the circle of fire below him began to take shape, soon engulfed in flame. He tugged twice on the rope. Again, the rope began to lower him down closer to the circle of fire, Dir'grar's eyes scanning down below him, trying to check inside the circle.

Indeed, there were daemons that were inside the circle as well, somehow trapping themselves in the circle of fire. And now they were part of Dir'grar's job. Just a dozen feet above the daemons, he tugged the rope, pulling the knot loose as well, the ground below him rushing up at him.

Dir'grar unsheathed the short sword at his hip, the torch out in front of him as he landed. The daemons were still lost amid the flames but came to attention when they smelled Dir'grar's flesh. They leapt at him without hesitation. Nevertheless, Dir'grar was already arching his blade out at them to catch them in mid-air. Two were cut out of the air and then he waved the torch at the other's, three behind him, forcing them back into the flames until they leapt at him, his blade striking a ferocious blow, their shadowy forms slumping to the cavern floor at Dir'grar's feet. He kicked the shadowy forms out over the flames, watching as the other daemons around him jumped up and down, trying to see inside the wreath of flame he had formed around himself. He watched as the rope disappeared into the darkness above him.

"Well, I'm here until they get here." He pulled another water skin out into the flame, watching as the flames leapt at the shadows, at the darkness around them and, for the first time in over five centuries, the curse of the caverns that had housed so much hatred. Dir'grar was the first to fight off the darkness…and he was winning.

26

It had been two days since the sudden appearance of a fisherman named Falwen Sanse at the guild hall as well as the sudden death of Scribe Gilden Felves and still none of the scribes could make sense of it. The old fisherman had simply shook Falwen's hand. There had been no secret incantation, no spell of any kind. Falwen seemed to be just a normal fisherman. It was all so very confusing to the scribes, who were of a simple nature; the outside world of dramatic occurrences and death was not for the tame at heart, as were many of the scribes, especially those that had been living in the great library for all of their life.

Of course, many say that Falwen was on the verge of collapse and, quite possibly death, but no one took the rumors serious; at least, not until now. In less than a day, the scribes had selected two scribes that were close to Scribe Felves to secure his property and, amongst his things, a will was found. Within a scroll case, there were specific instructions on how the proceedings of the reading of his will should go, how it should work, and who were allowed to attend. Pages upon pages of details were found as well as an inventory list of all of Gilden's belongings.

For a moment, it seemed to everyone that Gilden almost knew that he was going to pass away sometime soon. For a scribe, this sounded a bit absurd. But Falwen did not take the idea lightly.

He had been told to come here and find a scribe by the name of Gilden Felves. But what to do once he got here, he did not know. 'Find out a human by the name of Gilden Felves', Divlo had said, as Falwen was standing by the shore, the fallen body of Greditto having washed up on the rocks. His task had been only that. And, as he sat in the guest room he had been given by the guild, he hoped that the reading of this scribe's will would answer some of the questions that needed answering, at least in Falwen's mind.

Falwen lay back on the bed, his thoughts suddenly drifting to his family far off on the western shore.

I wonder what they're doing, he thought to himself, picturing his children playing in the surf while his wife walked along the sandy beach.

Oh, to be there again, Falwen noted, *would be something of a miracle.* With the knowledge that he had at hand, he knew that it was not as simple as that. The grand scheme was nothing to tamper with. Be it that Falwen had lived most of his life without ever receiving the grand scheme; he was terrified of the idea of actually losing it and never getting it back.

Though he did not know what his grand scheme was, he had been given a direction by his own angel, Divlo, and knew that he could not be steered wrong by him. In all the years that he had asked and prayed for guidance, Falwen's ships had never strayed from their path and it led him here to where he had been for nearly three decades, over half of his life, staying with his family.

His wife and children were the only things that mattered to him now. And, from what Divlo had said to him, it was imperative that he ensure that his part of the grand scheme in this world was met. 'The things you do from this point on will change the history of all on Ar Solon.' The angel had spoken these words and they seemed now to be etched in the fisherman's mind forever.

Yet, still, he feared for long moments that there may be no end to the amount of responsibility he may be given, praying to his angel that had given him his strength in his younger times to give him clarity of mind now.

Falwen let himself sink into the bed, the soft sheets and airy room slowly pulling the ache and pain from the last day's adventures from his bones. He began to drift off to sleep, to feel himself lighten somewhat from the stresses of the world. For a moment, his mind and body were at peace. He had heard of the healing properties of the scribes and how it was said that one that becomes a scribe never turns from their trade. Many had attributed it to the magikal properties that are bestowed upon them by the Creator for giving up their lives for a great service; others say that scribes, once turning from the daily life of an inhabitant, do not know how to turn back to their former life so they take on the trade as a service for life to keep themselves alive and continually pressing towards something greater.

This something greater that those talked of, those magikal properties those spoke of, all seemed to be unsubstantial reports, either by local drinking patrons or a vagabond, wanderer or trader that passed through the town every season or so, passing along wares as well as stories of great adventure. Falwen felt as though he were one of these great stories that people told about. Though he may only be a minor character in the great stories that were told, he felt that he would play an important role.

He could almost see the quill moving in his mind, words upon words filling the pages, his history and the history of others around him being written. He pictured himself sitting in a chair in a remote location, his eyes focused and hard on the pages in front of him, turning page after page of written pages, only to find one page left in the book in front of him. His hand lifted from under the book, holding out the ink quill as if it were a weapon, stabbing the end down deep into the book, carving letters into the final page. The ink swelled up in the tip of the quill, emptying out onto the page, seeping into each carved letter, the ink filling up the letters until, finally, it was finished. Falwen looked down at the last page and gasped. The word bit into his very soul:

...FOREVER....

Falwen jolted awake suddenly, a light tapping sound echoing in his room from someone knocking on the door. The word still echoed in his mind, the dream still pulling at him, nevertheless the fisherman managed to pull himself up out of the bed and opened the door. A young scribe stood looking at him anxiously, hands squeezed tightly together in front of him.

"It is time, Master Sanse. The council is ready for the reading of the will, sir. Please follow me."

In moments, Falwen had slipped on his boots by the bed and straightened his clothes, doing his best to maintain a suitable appearance for such a ceremony.

Two days had gone by and Falwen had become somewhat apprehensive at the long wait, his eyes darting from scribe to scribe as he walked down the long, quiet hallways. All of the scribes were dressed in either brown or grey robes of the scribe order, their feet shod in a simple sandal that tapped against the floor as each of them moved past him.

They wear such simple garb; such quiet souls they are. I don't see how they do it, Falwen thought to himself, watching as he and the scribe turned another corner and continued down through a narrower hallway, a number of doors on each side passing by them, the scribe eventually stopping at one of the doors on their left. On each door, there were a series of undecipherable codes on the door, each on a plaque. Falwen looked at the scribe and motioned to the plaque on the door before the young scribe opened it.

The scribe whispered in response. "All head scribes of the order have an office in which they conduct their business. This code on the door signifies their rank and time in service to the order. It is written in Parthenian. It is a language that only the scribes use on Kariyl."

"Parthenian," Falwen exclaimed, somewhat louder than he expected, the word echoing down the hallway. He quieted his voice somewhat. "Isn't Parthenian a language and history that all of Kariyl is forbidden to delve in?"

Falwen could tell right away that the scribe was hesitant to answer. The young scribe tried to look for an answer, his eyes darting down to the floor momentarily. "Master Sanse, maybe it is not the best time to be speaking of these things. Scribe Felves' will is about to be read and we must have our mind on other matters; the matters at hand if that is okay with you."

Falwen could tell when someone was trying to change the subject. The fisherman put this oddity of conversation away for another time. He nodded in agreement.

"My apologies, scribe."

"None required, Master Sanse." The scribe motioned to the door. "Shall we?"

The fisherman nodded. The door opened and they stepped inside.

The first thing that the fisherman took notice of was the smell within the room. It smelled what any room full of years of books would smell like; dry and musty. The room was full of the smell and, everywhere that Falwen moved, the smell permeated his nostrils. He looked in front of him and, for a moment, the light from a number of candles in the room flickering, he thought that he saw several people sitting in front of him. Once his eyes grew accustomed, however, he noticed that there was only a single man sitting at a great table in the middle of the room, his hands on a scroll parchment that was rolled out, the scroll almost reaching from one end of the table to the other.

The scribe in front of him wore grey robes of the order and wore a pendant around his neck, his bald, smooth white head reflecting the candlelight here and there, his eyes cast in shadows due to his thick, overhanging brow. He looked almost menacing for a moment. The young scribe bowed respectfully and backed out of the room, closing the door so that Falwen and the grey-robed scribe were in the room alone.

The scribe spoke. His voice was thick like smoke. "Have a seat, Master Falwen Sanse. I have been waiting to see you for some time since your arrival here days ago."

Falwen was surprised to hear that. "Really?"

The scribe scooted a little closer up in his chair behind the desk. "Oh, yes! What I have found in Scribe Gilden Felves' possession is quite interesting. However, I find your arrival here quite disconcerting. After all, Gilden passed away the moment that he met you."

Falwen was taken aback at the direct accusation, especially after how nicely they had treated him the past few days until this moment. "I'm sorry, I didn't quite catch your name, Scribe….."

"Head Scribe Ja'wan. I am head advisor here while Head Scribe Tollins is away."

"Well, Head Scribe Ja'wan, I'm afraid that I know little about the mysterious death of Scribe Gilden Felves. I never even knew the man. I take offense to what you say, sir."

"Indeed, you should, Master Sanse. However, I feel that it is my responsibility to maintain a respectable work place for the scribes here and, since the death of one of our most prized scribes happened during the time in which I am in charge, I feel it my responsibility to question the one person that may know something about his death….be it that you are the sole bearer of his property."

Sole bearer! This can't be! I don't even know this person! Falwen's heart began to beat harder and harder against his chest. He could feel the beads of sweat begin to form around his hairline and in between his shoulder blades. "I don't know what to say."

Scribe Ja'wan did not seem to believe Falwen at all. His eyebrows furrowed at this answer and he then turned his attention to the scroll in front of him, turning it slowly around so that Falwen could see it. Throughout the entire scroll, Falwen's name appeared, almost covering the scroll paper, a number of detailed instructions on what to do with the possessions given throughout the will. One word in particular stuck out:

AGNAR.

Falwen began to protest. "You're not saying that I have to go to Agnar? That's such a long journey north; not including the danger. I wouldn't go up there with a dozen well-armed Golettan soldiers."

"Well, you don't have to because it states that you are to go alone. There are, in fact, a number of stipulations in this will. It also states that, if you are not present during the reading of the will, then a messenger will be sent to bring you here and deliver the goods. This is your task, Falwen. It seems to be set in stone; it's almost as if you have a grand scheme of sorts given to you, Master Sanse."

Falwen almost jumped in response. "What did you say?"

Scribe Ja'wan was a little startled. He scooted back in his chair a bit.

"Master Sanse, I mean no offense to you, sir. In fact, you seem like a nice enough fellow. It's simply this: we here at the scribe's guild have never seen nor heard of anything like this before. We are, in fact, trying to figure out how this came to pass at such an opportune time for both you and Scribe Felves. Master Sanse, do you understand that you came on the day that Scribe Felves passed away and were soon found to inherit everything that this man ever owned, and you say that you've never met him before in your life? I find this to be quite strange. In fact, if this scroll were not signed by him and written in Gilden's own hand, I would say that there was foul play here." The Head Scribe paused, looking down at the scroll. He then took a great, deep breath and continued.

"However, of course, there is nothing I can say. Since this is a legal document, I am obliged to honor this contract and send you on your way."

"Thank you for the understanding, Head Scribe. I do not come here to make problems."

"Then why, may I ask, did you come here?"

Falwen could no longer hide the truth. Nevertheless, he felt inclined to protect himself and the presence of angels on the land of Kariyl. "I come here simply because it is my purpose to."

Head Scribe Ja'wan chuckled loudly. It was the first time Falwen saw a smile pass the grey-robed scribe's face. Falwen didn't find anything funny at that moment. In fact, he still felt a little bit defensive; being accused and excused in almost the same breath didn't do too well for his spirit.

"What's so funny, Head Scribe?"

"It's just what you said puts me in a state. It takes me back to years ago. I almost forgot about the conversation until you spoke those words."

"What words were those, exactly?"

"When you said, 'I come here simply because it is my purpose to.' Scribe Felves said those words almost 50 years ago when he came to the Scribes Guild. I was a young man at the time, working on my guild lessons, but I was there when this old, disheveled man came wandering in. He promised that he would bring the guild to a new age and bring about a change to the Guild that we had never seen before. And he did just that. He showed us copying methods that cut the time almost in half and ways of preparation of tomes that would keep them preserved for far longer than we could ever imagine. How he got the information to all of these things, we never knew. But we kept him on ever since."

"And did you believe him?"

"About it being his purpose, Master Sanse? We never knew what his purpose really was. He spent much of his time writing his own stories in his personal quarters. No one ever bothered him until just recently."

"Until recently?"

Head Scribe Ja'wan was hesitant to answer. It was the same look that the young scribe had given Falwen just outside the doors moments before.

"There are some things that need to remain a secret to the guild, Master Sanse. You have no part to play here at our guild. Maybe when you get to the guild in Agnar, you can ask them questions about Scribe Gilden Felves."

"Is that where Gilden has stated to take his things?"

"Yes. There is a small guild house in the Upper Agnar that we send supplies to every season or so. They are very resourceful, those dwarves. We never thought they'd be good scribes, but they are very diligent. And, with their ability to see in the darkness, they work well into the night and don't use many resources as we do here at our guild. You will be safe enough going on your own. I will let you read the will for yourself. The wagon is already loaded and ready once you feel rested enough to begin your journey."

"Wagon? Why would I need a wagon?"

"Apparently, you don't know Gilden as well as we all do here. He has quite a collection of things. And he wishes his body to be transported along with his supplies. He has stated that he wants to be buried in the Agnar Forests just north of the Agnar Guild House." With that said, Head Scribe Ja'wan stood up from his chair behind the great desk and made his way out of the room, not speaking another word to old fisherman, closing the door softly behind him.

Falwen sat for a moment, trying his best to understand what just happened.

Apparently I don't know Gilden. Of course I don't know him! I don't know anyone here. What is all this about?

Gilden took a long look at the will written on the scroll in front of him, not wanting to read it but knowing that he should. *What is it you know that I don't, Gilden Felves?*

Falwen pulled the scroll closer across the table, looking down at it. Pages upon pages were written by this scribe, small maps drawn on a thicker set of parchment for directions to the Guild at the Upper Agnar, even an inventory list of his items had been made, categorizing everything that the scribe had secured since his arrival here at the guild.   Falwen Sanse continued to read the will.

'The Last Will and Testament of Scribe Gilden Felves:

The following will and testament has been written with the sole proprietor in mind. The name of that proprietor is Falwen Sanse. He is located in the small town of Simmer Lo, just north of Goletta. He has been tasked with taking my belongings to the Upper Agnar Guild. Arrangements have been made with the Upper Agnar Guild to care for my possessions. Someone will be there to care for my things....' Falwen continued to read on, still not knowing what to say about the knowledge that Gilden had about him, yet unable to let his eyes move away from the scroll in front of him. It was almost as if he were urged to continue.

*　　　　　*　　　　　*

Dir'grar watched as the last checkpoint guard lowered himself down, watching as the mass of daemons tried to come at him.

Rynen untied the rope from his waist and straightened the armor he had been given, pulling out both of his short swords at his waist, waiting for the signal to move forward. Several bandages were tied and double bandaged around his waist and all over his arms under his armor, his tunic still bloody from the attacks earlier, which made him look a mess compared to the others. The sleep that he received, however, was much needed. He refused to stay behind and, as he looked at Ermoor by his side in similar armor, he knew that there was no way that they would ever stay behind. At this moment, the battle that they were fighting was personal. And there was no way that they would wait for repair of their worn bodies or clearance from Kalir. But Kalir already knew that. He smiled at the two checkpoint guards at his side now, looking to Dir'grar for the next part of their move.

Dir'grar hefted a barrel over his head with both hands and tossed it into the daemon crowd ahead of them. Kalir tossed the torch in after the barrel. Once the barrel shattered, the oil spilled forth and lit the entire cave as well as the daemons in front of them, the checkpoint guards pulling out a number of spears from a supply bag they had brought down with them. Dir'grar held up the fish netting and tossed it into the piled of daemons in front of them.

"Checkpoint guard, now!" The checkpoint guard, nine members including Dir'grar and Kalir, pressed themselves together and pushed forward against the daemons, jabbing at the captured daemons in the netting as they struggled, jabbing one after another, Ermoor and Rynen watching for random daemons at the corners of the netting. Dir'grar grabbed another barrel from the supplies and moved forward, tossing another barrel into the daemons, Kalir following with a lit torch.

Again, the cavern lit up, and again the checkpoint guards surged forward, spears at the ready, cutting a swath through the daemons, their protective armor keeping them alive, their sharp wits keeping the enemy at bay.

Never have a checkpoint guard worked so fluently together, stepping forward, attacking, parrying the enemy; they all seemed to be one great machine moving together, they spears poised at the ready. The daemons sensed this and began to withdraw; somehow, they knew that this was a trap.

The number of burnt daemon carcasses had become an excessive amount around the other daemons and the smell was sickening. Daemons crawled over their brethren's burnt shells and back into the caverns that they had come from, Kalir ordering the checkpoint guard to rush them back even more.

Numbers of daemons fell in the retreat and never recovered, their bodies littering the ground as well. Soon, the cavern floor stopped moving and all that was left were smoking shells of daemons, Dir'grar scattering a number of makeshift torches into the corners of the cavern to light it up even more.

The cavern was so much larger than they had ever seen. At no point in time did Kalir expect to see so many cavern entrances all at once. There were dozens of entrances piled together, some high up on the cavern wall while others were just spaced far enough between others to actually be separate. Kalir spent little time looking around and ordered his team to gather the remaining supplies and move out. He pointed to the cave the daemons had retreated into.

Dir'grar hefted two barrels onto his shoulders. He looked into the cave. "Aren't we going to wait for the rest of the crew to get here?"

Kalir shook his head. "I trust you all. The others will follow our lead. Ranyll does not have time on his side, Dir'grar. It has already been long enough of a wait. We must move quickly if we are to even have an effect on the daemon army."

Dir'grar nodded and then motioned to the others to follow, the seven remaining passing by the smoking masses of daemons and the still-lit fires that continued. They moved into the tunnel and began their descent into the daemon's nesting caves.

27

Triggle and Ilthen looked ahead to the lit pathway just in front of them. It had been some time since they had seen any light. They didn't know whether to think of it as a good omen or a bad omen. In fact, as they looked back at the faerie army that moved silently behind them, they could not think of anything as bad right now. It had been somewhat of a close call back in the tunnels with the daemons, Triggle knew, but he kept his head on straight. At least, that's what he continued to chant to himself inside of his mind.

He knew it wasn't the best thing to lose his sensibilities in front of a lady, especially one that he had just met and was faerie kin to. It was not proper at all. He looked now over at Ilthen, her eyes deep and focused on the tunnel in front of them. Triggle smiled slightly, a little mischievous thought drifting through his mind. Ilthen caught the look, too, and blushed a little, thumping him smartly on the arm with the flat of her dagger.

Triggle rubbed his arm in defeat. "Ouch! What was that for?"

Ilthen pointed to Triggle's head then to the tunnel ahead of them.

"For everything that is floating around in that head of yours and for it not being on the cavern in front of us. Don't you hear them?"

Triggle shook away the thoughts and listened closely in front of him. He could almost make out something just ahead of them.

It was a noise, without a doubt.

He just didn't know what it was. For a second, it sounded as if it were a skittering or a movement of stone against stone. He listened for another moment and then heard nothing. He looked to Ilthen.

"Whatever it was, it seemed to come and….." Then he heard another sound. It was a sound that he hoped that he would never have to hear for the rest of his life, as long as his little faerie life would keep him safe; it was an intense harmony of clicking sounds echoing from the passageway just ahead of them. Just behind them, Triggle could hear the shuffling of faerie feet and felt a slight nudge from the nose of the lead unicorn.

I believe it is time for us to move forward, Triggle.

The Miftle faerie whispered lightly now. "But there are daemons ahead of us."

Exactly. That is why we must attack them before they can attack us. Do not be afraid, Triggle. We are stronger than they will ever hope to be. And, besides, you do not have to fight them alone anymore, my kin. We are here to help you.

Triggle could see, out of the shadows behind him, the hundreds of faeries that sat, motionless, while the lead unicorn nudged Triggle forward, the Miftle keeping his gaze away from Ilthen for the moment.

I need courage, Triggle told himself, looking down the passageway that was filled, red daemon eyes shifting back and forth through the darkness, the Miftle faerie's hand sliding toward his flask. It was full now, the Miftle faerie wanting so bad to take a sip.

Just a little sip, to take the edge off.

No, my friend. You have far greater powers to wield than a simple flask of spirits, Triggle. Remember what happened at the Dwarven shield.

You were there, Triggle questioned.

I was not, Triggle, but we felt your powers come to life. The greater faeries can always sense it. Just as we sense Gwenzel's powers right now. He lives….he lives and he needs our help.

Triggle's hand drifted away from the flask and he lifted his hands up in front of him.

The sudden clicking in front of him began to get stronger. He could see the red slits begin to move toward him; they took notice of Triggle and Ilthen just behind him, their claws clicking almost in unison, they maws opening forth. They scuttled on the floors and many of them traveled across the ceiling of the passageway, hordes of daemons shifting their attention from the darkened cavern to the living, breathing Miftle faeries that seemed to be alone and for the taking. But then their red slits caught sight of the unicorn.

The great white beast stood over the two Miftles, it's great mane and horn waving as it snorted and pawed at the cavern floor below; the great horn surrounded by a magikal fire. The lead unicorn surged forward and the hundreds of faeries followed suit, many of them flying forward, others riding on the backs of other great faerie creatures; Triggle, Ilthen, and the lead unicorn moving forward into the horde of daemons without hesitation. Triggle felt the magikal fire course through his veins, stronger this time than before, the passageway around him lighting up as his hands lit the way for the others in his party.

The daemons stood motionless for a moment, wavering from their intended position of maiming and devouring the two Miftles, watching as the tunnel ahead of them became covered by the massive amounts of faeries from the Faerie Homme come to finish the task that had been left alone for some time since The War of the Races. Several cries from the faeries echoed Shilinda's name as well as the names of others that had fallen in the Wilden Marsh, their spirits high and soaring, their weapons poised and at the ready.

The daemons faltered and broke their ranks, scattering throughout the passageway, trying to look for an escape route. But there was none. Sprites flew through the tunnels, tossing handfuls of fire dust over the daemons, sending the scurrying into the faerie army, the fire dust lighting the tunnel so all the faeries could see the daemons. The fire dust tore at the forms of the daemons, sending them reeling to the floor. The daemon horde collapsed in moments under the weight of the great faerie army, Triggle, Ilthen, and the lead unicorn still holding the front of the line, Triggle's magikal fire lancing out through his fingertips at the daemons. Once it surrounded their shadowy forms, they seemed to dissipate and turn into nothing. There were no remains, no skeletons on the floor.

The massacre of the daemons was not a massacre at all. As the faerie magik from all of the faerie kind touched the daemons, the daemon forms just seemed to vanish as if they had never been there at all.

Soon, the passageway was clear and the faeries had broken through, leaving no daemon alive or letting them escape to tell the rest of their kind, who might be hiding anywhere.

Triggle's face twisted is disbelief. "That's strange. Why did they just disappear like that? Every battle that I have been in so far that has never happened."

The light from the lead unicorn's horn began to fade, leaving the passageway somewhat barren and cold. It approached Triggle and Ilthen a little closer.

My dear Triggle, you have been too far from the rest of your kind. We, as faeries from the Faerie Homme have known this for some time. Whenever there is too much light, darkness cannot exist.

Triggle still seemed confused. "I do not understand."

The unicorn began walking them ahead in the passageway.

We shall talk along the way. However, we must not tarry. We are close now, closer now to danger that we have been in some time.

The faerie army moved through the passageways as silently as they could. The battle with the daemons had left many wounded, but none had died. Many were beginning to feel fatigue for moving at such a quick pace. Faeries, in essence, were not purpose-driven creatures. They had been known in stories to fill their days with frivolity and fun just to pass the time; the only purpose in their lives had been to enjoy each moment in life and keep away from the inhabitants for all time. Now, both purposes seemed dismissed and wiped from their minds completely, replaced with the emptiness and pain from the loss of their beloved Shilinda.

The day wore on and the pace did not slow, even for those that began to fall behind. The faeries made a pact that they would never leave another faerie behind; with each faerie that began to fall behind another faerie went to help.

*   *   *

It was far darker than it had ever been in a cave so far, Ranyll decided to himself, stepping back into one of the caves that they had come through only a day earlier, his mind drifting to what lie just ahead of them.

The Dwarven Crag, he thought to himself. Ranyll had thought that it was a nightmare of some sort that he had escaped but, when the dwarves stated that they would have to go back the way they came due to the mass number of daemons approaching from the other side, Ranyll almost felt like facing innumerable odds with the daemons instead of seeing the Crag again. He watched as Arntheer moved ahead of the rest of the party and lifted his hand for everyone else to stay where they were.

It was pitch black and Ranyll couldn't see a thing. D'meir seemed to be feeling the same as Ranyll, for he sat on the human's shoulder, its small claws digging into the young man's skin through his clothes. By now, Ranyll knew what the certain signals meant that D'meir gave him from time to time. This one meant both to stop and that D'meir was afraid. Since he was standing still, Ranyll knew that D'meir was afraid. The young man wanted to comfort D'meir and say something but he was afraid to move for what he heard up ahead in the tunnel; it was a soft clicking. It was a daemon.

The clicking did not echo within the tunnels as it had done before; it was far too quiet and too cramped for that. They were in a small chamber, just big enough for a dwarf to make it through without bumping its head; however, all dwarves had to take off their helms and move carefully because the ceiling shifted every now and again, bringing the roof closer down on them than it had been. Ranyll disliked this very much but he dealt with it the best he could; he kept his hand out in front of him most of the time, watching for those points in the ceiling where it lowered over time, in hopes that he wouldn't come in contact with it again and make another knot on his forehead.

In the time that they had travelled together, Ranyll had learned a little about Arntheer and his crew of dwarves. He knew that Arntheer was the leader and that, during any bout of indecision, he was ready to take a stand and make a move. Oagthor called him brash when the younger dwarf had decided to go back the way they came. 'We might be cornered, trapped on both sides, if we go back the way we came,' Oagthor had said, grabbing at his thick beard with his calloused hands, an apparent sign of stress, Ranyll noticed.

But Oagthor and Rathor gave in to Arntheer's demands in the end; soon the caravan of dwarven soldiers, the human boy and the fire fox were all going back the way they had come, regretting every step yet knowing that this was probably the safest way for the moment. Now Arntheer had his chance to prove himself. He knew that the lone daemon was lost in some way or a messenger daemon; the creature seemed to wander around, looking for a place to go and never finding one. Ranyll knew that the only thing that

the rest of the party could do while Arntheer followed the daemon was wait;

wait and rest. And Ranyll did just that without prompting or hesitation.

Soon, the young man was asleep against the side of the tunnel they had

stopped in, D'meir following suit, the fire fox curling up into a ball on

Ranyll's shoulder.

For a time, Ranyll's mind was clear. It was not corrupted with the great

creature, Scarwol, which D'meir had explained to him about earlier. Instead,

it was filled with the dream of a place. This place had come to him in

images, in small slivers, like the light from a distant window, slowly but surely

the light of the early morning creeping into the room, allowing only a slice of

the world outside then, all at once, the full breath of the morning would

come. The world inside Ranyll's mind seemed to coalesce around into the

forms of clouds and smoke, shifting this way and that. Then, as if it knew

that Ranyll were watching it, it began to take on a shape and form of a

location.

The location was deep inside a labyrinth of vines and reeds, thick-trunked trees that
grew low to the ground but in various numbers throughout this area.

Ranyll had never seen this place before but, for some reason, there was so

much of it that he could not deny what the world had and allowed it into his

mind. Ranyll continued to dream.

There were also great towers that were rotten and falling in amongst themselves, a world
that had been created ages ago but was now disappearing in the wild world around it.
Ranyll grew afraid at this thought, knowing, for some reason, that this world of the wild
would come about. He had never been in the wild and knew not how to combat it.
Suddenly, as if by magik, the world shifted and threw him into an underground lair, a

world that was unknown to many men, cobwebs and darkness were all that were found as he was pushed through a set of great caverns. A history of worlds had come and gone through these tunnels as well, but Ranyll knew not the names of any of them or the faces. All he could see was the past and how it reflected its light upon the present, a world away but suddenly in his face, here and now, a new light moving through the tunnels. It was as if he were seeing what had transpired as it happened, years ago. He could suddenly feel the presence of someone near him.

Ranyll awoke to the sound of clicking in the caves ahead of him, his eyes clouded with sleep, his ears full of screams of war and sudden death. He looked in front of him but all he could see was darkness and, in the darkness, movement of the others in his party. He heard one voice; it was the voice of Arntheer.

"They are attacking! Grab your weapons! They are here without warning!" Inside Arntheer's voice, Ranyll could hear panic; it was a panic he had never heard in Arntheer's voice before. Ranyll lifted himself to his feet in moments, pulling his father's blade free from its sheath. He prepared for the worst; and the worst is what met him.

In a single sliver of a dwarf's torchlight, he could see a massive army of daemons moving forward, the dwarves doing their best to combat it. The young man could feel the Dwarven Crag take hold of his heart through all of this, his courage wavering in the dim light, his eyes trying their best to focus on a villain in front of him. He looked to D'meir, who had been at his side through most of the journey, and was without a friend. D'meir was gone, nowhere to be found.

Oagthor seemed to be in the thick of battle and it was nothing for Ranyll to do but charge into the fray, into the thick of battle, with but a war cry and a raised sword of a time long gone, his eyes trying to focus in front of him as he pushed forward.

In moments, he could see his enemy; the red slits were like targets for him. Ranyll lifted his blade and dug his feet deep into the cavern floor, impaling a single daemon with his first strike, his sword scraping against the floor in front of him. He stopped and watched as the struggling daemon tried to escape his sword. Ranyll slammed his sword to the ground, wounding another daemon, eventually killing the daemon impaled upon his own blade.

For long moments, Ranyll tried to focus himself in the battle and seemed to see none of the party that he had traveled with; that was, of course, not until he saw Arntheer. The leader of the dwarven garrison had slipped his double axe from its sheath on his back and began swinging in wild arcs at the daemons that filled the cavern, flinging their dark forms into the air with a swift stroke, one massive swing after another, Arntheer trying his best to uncover a fallen dwarf from the daemons that began to surge forward.

And Arntheer's attempt was forfeit; a wave of daemons began to surge forward, like a tide of darkness within the cavern. The darkness blotted out all light and, for moments, Ranyll saw nothing save the dark red slits that were what he felt would be his death sentence. He had fought the daemons for such a long time now that is was all that he saw. He found that, in some way, that he could never escape from his fate of dying at the hands of the daemons. He could make out Oagthor and Rathor in the wave of darkness. They had been caught up in the army of daemons and struggled as best they could to try and escape the daemon's claws as they clicked wildly, their weapons swinging at anything that was a dark form or mass around them.

Much of the garrison had fallen underneath the daemon mass and there were only five dwarves that Ranyll could see now. Oagthor and Rathor were several feet from him, their weapons hacking at the mass as it moved against them. Arntheer had managed to pull a dwarf up from the surging wave of daemons with the help of Tharnin; Geldif's cut and bleeding form surfaced with a daemon gripped in each hand, his thick fingers trying their best to strangle the daemons to death. The daemons in his hands soon were still and he threw them into the fray, balling up his fists to fight the rest before him.

Ranyll felt a sudden desperation come over him. He knew that there was nothing more that he could do yet he looked for any help that he could get to take him away from the scene before him. He called out for his friend.

"D'meir! D'meir, where are you?"

For a long moment, the only thing that he could hear and see was the remaining dwarves and the daemons. Darkness began to overtake his heart and what remained of his spirit. He lifted his sword in one final attack as the daemons began to overtake him completely. Ranyll's sword jabbed down into the forms of the daemons as they overtook him, their shadowy claws tearing at his legs, clawing at his knees and ankles as he began to feel himself lose balance, his feet coming up from the cavern floor a bit with each rush of daemons that clamored after him.

He slammed the tip of the sword down into as many daemons as he could over and over and, as he did, he saw something spark in front of him. It was a light spark at first, the blade of his sword almost leaping out at him, a red outline of his blade beginning to take shape. He knew that he had struck no surface that made this occur, for the entire floor was simply the cavern floor and nothing more. Ranyll thought he had seen a trick of the darkness at first, yet it began to take shape even more in front of him as he grasped the handle tighter in both of his hands. He looked up at the wave of daemons. They began to waver a little, shifting on top of one another instead of constantly flowing over one another.

Not far, Ranyll saw D'meir and his fire trail begin from the corner of passageway, appearing quickly, a trail of fire shifting and moving straight for Ranyll.

D'meir's voice invaded Ranyll's mind.

Ranyll understood now what the light was. It wasn't the sword at all; it was the magik that D'meir had given to him when saving him. Somehow, it had begun to take shape and it formed around Ranyll's sword as he fought. This time, more focused than before, Ranyll raised his father's sword above his head and, closing his eyes for a moment, fell into the magik that coursed through his veins. It flowed like a fever flows; strong, virulent, exploding through unknown passageways in his mind, searing and burning every sense in his body as it moved, serpentine, through his limbs.

When he opened his eyes again, there was light, a rippling orange and yellow glow coming from above him. As he looked into the air, his father's sword was wreathed in flame; a magikal flame that startled and drove doubt into the mind of his enemy that surrounded Ranyll and his party.

The flame burned at the very core of each daemon as it touched them, sending them reeling into one another, desperate for escape, D'meir and Ranyll cleaving an opening for the dwarves to escape behind them, Ranyll swinging madly at the daemons with both hands gripping the flame sword, the flames encircling causing no heat or pain to Ranyll yet sending the daemons into a frenzy. Ranyll could also feel the flames channel themselves through his body, cycling itself over and over again as he kept hold of the blade. The young human knew that he could not maintain the magik for much longer. The party needed a plan; something that would get them away from the daemons and into safety until they could formulate a better plan. Not far ahead, Ranyll could sense the Dwarven Crag, looking through the daemons to see the same small pathway they had taken to exit through only days before. Ranyll looked to D'meir and motioned to the passageway.

"D'meir, let us lead them to the Crag and over it. Once we do that, we can rest and regroup." D'meir nodded in agreement and the dwarves regained their footing and their other fallen party members that were able, totaling to just over nine dwarves.

That's almost half that we lost, Ranyll thought to himself, the image of so many faces never appearing again beginning to upset him greatly. He had never lost anyone or anything before and did not know how to feel. He looked back at the bodies of the fallen dwarves only to see Oagthor rush to his side, grabbing his shoulder.

"Not now, Ranyll! We shall mourn the dead once we affirm that we are still alive. Focus, Ranyll! Get us free of this abominable place! You can do it!"

And, in that moment, Ranyll knew that he could. He saw the other wounded dwarves pull themselves up to his side, watched as they took a fighting stance with what weapons they had left next to him, their eyes bearing into him, giving him the acknowledgement that he needed to continue. No longer were Ranyll's footsteps in doubt, but each step he took was with renewed fervor, a confidence in himself and what D'meir had given him would see them through. As the daemons began to retreat, the dwarves rushed forward and attacked them, hacking and slashing into the shadows that moved further and further into the passageway where the Dwarven Crag lie, the dwarves stepping over the fallen daemons as they continued their assault.

Ranyll was there, by their side, his sword alight with a magikal flame, cutting a swath through the fear and doubt of the daemons as D'meir caught any that he missed in their surge forward to the Crag. Soon, the Dwarven Crag was in sight and Ranyll could feel the pull of whatever lay down within it; but there was something else in view. With the renewed light of the flame sword, Ranyll could see a small party of daemons in movement not so far from the other side of the Crag, moving down into the Crag. And, within the party, the daemon TSeT held Gabriella tightly to his side. They disappeared down into a corner of the Crag.

Ranyll felt a flurry of excitement overtake him and he rushed into the daemons, the flame clearing a path for him, its light a brighter orange hue that it had ever been so far. D'meir followed behind him and the dwarves began to move in his direction.

Oagthor called out to the young boy. "Ranyll, what are you doing? We were supposed to be working together." Ranyll turned back just long enough to respond to Oagthor and wave them forward with him.

"It's Gabriella! If we can get her, then all of this will be over. She will be safe. She's been taken down into the Crag by a daemon. We must get her!" Oagthor stopped himself in his tracks, the other dwarves stopping just right behind him. Oagthor wiped the sweat from his brow and noticed Arntheer making his way forward to follow the human. Oagthor lifted his thick arm in front of Arntheer and stopped him.

Oagthor knew what Arntheer was going to say. He started before the young dwarf could begin. "Listen, young dwarf; you may be something at your garrison in Dardist, but the Crag is no place for anyone to go willingly. If we follow Ranyll in there, we're sure to be outnumbered. Besides," Oagthor turned around and pushed the remaining dwarves aside, hammering a death blow to a daemon's skull with the butt of his axe, "we've got plenty of work to do here. Ranyll will have to go it alone. I will not sacrifice the rest of my friends to the Crag, because that's what it is; willing sacrifices. I suggest you take an old dwarf's word for it, Arntheer. I usually don't give mine more than once!"

Arntheer was still heated from battle, his nostrils filled with the stench of the kill, his eyes wet from his fury over his garrison being torn to just a few of his closest soldiers. He looked back at the weary garrison of dwarves and knew it was true what Oagthor said. The young dwarf clenched his axe and nodded, watching as the remnants of daemons circled the dwarven party, the red slits for eyes expecting an easy defeat.

"I will take your advice, old dwarf, not just because you are right," Arntheer tossed his axe into a crowd of daemons who, in return fell to the cavern floor and died, "but because I want to hear the tales you have to tell in a fine tavern far from any cavern and pit of daemons. You have stories, don't you Oagthor? Or has your life been sedentary like the rocks that fill this cavern?"

Oagthor smiled through the dirt and blood, his beard showing a brilliant set of white teeth tinged with blood from battle. "I do, young dwarf. Many stories, though this will be the first I tell." Oagthor's laughter echoed throughout the passageways and even startled the daemons in front of them, that single moment allowing the dwarves to rush the daemons, toppling many over the edge of the Crag, Arntheer rushing for his axe, fists swinging against the hardened shadows, slamming into one and another until he found the handle and ripped it free from a fallen daemon carcass. The dwarves continued to battle for the top of the Dwarven Crag.

*   *   *

Ranyll could hear a dwarf's laughter echo into the Crag as he made his way down a rudimentary set of steps, further into the darkness. He was able to lessen his hold on the magik to where the sword glowed just enough so that he could see in front of him, D'meir lighting the steps at his feet, the fire fox's magik still coursing through its veins.

The fire fox, though continuing straight down the stairway, seemed lost.

"Ranyll, are you sure you saw Gabriella and the daemons come this way? I don't see anything."

For a moment, Ranyll doubted himself. Yet, he wouldn't allow it anymore. Still feeling the magik coursing through him, he increased the power of the flames on the sword, the Crag lighting up for the first time. The two were at the western side of the great Dwarven Crag, almost the same spot that Ranyll had fallen at, yet they were moving down a hidden stairway that started some feet away from the edge of the walkway.

The only reason that Ranyll had been able to get to it was because he had seen the daemons moving down into the Crag, their forms hopping from step to step. Now, in front of them, they faced and steep stairwell that hugged the western side of the Crag all the way down into darkness. And, just in the darkness, Ranyll could make out forms moving. It was Gabriella and the daemon party!

Ranyll began moving down the steps at a quicker pace, D'meir soon being lost behind a few steps. The fire fox, knowing this, hopped up onto Ranyll's shoulder and watched as they closed in on the daemon party, Gabriella soon coming into view. The angel looked back and had a look of surprise on her face as she saw Ranyll climbing down to her.

Soon, the darkness swallowed everything and Ranyll kept the flame sword in front of him, the world seeming to change right before him. He could feel something unstable at his feet and soon realized that daemons were upon him. He swatted at them with his sword but they were too close. D'meir dispatched himself immediately and arced through them with his magikal fire, their forms soon slipping into nothing, Ranyll continuing down the stairs. He could scarcely make out Gabriella and TSeT and a small number of daemons. Ranyll moved quickly on them, his flame sword swiping at the daemons just in front of him, the young man rushing for Gabriella as they fell.

The daemon TSeT was there in between them in moments, his flesh body barely holding together, the sockets staring out at the human boy and the fire fox as they tried to find a way past him on the stairs, watching as Gabriella was pressed against the wall, her hands clasped tightly around her arms in fear.

Ranyll looked upon the fleshy daemon and was disgusted. It had managed to keep itself intact throughout the change but, as time wore on, the body began to age and small pieces of it were missing, the eyes hanging wearily in the sockets. He spoke to the creature.

"Give her back to me, daemon, and we will leave and let you go unharmed." It did not answer, just stared blankly at them, the fleshy body rocking from side to side slightly in the darkness, its face shadowed by the light from Ranyll's flame sword. Ranyll reached around the fleshy daemon for Gabriella, who grasped his hand quickly, squeezing it tightly into her own. Her cold flesh was a fire within the young man, who felt the life he was entrusted with safe once more.

The fleshy daemon seemed not to take notice of Gabriella moving past him; it just stared at Ranyll's face, at his expression, at the look on the young man's face.

It was then that the fleshy daemon spoke. "You do not know why we hate you so, human? We hate you because every breath of life you life you rejoice in. We see each emotion and are incapable of any our own, except hatred and loathing for those emotions that we cannot feel ourselves. That is our curse."

TSeT lunged at Ranyll and the young man pushed Gabriella behind him on the narrow stairway, bringing his flame sword out to meet the fleshy daemon. TSeT writhed in pain as the magikal blade struck out and cut away his left arm up the elbow, the fleshy daemon losing its footing on the stairway, reaching out in desperation as it slipped off the stairway completely, disappearing into the darkness below. Ranyll held Gabriella close to him as he watched TSeT disappear into the Dwarven Crag.

Oagthor looked down into the depths of the Dwarven Crag and could see nothing, not even with the torch that he had lit or from the fire the other dwarves had going, tossing daemon corpses onto it, one by one. He could not hear anything either. It seemed that Ranyll and D'meir were lost in the darkness of the Crag. He had seen it many times, just never thought it would be the boy.

He looked over to Rathor. "Such an ignorant boy; couldn't wait until we cleared him a path; had to go running into the battle! Damn that boy! He may have ruined it all!" Rathor just stared at his old friend. Oagthor could see the glimmer of smile across his friend's face.

Oagthor was beginning to get flustered. "What? What is it? I told him to wait. I did."

Rathor just combed his fingers through his beard and wiped away the soot that had formed across his brow and helm, wiping it away on his breeches. "You of all people tell a young boy on a quest to wait, to hold until help arrives. Do you know how many times I've jumped into trouble with you because you did that very thing? And then you hold Arntheer back from being, of all things, another you? I can't believe you! If you say there's something special about that boy, then there's something special about that boy. There's no doubt about that."

Oagthor was befuddled. "Why do you say that?"

Rathor pointed down into the Crag. "See for yourself."

Ranyll, D'meir and Gabriella rushed up a hidden stairwell against the side of the Crag, the dimly lit flame sword in Ranyll's hand their light, daemons trailing just behind them.

Oagthor almost jumped in delight. "The boy is alive! He's alive and he's got the angel! Quick, someone, get me some rope so that we can bring them up from the stairs!"

He is our savior.

Oagthor could feel it in every movement he made toward Ranyll, could see it in the way that D'meir had followed the boy, from the beginning to now. D'meir had never doubted Ranyll for a moment. As Oagthor reached out for Ranyll's hand, the dwarf knew that he never would again either.

The darkness of the caves was intimidating. The long, thick-pillared corridors and the ancient runes and markings that lay inscribed across each wall seemed to make the world that the faeries flew through surreal. The four sprites had seen the markings of old before, but never had they seen so many; and so many so clearly carved, as if the centuries had not gone on here but let the markings remain in the same day in which they were written. There were no cobwebs or small pieces of fallen debris in these hallways as were in the others that they had been through; someone or something had made sure of that.

The sprites, Timber Fey and Lena Fey of the Glor Clan along with Ugeno and Fleet Mikteel of the Sifter Clan, had been tasked to scout ahead for any signs of daemons or the creatures that had stirred when they entered Wilden Marsh. Though they hadn't found anything, Timber Fey didn't feel quite at ease with the surroundings that they were in at the moment. There was no age, no dust, no decimation of the passageways around them, as if they had been well-preserved by an unseen hand.

The most pressing thing that made Timber Fey uneasy was not this but it was simply the fact that there were no smells within the caverns. Each cavern, each passageway, each small area that the faerie army had made their way through contained a number of smells and aromas and, when Timber entered these caverns with the three others from her scouting party, that was something that struck her as odd. The others took notice of this as well and, as they made their way through with their small hand-made torches from a collection of twigs, they saw nothing or no one.

Timber Fey knew this wasn't right. "I think we should go a little further and, if nothing is seen, make our way back as quick as we can to tell the rest of the faeries. In fact, Fleet," motioning to the slimmer, sharp-eyed Sifter sprite, "I think you should go back now and tell the rest of them that there's something here. We'll scout the rest of the area and catch up to you shortly." Fleet had never really spoken much, so the simple nodding of his head was understanding enough that he knew exactly what to do. He winked smartly at his Sifter cousin, Ugeno, and was off in a flash, the fluttering of his wings almost putting out all their torches in one swift gust.

And then there were three.

The cavern soon opened up to a large antechamber that rose up high above the three sprites to great heights, several sets of markings following up the wall to the beginning of the domed antechamber, then connecting to a circular pattern of markings around the rim of the dome. Within the dome, ancient carvings of a great battle were carved; the sprites could only see phantom shapes and faces with the amount of light that they had, barely making out a scene or two before it was lost in another portion of a scene as they passed by the domed area into a new chamber, the area around them closing in somewhat to direct them into a smaller passageway. They continued for some time down a long corridor that had no markings or carvings at all, but was adorned with pedestal upon pedestal of busts of great dwarven kings of the ages long past set on each side of them. The names of each king were inscribed under each bust, many with inscriptions under the name and dates of their reign.

Timber began to feel uneasy.

There was something amiss within these walls, the sprite thought to herself. *We should be making our way back now.* Just ahead, there lay a great set of closed double doors. From their vantage point, the doors seemed to be made of the same stone that the walls were.

Timber Fey stopped herself in the air, wings fluttering a little bit faster than before. "I think we should be going now, scouts. I think I've seen enough." But the other sprites almost insisted. They had seen the door, too, and faeries had always known to be curious. In fact, Timber Fey wanted to see what lay beyond the door but knew better. In the short amount of time that she'd been within the caverns where the daemons dwelt, she had never seen anything of this sort, so she knew that there was something at work here that was not good.

If it were good, then there would be a greeting of some sort or even some sconces on the wall lit up with a light; but there was nothing to greet them. And Timber knew what that meant.

We are not welcome here. No matter how much it looked welcoming, no one was welcome here, unless by invitation. And Timber Fey or any of the others had not received any invitation of any kind.

Timber could see the look of longing in Lena and Ugeno to see what was behind the door but she flew closer to them, waving her torch in front of them. "It is time we leave this place. What behind those doors is of no consequence to us." Once focused again, the sprites turned and began to follow their scout leader. No sooner had they turned away from the door that they began to see the fog appear, coming from underneath it.

It was not a smooth, quiet rolling of fog like on the Reune Lake in the early mornings near the Faerie Homme; but it was an urgent fog, almost forcing itself through the underneath the great stone double doors. Once enough fog had breached past the doors, it began to take a shape.

Timber did not wait to see what shape it took. Dropping her torch, she reached out and yanked the sprites forward and began flapping her wings as quick as she could, their torches going out in an instant. The two sprites complained.

"We can't see a thing! Hey, what's going on?" But Timber did not respond. She could feel their faerie wings begin to catch up with hers and that's all that she had wanted. Soon, the three were moving at a steady pace, none looking back, the three only focused on what lie ahead; more darkness and hopefully Fleet not far from sight, if they could even see him before they ran into him.

The air around them began to take on a smell; it was strange to them because the tunnels had no smell when they came through the first time, but on the way back was different. Just ahead, they could hear a faint fluttering, that of a faerie's wings not far ahead. With renewed hope, Timber urged the others forward, only to find that the sound was approaching them more than they were approaching the sound. Soon, they could make out a faint form flying right at them. They stopped and noticed that they were within the antechamber again. The great carvings of war could not be seen above them. Ahead, Fleet cried out one word that sent a streak of terror through their limbs.

"Trap!" And then Fleet vanished in a plume of fog in the shape of a great beast, its empty fog-filled eyes staring intently at the other three. It did not hesitate. It came at them relentlessly, having no limitations to its abilities. They rose as quickly as they could through the air and it continued to follow them, the great fog creature gathering speed quickly, almost upon them now. Timber released an ample amount of fire dust at the fog beast and it made itself dissipate into nothing before her, letting the dust hit the ground on the antechamber floor, lighting the room somewhat. The three sprites were now almost to the ceiling and there was no escape. It was then that Timber Fey had a plan. Getting the others attention, she grabbed a handful of fire dust and held it out before her. The other sprites took the hint and did the same. She called out to them.

"Follow it and do not stop!" They nodded and all three sprites released the fire dust, watching as the fog creature let itself dissipate into nothing. The three sprites took their chance and followed the fire dust down to the floor, watching as the fog tried to form itself around them but soon lit up by the fire dust when it came close.

The fog had become thick throughout the entire chamber now, coming in from both sides. Timber had little hope of escaping into another chamber. She held out the rest of her fire dust and threw it into the chamber hallway that they had first come through; the fog opened itself up, only to close up behind them as they moved forward.

At this rate, we will all be out of fire dust in moments, Timber thought to herself, her wings suddenly beginning to tire. She could feel the fog begin to take over around her and she knew this was her last stand.

Fleet had fallen so quick and he was the fastest of us all. We are doomed.

The only thing that Timber regretted at that moment was not being able to get the message out to the faerie army. She felt the fog enfold around her just as she was pulling out a handful of fire dust. It was a thick, blinding white fog; a hard contrast to what she had been seeing within the tunnel. She could feel the air pushed out of her little faerie lungs. She began to lose consciousness.

Ugeno Mikteel and Lena Fey watched in horror as Timber Fey was pulled into the fog, the small frame and fluttering wings disappearing before them, the last of their fire dust expended on the previous blanket of fog.

Now the fog came for them. However, the fog seemed different than it had been. All of a sudden, it writhed and swirled in front of them, bringing a new smell to their nostrils that they hadn't smelled in some time while in the caves; sweaty dwarves. The smell would usually disgust them to no end, with thoughts of sweat-soaked beards and dirty breeches, but at this moment, nothing smelled better to them. Just ahead of them, they could see the flickering of torches and a small group of dwarves led the way into the fog, waving a torch in each hand to separate it completely. And just behind them, a young human and a pale woman draped in a cloak, closely followed by a fire fox alight with its magikal fire, keeping the way clear in its own way.

The sprites could see the fog in front of them dissolve into nothing and the still form of Timber Fey and Fleet Mikteel on the floor not far from them. They had to fly in front of the dwarves to keep them from stepping on the other sprites.

The fire fox darted up to the front of the dwarven party. "I knew there was a Sifter Clan member here! I could smell your scent from the caves almost a mile back! What are you doing here?"

The sprites didn't have a chance to respond. The fog continued to trail around them, snaking its invisible fingers as close as it could around them, trying for a hold without being singed by the torches the dwarves held in their thick, round fingers. Even the fire fox's magikal fire could not keep them from drifting closer and closer, trying their best to find a way to form back into the fog creatures. It was not until Ranyll pulled his father's sword free from it sheath and set it on fire with his magik did the fog seem to retreat and, finally, dissipate completely. Once the fog had dissipated, Ranyll resheathed his sword and looked at the new faces before him.

Timber and Fleet soon came to and saw what had saved them; a dwarven party escorting the angel Gabriella and the human boy they had heard so much about. After listening to the fire fox's story and resting for a bit, they continued their way back the way they came; a different route than the dwarven party had come. They passed the way the dwarves had come and continued on to the faerie army, who were not far. Soon, the dwarves were in uncharted territory. They had seen the twists and turns before, but they had never ventured into the caverns they were in now.

The hodge-podge party had shifted somewhat since the original trip. Oagthor, D'meir, and the four sprites took the lead, with Timber Fey leading the way. In the middle of the party and the most protected, was Ranyll and Gabriella, the angel staying close to her protector than she ever had before, leaning on him at times, his cloak wrapped tightly around her shoulders for warmth. Taking up the rear were the remnants of Rathor's party and Arntheer's garrison with Arntheer and Rathor walking side by side. Arntheer looked at the old dwarf from time to time, finally disturbing the older dwarf enough to give in and question the younger.

"What is it, Arntheer? Why do you keep looking at me so? Do you fancy me, boy?" Arntheer stared harder for several moments before answering.

"No, old man, I do not fancy you, though the company I keep as of late have been my fellow friends more than the dwarven woman that I dream of at night. No, Rathor. I am just taking much of this as a dream right now. I mean, how is it we are alive? Do you ever ask that of yourself, or anyone else for that matter?"

The old dwarf chuckled a little bit before answering. He seemed to be taking his time with preparing his answer.

Then he simply said, "You are a young dwarf, Arntheer. You prove it to be so in your speech. No common-sensical dwarf would ask such a dumb question after they have come out of such adversity. A proper dwarf would thank the gods that they came out unscathed and prayed for a day when the honor of death would take them. Arntheer, I am thankful, yes. But any of the battles that I've been in, with the exception of bar fights, I would have been glad to die in because they all were in honor. Which leads me to believe, young dwarf, do you fight for honor, as is the dwarven way, or do you fight for glory like that of the humans?"

He could see that Arntheer was a little insulted by this. The young dwarf bit his lip and turned away for a moment, his hands squeezed tightly by his side.

Rathor spoke. "What, boy, do you have no tongue? Can you not speak your mind? Speak, dwarf! I am an aged dwarf and can take what you may say better than most."

Arntheer spoke between clenched teeth. "I hold back from attacking you because you are to be respected by what you do here for the city of Dardist, but you know nothing of what I've gone through and, by all means possible throughout my life, I have lived a full life for a young dwarf."

Before Arntheer could begin a new sentence, Rathor was upon him. The old dwarf ripped the axe from Arntheer's sheath and threw it aside, slamming a knee into the young dwarf's stomach, doubling him over.

Rathor continued by doubling up his fists and slamming them into Arntheer's face, sending him reeling into the cavern wall, where Rathor met him, the young dwarf out of breath and bleeding from the mouth.

The rest of the party moved to the fighting dwarves but Oagthor stopped the parties from interceding when he saw the intensity on his friend's face.

Rathor leaned in against Arntheer and pressed his forearm against the young dwarf's neck. "You insult me by not attacking me, boy! I call you a child because you are just that and have not seen the world from my point of view! When you have lived to my age, then you can say those words out of your lips! 'Lived a full life', what pride you have, boy!"

Rathor slipped free a dagger from his hip and placed it up against Arntheer's chest. "This is what I would get for looking at another person the wrong way where I come from. I am not Oagthor or any dwarf the likes of which you have ever seen. I have lived lives over and over again and still my time is not over. Be careful with your words, Arntheer, they are just as dangerous as that axe that you carry so proudly on your back!"

Soon Oagthor was by Rathor's side, but Rathor was already moving away. He looked to Oagthor. "Tell this boy that he should go see the world, Oagthor, and not hide in caves. That is what is wrong with our race in the first place; the other races think that we are cowards. And why shouldn't they; look, I have to come to their aid to help them. By the gods, Oagthor, a human boy is even helping our people!"

And that is when Oagthor smelled the dwarven spirits on Rathor's breath. It was heavy and it lay thick in the air around them. Oagthor reached for the water skin at Rathor's hip and noticed that it was empty.

Oagthor just sighed. "When?"

It was the last of their dwarven brew.

Rathor tried his best to look puzzled. "When what?"

Oagthor was more embarrassed than angry, a slight flush coming to his cheeks as he scolded his friend in front of the party. "When did you get so thirsty?"

Rathor stumbled a little when answering, sliding his dagger back into its place at his belt. "Since this morning; I couldn't help it, Oagthor. I've had an awful headache."

Oagthor looked then to Arntheer, who was picking up his axe. The young dwarf just sneered at Rathor, who, in return, gave him a little grin that poked out of his thick, black beard.

Oagthor patted the young dwarf on the shoulder. "Are you alright, Arntheer?" Arntheer wiped the small trace of blood from his mouth and finished strapping his axe to his back.

He didn't hesitate to answer. "I'm fine. Just keep that drunk away from me! I hate it when dwarves can't hold their brew."

Rathor countered, slurring in his speech a little. "I can drink with the best of them, boy. You watch yourself or you'll find me at you again for that mouth! I'm not some old dwarf from Dardist. I'm a surface dwarf and I don't need pretty little stories to prove myself. I'll prove myself to you now if you open that smart mouth of yours again!"

Oagthor pushed the drunken Rathor ahead of the rest of them, his friend rambling on about some time in an abandoned fortress in the mountains. Oagthor spoke over his ranting.

"Rathor will walk with D'meir and myself. We'll take the lead. The sprites say that we're not far from the faerie army. They're taking refuge in a cavern just up the way. We should be safe there to rest and replenish. We will talk about it all then. Let's keep it a little close. We don't want to be caught by surprise by anything. We're not in a safe place anymore!"

They traveled for some time before the sprites stopped them and led them to another tunnel that took them to the cavern where the faerie army had taken refuge to rest. As they entered it, however, the sprites were surprised to find it completely empty.

Timber Fey was almost overwhelmed with fear. "This was the cavern! I know it, I know it was! It was three turns right, four left, second tunnel on the right, then take a left down into the cavern. This is it."

There were, indeed, some remnants of the faerie army being here; hoof prints could be seen, the air still had some dust floating in the air from the previous occupants movement within the cavern. You could see the dust floating through the air within the torchlight. All of the tracks even seemed to continue through the cavern and out the other side of the cavern into a smaller tunnel, barely able for Ranyll to stand up in all the way. Oagthor looked to D'meir for answers.

D'meir looked at him in return. "They didn't tell me their plans before I left. I've been gone from the group for some time now. The sprites would be able to tell us something better than I could." The fire fox looked to the sprites for an answer but stopped short, his snout catching the scent of something in the air. He sniffed for long moments before confirming what he smelled.

"It's the creatures of mist again! I can smell them in the air. They are further ahead. There is a battle that wages as we speak." D'meir moved ahead and lifted his snout up into the air. Everyone around him grew silent and waited for him to speak again.

D'meir just looked at them. "Well, what are you waiting for? I don't need to sniff twice. I know what I smell and don't smell." And D'meir was the first one down the tunnel before anyone had a chance to get their bearings.

Not far ahead, a scuffling and outbreak of shouts, screams, and cries rang out into the air, Gabriella huddling close to Ranyll while the dwarves in the rear began to move forward, soon passing Ranyll and Gabriella altogether, each dwarf pulling their weapons out to prepare for battle.

That's when the fog began to roll in. It wasn't after the sprites this time, but it came for Gabriella and Ranyll, shifting this way and that past the dwarves, bypassing D'meir completely. The four dwarves that held torches began to wave the flames at the fog, making it break apart and even the wisps of it began to dissipate altogether, yet it still came after Ranyll and Gabriella. The fog began to form itself together in between the party and Oagthor grew into a frenzied panic.

He ran towards the thicker fog with his torch in hand.

"Quick! Don't let it form together; torches, torches quick! D'meir, help me on this side!" And all suddenly knew what the fog was trying to do. It had begun to form a wall between Ranyll and Gabriella and the rest of the party. It started at the floor and was already up to several feet; a hard, solid wall of fog forming between them.

In moments, it had formed up almost to a dwarf's height and it continued to the ceiling. D'meir lit up, the magikal fire of the faerie kin surrounding him, but it did not even penetrate the thick fog that was quickly closing them off from Ranyll and Gabriella. There were only a few feet left before the fog wall closed completely. Oagthor looked to Ranyll and nodded, the young man nodding in return. He pulled out his sword and lit it afire with the faerie flame, slamming the sword into the fog wall. The blade bounced off harmlessly. It was as if the fog wall had become a smooth, shifting wall of marble.

The faerie battle with the fog behind them began to rage into the cavern before them. Oagthor looked to D'meir, the fire fox still ablaze with his magikal fire. When D'meir saw the look in Oagthor's eyes, the fire extinguished around him. Oagthor picked his friend up, both of them watching as the fog wall closed, only a foot or so remaining within the wall for them to see.

D'meir nodded to his friend. "I will promise to keep them safe, Oagthor. I know what faith you hold in Ranyll. I always knew, my old friend."

Oagthor stroked D'meir's head one last time and tossed him through the small space in the fog wall, watching as the last of the fog formed together and blocked out the three of their party on the other side completely.

Oagthor turned and faced the rest of the party. "Let us join this battle that wages almost upon us. Let us find another way to the angel, Ranyll and D'meir. Maybe with the faeries' help, we can get them back." The party moved forward, all with a heavy heart but with renewed vigor that there was still hope.

As soon as the wall formed behind them, Ranyll, Gabriella, and D'meir saw the shifting begin to take shape within the fog. It began to coalesce into something far worse than a simple wall. Ranyll now knew the purpose of the wall and why it had been formed between him and the rest of the party; no escape. He did not know the way back through the tunnels as the sprites did;

he vaguely remembered the way to his uncle's checkpoint, and that had been following the river. Indeed, the fog seemed to have a sentience, and intelligence like no other fog he had ever seen before. And, as the great fog creature began to exit through the fog wall, he knew that his no escape theory was no longer just a theory, but the truth.

The fog creature grew to an enormous size; almost six feet in height. It dwarfed the three easily with its height and its immensity. It seemed to take up most of the cavern from shoulder to shoulder. Each great paw came through the fog wall, one great clawed paw after another until, finally, the creature was upon them. It did not hesitate to move towards them; in fact, it did not even seem threatened by their weapons.

Ranyll moved Gabriella behind him, his flame sword between himself and the fog creature. D'meir was at his side as well, the faerie fire ablaze around him, his body low to the ground as if he were about to pounce.

"Gabriella, I need you to move slowly through the tunnel behind us and find a safe place." Gabriella nodded nervously and let go of Ranyll's hand, watching the great fog creature as is moved towards them, Ranyll and D'meir retreating slowly together. However, Ranyll noticed the strangest thing; the eyes of the fog creature did not move from him.

As Gabriella disappeared down the tunnel and into another one, the fog creature kept its great eyes focused on him and him alone. It did not even bother to look at D'meir, whose flame had become larger and more prominent, each step the great, smoky behemoth took towards them.

Ranyll held the flame sword up at the fog creature, which seemed to flinch for a moment, then recover, moving closer and closer by the moment. "D'meir, this creature is not after Gabriella."

"I know, Ranyll. This creature has come for you. It is a servant of Scarwol. There is something he wants from you."

"What is that?"

"Let us not wait and find out." The fire fox leapt at the fog creature, its flames arcing straight into the creatures' eyes, blinding it momentarily.

D'meir cried out. "Strike, Ranyll! Strike now!"

Every thought in the young man's mind was about to explode. He still remembered the hold that Scarwol had upon him; it was still somewhat fresh in his mind. He looked at the great fog creature as it reared back in what seemed to be pain. It lifted its front two paws up in protection and, as it came down, Ranyll prepared his attack. He drew the great flame sword back behind him to take a swing, the flames turning from an orange to a white-hot. As the fog creature came down upon its front legs, Ranyll swung for its head.

29

The northeast trek had become something of a blur to Falwen Sanse since his departure two days ago. Falwen had never been anywhere but on the west coast of Kariyl, yet he decided, after the first day of traveling, that he hadn't missed much. The trail that had been chosen by Gilden's directions showed him the most barren landscape he had ever seen in all of his travels. He had traversed through much of Parthenia's coast when he was younger, even ventured on The Forbidden Islands far west, but he had never seen such emptiness in all of his time here on Ar Solon. It was as if no one dared to venture north at all. In fact, he had passed no one in the past two days on this trail, checking and double checking his instructions to make sure that he had not taken an incorrect route.

The landscape was nothing but a few small stunted trees and small patches of grass throughout his journey so far, with a touch of some man-made signs or road markers that had become worn and faded over time. He had heard much of Agnar and the dwarven people that lived there, but never had he heard of them being scribes or even in a guild of scribes for that matter.

What do they write about, Falwen asked himself, looking back at the wagon full of supplies, taking note again of the numbers of sealed boxes with Gilden's own personal seal upon them.

I'm sure they will be interested in what I have in my possession. Falwen didn't pretend for a moment that those sealed boxes weren't filled with books. In fact, he knew that they were. What the books contained, Falwen couldn't imagine, trying his best to steal a peek at them throughout his last few stops.

However, the boxes were latched and sealed and, in the instructions that were given, they were not to be tampered with or opened until they arrived at the Agnar Guild of Scribes.

There must be a reason for this, Falwen thought to himself, leaning forward a bit in his seat to straighten out the stiffness in his shoulders and back, his hands holding tightly the reins as he shifted from side to side.

The two horses that pulled the wagon, Monk and Feebs, carried on their usual banter back and forth, huffing and neighing every so often, the only conversation Falwen having heard since leaving the guild.

"I'd even consider having Scribe Ja'wan here to talk with," the old man said aloud, the horses' ears pricking up in response, their pace shifting slightly. His voice almost startled himself in the waning sunlight, watching as the last of the light began to sink behind him in the west, almost falling into Alvanus Sea behind him.

Ahh, the sea, he thought to himself, *the very thought of it brings me back to my senses. It's about time for a stop.*

Falwen slowed the wagon down a bit by pulling on the reins, the wheels bumping off of the main trail to a little spot not so far from the main thoroughfare. Falwen laughed when he thought of the small road actually being busy.

"They would probably have to build an extension to the road in order to facilitate any more traffic than there is now." Somehow, his own voice calmed him a little, which is something that he needed, the thoughts of the daemons he encountered in his short time on his journey forever staying in the back of his mind, his eyes darting to and fro in the darkness from time to time. He had learned to stay alert, even in the darkness, just since encountering the one on the shore.

It was as if a chill of fear was forever etched on his mind, which connected to the hairs on the back of his neck, which stood up every time he thought of the daemons and what they were capable of. Again, he thought of the still form of the angel at the shore, the waves lapping at his decimated corpse. Falwen tried his best to keep the image from his mind but, as the sun sank over his shoulder and cast the world around him in shadow, he had trouble of thinking of anything else. He climbed down from the wagon and stretched his legs, checking the straps and pulleys connected to the horses on the wagon.

He looked at the two horses who, at the time, didn't seem very interested in him at all, their attention on a small tuft of grass at their feet.

"Maybe I should start a fire. What do you think?" But the horses did not say anything; not even a neigh or a whinny broke from their pursed lips. Falwen soon turned his attention to the wagon, untying a side of the canvas to get to his usual nightly gear, which he had arranged in a small pile in between the sealed boxes, a small bedroll and a handful of other supplies in his hands and he prepared for his nightly stay on the ground. Soon, the handful of tinder that he had kept in his wagon was lit and he fanned the small flame with his hand, adding more tinder once the flame hand engulfed several small sticks and twigs. He rubbed his hands together for warmth and held them over the fire.

He looked back at the horses. Monk and Feebs had finished chewing at the tuft of grass on the ground.

"There, that's better, isn't it?" Again, no response. Yet, they did stare for some time at him without moving. This did not comfort him in anyway. In fact, it kind of disturbed him a little bit. Falwen continued with his nightly preparations and was soon sitting by a roaring fire, a small pot hanging over the flames, Falwen stirring a broth he had made from some of what he had eaten earlier today. The old fisherman tied the feedbags onto his horses and sat back down, pulling his cloak tightly over his shoulders, trying to break the chill that had come over him. But it had yet to break the chill. In fact, nothing seemed to do it. The thoughts of the daemons had begun to take over his thoughts.

And that's when Falwen got the idea to open one of the sealed boxes. He did not hesitate. In one quick motion, the old fisherman lifted himself from his seated position, moving just past the horses and to the wagon, where he retrieved his hooded lantern. He went back to the fire and lit it, moving to the back of the wagon. Unfolding the back flap, he lifted himself up and into the wagon, panning the lantern up above the sealed boxes. He shifted the boxes back and forth, testing the weight, looking for any differences in the boxes, but found none. There were twelve boxes that looked, weighed, and were completely the same as one another; and all of them seemed to be quite heavy. In fact, Falwen could barely lift them. It was the best that he could do to push them from side to side.

Now he didn't know what to do. He didn't want to risk a lot of trouble just to keep himself from thinking bad thoughts. He bypassed the sealed boxes and moved on to the other items in the wagon. All of his own supplies were still neatly piled next to the remnants of the campsite supplies. There were three food crates filled with random items that Falwen could prepare along his journey to the Agnar Guild. And then there were two other crates he had yet to investigate. They were not sealed as the other boxes were so he moved through the wagon to them, setting his lantern down on a nearby box. He lifted the box lid of the first box. It was a much smaller box than the others that were sealed; about half their size. He couldn't see inside the box because it was so dark so, grabbing his lantern, he peered inside.

There lay, in the center of a handful of packing hay, a thickly-bound brown leather book. It was a tome, for Falwen had seen these before in the guild during his stay. And, lying next to it, were a quill and a single, corked well of ink. It was a mystery to Falwen how the bottle had not spilled during his journey, for he had traveled over much rough terrain. But there it lay, not a single drop of ink spilled, the cork on the top still tightly sealed. Falwen reached down and picked up the tome, the weight of it a bit overwhelming, his aged fingers gripping tightly around it as he slid the box lid back in place, the lantern and the tome in his hands as he exited the wagon. He sat back down by the fire, extinguishing the lantern completely, the fire still brightly lit in the early evening. He opened to the first page. On the inside page, there was an inscription of sorts, a simple name and dates of whom and when the tome was written. It was written as follows:

This tome of Ar Solon was written by the hand of Gilden Felves, The Third Chronicler, yet was not finished by the same hand. The Fourth and Final Chronicler, Falwen Sanse, shall complete this tome and all the tomes that remain. This is thy will and it shall be done. I have fulfilled my promise and completed to my appointed time. The remainder of the history is now in the hands of Falwen Sanse.

It was simply a beginning, but it was something of a puzzle to Falwen as he read it, over and over again.

Chronicler? What or who is that? Apparently Gilden Felves was a Chronicler of some sort, but his work was more of a copier and not a full-fledged scribe that traveled, from what the other scribes at the guild had said. What was this all about?

Falwen continued onto the next page. This time, the words were written in the smaller penmanship of the scribes. This page began the tome itself.

It had been many a day since Ranyll had seen Gabriella. And it was now that it was somewhat difficult to come to terms that he had, indeed, rescued her, having her next to him now. They rested in a cavern for the moment, the rest of the party resting as well, several dwarves taking first shift, guarding both sides of the tunnel, their thick forms blocking much of the tunnel so only slivers of the tunnels past them could be seen.

Ranyll knew that the daemons were going to attack. He knew this and feared it all the more, knowing that he had suddenly taken their most prized possession; something that The One had sent them on a mission to find. Ranyll knew that this was no easy feat. He had been given a great power as well as a great task; to save the angel at all costs. Of course, no one had really given him the task. He had appointed himself all along and, throughout many of those moments traveling, regretted that he had ever took on the job of protecting Gabriella from the daemons that searched for her day and night.

It all seemed familiar to him now, the old man letting go of his hold of the tome a little, letting the weighty book fall into his lap.

This is part of what I have been going through myself, Falwen through to himself. *But I wonder if there is more to the story.* He skimmed through the pages to the end of the writing, which was barely midway through the tome, his eyes darting to the last few lines on the page.

To the garden, he thought. Gilden Felves scanned the room for his thick walking robe and cane and made his way for them both, taking great care not to pull down the drying pages that floated like phantoms of the future throughout his room. The Chronicler grabbed his robe and draped it over his shoulders, tapping the cane down on the hard, stone floor. It echoed in his room and down the hallway repeatedly as he disappeared down the dimly lit corridors to the meditation gardens.

"I know where this is going!" Falwen read the last lines of the page and saw himself enter into the story, reading as Gilden fell dead at his feet, the old fisherman almost reliving the scene all over again within the page. Then he looked to the next page for answers.

Empty.

"What now? Where is the rest of the story?"

Whether it was deep into the night and the fears of the daemons had not subsided fully, Falwen did not know, but somewhere in the darkness, an answer to his question came. There was a loud thump near the horses, as though someone were tampering with the sealed boxes in the wagon. Falwen nearly dropped the tome down in surprise when he heard it again, this time a harder, more urgent thumping sound that came from inside the wagon. As if by instinct, Falwen's hand went to the sword at his side. His rough, worn fingers gripped the handle lightly as he slid it out of its sheath, taking step after cautious step back to the wagon.

THUMP! THUMP, THUMP! Falwen could not see inside the wagon, but knew there was something making that noise. He lifted the tarp up on the side where his personal belongings were. Just then, something jumped out at him and slammed into him full force. Falwen felt a box smash him in the face, knocking him backwards and away from the wagon. The box fell and broke into several pieces upon the ground in front of him. The noise jostled the horses, who woke from their sleep, only to make more noise at having been awakened.

The old fisherman's sword had slipped out of his hand when he tried to cover himself and now it lay within arm's reach of him, Falwen slowly wiping the sweat from his brow with his hand. His hand came back with blood. The old fisherman could feel a small cut that had opened up on his forehead from the box, now looking around at the contents that had been spilled around him. It was the same crate that the tome had come from, yet the only thing that was in the crate was the glass inkwell that had been packed away with it. He picked it up. Falwen looked around for the quill. He had not seen it fall with the crate and could not see it now.

What had caused the crate to fall, Falwen wondered, lifting himself back up.

The horses had quieted themselves somewhat and Falwen began picking the shattered pieces of the crate up around him when he heard it. It was a scratching of sorts, similar to the clicking of the daemon that had come after him at the shore. It was a sporadic scratching that came in long bursts for a time. It sounded like something trying to get out or all of those old ghost stories about someone scratching at the window panes for the little children on the other side. Falwen knew that he was no child, but in no way did he want to find out what was on the other side of his window pane. The old fisherman was better left in the dark on this one, but he knew that the scratching had not stopped in some time since he stopped to listen. He did not think it was planning to stop, either. He picked up his sword in his free hand and made his way around to the sound of the scratching, which came from the front of the wagon, where the fire was still burning brightly.

It was the quill. The unmanned quill was floating just above the tome, its pointed edge flowing and dipping across the pages as if there were a person writing with it. It moved with purpose and did not linger long, even to turn the pages, which it did periodically with the edge of the quill, floating back to its place on the next page to continue.

Suddenly, it stopped. It floated above the page it was writing on, then flew straight at him. Falwen lifted both of his arms to protect himself, but it was too late. It hit its target without even thinking; the cork to the ink well that lie in his hand. The cork popped out and fell to the ground and the quill, right in front of Falwen, dipped itself in the ink and flew back to the tome to begin writing again.

Fascinating, truly fascinating! Falwen was without words at the moment. He approached the fire and leaned over the tome that he had left on his blanket, watching as the quill performed its duties without hesitation, in perfect penmanship. Whose penmanship, Falwen did not know, but it was a very neat and elegant hand that the quill wrote with. The old fisherman put his sword down on the blanket next to the tome and sat down next to it, reading the first few lines of the page that it was writing on.

"Strike Ranyll, strike now!" Every thought in the young man's head was about to explode. He drew the great flame sword back behind him to take a swing, the flames turning from an orange to a white-hot.

Falwen's mind lingered on that name for a moment. The fisherman from Simmer Lo had never heard the name but the name seemed to be of some importance. He did not know why, but he got a feeling when he read the lines again, over and over, as if they seemed more true the more that he read them. And, indeed, it was as if he could almost visualize the scene in his head when he read them over and over again. He watched as the story put itself together in his head, of the great fog beast, the lost and frightened Gabriella and the fire fox D'meir as it defended them with its life. Falwen could see the old, dwarven tunnels materialize before him, the darkness enveloping him and, before he knew it, he reached his left hand out to the quill and took hold of it.

Suddenly, he was there with Ranyll. His eyes adjusted and the fog beast was rearing back from the attack D'meir had just given it. Falwen felt the vibrations from the quill as it scratched on the blank page in front of him.

*   *   *

The Fog Beast reared back in pain as Ranyll's flame sword bit into its solid form, the creature shaking its head in hopes that the wound would go away. Ranyll struck again, this time at one of its great front legs, letting the flame sword bite deeply into the thick-skinned Fog Beast. It wailed in agony, stomping its massive paws at Ranyll, the young boy trying his best to stay on his feet as he retreated. He lifted his sword up in front of him for a buffer from any attack the Fog Beast might try and watched as D'meir moved up in front of him, between him and the creature.

"Ranyll, take Gabriella and go! You must go now before it's too late!" Ranyll refused. He couldn't leave D'meir here by himself.
"I won't leave you, D'meir! We must all go! This beast cannot defeat us as long as we stay together."

D'meir did not accept that answer. His flaming form lashed out at the beast to keep it back and he looked back at Ranyll one last time. "This is my duty, Ranyll, to protect you. It has been since this journey. Just as yours is to protect Gabriella; mine is to protect and defend your safety at all costs."

Ranyll was shocked and dismayed. However, it all made sense now. All of those times that D'meir had been there to save him, all of those times that D'meir had used his magik to heal him and keep him safe. He had done that for no other, not even Oagthor, and the dwarf and D'meir had a history together!

Ranyll nodded in agreement. He eased the fire of the sword in his hand and disappeared down through the corridor he had sent Gabriella only moments earlier.

Not far down the corridor, Ranyll noticed that the tunnel opened into an old cavern, a sanctuary of sorts; great, crumbling columns reaching high into the darkness above him. There were at least two dozen of the carved pillars that spiraled up into the top of the cavern ceiling; while some had fallen, others still remained, the last of the silent guards that kept the abandoned halls clear. There were a number of old crates and ancient devices that lay rusting not far from the edges of the darkness, hunkering old pieces of relics that had collected dust from age and time. Behind one of them he found Gabriella, hiding. She moved from behind the pillar and came out into the light of Ranyll's flame sword.

"Where's D'meir?" The fire fox was nowhere in sight. Ranyll reached his hand out to Gabriella and she took it gratefully, looking around at her dimly-lit surroundings.

"He's holding back the fog beast so we can get away." Ranyll found it hard to believe it yet alone say it, yet he knew that D'meir was full of surprises. The young man looked for a place to hide. Gabriella looked over at him in the flickering light.

"Where are we, Ranyll?" It took several moments for Ranyll to answer. He looked around again, this time a little less rushed now that he had Gabriella by his side, taking in his surroundings. In the histories he had read back in Telgin, it told of the dwarves and the many fortifications that they had built within the mountains. The books also spoke of safe holds, or sanctuaries, that dwarves could hide in, taking refuge from danger, either from something attacking them or from the elements themselves. This looked like one of them. There were two exits; two great sets of double doors that could only lock from the inside.

However, it seemed as though the sets of double doors had been decommissioned, Ranyll taking note that both sets of doors were off their hinges and on the floor, a pile of dust and debris covering the once great entrance doors.

"We're at an old dwarven safe hold. It looks like it hasn't been used in some time, though." He looked over at the stacks of old, rusted weapons on a weapon rack nearby, then to several boxes of supplies, which looked as though they had diminished with age and time as well. The only thing that looked of use was the wood from the boxes. Ranyll began to move towards it, taking Gabriella with him by the hand.

"I have an idea. Help me with the scraps of wood. Grab as much as you can and come with me."

They let one another's hand go and began grabbing as much old, dried wood as they could. Ranyll hoped this plan worked. Moreover, he hoped he would have time to implement the plan before the fog beast came.

*   *   *

Oagthor and the rest of the party of dwarves watched as the fog barrier close around what hope they had; D'meir, Ranyll, and the angel Gabriella being swallowed up by the foggy mist in between their party. Oagthor turned to the rest of them, a sudden sadness in his eyes at seeing his friend D'meir go. Oagthor had several of his men use their torches against the fog wall, but it did not separate or give like the fog creatures had done earlier. Oagthor even tried poking at it with his axe, yet that did nothing either. He looked to the rest of the party.

"Let us help the faerie army and maybe they can break this barrier with their magik. We have no time to waste. The longer we are separated from them, the less of a chance they have to live." The dwarf hated to put it like that, but he also knew that there was no time for error. If something was going to be done, it must be done quickly and it must be done now. He looked at the rest of the party and at the sprites, who flew just above his head. He urged the party forward into the thick of battle against the fog creatures and the remnants of the faerie army.

Oagthor had never seen a faerie before in his life, not until D'meir, but soon saw more than he would ever need to see for the rest of his time on Ar Solon. He saw unicorns, sprites, brownies, Miftles, and a number of other faerie creatures that he didn't know the name of standing against an unbeatable force. However, the dwarf noticed, the faeries had found a way to defeat the fog creatures.

As the creatures formed in front of them, rearing to attack, the only way they themselves could be attacked was if they were in solid form and took a shape. Of course, this did not defeat them in the manner of defeating an opponent and seeing them die, but it did weaken the fog to where it would retreat and have to reform into something else which, to the dwarf, seemed an exhausting task. Nevertheless, the faerie army continued forcing the fog back. Oagthor gathered the dwarves together and prepared their attack. He handed each of them the remaining torches from his pack, taking two for himself, and lit them from the last two torches that were still lit.

"The faerie army cannot continue to fight the fog creatures like this. The faeries will be defeated eventually because the fog does not give. Let us make it give! You know what fire does to the fog, let's push the fog back and give the faeries a rest so they can work on the fog barrier."

The dwarves moved in quickly; they did not hesitate like humans or elves, unconfident in their actions; the short race of beings knew what they had to do and it had to work. The plan did work, indeed, much to the faeries pleasure, giving them a chance to pull back from their attack. Oagthor approached the unicorns as he waved the fog away with his two torches, his axe strapped across his back.

"Unicorns, I need your help. I am Oagthor Axeblade and I was escorting Ranyll and Gabriella before we got separated. The fire fox D'meir is there with them but there is a fog barrier that is between us and them. We must get through it."

Not seconds after Oagthor spoke, the unicorns were en route to the tunnel behind them, soon at the fog barrier. The dwarf smiled and continued to wave the fog away with the rest of his party. The scout sprites reunited with the faerie army and told what had transpired in their patrols through the tunnels as the faerie army rested for the moment.

Soon, the barrier was down and Oagthor informed his dwarves to continue while he went to find Ranyll, Gabriella, and D'meir. Two unicorns went with him as well as Triggle and Ilthen, riding on the backs of the great, magikal creatures. The unicorn that was left kneeled so Oagthor could climb on as well. Oagthor nodded in thanks and did his best to hang on for his life.

*   *   *

D'meir darted through the tunnels, using the last of his magikal fire to show his way in the darkness. Ranyll and Gabriella were nowhere to be found, which is exactly what he wanted. The fire fox had agitated the fog creature something fierce, the great fog beast doing its best to try and catch the small fire fox; but, having no luck, it only frustrated the beast further. Now its nostrils flared in anger, its stride keeping pace with the magikal fox's speed, almost catching him at moments.

D'meir ran further through the tunnels until he came to an open cavern. In moments, he knew Ranyll and Gabriella had been there. All around the cavern, great fires had been lit, covering the cavern in a dim light, shadows reflecting off the pillars that reached to the top of the great domed ceiling that had begun crumbling over time. D'meir knew it. This had to be the place to take his stand against the fog beast. With most of his energy depleted, the fire fox was beginning to become exhausted with the chase. He turned the corner into the cavern and darted through the great pillars, noticing that this slowed the fog creature greatly. It had to focus on its movements not to hit the pillars. D'meir noticed that Ranyll and Gabriella were not in sight in this area either. The fire fox turned around to face the great fog beast that was not far behind him at all.

"This is the last of it, creature! You shall not leave this room! We shall deal with one another here until it is done!" The creature seemed to understand what D'meir was saying to it. It took two great steps and slammed a shoulder into the pillar on its left, shattering it into pieces, several great stone blocks slamming down not far from the fire fox. The fire fox jumped away from the debris and climbed on top of a fallen piece, staring long at the great fog creature before him.

"You have nothing that can defeat me, creature! I am a fire fox from Dree! I am here as protector and you are in my way from achieving this. Get out of my way!" D'meir darted up a pillar and allowed the fog creature to see this. The fog creature darted after him, slamming into the pillar, the great stone pillar crumbling under the beast's weight. It tumbled all around the fog creature and D'meir shot into the air just above the creature, landing on another pillar not too far from the last. D'meir moved a little further up the pillar and taunted again.

"Again, you are a weak being and can't even be in the true world for long. You have to shift in and out of worlds. You have no substance, foggy dog! Your master has you on a short leash!"

The fog creature seemed even more perturbed now at the name calling and reared back to slam itself into the pillar. It lunged for the pillar. On this signal, D'meir prepared to jump. The fog creature stopped just short of the pillar and tapped the pillar with its shoulder, D'meir jumping out and away from the pillar, though he just realized that it was not falling like the others. The fog creature knew the fire fox's plan.

The great fog creature leapt up into the air and wrapped its teeth around the fire fox, bringing it down with him, its jaws tightening on its prey. That's when D'meir used his magik. He felt his paw snap between the fog creature's teeth and knew that his front paw had been injured, lighting himself up in a great magikal flame. The fog creature howled in pain and spat the fire fox out, lapping at its own maw in pain. It came at D'meir just as he touched the ground. The fire fox leapt back up with its back paws, grabbing onto a pillar with its one front paw that wasn't injured. Just as he found a hold, the fog creature slammed its shoulder

D'meir continued to hang on with his three useful paws as it fell, waiting for the fog creature. It came at him now, directly under the pillar as it fell, jaws wide and waiting for the fire fox to fall. The fire fox leap out and in the direction of the great pillar as it fell, the fog creature jumping away as well.

D'meir felt the jaws wrap around him once more and, this time, did not let him go when his magik erupted around him. It clamped down on his small form and continued to squeeze, the fire fox crying out in pain as he felt his small form collapse under the weight of the jaws of this creature. In another moment, the pillar made contact with the airborne fog creature and slammed it down into the cavern floor, blowing the air and the fire fox from its jaws, several sections of the pillar rolling aside in the dim firelight.

D'meir lay still on the floor.

Oagthor watched as the pillar struck both the fog creature and D'meir in mid-air and sent them tumbling onto the floor together, dust and debris flying up as they made impact not far from him. The dwarf felt his stomach drop at the sight of this and commenced to climb over and around the fallen pillars to reach his friend. The unicorns were unable to traverse in the middle of the cavern and had to go around the fallen debris, carrying both Triggle and Ilthen to the other side.

Oagthor reached the still form of D'meir and saw that the fog creature was, indeed, still alive but trapped underneath the fallen pillar. It was within reach of D'meir and continued, in its solid form, to come after the fire fox. Oagthor approached before the fog creature could respond and slipped his axe free from its holder on his back, taking a swing right at the creature's head. The fog creature turned just as the axe hit its mark, slamming its head down into the cavern floor. It lay still and, in moments, dissipated from view, the pillar shifting and falling onto the floor as well. Oagthor retrieved his axe from the floor and watched as the weakened fog shifted and moved away from view.

Oagthor reached down for D'meir. The small form of the fire fox was barely recognizable. He had fallen from the mouth of the fog creature and landed hard on the ground, blood and dirt mingling together, matting his once bright fur together in clumps. The dwarf could feel a faint pulse in the fox's body and Oagthor did his best to hide his concern from his face as he spoke to D'meir.

"It's going to be alright, my friend. It's going to be just fine, you'll see." He smoothed the matted fur down on D'meir's head and continued to stroke him behind the ears, where he had always known it had given him comfort.

The fire fox looked up at Oagthor.

"It's alright, my friend. I was chosen for this path. I've done my part. Ranyll and Gabriella are away from here as it is planned. They are on the next step of their journey."

The fire fox coughed and that cough seemed to tear into his entire frame, his paws and tail twitching in response to the pain.

The dwarf looked down at the fire fox, tears in his eyes.

"But what about us? What about our adventures together? You can't forget those, can you?"

D'meir smiled though he was in pain. He laid his head back down and rested for a moment. Then he spoke.

"I have one last journey to make, Oagthor, and I'm afraid that you cannot make this one with me."

Oagthor knew it was the last time he would see his friend alive again. He had become, over time, a cold and unfeeling dwarf due to the ways in which the world of Ar Solon had treated him, but his insides grew soft now. He leaned down and cradled D'meir's head in his hands, kissing his forehead gently.

"I will not forget you, my friend. I will not forget you; and I will avenge you."

D'meir smiled. His voice was just a faint whisper now.

"I would not expect any less from a dwarf."

The two unicorns as well as Triggle and Ilthen were standing silently behind Oagthor and watched as the life escaped from D'meir's still form, the fire fox no longer speaking or breathing; the faint glow the fire fox had as protection now faded from view. They were silent for a time after that, the dwarf still close to the fire fox.

The faeries could hear a faint mumble coming from the dwarf's lips and, as they listened, they recognized it as a prayer. It had been long since they had heard a prayer. But as quickly as it began it was done, Oagthor standing back up to his feet, the dwarf retrieving his axe and torch that had fallen not far from him.

The unicorn was the first to speak.

"I am sorry for your loss, Oagthor Axeblade. D'meir…."

Oagthor interrupted.

"We will have time to mourn later. We must find Ranyll and Gabriella before more danger has befallen them. Come, let us go. We shall bury and mourn the dead once this task is finished."

The dwarf gripped his axe tightly and felt the stomp of hooves behind him moments later, followed by the tapping of the Miftle's boots on the ground as well, moving into the next chamber past the fallen pillars.

30

It had been four days of nonstop travel for Head Scribe Devver Tollins and Scribe Henzell, the wagon ride a taxing one to their purpose. Devver's driver, Jennings, had urged them to stop at a small town with an inn and stable to feed and water the horses, but the head scribe would not hear of it. After seeing what he had seen on the roads he travelled, closer and ever closer to danger, he admitted to himself that there were things that were beyond his control. He had set out to do something very specific, and to take a rest and stop now could possibly jeopardize everything. They were very close to their destination.

Within the book head scribe had within his possession, it spoke of a cavern entrance not far from the Tirapoor Channel, only a day's ride from Reune Lake. It gave a specific piece of landscape and scenery within the tome that was explicit in detail and, as the wagon slowed down, Head Scribe Tollins began to grow uneasy.

They were almost there.

He knew of the dangers that lurked on the continents of Ar Solon, though he had never much cause for alarm in his own routine world of scribe duties; however, he had seen recorded many an atrocity in his time as a head scribe that made the hairs on the back of his neck stand on end.

Jennings was soon there at the wagon's door to open it and set the stairs up so the Head Scribe and Scribe Henzell could climb down off the wagon, which rocked back and forth slightly as they exited. Before them was the Tirapoor Channel.

It was still a beauty to behold, Head Scribe Tollins thought, watching as the great river flowed before them, the channel a single flowing river, clear of debris and age with the help of the checkpoint guards that patrolled and cleaned the area. Of course, the western half of the Tirapoor Channel did not require as much work as the eastern half, the western being only half the size of the eastern side opposite of the Reune Lake, much of the Tirapoor Channel flowing into smaller streams and a few lakes collected here and there in the western half of Kariyl.

Scribe Henzell stretched and walked closer to the channel. Head Scribe Tollins stood where he was and searched the area with his eyes. Soon, Jennings was at his side, tightening his belt at his waist as he shifted the scabbard at his side until it was comfortable. He looked over at the Head Scribe and nodded in the direction of the younger scribe.

"Does he know why we're here?"

The Head Scribe took a moment to answer. "To tell you the truth, Jennings, I find it hard to find out why **I'm** here, but I am." He paused, looked down at the tome in his hands, studying a page or so, then looked back up in the direction of the Tirapoor Channel.

"As for Scribe Henzell, I feel that he will do fine with this mission. I picked him because he needed experience. However, he does not need to know everything about the mission. He knows enough."

Jennings nodded to the answer, thinking it through a bit. "Well, Head Scribe Tollins, it's been a pleasure working with you. Whatever happens here, I want you to know that. We've been through a lot in these last few years."

Devver nodded in agreement, closing the tome and sliding it back into his bag at his hip. He pulled the leather flap over the top of the satchel and tied the leather cord tightly. Devver then walked back to the wagon and reached inside, putting on his own belt, fitting the Golettan scabbard and matching blade in its place at his side.

"Many adventures you and I have taken, yet none so as important as this one. At least, I hope that is the case. One can never know."

Jennings looked puzzled. "How do you mean, sir?"

Devver closed the door to the wagon and began walking towards the channel. The Head Scribe pointed over to a corner of the channel that was clustered with a number of large shrubs and bushes. Not far from where they stood, there was a small suspension bridge that floated above the roaring channel below, used mostly for checkpoint guards to catch passing debris and cross so they didn't have to swim or ford themselves across.

"I will have to explain it to you later, Jennings. I think we've found what we're looking for."

Head Scribe took the lead in the crossing of the suspension bridge, which was made for one person to cross at a time. There were two ropes that hung at the sides of the suspension bridge for those to cross with. Head Scribe took his time and tried his best to keep himself looking up and not at the roaring waters below him. He looked back once to see both Jennings and Scribe Henzell watching him intently, then looked back to his present state and continued on. Once he reached the other side, Devver turned and waved the other two forward. He looked over his shoulder at the clump of bushes not far from him.

"Just as I thought," he remarked, noticing a small entranceway dug into the ground that was well-covered and unnoticeable unless, of course, you were looking for it.

Jennings and Scribe Henzell made it across safely and soon the three of them were moving clumps of trimmed brush from the entranceway opening, watching as Head Scribe Tollins reached his hand down to the heavy circular door and tugged at the iron rung connected to it. It didn't budge. Head

Scribe tried again but, to no avail, it did not budge. He looked at the other two for assistance.

"I believe, if we all pull together, we can open this door. Here, let us try." Devver moved aside a bit and allowed enough room for the two others in his party to pull with him. With a single tug, the door was pulled free and swung outward, the hinges holding it in place against the ground, small pieces of debris and leaves falling inside the hole. The three of them looked down into the hole that held a small set of grey, stone stairs that led down into the darkness in a spiral.

Devver spoke up then, more true than he had ever spoken before. "It's true! It's all true, gentlemen! The tome says all of this. I have read to here in the tome and it took the three of us to open the door, that's why I said it in such fashion. This is incredible! It is as if we were guided here and the world has already been written."

Jennings looked confused. "So, what you're saying is that **everything** that we've done has already been written and we're just playing it out as we go along?"

"That's exactly what I'm saying!" Devver wiped off his hands from the door handle's rust and age that had been covering it and untied the satchel at his side, pulling out the book. He opened to a marked page about halfway through and began to read.

" *'And it was there that the party of three stared down into the great door that was the entrance into what lay next in their adventure, the head scribe relating to the other two the events that had transpired up until this point and how it had all been written before. He knew that the others would have trouble believing him so he took the tome out for proof and read to them a passage or two before closing the great book.'"*

Jennings just shook his head. "That's incredible, Head Scribe Tollins. What does it say that we do next?"

Devver looked down at the tome and read a bit further on his own before continuing out loud. "It says that we light a torch from our packs and continue down the stairs to find something important to the mission as well as the fate of all of Ar Solon."

This made the two in the party very somber, almost in a meditative state, scared to say anything due to the fact that what they said would be documented, but also too excited about what they would find down in the tunnel that they hadn't much to say.

Soon, the torch was lit and Devver led them down the grey, stone steps, each step spiraling down and down into darkness until, finally, they came to a small entryway with a wooden door in front of them.

Jennings almost jumped with excitement. "Now what does the tome say that's going to happen?"

Devver quieted his driver with a wave of his hand as he leaned against the wooden door, his ear to the door, listening for any sounds.

"I've not read past this point. If I were to continue to read ahead, it would be hard for me to follow the directions exactly and I am afraid I could change the future irrevocably because I've altered history as it is being written. One must be careful not to read too far into one's own future. It can damage what may actually happen and could possibly send events spiraling into chaos."

At this, Jennings stepped back away from the door a bit, looking at Scribe Henzell and then at the Head Scribe, waiting for them to make their move.

"I want no part in changing the world irrevocably, Head Scribe. Do you mind if I stay right here while you and your assistant go in without me?" The Head Scribe nodded and handed his torch to Scribe Henzell, the elder scribe taking the tome back out from its pack on his hip, opening it back up to the marked page. He read aloud.

"For many moments, Head Scribe Tollins and the others in his party stood, transfixed at the door, waiting and hoping at the same time that the tension that held them at bay would soon subside. Devver reached out his hand and pressed his fingers against the door, pushing slightly. The door opened easily enough. Devver looked inside and saw what he never expected to see...."

Devver then dropped the tome on the floor and pushed Scribe Henzell aside, pressing both of his hands against the door, the door giving as easily as it said it would, the Head Scribe waving away the dust that the movement brought up.

"No, this can't be! No, there must be a mistake!" He walked into the empty room and looked around. It was a small, square room, all of the four sides even and made of smooth granite. It looked like a storage room that hadn't been used in some time. Scribe Henzell and Jennings walked into the room, Scribe Henzell panning the torch around at the small space they inhabited. The young scribe looked to his mentor for guidance, his face awash in confusion.

"What are we supposed to be looking for, Head Scribe?"

Devver Tollins did not know what to say. He was at a loss for words. Making his way back over to the tome that he had dropped at the entranceway, he snatched up the tome and brought it into the room where he could see the writing, just under the torchlight. He continued yet his voice was not nearly as strong as it had been moments earlier.

"...Devver looked inside and saw what he never expected to see....an empty room. It was barren and had been barren for some time since the Treaty between the Races. It had been a storage room for supplies and weapons if there was ever an ambush or the parties were ever in need of assistance and did not have shelter for the night."

Devver took a deep breath and stared at the tome in front of him for long moments, silent. Never had Scribe Henzell seen Devver so rapt in thought. Neither one of the party said anything to him while he thought, though they did look around the small storage room for some time, taking their time to feel the walls, to touch the cold, granite floors, even to look at the cracks in between the walls to see if there were any secret entrances or compartments that could be found in the dim light of the torch that the young scribe held.

Nothing.

Devver began thumbing through the rest of the tome then, looking and, finally, finding the last page of the tome that had been written in. He began to read.

"'It was the intent that you, Devver Tollins, were to leave the guild so that the most important thing could occur; that the next Chronicler could take his place. Though I have the utmost respect for you, Head Scribe Tollins, you would not allow what must happen to happen in front of you; many of the tomes that I own are now passed on to the next Chronicler. Yes, it was true; I was the Chronicler of all of Ar Solon, that secret cannot be kept any longer. Yet, the journey through the harsh country and the seclusion that the next Chronicler has will distance and protect him from any that know about him. He has taken all items that belonged to me, including my own body to be buried in secrecy from prying eyes. Do not attempt to follow. Your story ends here, Head Scribe Tollins, as well does your party's story. Return to your guild and forget that you ever knew a man by the name of Gilden Felves.'"

With these final words, Devver closed the tome and slipped it back into the satchel at his side. He looked to the others and nodded to them in acceptance.

"Come, Scribe Henzell. We tarry here too long. It will be getting dusk soon. We must be getting back to Goletta. Jennings, once back across the bridge, we must begin our journey back as soon as possible. I must see to my guild."

The others said nothing, simply nodded, following him out of the room, the door closing behind them.

The outside now seemed bleak and dark though there was still light present, the sun breaking over the trees in the west, not far from their horse and carriage. They made it across the bridge with little effort, Devver taking a look back at the passage that they had been sure to keep hidden as they had found it.

For what, Devver reminded himself, *there is nothing there for us there. It was an empty room shown to me by a deceitful tome.* Devver almost wanted to hit himself in frustration, for being such an idiot when he was and had been educated and not the type to get caught up in such adventures. It would be years from now that the treasure inside that room would truly be found. Many have searched for the treasure contained within that room but many, just like Devver, have come up short.

Just once, Devver thought to himself, *I would like to have been part of an adventure.*

It was a quiet ride home.

*   *   *

Kalir and his checkpoint company had been walking through what seemed like the same set of tunnels for the last two days and not come up with anything, almost feeling as though they were circling the same tunnels over and over again. It was as if something were not letting them through the darkness. They had cleaned up the tunnels at the beginning of the passageway, which had been thick with daemons but, as they travelled further into the passageways, there were no daemons to be found. It was as if the creatures had vacated and moved to another location. In fact, they had seen nothing since entrance into the cavern.

Kalir noticed ahead that there were another set of tunnels that branched out and separated into more snake-like passageways all around them. It had been the same throughout their trek into the passageways. Kalir looked at the four different ways and separated the team of nine into three teams; Kalir, Dir'grar, and Taldin, then Mareev, Rynen and Ermoor and, remaining, were Andarin, Lincoln, and Fitts. All were somewhat seasoned checkpoint guards with the exception of Rynen and Ermoor, who were still finishing up their training.

One passageway remained unchecked for the moment. Their drill had been easy; walk a good distance, around 500 paces, if there is no sign of anything within the passageway, mark it and return back to point to check the other passageways. This worked so far, Kalir and his checkpoint guards had not found any of their markings within the time that they travelled.

All of the team checked their gear and prepared to separate, taking out their marking chalk from their bags. Kalir looked back at the passageway they had just come from, checking the markings on the wall again one last time before beginning his decent into the next passageway.

He smiled at the rest of his guards.

"Good luck, my guards. Be safe and hurry back. We have no time for playing within these passages. For all we know, the dwarves could have laid traps for unwelcome visitors."

"Or the daemons could be lying in wait for you at the end of the tunnel," Dir'grar added, hefting a spear up over his shoulder. "And then where would you be?"

Taldin raised his hand to answer. "Dead, sir?"

Dir'grar didn't find his joking funny. "Yes, Taldin, you'd be dead. Enough with the funny stuff. Let's do what Master Ranolf says and get back here in one piece. Got that, Ermoor, Rynen?" Dir'grar winked and loosened a smile from his face a bit under the great black beard.

Rynen and Ermoor didn't respond. They had been teased about much of what had happened, as if trouble had just found them, over and over again.

They couldn't help it that they got a piece of the action out there and had trouble handling. Ermoor thought to himself, *anyone who had to deal with what I've dealt with would have trouble.* He looked over in Dir'grar's direction. *Except Dir'grar, of course.*

The three teams split up and began searching the passageways. Rynen's group came up with a dead end about 300 paces into it, Mareev drawing an X at the end with his marking chalk, the three of them heading back. Andarin's team had made it 500 paces and beyond, yet they had seen nothing at all. Even the dust on the passageway floor had not been disturbed. They marked their passageway with an X and continued back.

Kalir's group moved forward into the passageway, the dim torchlight filtering out small markings of dwarven make, Kalir taking the lead with Dir'grar shortly at his side, Taldin taking up the rear. In 300 paces, they had found fragments of wall littered and strewn about, with a number of daemon bodies littering the way as well. The fragments came from a small passageway just big enough to fit into not far from where the bodies lay, Kalir taking an interest in something for a change. He moved closer to the small passageway, shoving his torch in the hole, looking up into the small passageway, which took a turn up into the ceiling of the passageway, a small glimmer of light filtering through the hole from a distance away.

Dir'grar almost pulled Kalir from the hole. "What are you doing, Kalir? Are you mad? You don't know what's in that hole."

Kalir smiled.

"There's only one way to find out, isn't there?" He handed Dir'grar his torch and pulled off his pack, taking out the small dagger at his side. He tucked in his tunic a bit more and tightened up his belts and straps. It was a tight passageway. He doubted very much that Dir'grar could fit in it due to his size.

"I'll be right back, my friend."

Kalir slid into the passage and shimmied through the space, leading with his hands, dagger in hand, and was soon out on the other side, out of view from his group.

It didn't take long before Dir'grar began to worry. He looked into the hole and waved the torch inside it a little to get a better view. "Kalir, what is it? Kalir, do you hear me?" Suddenly, Kalir's head popped down into the hole, waving away the torch with his dagger.

"Get the others. This is the way." He looked at Dir'grar. "My friend, I don't know how you're going to fit in here."

Soon, the rest of the checkpoint guard were making their way up and into what could only be called The Great Hall. Kalir had been here years ago when he was just a child with his father, trading wares to the dwarves before the treaty had expired. The Great Hall had been great at one time; but now, it seemed to be dilapidated and run down. The great pillars that had been made for the great dwarves of the times were faded and worn; even some of the great dwarven statues carved within the pillars were missing faces, hands, and other limbs, only pieces of what was once great.

Dir'grar, having a difficult time getting through the hole, smashed the tunnel open even wider with an old statue Kalir had found in The Great Hall, the great man stepping out of the hole on his own, the dwarven statue head still gripped tightly in his right hand.

Kalir looked to his men, somewhat disappointed for them. "It is a time of despair when these halls are empty, my friends. This was once a great hall that was filled with commerce and trade. Now look at it. It is a shame."

The Great Hall had been built as a thoroughfare when elves, dwarves, and men could trade freely between one another; now it was abandoned and hallowed out. Kalir and his checkpoint guards made their way through The Great Hall, trying their best not to disturb the layers upon layers of dust that had accumulated on the ground and the objects littered about, Dir'grar leading the way, torch in hand.

Kalir and the others noticed that the daemons had not demolished the things that had lain here for so long like the other things that they had touched. Much of what the checkpoint had passed was strewn about without care or thought, almost as if the daemons were gremlins of sorts, laying waste to whatever they could get their hands on. However, here was different. It was as if there was a sort of reverence here; as if something were here that they gave homage to by not touching anything except for the floors on which they had tread, leaving a small trail behind with their footprints.

Whatever it was, Kalir thought to himself, *I hope it keeps them at bay long enough for me to find Ranyll.* He looked ahead in The Great Hall for any movement but didn't see any immediate danger. Nevertheless, he couldn't take any chances, especially with what had happened with Ermoor and Rynen; it was as if they were a bad luck charm or had become a target of sorts. Kalir kept them close to him now, walking at a little quicker pace to take up the space between his group and theirs.

Taldin and Dir'grar looked a little concerned. Dir'grar moved up next to Kalir.

"What is it, Kalir? What's got you spooked?"

"Could be nothing, Dir'grar. Bring the groups in closer, that's all. I feel something here. I think we're close to something. I don't know what it is."

"Too quiet," Dir'grar questioned, looking around at the once great halls of the races, taking note to himself that the races during the treaty used to take great care at where they met. Many had stated that The Great Halls were lost to all, that they had been blocked and covered up so that none could relive the pain of what happened there some time ago. Dir'grar agreed. He didn't want to be here at all either.

Kalir simply shook his head.

"It's not that, Dir'grar. It's something else. There's a memory here; something I remember. This place was a significant place of evil. Something awful happened years ago to make everyone leave."

"You mean the massacre of The Great Halls?"

Kalir's eyes grew wide with recognition.

"Yes! I remember now! It was the year Ranyll was born. The Treaty between the Races was broken here! There was a massacre that occurred within these walls." Kalir looked around at his checkpoint crew and scanned the area around them for anything that moved, clicked, or scurried across the floor.

And that's when Kalir heard them. He had been so engaged with the past that the present was happening not far from him and he didn't even pay attention to it. It was two voices that somewhat melded together. In the dim light of The Great Hall, Kalir couldn't make out where they came from, but he could hear them.

The checkpoint leader put up his hand once and the guards went silent. They knew the signal and heeded its warning with complete obedience. No one moved, spoke, or did anything to break the silence of the area around them. This had been done many times throughout the checkpoint guards training as well as real-life situations. Many a time, Kalir had kept them silent for what seemed like hours, listening to the sounds of the forest, checking to see if all were right with his checkpoint. However, this wasn't Kalir's checkpoint. But that didn't mean that Kalir was any less efficient.

Master Kalir Ranolf listened for several moments, called out to his group, and then darted for a dark spot on the west side of the Great Hall, the two in his crew following quickly behind. The other groups could barely make out what Kalir had said. Once they understood, the rest of the groups closed in as well, watching as their checkpoint leader climbed down into tunnel, using his torch for light to traverse further into it.

Ranyll and Gabriella made their way through the passageways, not bothering to look back, not wanting to more than anything. The Fog Beast had reared its ugly head and, though Ranyll hated to think that D'meir was alone in fending this creature off, knew that his responsibility lie elsewhere. He look at Gabriella now, who was flush and out of breath, her eyes wide with fear, small hints of the possibility of escape at the corner of her eyes. She looked at Ranyll staring at her and stopped.

"What is it, Ranyll?" It had been a long adventure to get to Gabriella and he had not a chance to fully look on her since the daemons had taken her. He could feel the pounding in his head from running a great distance with little fresh air in these caves. Being in the caves were indeed taking a toll on him as they would anyone who is not used to breathing the thick, dirty air. Ranyll leaned up against the nearby wall and took deep breaths, trying to steady his breathing. He smiled to the angel and put his weight on his sword, tip pressed into the cavern floor, Ranyll taking comfort in the moment.

"It is the first time I've really looked at you since I got you back."

Gabriella was silent for a time. She stared at the young man with the same look that she had on her face when she had given herself up to save him and Gwenzel. There was the sad pair of eyes, which took over the strong, solid cheek bones that surrounded the petite nose in between them. Gabriella still had a smile upon her face but there was something strange about the smile, something far away; far away from the dwarven caverns filled with daemons and ancient evils that far surpassed any common day that Ranyll could muster up in his mind.

"Ranyll, you have been a great protector." Ranyll just shook his head.

"No, I haven't Gabriella. If that were the case, then I would never have let TSeT take you from me. No, Gabriella, I haven't been a good protector. The others in the party just didn't say anything, but I know it to be true."

Gabriella moved closer to Ranyll, somewhat cautiously, her eyes darting here and there in the tunnel ways around them. She placed her hand on top of Ranyll's, his grip tightening on his sword instinctively.

"Someday, Ranyll, all of this fighting and running will be over for you and your family. Now is but your moment to show who you are and what you stand for. As an angel, I can at least tell you that. Your mind knows of the grand scheme and it flows strongly within your veins. Whenever you feel perplexed or confused, remember that. Let those words comfort and calm you. Ranyll, for you, there is much more ahead." She paused.

"Ranyll, I never told you what my purpose was here on Ar Solon, what the Creator had instilled within me, did I?" Gabriella looked intently on Ranyll, waiting for his reply.

"What do you mean, Gabriella?" The conversation seemed to take a weird turn. Ranyll looked and around him and could see nothing but the bitter blackness of the tunnels. He had not heard D'meir or the Fog Beast approach at any turn. For the moment, they seemed to be safe.

She continued.

"Each inhabitant as well as each angel was supposed to be instilled with the grand scheme of the world as well as their purpose. Most inhabitants weren't; that is why this world suffers as it does. Well, all angels have a purpose and are known by that purpose. For Greditto, he was the angel of song and music, sent down to the world of Ar Solon to instill these things to further the inhabitants in their own grand schemes."

Ranyll gripped Gabriella's hand tightly. It all came to him now. He looked at Gabriella in surprise.

"So, that means that, if Greditto passes on and no other angel takes his place, then ….."

Gabriella finished. "Then inspiration for song and music is gone forever. What is here now shall be here forever and nothing more."

Ranyll was in shock. He knew nothing of the severity of such consequences.

How could the Creator allow the death of such wondrous things on this world? Ranyll stopped his thoughts short. He looked at Gabriella again.

"Shilinda, the angel of faeries, she has passed also. That means that there will be no faeries to multiply and inhabit the land either. That means, what is here on this world is here and there shall be no more, correct?" Gabriella nodded her head in agreement.

Ranyll remembered seeing the faerie army and knew that that was all that was left; and there were so few left. This was all too much for Ranyll. He leaned his sword against the cave wall and grasped Gabriella by the arms, pulling her close. He brushed her face with a hand. Suddenly, Gabriella had become something foreign to him, almost intangible in his eyes. He knew he had known her and could see her now, but the idea that he was simply another inhabitant played inside of his mind.

"And what powers do you hold in this world, angel? As an inhabitant, our world is falling apart and you are simply watching the demise of an entire population and keeping all of this to yourself?" Ranyll could feel the frustration well up inside of him, could feel it all wanting to cascade out of him and press against Gabriella, but he knew where his anger and frustration needed to go. There was only one that deserved it all.

Gabriella enclosed Ranyll's hand with her own, trying her best to soothe the inhabitant in front of her before answering.

"Ranyll, there will come a time when you will understand everything that is going on around you. You will be strong with purpose and many will follow you, even ask you for guidance and healing of their own afflictions. That time is not now. You are feeling what you feel now because this is how it must be. There is no other way." She paused again.

This time, she withdrew her hand and moved away from Ranyll, the young man letting her go. She drifted only a few feet from him, but the disconnect was as strong as it had been just a moment ago.

"I never told you what I did because I did not know how to tell you. For you, it may be easy with your thoughts and feelings, but mine have jumbled up on me and played tricks on me many times. It is a thing, these feelings and emotions that I have, and they cannot be trusted. To speak out loud, to tell you what I am telling you now, is the best possible truth for me." She paused for a long moment.

"Ranyll, I am Gabriella, angel of dreams and visions. It has been given to me in a vision that you, Ranyll Tolver, are my grand scheme, my purpose in this life. These moments that have been given to me as a mortal are for you and my purpose is to prepare you for your life and what lies ahead." Ranyll was about to speak when someone else did in his stead.

"You say too much!" A voice in the darkness interrupted.

Ranyll saw the fear in Gabriella's eyes take shape as she turned to where the voice had come from, both of them staring into the darkness. For a time, there was no further conversation, yet Gabriella knew who lay in the shadows.

Ranyll's blade flashed in the darkness, but before he could think to cover it in a magikal flame for light, the voice made his presence known in the dim light of the tunnel. A human man, his face clean and shaven, his shoulder-length hair well-kept and swept behind his ears, walked out into the darkness, his eyes flashing at Gabriella who stood before them, then met up with Ranyll's, piercing and strong. Ranyll didn't have to guess who this was. He lifted his sword up at The One, his sword hand steady and tightly grasping his father's sword.

"Ah, the one and only Ranyll! I must say, you are not what I expected; someone taller maybe. Yes, that's it. I expected a man, not a simple youth such as yourself. What are you, all of sixteen summers…."

"…seventeen summers," Ranyll corrected, putting himself between Gabriella and The One.

"My mistake, Ranyll. My apologies." The One looked at the blade in front of him, only a few feet away, and then back to Ranyll, smiling the entire time.

"Your father's sword? Really? Well, you must be proud, Ranyll Tolver. It's not every day that you get to have an artifact from the past, especially one with such distinguishable background." The One seemed to take pleasure in being sly even though he had a sword pointed at him. His eyes did not waver from Ranyll's gaze. The One continued.

"What does it feel like, inhabitant, to know that you are to be the cause of this angel's death, no matter how hard you may have worked to get her back? How does it feel to know that, boy? That is your true name, right? Boy?"

Ranyll could feel his blood boil, yet at the same time, he had such a deep sense of fear within him he knew not what to do with himself. He told himself to be courageous, to keep from wavering in the face of fear and he did so, almost blindly, trying his best to stare through the visage of The One, right past him. However, what lay past The One could be taken as just as bad, if not worse.

The tunnel was not completely dark behind The One. Small, red slits that were eyes blinked out eagerly at Ranyll and Gabriella, the entire tunnel was filled from top to bottom with daemons, stacked on top of one another, all of them crowding each other, trying their best to get a spot to watch, almost emphatically, as Ranyll and Gabriella looked for a way out of this situation.

But there seemed to be none; save the glimmer of light that trickled just behind Ranyll and Gabriella. The hope had not faded, not faded for them completely. Ranyll managed a quick glance at where the light was coming from and then back to The One and his daemons.

The One had not moved; not even blinked and eye. He stood, statue-like, while the daemons wriggled and writhed behind him, a grotesque scene unfolding before Ranyll.

This was the end, Ranyll thought to himself. *This is where I take my last stand and where The One takes his first stand against Gabriella's protector.*

In the tunnel behind him, Ranyll could hear voices; human voices. There was someone coming to save them; save him and Gabriella. He just hoped that they made it in time.

31

Arntheer and the other dwarves used the last of their torchlight to light the random sconces on the walls, keeping the tunnels lit while the faerie army collected their dead and dying. The fog had crept away after the breeching of the fog barrier the unicorns had broken through, the dwarf finding something very wrong with that from the start.

"Something is happening, I know it. We are missing something here. Any word from Oagthor?"

The scout sprite shook its head in defeat.

"Nothing yet, Arntheer. He and the unicorns are backtracking their route, but they can't find Ranyll or Gabriella and have no trace of which direction that they went in through the tunnels. It was almost as if they just disappeared."

The dwarf doubted it.

"Yeah, that or something is trying its best to hide them from us." Arntheer had noticed throughout their travels through the caverns and tunnelways in the last few hours, they were not able to find their way back through to the exit; even their tracks in the dust had been if they had never come through. The other problem was that the markers that they had used, the simple chalk marks on the walls, had somehow disappeared by the time they came back through the tunnels. Arntheer knew a few twists and turns to get back on the original track back through, but he didn't know the entire way back and, after a few paths of going the wrong way, had decided to go back and regroup with the faeries.

Yes, something was controlling these caves. Whatever it was, they needed to take care of whatever they could to get rid of it and escape before they began to rest or lose their supply of food. It didn't seem to be a battle of strength anymore, Arntheer decided, but a battle for survival. The battle between the fog creatures had become a stalemate, with no one really conquering any ground or taking lives and Arntheer knew that, whoever controlled these creatures of fog, knew something about survival. In fact, he was betting that it knew a lot more than it was letting on; this is what Arntheer feared most. There was something that was going on around them that he knew nothing about. As a dwarf, he had been a fighter and a guard in Dardist for most of his young life; he never knew anything more than that.

However, Oagthor Axeblade was a seasoned fighter. He had served many terms as a representative for the dwarven colonies that lived outside of the mountains and had seen to it that he traveled a great deal, taking pleasure in the visits to the other races, trying his best to clean up the messes that were made when the treaty had been broken all those years ago. Even Rathor had some experience in these matters, at least more than Arntheer had. The dwarf looked around at the calmness of the situation and at the faeries that rested throughout the tunnels, spread out, many of them sleeping, a selection of them taking watch at each entry way and exit that was accessible.

Arntheer looked over at Rathor, who lay sleeping not far from the rest of his dwarven party, his small pack tucked under his neck to cushion the wall that he leaned against. The older dwarf seemed dead to Arntheer. He did not move, did not even seem to breathe; he seemed as if he were in some sort of trance with his eyes closed. Arntheer approached and, when he did, Rathor's facial expressions shifted slightly.

He spoke, his eyes still shut. "What do you want, dwarf?"

There was concern in Arntheer's voice. "Why are we here, Rathor?"

It took a moment for a response. "What?"

"Why are we here, right now, in these tunnels?"

"Because we followed the only way we knew to get here. Oagthor had all of us patrol the passageways, you know that. This was the only one that was leading somewhere."

"Why did the rest of the tunnels just end? Did the dwarves never finish what they started?"

Rathor shifted in his place and lifted an eyelid. "Dwarf, if you've come to have conversation, I'm of no use to you. I was sleeping, Arntheer. Sleeping! Maybe you should think about some as well." Rathor's eyes closed and he shifted a little to get more comfortable.

Nonetheless, Arntheer pushed his point further. "Rathor, if we took the only way to get here, then those tunnels that were dead ends were all started but never finished. Is that even possible?"

"Dwarf! I don't know what you're getting at. After all, these are your caves; shouldn't you know your own caves? I've never been here before."

"And I've never been in these caves before either! This is not on our maps back in Dardist! This is something we never knew was here. It was as if something opened up a way and let us in just so it could trap us inside. I'm telling you, Rathor, I don't like this. Something is wrong with the way we're looking at things if we can't find Ranyll and Gabriella, who were just here with us hours ago!"

Rathor seemed to get the young dwarves point, but only just a little. He nodded his head in agreement. "You've got a point there. No one's questioned that point so far. We are lost, but the only thing that we can do is continue to chase our tails and hope that we find a passageway."

Rathor paused. "Bring it up to Oagthor when he comes back. We'll see what we can do then. Right now, you should get some sleep. You'll need it."

But Arntheer didn't feel like sleeping. He knew that there was something amiss in these caverns that they seemed to be trapped in. The caverns, indeed, were strange, but in no way did they have any markings of resemblance to any caverns that he had frequented as a dwarven child or now as a patrol guard in the town of Dardist. Time and age did not spill across these caverns as they did so many others that he had seen; it was if they had been maintained and preserved by someone or something and kept in a vacuum for generations. Even the air, though dank now due to the battle that had waged, thick with blood and sweat, had a smell that was different than that of the air in the caverns that connected to Dardist.

With that, Arntheer did what he always did when something perplexed him; he took a walk. Breaking from the rest of the search party, the dwarf loaded up his small satchel and supplies in his arms and began to comb the caverns again by himself, making sure not to attract attention. He didn't want anyone coming along with him or to know that he was gone.

I will be back shortly, he told himself, hefting up the last of his supplies; some digging tools, bags, and a length of rope neatly knotted and tied around itself. The other dwarves had released the supplies that they carried upon the others after the battle had calmed somewhat, using what they could to dispose of the bodies and debris that lay strewn across their way. Arntheer would find out what and where they were and a way out of this trap, whether or not anyone believed him about it. However, he resolved, it was alone that he'd have to do this.

It had been only a short time since Arntheer left the others when he noticed that the smell of the old caverns had come back and, instead of the dead end that had been recorded on the maps given to him by the other guards, there was an open passageway that disappeared into the darkness far ahead of him.

He stopped for a moment, limiting his movements, listening to the darkness around him for a moment. The darkness seemed to say something to him; seemed to whistle and chant to him what lie in wait, what was hiding in the corners, ready to strike once it saw him. It lasted for a single moment and then was gone from his eyes, the only thing catching in his ears being his breathing in and out of the strong, flavored air around him.

Just then, a single light flashed from the darkness and his eyes caught the glint of a blade ahead of him in the passageway, his hand making for the small hand axe on his back. But it was too late. The flash of the blade ahead of him had only taken moments, but the bearer of the weapon was now within eyesight and closing in by the second.

Oagthor, his eyes flashing wildly in the darkness, came directly at him, Arntheer doing his best to capture Oagthor's attention and not mistakenly get attacked. He waved his hands out away from him, trying to flag Oagthor down, but the elder dwarf still came, his eyes fiery and wild, his hands gripping his battleaxe tightly, his mouth wide open and crying out what could not be shown in his shadowed features.

Arntheer backed away at this point, reaching for his hand axe at his back, his fingers fumbling for it wildly.

He means to take my head off, Arntheer agreed, his back pressed up against the wall now as he felt the handle of his axe in his hands. He freed it from its sheath, only to see Oagthor a moment later, his axe flung freely from his aged hands, the weapon spiraling directly at Arntheer. The dwarf then heard what Oagthor spilled forth from his mouth. It was not a battle cry, which many dwarves give their foes before the deathblow, but a curse on a name that echoed in Arntheer's head.

"SCARWOL!"

Arntheer saw the hate in Oagthor's eyes as he closed in on the younger dwarf, the axe slamming into Arntheer's body, flinging him back into the wall behind him, his head jerking forward from the attack.

*　　　　　*　　　　　*

Arntheer lifted his head up from the ground and felt a number of hands on him, bringing him to, some slapping at him while others simply pulled him from the fog that had its hold on him. When the dwarf opened his eyes, the blinding fog was still there, as it had been when it surrounded him when the battle began, at the side of the faerie army, fighting off the fog beasts as best he could. However, the fog beasts were not easily defeated.

Arntheer could feel the wound he had taken in his chest from the battle with the fog beast, yet looked around for Oagthor and his airborne battle axe, only finding the concerned faces of his garrison as well as Rathor's blank stare as he stood over him.

"You okay, Arntheer?" The old dwarf did not wait for a response. "You okay, Arntheer? Curse you dwarf, answer me!"

Rathor looked to the others that still had their hands on Arntheer, waving their torches around him to keep the fog from coming back. It drifted off from his chest and veered away from the torches completely, soon rolling down past his waist and, finally, to his feet, one of the garrison dwarves closing in on with a torch of his own, finally sending the fog away, it dispersing into the air about them.

"Oagthor! He came at me! I couldn't stop him!"

Arntheer did his best to stand on his own. The wounded dwarf winced in pain as he felt the wound take hold of his body, the young dwarf grasping at his chest, his fingers touching the wound almost immediately. Arntheer's tunic had been torn through as well as the small set of mail and the leather vest that accompanied it, a clean set of three, bloody claw marks clearly defined across his chest. He let himself drop back to the ground, the dwarves around him continuing to pull him away from the battle which still raged from all sides.

Rathor was still by his side. "It was lucky you took that damage, dwarf, because the fog beast had a good hold on you. The only reason you're alive is because you went limp and fell out of its mouth."

Arntheer tried to respond but couldn't. The pain was nearly unbearable. He could feel himself drift off from his present place as the rage of war began to subside and die around him, the tunnels hindering him from hearing the rest of the battle. He spared a couple of glances at the tunnels around him and watched as he was finally laid down against a cold tunnel wall, the insides of his mouth sticking together as he tried to speak.

"I….I think I can…..stand." However, when Arntheer tried, the pain shot through his body and he collapsed onto the cold, stone floor. Rathor and the other dwarves rushed to his side, the eldest dwarf taking a look into Arntheer's eyes. They seemed somewhat glazed over and rolled back into the dwarf's head, still shaking from the pain.

Rathor shifted in his placed in front of Arntheer. He looked to the other dwarves around him, knowing that he could not count on them for much, with the exceptional brute strength that they had given in the previous battles that they had fought together in. However, he looked to one of them for a job.

"Find a flying sprite in the battle. Have them come and use their magik on Arntheer. I will do what I can until they arrive." He paused and began to tend to Arntheer's wounds. Rathor looked back up as the dwarf left. He added, "…and make it quick. I don't know how much time Arntheer has."

Arntheer had come back somewhat from wherever he had went, smiling at the old dwarf next to him. He reached out a bloody hand to Rathor. The old dwarf took it, squeezing it to his chest, tapping lightly on Arntheer's arm.

"It's going to be alright, Arntheer. We found where these Fog Beasts live. It shouldn't be too much longer."

Arntheer just smiled, gripping Rathor's hand tighter.
He managed a few words. "I don't hate you like you think I do, old dwarf."

Rathor felt Arntheer's grip loosen in his own hand and saw the dwarf slip away from him. Rathor squeezed back into the bloody hand of the dwarf who now seemed to grow cold with every moment that passed.

"Hold on, Arntheer! Help is on the way!" The only thing the other dwarves could do around was stand and watch in disbelief as another of their kin seemed to slip away before them.

*   *   *

Oagthor hefted his axe onto his shoulder and trudged on through the darkness. He had left all of his supplies behind in an effort to make better time and catch up with anything and everything that would come into his path. The dwarf had long lost all sight of the quest and looked now for something more to satiate the anger that welled up inside of him. He had even left the unicorns and the two Miftles behind, taking a number of different tunnels to lead them off his trail. Holding back the tears the best way he knew how, he called out to the creature that he knew by name.

"Scarwol! Scarwol! I will kill you, you lowly creature; you and your Fog Beasts!" A sense of deep loss had fueled the dwarf's movements forward in the darkness, however, the bile welled up inside of him seemed to escape every so often, Oagthor's axe drifting out against the quiet hallways, slamming small fragments of wall across the well-manicured floors. He looked ahead into the darkness and saw nothing, save the next hallway that offered no new solution.

This is my task and mine alone! None will get to savor this moment with me.

Oagthor tried to forget D'meir and how the creature had fallen not but moments ago, yet it was all he could think about. D'meir lay shattered at his feet when he had approached, and for what? Oagthor had to keep from screaming in anger.

The boy! This was all because of the boy and his quest to find the angel! Curse that boy! Curse him! Our savior? Oagthor scoffed at the idea. It would take more than survival from an army of daemons for Oagthor to be convinced otherwise that this boy was something more. His mind drifted to the small creature again. The fire fox had been so much a part of his life, the dwarf had trouble remembering when he didn't think on the small creature that had gone on so many adventures together with him, having saved him from a fate worse than death several times over.

The dwarf passed into a number of chambers and passageways then, without really looking into them, knowing by instinct when the attack would come.

It would be foggy, he thought, *and the air will taste different, as it had in the tunnels fighting with the faerie army.* It had sort of an ancient dust taste that seemed to float around him before the Fog Beasts attacked.

Soon, his anger-laden journey came to an end; a dead end. Directly in front of him, the dwarf doing his best not to blink, a temple had been carved into the face of a rock wall, much of it crumbled away now; however, pieces did not lay strewn across the ground as he half expected them to be. The ancient faces carved into the temple stared down at him.

They were not dwarves, not humans, not even elves looked at him now. *These were the faces of the Gods*, Oagthor knew, for the eyes always seemed to be trained and fixed on him at every moment. There was no large debris from the shattered temple lying about; the floors were clear around the temple, just as they had been in the last few miles of tunnels that the dwarf had traversed through. The dwarf knew where he was; knew what lay inside just ahead of him.

It was Scarwol's temple. Many storytellers had spoken of this accursed place in their travels, yet none had actually seen it.

Oagthor made his way inside without a single thought; the only thing coursing through his veins at the moment seemed to be hate. Hate filled his eyes; hate filled him up to the very core. He half expected an attack and, when it did finally come, he welcomed his chance to release the bile that fueled him forward.

The smell of the Fog Beast filled his nostrils before he saw the mist roll in. Oagthor saw the creature begin to take shape; he knew it would only take moments and then it would be upon him.

"This is a waste of my time, Scarwol! I want you! Why send your minions?"

The Fog Beast formed in front of Oagthor as he spoke, the dwarf looking up at the temple stairway at the Fog Beast that seemed to, at first, roll down the steps until it stood and took full form in front of him now. The dwarf did not budge from his spot. He leaned his axe up over his shoulder and sifted through his pouches at his side with his free hand, producing a small pouch out in front of him. He unraveled the small string from around the top of the pouch and watched as the Fog Beast approached him, its maw spread open to take him into its mouth in one quick bite.

The dwarf continued to call out to Scarwol.

"I'll just take your dogs down one by one until I find you! I've got time, you accursed coward!"

In that moment, the Fog Beast leapt forward. Oagthor shook the pouch out in front of him, the fire dust scattering in the air in front of him, clinging to the Fog Beast. As soon as the delicate dust made contact with the Fog Beast it erupted in flames, giving the creature more solidity than before. Oagthor slipped the small pouch back into his belt, gripping his axe with both hands, watching as the Fog Beast reeled back in pain and surprise. Oagthor leapt forward, axe cleaving into the great fog creature, silencing it with blow after blow, Oagthor checking the stairway and the tunnels behind him for more. He smiled, watching as the mist retreated back up the stairs, his short legs carrying him up just behind the mist.

"Is that all, Scarwol?" Still, Oagthor heard no answer from the creature. The dwarf continued his search.

*   *   *

The torches did better at alleviating the tension that Ranyll had about facing the One and the daemons alone, yet it worked as a double-edged sword; once in the torchlight, it showed how many daemons there really were, which was more than Ranyll could ever imagine fitting into one passageway.

Arms, legs, claws, and contorted faces covered every space of the passageway behind The One, red slits blinking almost in unison, watching with rapt attention the other humans that moved closer down the passageway behind Ranyll and the angel.

Suddenly, a voice called out. "Ranyll, is that you?"

Ranyll nearly dropped his sword in surprise at hearing his uncle's voice, turning quickly to verify that it was his uncle, yet returning back to The One and the daemons that waited behind him.

Ranyll called out while keeping his eyes trained in front of him. "Yes, it is I, uncle."

Kalir and a small number of others materialized from the torchlight behind Ranyll and Gabriella, looking almost immediately on the man standing in front of them, an army of daemons waiting to strike. The One just smiled when he saw the others.

"So, now I guess we have an audience, isn't that right, Ranyll?" The One did not wait for a response. He continued. "I guess I'll have to kill them as well."

Ranyll's gaze drifted suddenly to his uncle's, whose eyes were still trained on the sight before them all; then Kalir fixed his gaze on young Ranyll's and motioned his gaze back to The One. In that one gaze, Ranyll seemed to know what his uncle wanted.

I will be fine, Ranyll, is what the gaze had said to him.

Gabriella was the one to speak next. "You do not need to take their lives, Darien. They are innocents."

The One interrupted. "So are we all, angel! I tire of the petty squabbling, the symphony of wailing and whining above me, angel. I will be rid of them all now! I've waited for this chance for some time, even killed your own kind for a chance at this. You are the next step for me."

Gabriella took a step forward towards The One. This threw Ranyll and the others into near hysterics. Ranyll lifted the tip of his sword out and closer at The One, which seemed to do nothing at intimidating the figure in front of him; The One stood where he had been standing, looked the way he had been looking. His pale, gaunt features seemed to reach out to Gabriella and she moved a step closer.

Ranyll reached for her. His hand hit her cold skin and the young man almost withdrew with surprise, yet he pushed past the cold and squeezed her arm tightly.

"Gabriella, no!" His voice seemed to yell out in his mind but it came out as a whisper on his lips. Gabriella seemed far away now, seeming to slip further and further away from the reality that they had known together. In moments, she had changed and looked the way he had seen her all those ten-days ago, when she had first come to him at Telgin. She was the same dream-like apparition that she had been then. She stared into his eyes.

The world spun for Ranyll. He knew that he was in the same state that she had put him in when they first met, yet Ranyll tried to fight his way out of it this time. Something was happening around him. The One, the daemons, Kalir and the others; they all seemed to drift away from him now; the only thing Ranyll could see was her face, her eyes, the depths of them as they surrounded him at all sides.

His voice came out broken then.

"What are you doing, Gabriella?" Pieces of his own words shifted around in his mind and, as Ranyll spoke, he realized it took much effort for just a few words.

The angel did not respond, her form unclear, almost transparent in front of him.

Gabriella moved towards him, her hands reaching out to his sword in front of him, moving it aside with ease; Ranyll did not fight against her. Gabriella moved closer to him. In the back of his mind, an echo screamed out in warning, but he could not fight against what was happening.

Just behind Gabriella, he could see the darkness shift suddenly. Ranyll could feel his sword shift in his hand. And then Gabriella's eyes shifted once and a look of pain splashed across her face.

And then the dream was suddenly gone.

The darkness took over and The One's panic-stricken face was the first thing Ranyll saw. The One approached Ranyll and the young man prepared for attack, trying his best to lift up his sword in defense. However, it would not move; there was a dead weight on the blade. Ranyll looked down in front of him and Gabriella lay on the end of his sword, her hands grasping at the hilt, her bloody hands around his own.

Ranyll's heart nearly stopped. Around him, the world exploded in sounds and movement, Kalir and the others taking up a defensive position around him as The One charged at him, the daemons seizing their moment to go into a frenzy; The One released his hold on them and they moved with such ferocity that they were nearly a blur as they attacked.

Gabriella was still holding tight to Ranyll's hand, her life ebbing away in front of him. The world seemed to crumble down around him. The One was as near as he had ever been, eyeing the fallen angel at Ranyll's feet, his eyes fixed upon the sword that lay embedded in Gabriella's stomach.

The One reached down to Gabriella and began to lay his hands on her when Ranyll slipped his dagger free from his belt and slashed out at The One.

"With my last breath, I will see to it that I bury this into your chest if you move but a hair closer!"

The One's gaze focused then on Ranyll. His look of panic seemed to slip from his face and he stared at the young man for a time.

"You have what I want, young man. There's nothing you or your friends here can do to stop me from taking it from you. I will have what I want."

Ranyll had felt the cold chill of defeat enter into his mind throughout this journey, but never had it been as defined as it was now as he stared back at The One, dagger shaking in his hand, Gabriella's grip loosening on his sword hand as she slipped away from him.

Kalir moved next to him then, waving a well-burning torch at The One. The sudden torchlight jolted Ranyll back to his senses. The One stared at Ranyll for a moment longer then began to back away from the torch in Kalir's hands, watching at his daemons were being held at bay by the others from Ranyll's group. He stood up slowly and stared at Kalir defiantly.

"You are a brave and foolish man, Kalir. There is no hope yet you stand here, waving your fire at me like the first inhabitants of the world did; they were not clever, but they at least knew their limitations. You, however, do not. I will kill you myself!"

The One reached out his hand and plucked Kalir up by his throat before the human had a chance to react. Kalir dropped both torch and sword and grabbed at The One's arm, trying his best to break the hold. Ranyll's uncle began to gasp for air.

The daemons saw this and began to push against the makeshift barrier of the others, testing the torchbearer's reflexes, some of them darting past the fire of the torches and into the ranks of the humans. Soon, the ranks fell back and the daemons moved in closer, almost near Ranyll now, eyeing him and the fallen angel with a ravenous look across all of their faces. Their master was the only thing that kept them from moving on them.

The daemons were gaining strength from watching The One take the victory! Ranyll could see the tide turn in a matter of moments; he knew that this was the moment that he must take action or there would be nothing left to fight for. He stared down at Gabriella and, to his surprise, she was looking up at him as well.

She relaxed her grip on his sword hand, her cold fingers slipping to her sides. Ranyll knew that she was about to pass away; he could see the brightness in her eyes fading more and more, yet she continued to stare into his eyes as she drifted away. Her left hand reached out to touch his face. Her fingers caressed his cheek lightly and then slipped away, only to return to at her side; still, motionless.

Gabriella used the last of her breath to speak to Ranyll. Her voice was a faint whisper.

"I will always be with you, Ranyll. It is your time. From here on until your death, you must prove your worth." The angel's eyes fluttered closed and her head shifted with the weight of her death and turned away from him.

Ranyll could hear his uncle choking on his last breath, the daemons rushing in on the others; the young man hesitated at first, then pulled his father's sword free from the fallen angel and felt the magik D'meir had given him flow through the blade. The blade of the sword erupted in a blue fire and The One, as well as his daemons, hesitated. However, Ranyll did not.

The young man felt his heart break inside of him as he left Gabriella's side, his sword arcing out at the daemons first, slicing through several of them, before standing in front of The One, his uncle nearly unconscious in a chokehold. Ranyll struck out against The One, swinging the flaming sword at his arm; the blade slammed into it with such force it could have cleaved through wood or stone; yet the blade merely bounced back at Ranyll, The One dropping Kalir to the ground. The master of the daemons reached for Ranyll, his other hand moving defensively to where Ranyll had struck him.

Under The One's hand, Ranyll could see the fabric take on a red stain quickly. Even The One looked shocked to see it. A twinge of pain fell across The One's face as he stood, trying his best to regain his composure. He reached for Ranyll but the young man's blade met him again before he could get any closer. Ranyll struck out, this time across The One's face, watching as a cut opened across his right cheek, a red line of blood dripping off his chin in moments. The One backed up from the flaming blade, his hands out in front of him, almost pleading. He reached up to his face and felt the blood, looked at it on the tip of his fingers.

The One was furious. The daemons stopped their attack against the humans and moved away from the torchlight, many of them filling in the gap between The One and Ranyll; however, Ranyll kept his blade trained at The One, nearly close enough to strike him again.

"There is something about that blade, boy; something I can't quite put my finger on."

"I can let you feel the sting of it again if you like!" Ranyll swung again but, this time, a daemon launched itself in front of The One, taking the flaming blade full to the chest. The creature wailed in pain as it hit the ground at Ranyll's feet, cleaved nearly in two. More daemons came to The One's side, many blocking Ranyll's way in front of him completely. Now, there was no way to get to The One. Slowly, the daemons began to surround the young man and his fallen angel.

The seconds turned into minutes; the minutes into hours. Time seemed to slow at a snail's pace. The world that Ranyll had known seemed to freeze in front of him. In the absence of time and thought, however, one thing could be heard. The chattering and clicking of the daemons were silenced by this sound and The One's face grew pale and cold when he caught the sound in his ears, turning slowly back behind him to see from where the sound came. Ranyll was sure that the noise came from the tunnels where the daemons had sprung forth yet, something else came from the passageway that was nothing Ranyll had ever seen. A cloud, thick like that of the Fog Beasts that had roamed the passageways earlier, rolled in from the passageway, yet with purpose that none could understand until the creature that controlled the cloud let itself be known.

Once seeing it, Ranyll and the other humans dropped to their knees.

Epilogue

It was my angel, Falwen had written on the page, a journey of words having been written well before these in the last few hours, yet the thought of Divlo returning again during Falwen's lifetime was something the fisherman did not expect. The words that flowed across the page that night by the fire seemed, for Falwen, to be something of a calling, a necessary step into his own grand scheme and, as he looked down at the pages of the tome before him, seeing Divlo's name written across in his own hand, he knew now what his purpose was. The Chronicler, whoever that was, was now a part of him.

He had taken a break moments earlier, resupplying the campfire with wood from the woodpile nearby, gathering himself up close to the fire for light, the quill moving across the page almost feverishly in his hand. He had never been a writer before but, for some reason, it didn't seem necessary at all right now. Falwen felt the flow of time move through him and watched as the moments played out onto the page.

*   *   *

The words had been stolen from his mouth, for Ranyll knew not what to say to a being such as this. His eyes glanced over at Kalir and the others and then back to the angel that stood before them, separating them from The One and his daemons.

The angel wore a thick, brown robe and had a well-groomed beard that hung down over his robe, almost to the silken cords that wrapped around his waist as a belt. His wings spread out across the cavern, the white blanket of feathers on both sides almost touching the walls, blocking out The One and his daemons completely. Ranyll had seen an angel before, both Gabriella and Greditto, but the angel that stood before him now seemed to glow with a presence that the others of his kind did not have. The blinding light that penetrated through the darkness of the tunnels began to fade somewhat, yet the brightness remained around the angel, the great being moving closer to Ranyll.

Ranyll looked up into the angel's face and what he saw there made the ideas fumble inside his mind, making it hard for him to speak.

The angel's face was full of sadness. The young man knew what sadness was, had seen it a number of times on the faces of those around him, yet he had never seen the immense sadness that could be held in such a being full of beauty and grace. The bitterness that Ranyll held towards the world around him seemed to vanish for the moment, replaced by what he saw in the bright yet saddened eyes of the angel in front of him. Ranyll had seen sadness such as this only one other time; when he looked into Gabriella's eyes all those days ago, when she had left he and Gwenzel to follow TSeT down into the caverns. Gabriella alone had shown such a sadness and Ranyll never thought he'd have to see it again.

The angel before them seemed to eye them all for a moment then turned to The One and his daemons. He turned away from the humans and covered the full area of the tunnel with his wingspan so the humans could not see beyond. In moments, the angel turned back around, his wings fluttering slightly, slowly curling up behind him, tucking into themselves behind his brown robes. As they did, Ranyll and the others noticed that The One and the daemons had vanished completely, leaving no trace of having ever been there. Not a daemon body littered the ground past the angel. The tunnelways behind him were clear, as if they had been cleaned by hand. The angel approached them.

"My name is unimportant yet my purpose requires the attention of all here!" No one had dared to speak. The group of humans continued to listen, scared to move dare they might miss something of what the angel had to say.

He continued. "I have only come for the angel; that is my purpose here on Ar Solon. I collect what does not belong here and am taking it back to where it belongs." The angel then moved towards the fallen form of Gabriella just past Ranyll. However, Ranyll was not so obliging. Holding out his blade, he moved to stop the angel. Ranyll's voice came out as a whisper.

"How do I know you're not like the other, the one that put her down here? How do I know you just don't want her for yourself?"

The angel smiled. This was the first time the expression had changed in the angel's face.

"I see why she chose you, Ranyll. She risked a lot for what you have welled up within you. You are right to ask that. Greditto, the angel you speak of, will not bother anyone again. He has passed on to another realm. I do understand your concern for this, but there should be no concern here, not at this moment. What should concern you is your future ventures, Ranyll."

The angel then moved past Ranyll and to the still form of the angel Gabriella, hefting her up in his arms, pulling her body close to his chest. He turned to the rest of them.

The angel continued. "I cannot say much to you, Ranyll, but I must say that you have a journey that has been laid before you."

The angel looked at the others.

"**You all do**. Much of what has transpired before you is only the beginning. There is a reckoning that is coming. Do not trust this based on what I say; take a look for yourself. The One is busy these days. The world needs hope, the world needs dreams. Without Gabriella, there is none to give it to them. What will Arsolon do without hope and dreams?"

All were quiet. None in the group knew how to answer. The angel answered for them.

"Well, humans, you are about to see what happens when there is only a sliver of hope left in the world you inhabit. Hold on to what you consider dear to you, for it may be the last time that you have it."

Ranyll felt the whole of Ar Solon come crashing down around him as he heard those words. He felt the weight of the sword in his hands for the first time in days. It seemed as though it were made of lead. He let it ease its way down at his side as he tried his best to breathe. No matter what he did, he could feel the uneasiness of what the angel said to him tear into his soul with the force of a rain storm. The questions in his mind seemed to collect together and culminate into one question. It spilled forth out into the open just as the angel turned to leave.

"Then why don't you do anything, angel; why don't you help us?" The angel stopped where he was and bowed his head, his beard curling into Gabriella's lap as she lay in his arms.

"I have done as much as I am allowed, Ranyll. As you know, Gabriella was left here because she affected inhabitants in a way that is not allowed by angels and our ways. The law forbids it. Ranyll, I **have** done something. I kept you and your friends alive. That in itself is something that should have been a fate decided by you and the situation in which you were in, yet I took it upon myself to come now and fulfill my duties by collecting Gabriella. What I have done has not been seen as an act of intrusion, but if I stay any longer, it will be. I must go now."

And with that, the angel vanished in front of them, a single flap of his great wings sending him spiraling up into the same light in which he arrived, Gabriella disappearing with him.

*   *   *

It was another few days before Falwen reached the Agnar Mountains. Days had gone by and it seemed that he would never reach them; Falwen always looking out into the sunset and saw the same mountains, the same landscape, none of it ever getting larger or close in any way. It wasn't until the morning sun brought a different sight; he actually saw himself moving closer to the mountains.

It had been a hard journey. Throughout his travels after the night at the fire, Falwen had to stop and make camp for the night so he could write, the flow of images coming to him like a flood of memories of an old friend, of an experience that he will never forget, always reliving it in his mind until he wrote it down.

However, these images were of nothing that he had ever seen in his life. In fact, these images weren't about his life at all; they were about the lives of others.

Nevertheless, for the last few hours, on each road towards the entrance into the mountain chain of the Agnar Mountains, he thought about his family, about his life of fishing and living on the coast as a simple man with a family. He also thought about how fast it had changed and how things looked so different to him now. He had found something within him that he had been searching out for years, hoping one day that he'd find it, yet never really believing that he would.

The doubts in his mind about him being able to be The Chronicler came at him in small glimpses as the remembrances of the expression on Gilden

Felve's face as he stood there, staring at Falwen, before finally passing away into oblivion right there before him. What he saw in those eyes showed him now of **his** possible future and what he might have to endure along his path of life that he took.

The setting sun later that day brought about small bits and pieces of outlined mountains ahead of him, Falwen looking into the opening of the mountain chain as it rose up all around him, his wagon making its way over the rocky terrain the best it could.

He had been able to see the mountains as they rose up throughout most of the day, but as the day wore on, Falwen knew that he would have been lost if Gilden had not drawn him a map to show him where he had been destined to journey to. The directions that Gilden had left behind were explicit, down to the pathways to take once inside the mountain chains so he would not get lost.

Falwen decided to camp at the opening of the Agnar Mountain trail and make it the rest of the way into the mountains in the morning, when he had rested more and could see in front of him without the use of lantern light. Once stopping the wagon, the fisherman made his way to the back and took out his writing tools and a small bundle of wood that he had collected on his last stop. He gathered some small stones to make a fire pit and began his nightly duties of cleaning, feeding, and watering the horses.

Soon, Falwen was again sitting by the fire; the quill, inkwell, and tome were in front of him, waiting to begin. It took only moments for the scene to escape from his mind.

*   *   *

It had been several ten-day since the death of Shilinda, the Queen of the Faeries, and still no faeries had returned from their hunt for The One and his daemons. The Faerie Homme, which was once populated by a considerable portion of the remaining faeries of Ar Solon, now sat empty.

Hollow, like that of a cocoon left by a caterpillar after moving on to its next stage in life. The faeries had been hunting and scouring the caves below the mountains for several ten-days now, cleansing the world of the Fog Beasts and daemons that they could find, trying their best to work with the dwarves to rebuild what had been lost to the dwarves in Dardist for so long; freedom from fear of attack.

The flames and fires that had been lit and burned the dwarven town had been extinguished with the magik from the faeries and the dwarves, for the first time in the last few seasons, began to rebuild and make hope a priority on their list, the stresses of the daemon threat somewhat extinguished for the moment.

The faerie population from the Faerie Homme at Reune Lake had dwindled down to a much smaller number than what had originally set out that day once finding out about the death of their beloved faerie queen. They had yet to find Gwenzel, Tristle or Drigno, but never stopped their search or gave up hope that they were alive. The dwarves in Dardist, after a formal introduction and explanation by Arntheer, Rathor, and the others in the party that had fought alongside the faeries, became close with the faeries. Within a short amount of time, many were inseparable with the magikal creatures, soon moving through the caves with them, the search parties for Gwenzel and the sprites continuing, but the search for daemons continuing as well.

In the midst of these searches, The One, knowing it was not in his best interest to be found by these creatures, followed the underground caves south, closing them up behind him so none could follow, a thick cluster of daemons staying with him, keeping themselves closer than usual after the close call with the human called Ranyll and the angel Divlo.

The One sat now, looking at the smooth surface of the ground where Kariyl had swallowed up Shilinda, his eyes tracing over the spots in which they had fought, looking at the remnants of the tree that had fallen, at the dirt tracks they had made. He had sent the daemons back below so he could meditate, which he had been doing more and more lately, yet he did not know why. He stared around at the dead and dying forest, many of the trees around him already dry husks of their former selves, and felt the emptiness inside of him grow, well-like, swallowing up the hatred, the hope, the care, the feelings that he had glimmers of earlier those months ago when he had touched her again for the first time in what seemed like centuries. All of that feeling fell down into the well that was his soul.

He did not stir when Divlo stepped out of the tree line not far from him. In fact, he knew that the angel was there, watching him. The angel had a somewhat somber appearance this time; not as he had when he appeared in the caverns all those months ago. Yet, he came with a purpose, just as he did when he had collected Gabriella.

"So, this is where she fell then, Darien? This is where it all happened?" The One didn't respond to the angel's question.

"Darien, this is where she fell, is it not?"

"That's what she called me, Divlo. She called me Darien." He paused for long moments, staring at the ground, his feet kicking at the small debris that lay near his feet, as a child does when they're scolded by their parents.

"That is your name, Darien. That is what your friends call you. Whatever happened all those years ago, you must let it go. You know that, don't you? You can't hold the hatred you have inside. It will kill you." Divlo continued. "You saw what it did to Greditto."

The One looked up at the angel, his gaze hard and solid. "You, an angel, take a slight at another of your kind? Is that how you have conversation with others, Divlo, using the downfalls of others to make you feel better? I killed him because he was of no use to me."

Divlo just shook his head. "Greditto was dead long before you killed him, Darien. You took away his pain, that is all. His love had been slain years ago and his illegitimate child was considered an outcast among her own race. It was easy to find hate inside of Greditto. You say that you know much of the world around you but you still don't see what is going on around you. There is hate built up all around; not just in your underground caverns full of creatures without souls, not only on the surface of Ar Solon, but in the clouded world, too. You think you are the only one that has troubles. We all have troubles, Darien; we just deal with them and continue on in our duties."

"I continue my duties, Divlo, as I have begun them, so shall I see them till the end!"

"So, you continue the same path then, do you? Nothing that you have seen here in these many months has changed the way that you feel about Ar Solon?"

The One clenched his teeth when he spoke this time, pulling out a dark dagger from his cloak that hid much of his frame. He pointed it at Divlo and everything around him.

"Nothing I could ever see here on this world would ever change my path! I do not waver! I will not stop until everything here is gone! Neither you or your precious Creator can stop me!"

"You know it is not our will to do so, Darien. We continue in our paths as you do yours. I cannot stop you from your course of action just as you cannot stop me from mine. I will not waver like Greditto or Gabriella did. I have a resolve, Darien, much like you do right now. I will not fail in my tasks, be they large or small. They are mine and that means much to me. You were once a great being, Darien. You still are, yet you've lost your purpose in life just as the inhabitants around you have. And, for that, I'm sorry."

The One did not return to the conversation or push it any further. His hatred and loathing seemed to slip away from him at that moment and he slipped the dagger back behind his cloak and into its hiding place. In another moment, The One was gone, the hidden passageway closing up behind him, leaving Divlo to his work.

Divlo looked at the sky, up into the clouds, trying his best to remember his way home. It had been some time since he had seen his home above the clouds and now, as he began his work, he knew that it would be some time before he would see it again.

The angel began, at first, with a simple wave of the wrist, the start of a well-formed movement in a series of movements, then continued with a series of inaudible words, the chant escaping his lips, directed at the ground where Shilinda had been taken by Ar Solon. In moments, the shape began, a light mist swirling around in front of Divlo, at his command, taking a form other than that of mist. Soon, a sparkle rose within the mist and coalesced, bringing the form almost to completion. Divlo ceased the chanting and moved forward, his hands moving into the mist; forming, molding, creating the substance that would soon be the monument to Shilinda.

This had happened one time before, Divlo recalled, remembering how an angel had been lost to the world without another angel coming to take them back to where they belonged. It was before Divlo took the helm of the position in which he now held, in a time long ago when the world was still new, when the clouded minds of the inhabitants did not have such a hold on Ar Solon.

The statue that had been made was one of the more beautiful things created in all of Ar Solon. It was still on the surface, on the continent of Parthenia, the populace on the continent taking comfort in knowing that there was someone always there watching over them. The Parthenians had lost their belief in something more, worshipping the statue as an idol, but Divlo knew where the error of their ways was and knew that, in time, much would fall into place in Parthenia.

He looked at the statue in front of him as the mist cleared around it, taking a quick side glance at his work, critiquing the very fabric of creation to ensure that it captured Shilinda within the statue, keeping her spirit alive by recreating the angelic being forever within the milky surface of the white, marble statue.

"I can guarantee it, Shilinda, you will not be forgotten. Just because you are not with us, angel, we will remember you up above. Let this statue serve as a reminder to those down here; the faeries, the inhabitants, those on a journey that are hardened by the world around them. Let this serve as a reminder that there is still compassion; give it to them when they ask, Shilinda. Be their guiding light in this world filled with darkness and doubt."

And with that, the angel Divlo departed from the statue, moving from the scene with swiftness that none could comprehend. He lifted himself into the air and headed for the continent of Parthenia, intent on his next task at hand, looking down once more to take sight of the statue of Shilinda, angel of faeries.

*   *   *

Nearly a season had gone by when Ranyll found his way to Reune Lake, taking refuge in the tree line from the snow as it continued to come down on him from all sides, his thick cloak and hood covered with more than an inch of snow. He could barely see in front of him for the thick blankets of snow that came down on him and the rest of the inhabitants of Kariyl. Many he had spoken to along the way said that this was the worst snow that they had seen.

Indeed, Ranyll thought, he had never seen this dark of a winter season in all his life.

The snow had piled up around the statue but the beauty of it seemed to echo across the frozen lake and over the snow-covered landscape around him, Ranyll shaking free the accumulation of snow on himself and his satchel on his back, brushing most of it off with the walking stick he had acquired while visiting his uncle, just a ten day earlier. He took a quick swig of the sweet brew Rathor had given him from the water skin at his side and corked it back, returning it to his side. The brew gave him warmth enough to continue on his task, his gloved fingers brushing off the statue, clearing away the snow from its still form, its crystalline skin glimmering in the early morning light. Though there was little light due to the snow that continued to fall, the little bit of light seemed to catch in the statue's form in front of him, blanketing the rest of the land around him in a shadowed light. The sun seemed to give favor to Shilinda at the moment.

Ranyll smiled when he thought of the idea, remembering his brother Tim and how he had spoken on such things not long ago, sitting on the grass next to the Tirapoor Channel. Those days seemed so long ago, when Ranyll knew very little about Ar Solon and its ways. The young man shook those thoughts off just as he did the snow and laid his walking stick at his side, kneeling down. He looked up at the statue and spoke.

"Gabriella spoke of you once, Shilinda. She stated that you were her only help, her only guidance here on Ar Solon. It was more of a whisper, an afterthought; at least, that's what I thought until I met many of the kind you favored. Now I am here, asking what Gabriella had asked all those seasons ago. I need your help, Shilinda; your guidance. I have been having dreams these past few weeks. At first, I took them as the past journey making its way out of my mind, letting them pass through and be forgotten forever in the world of dreams that all inhabitants have. I took them for nothing more than that."

Ranyll's hand went then to his father's sword at his side. He felt the handle of the great, aged blade, his fingers tracing the outlines of the fine craftsmanship of each contour made for the wielder's hand. He continued.

"Then I realized that I am the only one that dreams. I know of no one that dreams and Gabriella is no longer here. Things here on Kariyl are getting worse, as the angel in the caverns had foretold, and I believe these dreams to be visions of a future that will come to pass."

"I come to you for guidance, Shilinda. I seek the one that told D'meir that I was the chosen one. D'meir spoke of it several times when we traveled together, yet he never made it known who it was that told him. Oagthor even believed that I was something more than what I am now. I would like to know of this for myself. That is why I am going to search out this person and find out how they know this. Maybe I can get answers to the many questions that plague my mind at night before I sleep and even continue in waking dreams."

"I have the dwarf, Oagthor, in my dreams as well, Shilinda. I believe that he will have a part to play in this and I need you to guide me to him, Shilinda, so that he may help me in this journey that I am about to take. I know that he and D'meir were very close before D'meir passed away protecting me. I have not seen Oagthor since that day. No one has seen him. Please keep him safe so that I may find my way to him. That is all I ask."

Ranyll bowed his head and continued to kneel on the snowy ground for moments longer, completing a prayer and farewell to Shilinda and the past journey, clearing his mind for the present journey at hand. He lifted himself from the snowy ground before Shilinda and touched his hand to the smooth surface of the statue by the hem of Shilinda's robe, closing his eyes in thought.

The images, small glimmers of places, people and things, seemed to slip out of focus, as it always did as of late. Then, as quickly as it slipped away, a single image caught inside of his mind; *two great, stone pillars, connected by a stone archway, a series of mountains clustered closely together just behind the pillars. The snow had settled on the mountains and the pillars, blocking out the sign that the archway usually shone.*

However, Ranyll knew where this place lie; he had heard of it in the travels of the Telgin marketplace vendors many times; this was the Agnar Mountains, home to the dwarf lords that still reigned over their territory. Ranyll had heard of this place in the conversations between Rathor and Oagthor, but that was all that he really knew. He knew nothing of this place.

Picking up the walking stick at his side, he wiped the snow from his cloak and hood again, kicking it from his boots as well, trudging through the snow past the statue of Shilinda, the frozen lake behind it and, soon, moving north, towards the Agnar Mountains, in search of his friend Oagthor, for answers, and to find D'meir's informant on matters of his own fate.

The young man hoped that this journey held something more for him than just the loss of innocence and the only thing he had ever been in love with. It seemed to him that all friends had separated due to Gabriella's appearance; that they had all set out on their own journey, following the path set before them. Gwenzel and the two sprites had yet to be found, the army of faeries were still out looking for The One and his daemons; even the checkpoint guards that worked for his uncle had separated from the channel and began searching the forests for daemon breeding grounds, making sure that none were set up near populated areas.

Yet, for Ranyll, he felt as though he had to find his own path now; that nothing was set for him at all as it was for others. He knew that he didn't like this, this "growing up" adults called it; yet, it promised a number of things that Ranyll was still yet undecided on.

It had been months since that entry, yet Falwen read it over and over again, late in the night, when all the other scribes were sleeping and he could think out loud to himself without getting the looks that the dwarven scribes gave him ever since he came to this guild. The Chronicler knew that Ranyll had the hardest task of the entire group that helped Gabriella along her path of life here on Kariyl, yet he knew not how to help this young man.

In many ways, this boy reminded Falwen of his own boys, which he had not seen since the day he left his home, almost a year to the day. He had watched as Ranyll made his tear-stained return to his mother and younger brother after leaving the tunnels in Dardist and then, again, watched the tear-stained departure as the young man packed up what he could on his back and depart, just days later, trying his best to explain to his mother what he was going through.

She knew, Falwen told himself, knowing how all parents, at one time or another, find themselves staring at the child that they raised all of their life leave, taking with them a piece of their own heart, the emptiness sometimes unbearable for parents. Falwen knew about this all too well. He had seen his own departure as a young man tear at his mother's heart, sailing off to great new worlds and even greater adventures, always knowing that his mother would carry him in the back of her mind as she toiled away at her daily duties back home, always wondering if Falwen were okay, if he were succeeding in what he had set out to do.

Falwen closed the tome and lifted himself up from his chair and desk in the corner of his room, walking the tome and hooded lantern for light to his closet. He set the lantern down on the small mantle next to the closet and opened up the door, lifting the loose floorboards in the closet away with a small cord he had tied onto them all since he had come here, making it easier for him to climb down into the antechamber; something Gilden had not mentioned in his "detailed" documents to the next Chronicler.

I guess he likes to leave a few surprises, Falwen thought to himself, making his way down the carved, stoned steps, his light footfalls barely echoing in the long hallway beneath the guild. He had traded his fishing garb for a scribe's plain brown robes and leather sandals, having his robes made custom for him due to the populace of only dwarves that roamed the halls in the guild. Falwen knew that Gilden had picked the room for a reason, yet the new Chronicler didn't figure out why until he began to run out of room to store his secret volumes of the present and began stacking them up in his closet, locking it behind him every time he left his room.

He had heard of the rumors around the false copy that had been given to the Head Scribe in Goletta and didn't feel like having to deal with the additional penalties of having his own collection of writings being looked at with a suspicious eye by the dwarves. They were already suspicious about him coming to the dwarven writing guild; they needed only to find out whom he really was and that would be enough grounds to start an investigation into all that was in the books. Much of it would send the masses into hysteria, which is something Falwen didn't feel that Kariyl needed right now. He was happy keeping the secrets and took solace in such a place that surrounded him; the world seemed to stand still around him, with the exception of those in the tomes he wrote about every day, which seemed always to be busy.

After a few dozen steps, Falwen made it down to the library; his library. There were empty shelves built into the walls and wall sconces every foot or so, with a hook hanging in the middle of the room for him to hang a lantern, the room lighting up in moments once he placed his hooded lantern upon it. It was a dusty and unkempt place when he had first ventured down the stairway; the tomes had been too heavy and the first, flimsy wooden planks had broken under the weight, soon assisting him with discovering this vault for his own works. Once down here, he spent a few nights tidying up the place and, after bringing most of his things down out of the boxes that he had brought with him, made a home for the volumes that Gilden had left him.

The dwarves did not ask where the items went; in fact, they were somewhat happy with the idea of the eyesore of the wagon not sitting in the courtyard any longer. In fact, Falwen had not had a visitor inside his own chambers since he had arrived, with the exception of the dwarf showing him where he would be staying while he was here, which the dwarves did not question about either. Falwen thought about asking them why they did not ask much about his sudden appearance and then decided against it, thinking it better to remain somewhat distant from his fellow scribes until he himself were comfortable with the idea.

The Chronicler took a seat at his writing desk after he placed the tome he had brought down back in its place in the library just in front of him, looking down into the tome set out before him, several pages already written in; the one page open containing only the first few lines of the page.

Falwen had to stop and think on how he was to feel on what he was writing before he continued. He had the thoughts in his head for days, almost near a ten day yet, when he saw it on paper in front of him; he knew that this was happening and that it was not just an idea in his head. The idea of this terrified him greatly, knowing who and what this next tome was about. He had seen what this being was capable of and knew of its hatred for the inhabitants, but knew that the next few lines would most likely take him into the mind of this creature. He knew this would be one of the harder tomes in which to write without being completely affected by it.

The Chronicler read the lines in front of him again, shivering at the thought of what lay ahead for Ranyll.

Test was prepared to hate the human, Ranyll, for all time, but knew that the human would not make it until then. He had been given permission by The One to hunt the inhabitant down at any cost. The One did not specify what to do with the human; Test did not ask, either. It was better this way. In the last few centuries, Test had become adept at hunting down and killing inhabitants across the continent of Kariyl and Parthenia, changing in and out of forms to manipulate the world around him. Yet, this was the first time Test would actually take pleasure in it. He left immediately to begin his plan, which seemed to bubble and boil over in his mind, so many terrible things at once Test's own claw-like hands clicking together wildly in anticipation.

Author's Note

When I first began this story, I really had no intention of finishing it. It was a gift; the first chapter only and nothing more. However, within a year, I had revisited the story and seemed to find something more within its confines. I found a character that was struck down, left to the proverbial wolves, waiting to be saved. So, I saved her. It may not be the way that most see saved, but, with every ending to a long story, there will always be disappointments, hard times, upsets that you didn't expect to happen along the way. My decision to do these things had never really been my decision at all; something kept me writing. Day after day, I tried to figure out what was going to happen, just as entertained as a reader would be reading the novel, only to find out that those same upsets were my own; for the story had not gone the way I had wanted it to.

I always wanted good to thrive and triumph over evil. But, as I wrote the last few chapters of this book, I knew that the victory would not take place in this book. This was a single battle, a victory, but not in the eyes of many of the characters. The ones that you see at the end, still wanting some resolution; those are the characters that are not happy with my ending. They want the story to continue, however, they make the choice to continue alone.

I didn't have a plan to write a follow-up novel to this one; however, Ranyll and Oagthor's quest changed my mind. I realized that there were a lot of questions that they deserved an answer to and, almost immediately after I saw this, I began to write down the plot to the follow-up book. Of course, it couldn't be told in this novel; Gabriella's story was finished for the most part and, as a result of this, Ranyll's had just really begun. She had played her part by putting Ranyll in the place that he needed to be in as well as holding The

One back from gaining power, which is something that Greditto cannot say that he did. In reality, Greditto turned out to be worse than Gabriella in many ways. He just pushed his hatred for the world and himself onto Gabriella and rationalized the situation to the point where he could get the courage enough to strike her down.

He was the first pawn to be sacrificed on the chess board of this story. The end of the Ar Solon is near and these characters know it. They are more afraid than any will be in the novels to come before this story. I really hope that we will see more than just Ranyll and Oagthor in the next novel; who knows.

Certainly not me, I'm just the writer.

Read on
for an excerpt from
The Healer,
Book XXI of The
Chronicles of Ar Solon,
the follow-up novel to
Forgotten Angel.

Preview Chapter of
The Healer, Book XXI

Ranyll slipped silently past the daemons and made his way through the dimly lit catacombs beneath the city, lighting his flaming sword once he was away from them, hoping to come upon a passageway or hiding place before the daemons made it to him. He knew that the secret book room lay not far from where he was at the moment. From what the directions had stated on the map, he knew it to be this way and only a few steps further. Behind him, he could hear the excited pattering of the daemons as they continued their wicked parade toward him. It had been some time since he had dealt with a daemon, yet Ranyll knew what the daemons were capable of.

All too knowing, he thought to himself, taking quick, well-placed steps, his eyes scanning the tunnel in front of him. Beneath the chattering of the daemons behind him, he swore that he heard another noise.

It can't be Oagthor, Ranyll reminded himself, *he was still trying to get into the library. He knew nothing of the secret chambers beneath it. I hadn't a chance to tell him; that and our being separated had much to do with it.* However, Ranyll recalled to mind a few instances where Oagthor had been able to make an entrance when least expected. Ranyll continued on until the smell of m what lie ahead lay thick in his nostrils.

Ahead of him, still not completely visible with the light from his flaming sword, was the creature that the noise came from. A gelatinous form, cube-shaped, edged its way closer to him, its exterior shifting in the flickering light of Ranyll's sword, its transparent innards sucking in on itself to propel its spineless form forward, the heavy sucking noise blowing an air of stench into Ranyll's nostrils that nearly made him gag.

Ranyll lifted the sword up above his head to get a good glimpse of the size of this gelatinous cube. He had been warned about sentries patrolling the passageways, but he never thought he would see one of these in all of his days.

The gelatinous cube took up the entire seven-foot by seven-foot passageway in front of Ranyll. Though the cubes Ranyll had been told about had always been said to be a clear, transparent color, this one seemed to take on a grayish sheen, almost waxy, with limited visibility through to the other side. Ranyll, however, could see through vaguely to the other side and saw the other side of the cube collapse in on itself, the side closest to him writhing and sucking closer to him as well, the human taking a couple of steps back in response.

In doing so, Ranyll could hear the daemons approaching not far behind him. Yet again, he seemed to be on the verge of a dead end on all fronts, not being given much of a choice on either end.

Ranyll reached his sword out at the cube, the sword tip touching the cube. The flames at the tip of the blade submerged inside the gelatinous being and sizzled as they went out, the tip of the blade sliding into the cube, Ranyll feeling the weight of the creature moving throughout the blade to the hilt. The cube did not seem to take notice of the blade and kept moving towards Ranyll, more of the blade being submerged, over half of the blade in moments, Ranyll surmised, watching as the gelatinous form around his blade began to bubble and then sizzle, the inner form of the cube seemingly attacking the blade within moments of being inside the creature.

So it is true about their inner gelatinous forms, Ranyll concluded. *Their insides are their digestive system.* He knew that there was a reason he had studied all of those tomes back at the checkpoint when visiting his uncle.

Ranyll could hear the daemons drawing closer. In moments, there would be scores of daemons on him and even his magikal blade could not protect him against the small daemon patrol that crept eagerly forward.

I have to get through it....through it without dying. The human flung his pack off his shoulders and dropped it onto the ground in front of him, digging through it as quickly as possible. He pulled out some rope, his bedroll and, finally, the crossbow that the storekeeper had recommended to him, almost forcing it upon him at the shop. He hoped now that it would come to good use.

Loading a bolt into the crossbow's chamber, he laid the crossbow down, tying the rope to the end of the bolt. In another moment, Ranyll had stuffed everything back into his pack and sheathed his broad sword, slinging it over his shoulder. Ranyll bundled himself up the best he could. He put on the gloves he had from his pack, tied his boots tightly around his legs, and laced his tunic up to the neck. Lastly, he tied his cloak around his waist at the hem so it would stick to him. Any pouches he had on his belt he slid back into the protection of his cloak for safekeeping.

The cube had come rather close to him in the amount of time it took him to prepare himself, Ranyll backing up against the wall of the passageway now, the gelatinous cube almost to the point of turning within the passage. Ranyll picked up the crossbow and looked deeply into the gelatinous cube, taking aim for the far wall on the other side of the cube. He pulled the lever and the bolt shot through, slamming into something solid on the other side. The rope was still connected and stuck through the cube, Ranyll testing it by giving it a light tug. The rope still held. Ranyll flipped his hood down over his head and tucked it in over his face, wrapping the rope around his left arm several times. He could hear the skittering of the daemons now but let go of it in his mind, turning back down the corridor away from the cube once before turning back at it in full stride.

He sucked in a deep breath and then leapt into the cube, hands and head first.

The daemons turned the corridor just to see their prey disappear into the thick, gelatinous shape. Several of them hurried after, only to get stuck in the cube as well, their claws clicking wildly as they tried to cut through the jelly-like creature that now pulled them into itself. Soon, they were swallowed whole, the remainder of the daemons on the outside watching as their brethren struggled hopelessly for an escape.

On the other side of the cube, the rope went taut, shaking every-so-often from the weight of the human trying to pull himself through. Ranyll's head soon emerged, coated in a gelatinous waste, the cloak wrapped around him beginning to sizzle. Ranyll's hands then came through and grabbed for the rest of the rope on the other side, the gloves beginning to sizzle now as well. Ranyll's breathing came in gasps as all of his clothing began to smoke and sizzle on him. He pulled his shoulders through, then gradually to his waist, grabbed up more of the rope in his hands for the final pull. Using both of his gloved hands, he pulled his legs out of the cube, crashing to the other side of the floor with a splat.

Ranyll stood up and ripped the cloak off of him, tossing it to the ground as it burned away with from the acidic goo. He took a deep breath and bit his lip as he tore away at the rest of his outer garments; tunic, breeches, boots and, finally, his gloves, which seemed to almost disintegrate on his hands and he pulled the gloves off of his fingers.

He could feel the gelatinous insides of the creature still burning at his skin. Reaching into his pack on the floor, he pulled free a water skin and poured it over his hands, pouring the remainder over his head and shoulders and the other parts of the skin that burned, making a puddle of water on the floor for his feet to stand in.

He did not notice the figures standing just to the left of him in an adjoining corridor until they spoke. Two cloaked figures dressed in the robes of scribes, aged humans, stood on a set of steps right next to him, three heavily armored guards standing just behind them.

One of the cloaked figures spoke.

"What is it you want, young man? You have trespassed on sacred ground. Penalty for this is death. Speak, man! You have little time to explain yourself!"

Ranyll just stood there, still trying to recover from what just occurred when he reached back behind him, his sword not on his back. He looked on the ground next to him but it wasn't there either. He turned back to the gelatinous cube, which was already around the corner and could not be seen at all.

I have nothing to get it with, Ranyll thought to himself, searching through his pack for something, anything that he could retrieve his sword with. The sharp voice of one of the scribes commanded his attention.

"Answer me, young man; on order of death!" That's when the scribe's cloak caught his eye. In one quick move, Ranyll wearing only tatters and looking like a poor sneak thief, he darted up one step, ripping the cloak off of the scribe, retreating back to into the passageway with it. The three guards followed after him, the scribe's still in awe at such a display.

Ranyll wrapped his right arm in the thick cloak and looked into the cube as he approached it, making out as best he could the location his sword might be stuck in.

If it's not already dissolved, Ranyll thought, wincing at the thought of such an idea. *If there's anything magikal about that blade, it should be resistant to such things,* Ranyll concluded to himself, slamming his cloaked right hand into the cube, his hand searching for a hold.

The three guards came around the corner, swords at the ready.

They seemed to be waiting for a chance like this to come, Ranyll agreed, watching the smiles come across their faces as they saw him at a dead end, huddled against the gelatinous cube.

Ranyll smiled back at them. "One moment, fine gentlemen! Just let me explain to you. As soon as I get this…."

One of them interrupted.

"Listen here, boy! We don't have to do anything of the sort. You had your chance. Prepare for death!"

Ranyll had to face a grim fact; these men had no notion of letting him live or of allowing him to explain. It would have been all too easy for him to simply say to them, 'My apologies, gentlemen, but I am nearly melting due to your gelatinous sentinel here', or a simple, 'Pardon me but I have lost something of value within this monstrosity before us. Could you help me to get it and then all will be clear.' But Ranyll knew that the time for formality had ended long ago when he was tasked with such a mission as this.

I hope that everyone with manners and time on their side will understand…

He could feel the pommel of his sword in his hands through the cloak. In one swift pull, his sword and a mass of gelatinous goo came flying out, the cloak on his hand coated in acidic goo. Ranyll flashed them a quick smile and tore off a scrap of cloth from his undershirt, cleaning the handle off before touching it. He brandished the blade before them, the sheath falling off into pieces on the floor, burning up the rest of the way from the digestive acid. The sword was still intact; in fact, it did not seem damaged at all.

In moments, the passageway was brightened from the flames on the sword that erupted in front of the three guards. They began to back away.

…but if they don't understand, then this should at least get their attention.

Ranyll called out to them, still out of breath from all that went on around him. He left the cloak on the passageway floor and began to move forward, back to the stairway.

"I suggest you put away your swords, gentlemen."

The guards, still transfixed on the flaming blade, managed to hear Ranyll after he said it a second time, the guards backing up to the wall where Ranyll's bolt still lie protruding from it, remnants of the rope hanging off the end of it.

Ranyll looked to the two scribes, who now stood transfixed as well by the flaming blade before them. They looked at the young man as he spoke.

"My name is Ranyll Tolver, scribes. I have come from afar and am in need of your assistance. You are the only ones that can help me. I must gain access to the Island of Dree."

A look of terror flashed across the faces of the scribes when they heard the name of the island, the cloaked scribe pressing his hand up to his opened mouth.

"You cannot be serious, young man! It is not a place one travels to."

Ranyll nodded in agreement. He knew that the island was off limits to all of Kariyl, and all of Ar Solon for that matter. It had become a place complete with horror stories that rivaled those of Parthenian times, ages ago, when brutality had become the custom of the continent and the way of things. Yes, Ranyll knew of the dangers, especially of the ever-active volcano that became one of its primary features that kept many away; ash and dust for miles and miles. If you did survive against the unknown that lived there, the ash and dust would certainly be another challenge that stood in the way of safe passage into it.

"I wish I had another choice."

About the Author

Riley S. Brown has, for the last ten years, been working on his epic fantasy novels; a collection of over twenty-five novels all based on a land he had created several years earlier. He has written two novels, two screenplays, two books of poetry, and has worked as director, writer, and actor of a play performed at Volunteer State Community College in 2000 entitled <u>Bloodletting: A Vampire Love Story</u>.

The range of his writing is broad in genre; from adult fantasy to children's stories and horror, his growing interests peaked by his enrollment at Middle Tennessee State University in 2001.

Riley is also finishing treatments for several screenplays at this time as well. Two of them are horror films and another is a present day re-imagining of Lewis Carroll's *Alice's Adventures in Wonderland*.

Riley is presently in his fifth year teaching high school English and lives in Baltimore, Maryland.

<u>Coming Soon in The Chronicles of Ar Solon Series:</u>
Chains of Solace, Book XVIII
The Healer, Book XXI